What Happened at Yonder

'That way leads to Yonder.
It's a path less taken since the owners left'

What Happened at Yonder

William Paterson

FISH EAGLE BOOKS

Copyright © William Paterson 2021
First published by Fish Eagle Books 2021
Eshowe, Rosslare Strand, County Wexford
Republic of Ireland

Distributed by Ingram Spark worldwide
All Rights Reserved

William Paterson has asserted his right under the Copyright, Designs and Patents Act 1988 to be identified as the author of this work.

No part of this book may be reproduced in any form, by photocopying or by any electronic or mechanical means, including information storage or retrieval systems, without permission in writing from both the copyright owner and the publisher of this book.

ISBN 978-1-5272-8826-3

Typeset by Amolibros
www.amolibros.com

Printed by Ingram Spark worldwide

For Siobhán

About the Author

William Paterson, a journalist and author, was born of Scottish-Cornish parentage in Durban and grew up with his sister in an old colonial hilltop house, surrounded by virgin bush, with views of the Umgeni River and the Indian Ocean. He was educated at Michaelhouse, then the Durban School of Art in Natal and the University of Westminster, London. Upon his return to South Africa he spent most of his working life in the media. He is now settled with his Irish wife Patricia in Co. Wexford, Ireland, where he continues to write.

Acknowledgements

I am indebted to the kind people who provided a wealth of background material and guidance, without which this story could not have been written:
Ross Anderson for his kind permission to quote an excerpt from *The Forgotten War 1914-1918. The East African Campaign*; Dr Bill Bizley, author of the article "Unsung heroes: the trek ox and the opening of Natal" which appeared in *Natalia #34* upon which my description of oxen and wagons is based; likewise for permitting me to draw from his article "U-boats off Natal" which was published in *Natalia 23 and 24*, and which will surface in Book Three; Jan Bezuidenhout, Webredakteur of Landbou-weekblad and his colleague Koot Louw of Cotton South Africa for expert information about cotton cultivation; Alec Bozas, Chairman of T. M. Loftheim (Pty) Limited for his permission to use the store name of Loftheim's in these pages. Loftheim's is arguably the oldest company in Zululand and still going strong, nowadays as a property-owning company. Nadia Connolly for unstintingly assisting my editor with technical problems whenever required. Peter Croeser, Trustee & Administrator of the Natal Society Foundation in Pietermaritzburg, for his ready help in locating elusive information on matters-Natal; Reverend Michael Fourie, Rector of St. Thomas Anglican Church, Berea, Durban, and Sheryl Roberts, Parish

Secretary, for providing invaluable historical insights on the Old St Thomas Church, which still stands on the corner of Julia and Ridge Roads; Adam Hardiman, for helping with some German translations; Mark Henderson, owner of the Zululand Times printing company, who had no objection to my frequent mentioning of the newspaper of that name (no longer published), often called 'The Sausage Wrap', and for the assistance of Arthur Ashburner; Professor Shannon Hoctor, School of Law, University of KwaZulu-Natal (Pietermaritzburg) and his colleague Dr Rose Kuhn, Librarian (Law) for investigating regulations governing mandatory inquests in Natal during 1919; Allan Jackson and Gerald Buttigieg of *Facts About Durban*, an interactive website, who provided a lot of information and continue to mine the rich seam of Durban history; Clive Kelly, President of the Empangeni Rugby Football Club for guidance on scoring in 1919. The present ERFC grounds, Mick Kelly Park, are named after his father, Ronald Maitland ('Mick') Kelly. Although the club was formed in 1919, the rugby match described in this book is purely imaginary and has no bearing on actual people, venue or events; Brendan Lillis, retired banker, for cutting through the mysteries of local banking; Phil Mellstrom, Church of Scotland, on points concerning the order of a Scottish marriage service; Senzosenkosi Mkhize, Senior Librarian of the Campbell Collections for locating details of payments to Indentured Indians; The Reverend Sally Muggeridge, International President of The Malcolm Muggeridge Society, for insights into Malcolm Muggeridge's activities in Lourenco Marques during the Second World War, and allowing me to use Muggeridge's name in Book Three, although the narrative in the novellas strays from the actual facts; Yogas Nair, Editor of the *Mercury* newspaper, for permission to quote a report on Dr Simon Pooley's book on crocodiles (see Pooley below); for permission to mention KLIM®in several places. KLIM® is a registered trademark of Société des Produits Nestlé S.A., Vevey, Switzerland; Richard Nicholson, Manager, Economic Research at the South African Cane Growers Association (SACGA) for invaluable guidance on sugar cane cultivation, to whose name I must add those of Jayne Ferguson of SACGA, plus Chris Nel, Technical Editor, and Lloyd Phillip, Senior Journalist of *Farmers Weekly;* Katharina O'Carroll, for help with translation of German phrases; Emeritus Professor Howard Phillips, Department of Historical Studies, UCT for guidance on the dates of introduction of Social Anthropology at UCT; Dr Simon Pooley, Lambert Lecturer in Environment (Applied Herpetology) University of London and Member of IUCN Crocodile Specialist Group, for permission to draw from his observations on the Nile Crocodile in his book: *Don't get eaten by a crocodile: in South Africa or Swaziland*; Peter Roberts of the Zambezi Book Company, who provided invaluable information about the Victoria Falls Hotel, circa 1920, Rhodesian Railways' Zambezi Express and the introduction of Union Castle's 'Round Africa' cruises. He has published several books about the region, details on which you will find at www.zambezibookcompany.com and www.tothevictoriafalls.com; David Savides, Editor, and Kyle Cowan, journalist, *Zululand Observer*, helped to track down Ashley Peter, co-author of *Centenary of the North Coast Railway*, who had the facts at his fingertips about the Mtubatuba railhead in 1919; Eshara Singh, Senior Librarian – Periodicals, Msunduzi Municipal Library, Pietermaritzburg, for Spanish Flu newspaper clippings; Artur Stehli, writer in Schweizerdütsch; United Agents LLP on behalf of Jean, Lady Tweedsmuir, The Lord Tweedsmuir and Sally, Lady Tweedsmuir for permission to include eight words from John Buchan's novel, *The Thirty-Nine Steps*; Emerson Vandy, Papers Past Service Manager, National Library of New Zealand, for news material on Bolshevist atrocities in 1919 and the influence of Bolshevism in Natal; Dr Johannes Christiaan van der Walt, author of *Zululand True Stories* for allowing me to pluck and transmogrify some material from his fascinating book; Dr Regina van Vuuren, Assistant Director of Amafa aKwaZulu-Natali for invaluable insights into Zulu customs and traditional attire; Stephen White, Member of the Council, Clan Gregor, for reviewing passages about the Clan; Ms Mathilda van der Westhuizen, PhD, Agronomy, Agricultural Research Council Institute for Industrial Crops (South Africa), for providing precise information about the various stages and time frames in a cotton plant's development to maturity; Dalene Worrall for sending me a magnificent fistful of anecdotes gathered from her Zululand relations, many of whose memories have found their way into these pages in disguised form. I must make the point that this had nothing to do with the references to the Broederbond, which came from an entirely different source. Graphics for the railway map were adapted from an HTOL original and the book cover was by Tom Kelleher, ThINK, Wexford. The cover photograph is possibly of an assembly at the Ntambanana store. The map of Zululand in Africa was created by Àine Boland, also of ThINK.

Further thanks must go to Anna Baggallay for her dogged editorship – and occasional wildlife erudition which contributed in places to this book's accuracy; and Jane Tatam of Amolibros for taking this book from manuscript to print.

Characters

Donald Kirkwood
Brother, died France 1916
Sisters Winnie and Jean
Ntambanana settler
Judy Eriksen
Donald's original girlfriend/ Barbican
Toby Strafford
Good friend / co-farmer/ Anglo-Irish
Sisters Phoebe and Hannah
James (Jim) Bell
Empangeni farmer
Edna Bell
His wife
Emily Bell
Their daughter
Andrew Bell
A son
Nigel Bell
A son
Arthur Reed
Bell's Empangeni farm manager
Lucy Reed
His wife

Eric Schnurr
  Ntambanana cotton man / American
Marie Schnurr
  His French (Mauritian) wife
Sonya Broccardo
  Emily's good friend
Zeno Broccardo
  Sonya's twin brother, died in a shark attack in Book One
Joy Broccardo
  Sonya's younger sister
Paolo Broccardo
  Their father (Accountant)
Bianca Broccardo
  Their mother
George Moberly
  Editor, *Zululand Times*
Ivana 'Poppy' Popovic
  Typesetter / married Eshowe butcher
Jan Mocke
  Wagoner / wagon-builder
Johan Myburgh
  Tam settler
Herina Myburgh
  Wife, died of Spanish Flu
Susannah Myburgh
  Young daughter
Jean-Pierre Meyer
  Dinghy sailor friend (Madagascar)
Caroline Meyer
  His wife
Prudence Jardine
  Librarian, Daughter of Harbour Master

Keswick Jardine
  Prue's father, Harbour Master in Durban
Cordelia Jardine
  His wife, Prue's mother
Danielle Joubert
  Braille teacher, Durban
Pádraic O'Grady
  Retired Transvaal Irish Brigade
  Farmer, cattle expert
Kim Logan
  Logan's Import & Export
Howard Creighton
  SIS agent
Fritz du Quesne/ Alias **Capt. Stoughton**
  Opsaal Brandy salesman
Hubie von Weldenburg
  'Swiss' farmer
Frieda von Weldenburg
  His wife (Braille teacher)
Vishnu
  Indentured Indian servant
Deepika
  Vishnu's wife
Ivan Cohen
  Musical instrument shop owner
Masheila Reddy
  Daughter of indentured Indian at Bells
Luna de Villiers
  Prostitute, Medium
Layani
  Shangaan farm worker
Chinnamama
  Donald's cook at Yonder

Eben Brink
> Vet

Grizel Siedle
> Teacher

Verna Buckle
> With her husband, tenants of Chelmsford

Preface

Except for a few public figures, long gone, the characters that fill these pages are fictional, and any resemblance to actual persons is coincidental and unintended. The historical setting is reasonably sound but the towns, villages and landscapes depicted bear only a passing resemblance to the real ones.

The terms 'Kaffir' and 'native' are nowadays regarded as pejorative but were in common use at the time this story unfolds.

Prologue

– *setting the perspective*

"The extremes of climate and terrain found in East Africa meant that campaign conditions were usually very difficult. Given the dependence on subsistence farming and food imports, a well-organised system of transport and supply was absolutely essential to success or even survival. This was a considerable problem that had a major influence on the course of military operations throughout the war. Both sides relied heavily on human porterage and suffered heavily for it; in late 1916 and early 1917 both the Germans and British faced starvation on several occasions. In the end, the British with their superior resources partly overcame this limitation, although there was never an overabundance for the hard-marching columns deep in the virgin bush. All participants suffered severely from insufficient rations, medicine and equipment at one or more times. Extreme physical exertion and discomfort were the norm.

"The other dominating factor was disease. Malaria was the greatest plague for soldier and follower alike, with no one – regardless of rank or position – being immune. It caused enormous problems and disabled thousands for long periods, often permanently. Dysentery was second in seriousness, followed by pneumonia. Apart from the extremes of precipitation and aridity, human life was made miserable by the swarms of biting insects, parasites and dangers of wild animals. For domestic animals, the effects of the tsetse fly were even more devastating, and scarcely a beast survived the rigours of the campaign. Put simply, East Africa was an extremely unhealthy and uncomfortable place in which to fight a war."
Excerpt from *The Forgotten War 1914-1918. The East African Campaign* by Ross Anderson

After the Anglo-Zulu war had ended in 1879, the defeated Zulus were pushed into twenty-one reserves in Zululand, which lay between the Pongola River in the north and the Tugela River in the south, sharing its southern border with the British Colony of Natal.

Eighteen years of tribal turmoil and Boer meddling followed, before the Natal Colony annexed Zululand in 1897. In 1904, three hundred thousand acres of Zululand, held after the Zulu defeat as 'Crown Land', were thrown open for settlement by white farmers. Natal united with the Cape Colony, the Republic of the Orange Free State and the Transvaal Republic in 1910 to become the Union of South Africa, and in post-war 1919 further portions of the most fertile areas of Zululand were released.

A number of demobbed soldiers returning to South

Africa from the First World War East African conflict and the battlefields of Europe were offered roughly 1500 acres of land apiece to develop as farms, most notably 80,000 acres near Ntambanana, a dot on the map seventeen miles northwest of Empangeni, between the Mhlatuzi River and what was then known as the Imfolozi Junction Reserve, the high fever area set aside for wild animals in 1895, where the two winding tributaries of the Umfolozi River meet. Sixty-two Ntambanana farms were taken up beside the Reserve.

During a conversation on the overnight milk-train to Empangeni, Donald Kirkwood, one of the East African campaign survivors, had discovered that his future farm, which he decided to call 'Yonder', abutted that of one allocated to a Toby Strafford, an Anglo-Irishman and the only naval man among the new planters.

In Book One, *The Snake in the Signal Box*, Donald fell in love with Emily, an Empangeni farmer's daughter, and witnessed with her, Toby and Sonya a fatal shark attack on Zeno Broccardo, Sonya's twin brother, in the shallows at Richard's Bay, a remote fishing settlement on the shores of the Indian Ocean.

After inspecting the veld where his future farm would be at Ntambanana, Donald returned from Zululand to his pre-war job at a Durban bank, his initial appointment having been interrupted by four wartime years.

It was during this time that the friends witnessed the suffering caused by the Spanish Flu pandemic in Natal which was producing a rising tide of corpses. Conditions in the Cape were even worse.

While in Durban Donald was recruited by Howard Creighton in a small Pickering Street office belonging to Logan's Import & Export Agency. He was asked to monitor the suspicious behaviour of a 'Swiss' sugar-farmer, Hubie von

Weldenburg, and Fritz Joubert du Quesne, a pro-German Boer using the alias of Captain Claude Stoughton. Donald's occasional reports were to be posted to Prue Jardine, a Durban librarian who acted secretly for Creighton. He was to use a code based on random sentences found in a popular thriller published in 1915, *The Thirty-Nine Steps* by John Buchan.

He had bought a Model T Ford in Durban, which he named 'Kelpie' after the mischievous spirit that haunts the lochs of Scotland. His Zululand neighbour, Toby, had bought a Model T truck so that spare parts could be interchanged.

In far-off Russia, the Bolsheviks were struggling to gain control over the counter-revolutionary White Armies. The wholesale executions of the bourgeoisie and perceived sympathisers of the White opposition during the Red Terror were being continued by the Cheka secret police. Over half a million people were slaughtered, many with great cruelty. The ripple effect of the October Revolution was seeping through to South African trade unions, to the extent that local bolshevist literature hailed the African native as the true proletariat, much to the concern of Natal whites.

In March, 1919, the Anarchical and Revolutionary Crimes Act, commonly called the Rowlatt Act, had been passed in India by the Imperial Legislative Council. It led to rioting in the Punjab and other provinces, culminating in the British Indian Army's shooting of massed Baisakhi pilgrims in the walled public gardens of Amritsar.

The Rowlatt Act was designed to extend indefinitely the emergency measures introduced during the First World War, which allowed for arrests without a warrant and indefinite detention without trial.

The first shots of the War of Independence had been fired in Ireland, killing two members of the Royal Irish

Constabulary, and Eamon de Valera had been elected President of Sinn Féin.

In America, membership of the Ku Klux Klan had rocketed after the release of the silent movie, 'Birth of the Nation', with its portrayal of negroes as bestial simians.

Concomitantly, a resurgent movement was developing among many Dutch-Afrikaners still smarting from their Boer War defeat and an unsuccessful attempt to overthrow the government in 1914. The last had been trying to prevent the fledgling Union of South Africa from entering the conflict against Germany. Its leaders were in sympathy with German 'Social Darwinism', and sought independence from Britain. Envisaged was the permanent exploitation of the natives, Indians and mixed-race peoples through so-called 'Christian Nationalism'.

The Ntambanana settlers were ill-suited to meet the challenges of farming, about which they knew little. Nagana, a disease spread by the tsetse-fly, was decimating livestock, and labour was hard to come by; so much so that Natal farmers had resorted to employing indentured labour imported from India on five-year contracts. There were frequent reports of harsh treatment of the Indians, and disease was rife. While the official process of introducing indentured labour had stopped in 1911, thousands of Indian labourers had signed on for further years because they were too poor to break out of the system.

In the main, Zulu men refused to work on the land usurped by the 'white invaders', although the imposition of a £1 poll tax on top of the 14 shillings hut tax had forced them to seek 'men's work' on the Transvaal gold mines and the railways, away from Zululand.

Rural roads were few and far between, and transport within Natal relied heavily upon a limited rail network.

Those country roads that did exist were untarred and poorly maintained. The road from Empangeni to the Ntambanana settlement, for example, continued to deteriorate to the point that farmers had gone back to using ox-drawn wagons to get produce to the nearest station and mills, although a few intrepid motorists persisted in battling through.

Chapter One

It was chilly by Zululand standards when the early train from Durban pulled into Empangeni, and the Hlangazi and Nongidi peaks stood out clearly.

Donald and Toby had arranged to travel up together and had shared their compartment with a large blond Swede who introduced himself as Karl Lindqvist from Stallarholmen, and a man from Guernsey, Brent Renouf.

The Swede's limited command of English and his guttural pronunciation of the words he did know had made conversation difficult until plied with liquor in the dining car, when his tongue was loosened sufficiently for him to explain that, to gain experience of sub-tropical conditions, he was engaged to assist the Empangeni vet, Eben Brink. He was uninformed about the ravages of nagana.

Renouf, on the other hand, spoke endlessly about how he missed the Channel Islands, explaining at mind-numbing length the origin of his surname and how famous it was, then moving on to extol the virtues of the island's huge turkey oak. He was a forestry man seeking experience in the production of blue and red gum tree pit props for the Transvaal gold mines.

They were met as they stepped off the train by the vet and the owner of the gum tree plantations, and whisked away by their respective employers after much hand-shaking and goodbyes to Donald and Toby.

"Well, here we are," Toby said. "Shall we go and have a look at Frieda's legs? We have the transport, after all."

"That'll be an adventure in itself," Donald said. "At least the roads should have dried out; but perhaps we should make contact with the Broccardos first? Dreading it, but let's do it."

"Right! We'll take your Kelpie and we'd better go and supervise the unloading. I'll leave the truck outside Loftheim's to show off. We can book rooms at the Masonic Hotel later. I'm not keen on staying at the von Weldenburgs for anything longer than an overnight."

The leisurely pace of life in the village of Empangeni had returned to near-normal after the Spanish Flu outbreak, although the road surfaces were still giving off whiffs of Lysol, which became more pronounced as the day warmed up. An elderly white woman entering Loftheim's still wore a flu-mask and the Spanish Flu placards at the station remained in place. There was a notice outside the hotel to the effect that the kitchen was closed until further notice due to the untimely death of the hotel chef. The smithy's workshop was likewise closed.

Donald bought matches and some rice, tea, tinned bully beef, powdered milk, sugar and a tin opener in Loftheim's, just in case the vehicles broke down on the way to 'Tam and they had to survive overnight. For his part, Toby bought the latest Durban paper and stocked up with a mix of buckshot and birdshot for the twelve-bore he had acquired.

"I see they're trying to halt the export of food," said Toby, "according to an article I read while waiting for you. Local shortages, I suppose. May I read it to you?"

"Go ahead."

"As a result of dissatisfaction at the exportation of foodstuffs of which there are shortages, a special meeting of the Federation

of Trades decided to ask all affiliated unions to refuse to handle all foodstuffs for exportation from South African ports."

"I think that's reasonable. The country's broke since being forced to plunder the coffers for the war effort, and the Spanish Flu has done the rest. Far fewer crops were planted."

The frangipani blossoms had fallen and now carpeted the ground by the time the friends arrived and pushed open the Broccardo's squeaky garden gate.

Sonya's younger sister Joy heard it and came down the path to greet them, saying, "You'll find Mummy looking rather older, and Daddy is more absent-minded than when you were here last. He keeps on losing his glasses. Even Dumisane looks older. Sonya's gone back to varsity although she's struggling to cope and phones us often – when she can get through. Daddy visits Zeno's grave every day and I go along with him when I can."

Joy had grown in self-confidence and gave the impression that she was now 'in charge' of her parents and the household, young though she was.

Friends, no matter how close, can only sympathise with those who have experienced the unexpected death of a child and how it drags most parents down into a black hole of despair and loneliness. And thus it was with the Broccardos.

Although they did not show it, they were irritated by well-wishers who would recall the accidental death of some distant friend's young relative or someone unknown to them. While realising that such tales were efforts to establish rapport and sympathy, Bianca and Paolo would want to say (but never did): "We don't really care a damn about what you're telling us. What on earth has that got to do with the death of our son?"

What they actually did was to thank them and offer them

a drink or two, seated in deckchairs on the granolithic of the front verandah, which became slippery in wet weather.

After the visitors' departure they would breathe sighs of relief, saying, "Thank God they've gone," and talk about 'the old times' when Zeno did this or that, the difficult birth of the twins, or when all three children had become marooned in their rowing boat on the Nseleni River. The wind had changed direction and blocked their way with water hyacinth. Fear of crocodile attack was always present. The children had to reach down to pull aside the floating weeds while prodding the boat forwards with the oars, a laborious and dangerous process. It would have taken only a moment for a croc to snatch an arm and drag a child under water.

Once again, the Broccardos sat with Toby and Donald in the uncomfortable deckchairs under the mounted animal heads, with Joy taking up her post on the skin-covered pouffe, close to her mother. Their visit differed from the usual courtesy-callers, however, in that the men had experienced not only Zeno's death but the sudden and violent deaths of comrades-at-arms and the shock of their loss. Countering the enemy was less important than companionship shared or shattered.

This was the uniting bond of the Zeno tragedy. While the men had prepared themselves for possible resentment and rejection, all they sensed between them, and Bianca in particular, was a letting go…a floating away…a disentanglement and a fading.

"You'll share a drink with us, of course?" said Paolo as the telephone rang. "Ah, that must be Sonya. I'll tell her you two are here," he said, bustling off to the phone.

"Yes, yes. We are fine. We have two visitors, Toby and Donald. Would you say hello?" he asked, beckoning to Toby to come to the 'phone. "Yes? Well, here he is."

"Hello, Sonya. We called in to see how your parents and Joy are doing. We arrived from Durban this morning and are travelling on to Ntambanana tomorrow. Yes, they look fine, and Joy and Dumisane between them are doing an excellent job of controlling the household. Yes. She's seeing to it that they're eating sensibly, she tells us – and I am sure Dumisane is ensuring that too!"

"Yes."

"Could we write to each other, perhaps? Yes? That's marvellous. My address is 'Hadeda', Ntambanana, Zululand. What's yours? Well, more later through letters. I really look forward to seeing you soon, as very soon as possible. Take care of yourself, and here's your Dad," he said, handing over the handset to Carlo again. He had to bellow down the phone.

"You seem to like her," said Carlo.

"Yes, very much."

"Well, we wouldn't stand in your way," Carlo said. "You might be living only fifteen miles up the road, so if it came to anything, our daughter would be creating a home not too far away from us."

Toby was tongue-tied for the moment out of the sheer pleasure of hearing Carlo say that, and after they left Donald said, "You seem as pleased as punch all of a sudden?"

"Yes. We're going to write and Carlo said he would like the idea of Sonya settling down at Ntambanana. How's that?"

"That's quite a long furrow you'll have to plough, but she's a lovely girl. Who knows what Sonya will want? You know how women are…Don't twins usually marry twins?"

Chapter Two

Donald had been in touch with von Weldenburg from Durban, so the couple was expecting them. During the train ride to Empangeni he had asked Toby not to be taken aback at his expressing views that might be considered 'right wing', and asked Toby to imply to their host mild anti-British views from an Irishman's perspective. Not over-emphasised, but implied.

"For what reason?"

"I just want to watch his reaction – and Frieda's. I don't trust him, and wonder what he's up to."

The farm was several miles south of Empangeni towards the coast – off the same dirt track they had driven along on the fateful excursion to Richard's Bay with Zeno at the wheel. They had armed themselves with guest-presents – the careworn book, *Herrschaft und Knechtschaft by* Hegel, a bottle of Opsaal Brandy, and a large tin of Darboven coffee, "much loved by that Swiss man," he was told at Loftheim's.

Curved white entrance walls on the left of the track marked the entrance to the farm, with its name, 'Füllhorn', picked out in black metal letters above a metal cast of a cornucopia. Bountiful bougainvillea had taken hold, so that only the letters 'Füllh' poked through the growth. Toby got out of the car and pushed aside the shrub to make sure they had arrived at the right place. An entrance much further down gave access to the sugar fields and the Indian lines.

The thatched single-storey farmstead was at the end of a winding earthen driveway, shaded by forest mahogany and red-beech trees, and melodious with the calls of robins and sunbirds. On one side was a Braithwaite water-tank on stilts, surmounted by an extremely tall lightning conductor. A similar free-standing lightning conductor was to the left of the house.

When they got out of the Kelpie Donald stood in the wide sandy yard, fascinated by the darting of foraging black ants emerging from the ground, communicating with each other by touch and pheromone trails, and returning to the many ant-holes near his feet, while ever more ants emerged. It was a never-ending flow.

He thought that there must be at least a dozen different pheromone and vibratory 'words' which selected members of the colony understood. "An insect proto-language. Was Nietzsche right after all?" he thought. "Do ant teams serve overarching 'Uberants'?" He had read somewhere that all the foragers darting about at his feet were females and that male ants just lingered around the nest to be pampered and fed by them, before developing wings and flying off to mate. For the moment, he was transfixed. As this was a colony, he pondered, how did it keep itself distinct and protected from neighbour intrusions? Were there distinct dialects, and could one ant colony learn a neighbouring dialect so as to issue alarm signals on the intrusion of a common predator, like an anteater?

"Helloo!" called Frieda from the main doorway. After a round of 'air-kissing' and hand-shaking, she said, "Grusse! I see you like our pet ants. If you stamp your foot they swarm and attack. Just like Zulu impis. I saw you looking at our lightning conductors too. Ve get terrible, terrible lightning here and Hubie is scared of our thatch catching fire. There are more masts at the back in the trees, otherwise the trees are struck, he says. You have just missed him. He's on the farm. There has been trouble with Indian who run away. The police catch him and bring back to the farm just now. Hubie'll be back soon, soon. Come in, come in! Ve haf another visitor, Claude Stoughton. He's with Hubie."

One of the walls in the hall bore evidence of von Weldenburg's shooting prowess, with mounted heads of a wildebeest, a waterbuck, a duiker and a bush pig. Three stuffed purple-crested Louries were in a glass case on a hall table below them.

"What an interesting entrance!" Toby said.

"Ja. Hubie likes to shoot things. I don't – but what can you do?"

"For the farm, we were lucky. The estate was 'made good' by Herr und Frau von Breitenberg. They order roofs to be thatched but he die, Blackwater Fever, five years past. Buried on the farm. His wife she stayed but later give up and went home to Zurich with her kinders after the war was finished. So we bought the farm from her."

"Hubie knows members of the family, very illustrious in Switzerland." She gave the impression of not utilising her imperfect English very often but was warm and friendly, showing them to their rooms which smelt pleasantly of thatch.

She was a willowy five foot ten with intelligent eyes, high cheek bones and an easy manner, unlike the husband who they met up with again later, seeming to be perpetually on his guard and unbending, though willing to take the lead in conversations. Toby thought that Frieda's mouth was far too close to her bottom jaw – "rather like a sheep".

Captain Stoughton came as a surprise, as he was measurably stockier than Donald expected him to be, with a high brow, curly dark hair and impeccable English. Donald guessed that he was a shade over forty. He spoke little at first and gave the impression that he was weighing up the new arrivals.

They were sitting on the verandah under thatch. The house stood on a rise and the verandah gave way to a lawn bordered by red hot pokers, undulating fields being prepared for planting, and some low-lying hills beyond. Brandies and soda were at hand.

"If you come out to the front on a clear day you can see the sea from that kleine hügel over there," Hubie said.

"You came here to look at the farm and how we do things, but in winter the sun goes down early. We can see more in the morning light. Toby, you mentioned that you both planned to visit the Bells tomorrow at about lunchtime, so that will give us plenty of time for our farm inspection. We have ploughed and will be planting winter legumes to fix the nitrogen in the soil as soon as we can crush the god-damned weeds – the fluch und belastung of every farmer along with our unreliable Untermenschen and the weather."

"The grave of the owner who lived here before is on the farm just over there and we agreed to care for it, so perhaps we could stroll over just now before sunset to see that all is well? We must get back inside again before the mosquitoes come. Have you got quinine?...If not, we have plenty."

As they strolled to the grave, Hubie said, "My friend is even tougher than he might look. Believe it or not he rode by horse to Empangeni from the Vryheid district via Nongoma. Not bad for a brandy salesman, eh?"

"It would have been easier if I had been younger," Stoughton said, "but it was worth it. I saw a land as it should be. No railways, no roads – just a few tracks – and the pleasure of sleeping under the stars again. Of course, I had to keep a fire going to keep the jackals and hyenas away. Not my favourite animals."

"The only nasty moment was the crocodiles I met when I was preparing to cross a drift at sunset. I spotted one of them lying almost submerged right across the way I had to go. I thought it was a log at first."

"Ja. You never know where they are," Hubie said. "We see them in a stream that joins the Mhlatuzi River. Some lie on a sandbank but others hide in the reeds."

"So what did you do?"

"I shot him. Three times. All twelve foot of him. He reared up and struggled away to die and then I saw all the rest of them splashing and scuttling. I hadn't seen them before that. I rode across as quickly as the horse could pick its path while they were disturbed and got as far from the river as I could, before the light went. It was touch and go because the horse stumbled mid-stream and nearly threw me into the river. It was frightened."

"You must be careful of them where you are going to farm – them and bilharzia. Lots of crocs in the river there. Juss! They are cunning. They spend a lot of time watching what's going on around them. They notice where animals come to drink so know where to go when it's time to hunt."

"If you wash clothes or swim at the same place, the crocodile will know. If you often cross the river, or collect plants or catch fish at the same place, the crocodile will notice."

"When it's ready, it will sink below the surface without a ripple and then grab you when it gets close enough, crushing your bones in its mächtige kiefer, and drag you down to drown. Pfffft! If you see one on land, just back away slowly. They don't attack on land – at least not often."

The simple gravestone bore a roughly chiselled coat of arms and the legend 'Rudolf von Breitenberg 1868 – 1913. Moge er in Frieden ruhen.'

Hubie slashed at the weeds growing there with his stick and shouted: "Bloody khakibos! It'll smother us one day. We can hear it growing at night when we are in bed!"

"Have you done this for long?" asked Donald, after they had settled back on the verandah again. "I mean, representing a brandy company?"

"No. I got the job when I decided to return home after the European war. These are hard times and jobs are few and far between for people who are not farmers and have no land or much money, so I took it, for the time being."

"See any action?"

"You mean in uniform, in Europe?"

Donald knew du Quesne was in Brazil during most of the war, sabotaging merchant ships bound for Britain by secreting explosives into the coal. It was suspected that Lord Kitchener was dispatched by this means, when his ship HMS *Hampshire* blew up after leaving Scapa Flow in June, 1916.

"Yes, once when I was twelve I had to help fight off and kill some natives who were attacking the family on the farm, and in the second Independence War (you call the Boer War) as a lieutenant with Commandant General Piet Joubert. I fought against you fellows at Ladysmith, when I was put out of action by a British bullet through my right shoulder."

"After our Independence War I went to America where I managed to wangle a reporting job on the New York Herald, where I met the owner, someone called Gordon Bennett, at an anti-Prohibition drinks party. He saw me as adventurous – like that man Stanley he sent to Africa to find Livingstone. He offered me a job reporting on rubber matters in Bahia, Brazil…and there I stayed. I took no part in your European war."

Donald marvelled at du Quesne's ability to weave together a convincing farrago of fact and fiction. He thought that 'Stoughton' could easily convince anyone of the existence of Prester John, mermaids and men in distant lands who bore their heads under their arms. He said, turning to Toby as if to get his agreement, that he was impressed with Stoughton's courage and versatility.

"We'll drink to that!" said Hubie, and refreshed their glasses with brandy, adding soda from the syphon; whereupon Donald stood up, raised his glass and shouted loudly 'Opsaal!' in the form of a toast, making the dogs scramble up and escape around the corner of the house. Toby looked startled too. Frieda had excused herself by this time to supervise the preparation of dinner.

'Opsaal!' was to become a rallying cry in the years to follow among Dutch-Afrikaners, who remained hell-bent on throwing off the British yoke forever.

All had changed for dinner, with Donald having to dig out the only jacket he had to hand, a black and dark-blue striped Old Alleynian blazer which he had kept in his travel case. The gold thread in the crest was beginning to unravel.

Frieda came into the dining room after the men had gathered. She had changed into a black chemise dress with a waistline dropped to the hips à la mode and a hemline above the knee, with beige silk stockings above simple black pumps to show off her legs.

The impression on the men was evident. All eyes were on her, exactly as she had planned.

When they were seated she rang a small brass table bell for the first course to be served, upon which three be-gloved and uniformed Shangaans entered, with soup in a large silver tureen and a bread basket.

"We first have soup of Richards Bay oysters!" said Frieda brightly, and added, "I made the Brötchen myself," as one of the servants ladled the soup, another holding the tureen while the third offered Frieda's rolls from the shallow basket.

"First we say Grace," said Hubie, launching immediately into "Danke, Herr, fur diese deine Geben," catching the guests off-guard; then added: "We usually call it Rio-do-Peixes soup after the Portuguese explorers who found the Mhlatuze Lagoon at the Bay…'The River of Many Fish'. The lagoon is still jumping with them – and hippos and crocodiles and pelicans. But of course you have been there," he ended brashly.

The room was lit by candles on the table and tin wall reflectors, combining to create soft light and pale overlapping shadows. "We have a generator and batteries, but Frieda likes candlelight for dinner-time," Hubie said.

Outside the wire mosquito-screen, a chorus of crickets and very small frogs had started up. Moths and other night insects were fluttering against it, attracted by the light.

There was a large grouping of family photographs and small watercolours on the dining room walls – one was a daguerreotype of a balding man in a high collar and a waistcoat decorated by the chain of a pocket watch caught in a central button. His waxed moustache was turned up at the ends. Another was the head of a smiling woman with a long face like a greyhound, small horizontal slits of eyes and an enormous smiling mouth revealing large teeth. Below her was one of a woman in a white dress, in front of many arched house windows, reining in two large labradors, one sitting and the other standing and staring vacantly, as dogs often do when on a tight rein. Above those were unsmiling pictures, presumably because the figures had to hold their positions and expressions for the long exposures. There was one of a girl with puffy cheeks and a head crowned by a garden hedge of hair, another of a newlywed couple – he, fair-haired, in a uniform with a black collar, she, a brunette, in white with left arm entwined with his and her right dangling a modest bouquet of flowers at her side.

Next came fish, fresh from the Mhlatuzi Lagoon, accompanied by white wine, redolent of sandstone and granite, from a Constantia estate in the Cape, introduced by a toast proposed by von Weldenburg to his guests. It was followed by game, carved on a sideboard, as he described where he encountered the nyala in riverine bush near a watering pool.

"This red Petite Arvine wine I keep only for special guests as it has been impossible to get it from Switzerland, so it's from a dwindling stock we managed to bring with us; but it goes so well with the nyala, ja? We grow our own vegetables too so we do not suffer shortages."

"The white wine from the Cape you had with the fish I consider almost as good as the Chardonnay from Switzerland, which travels badly so I did not bring any with us. Although the Cape wine had to travel by train a long way, it has not suffered too much."

"Now, I must thank you again for the Hegel book," said von Weldenburg. "I have no doubt that it will reinforce my views about Untermenschen."

"Perhaps. But does not Hegel concern himself more with a notional 'elevation' of slave to the level of master? An 'erhebung'? Was not this the thread that attracted Schopenhauer and Karl Marx? I'm afraid I have very little knowledge of these things so I could be completely wrong; but I thought the book might just intrigue you."

"It certainly does. The influence of Marx brought about this second chaos in Europe even while it is enduring the result of the last one, so I will most certainly be interested to read the book. It is a case of 'know your enemy'. Of course, Frieda has completely differing views."

"What happened to the Indian brought back to the farm?"

"He was flogged."

"I see. And what will happen next?"

"He must work, but I have cut by half his food ration for a month."

"He must work with even less food?"

"Ach, it is not all bad, Donald. His wife works in our kitchen garden and you know how these coolies are. They steal food from under your nose. We have to lock up the mieliemeal, the sugar and the tea in the kitchen. He will not go hungry."

"Do they run away very often?"

"No. This is only the third; but the first one died later. When they don't fill their weekly quota, I cut their ration and their pay – so I suppose this could be the reason. They are lazy swine, you know."

"But are not the Zulus even lazier?"

"Ach! They just won't work at all. All they like to do is sit and look at their cattle. I don't even want them on our farm, but I have to have some. The Shangaans from the Mozambique border are better. Some people call them Tsonga."

"You are too harsh, Hubie!" Frieda said. "That is the why the Indians run away."

"The Indians I have encountered seem to work hard and some with great initiative; but I am told that the long-term effects of malaria make anyone seem lazy," said Donald.

"Perhaps. We were promised cheap labour, but it is not cheap when half of them vamoose and some of those that are left get sick and die."

"Mrs. von Weldenburg, are you still involved in teaching Braille?" asked Toby. "I remember you saying that you taught Braille to soldiers in a Swiss sanatorium."

"Frieda, please! Call me Frieda. Ja, I work in ski resort commandeered by Red Cross for wounded German prisoners of war, many blinded by gas. So I taught them Braille. The Red Cross kept other mountain resorts for Western prisoners with bad wounds too. Gas-blindness was bad on both sides. We kept them in Switzerland until the war finished. Sixty-eight thousands!

"There was lots of different gas but phosgene was the awful worst. It couldn't be seen – not like chlorine; but smelled like wet hay. Most died running away from the gas. Those that stayed and stood on parapets suffered not so badly, they told me. The men that lay down, like the wounded, suffered very bad, because the gas sank down into the trench.

"I saw men suffering from mustard gas. Fatal cases took about five weeks to die. The skin of survivors blistered and they were blinded. Also lots of bleeding inside and breathing painful. Like near drowning.

"Why are you men such brutes? You kill your animals more kindly than your human enemies! But because of my Braille training I observe many blind and nearly-blind people here, mostly natives. I am going to try and see what I can do. It will help me get past what I have seen."

"Ach, mein Gott, Frieda! We will be smothered by them if you teach on the farm." Turning to Toby and Donald, he said: "My wife always wants to do good works."

"Not true, Hubie! We must not waste any skill we have. Zat is all," and turning back to Toby she said, "Meanwhile,

I help Hubie with the accounts and the house. On a farm there's always almost too much to do."

Donald mentioned that he had, just by chance, met the secretary of the Durban Braille Society who was keen to establish contact when he mentioned Frieda's interest to her, and fished out of his jacket pocket a piece of crumpled paper with Danielle Joubert's address.

"I remembered, from our conversation on the Bell's farm, that you had expressed an interest in contacting the Durban Braille community, so I just scribbled down her address. I hope you can decipher my writing."

"Thank you. Zat is most kind. I will write to her as her advice will be useful. I believe zat all written languages here, including Dutch-Afrikaans, use the basic Latin alphabet – with extra letters for the diacritics."

They looked blank until she said, "By 'diacritics' I mean accents which can change the meaning of the word. But I do not know Zulu at all, so I will start with English and Dutch-Afrikaans (which I understand, but not perfectly) and even zat will be a big kopje to climb."

"And Fritz? What happened to your horse?" asked Toby.

"Sadly, I sold her in Empangeni. I think the risk of East Coast Fever here is too great to rely on a 'fourlegs'; so the rest of my travels will be by train – until the distillery decides that I've earned a car – not that a car will help much on the few bad roads you have here in Zululand."

"That encounter you had with the crocodiles must have been highly unpleasant. But you also talked about bilharzia when we were at the grave. Is it that bad?"

"It's bad in streams and rivers everywhere in Natal in the midlands down to close to the coast. Not so bad near the mountains, because the water flow is strongest."

Hubie joined in by saying: "Badenhorst's oldest child

got it, paddling in a spruit near here, where there are no crocs. Makes you sick and makes a child stupid; stops them growing properly. The parasite goes into the skin and sits in the lungs and liver. When it matures it infects the intestines and other parts. The only cure is buchu, a kind of bush with white flowers; but if you put ducks in the stream the bilharzia snails disappear too – don't know why. But then the black-backed jackals eat the ducks."

"How did you three come to know each other?" Donald asked.

"Well," said Fritz glancing at Hubie and Frieda, "That is a long story and too long to bore you with tonight. Let us just say that Hubie charmed Frieda away from me on wings of song."

Fritz asked whether either of them were married, and Toby replied that while there were intentions afoot neither of them had had much time for courting between 1914 and 1918. Fritz looked at them steadily and Donald would have given a fortune to know what was passing through du Quesne's mind right then. There didn't appear to be any sign of hatred for the two 'Englishmen'.

The party moved to the sitting room where candlelight was reinforced with pale electric light from a standard lamp, which throbbed with the revolutions of the generator in one of the sheds, and a log fire which helped take the chill off the early winter evening. Hubie's dogs had found the fire well ahead of the humans and were slumped across the hearth. Of the books and magazines on the generously-proportioned coffee table a newspaper titled *Völkischer Beobachter und Sportblatt* caught his eye because of the curious symbol on the masthead – a cross with hooked legs in a circle. The front cover also carried a grainy photograph of a young woman wearing a pearl necklace.

When he asked Hubie about the symbol's significance von Weldenburg replied that it was a 'sauwastika' and thought that it was a Buddhist and Hindu good fortune symbol.

"A Swiss friend posted the paper to me and it has just arrived, with a letter. He was sent it by someone in Germany – a friend of Grafin Hella von Westarp, who was murdered in München early this year by the Bolshevik Red Guard, part of the so-called Bavarian Soviet Republic. See, that's her picture. She was an anti-communist. The letter says that they just took her into a courtyard and shot her because she was a member of the Kapitalistischen Klasse. She was the secretary for the paper. Very sad; but I just read it for the sport pages."

He went to a large, dark Carl Ecke upright, opened the keyboard, lit the candles on the swing-out candelabras and sat down; then, looking at Frieda enquiringly, launched into a surprisingly well-played Schumann introduction before Frieda moved to stand beside the piano to sing 'Wenn ich in deine Augen seh' ('When I look into your eyes all pain and woes fade') – and they really did look into each other's eyes. The 'Englishman' guests sat surprised, impressed and silent. Stoughton's gaze remained fixed on Frieda.

At the end of the Lied, Hubie said: "The piano belonged to the last owners. The wife left it for us when she went back to Switzerland. She told us that it was brought by ship to Durban then loaded onto an ox-wagon to bring it to the farm. The missing piece of wood on the top of the piano has always been so, and was damaged by rough handling during its travel here."

"In the dry season it goes out of tune and we have to fetch the piano tuner off the train at Empangeni."

Another Lied followed before 'Stoughton' wound up the evening, laced by more Opsaal brandy and the glow of well-being, by fetching a guitar from his bedroom and playing from memory some favourite tunes he said he learnt while listening to the Bahia rubber-tappers. Some were work-songs, he said. For one of them, they would chant over and over the words 'Não venha para a Bahia' to a strange beat they called 'lundu' or 'samba'. He demonstrated the rhythm by slapping the top of the guitar with his fingers.

"Often, they would dance to it when work was finished for the day…a strange sort of shuffle. Three steps to two beats. Sometimes it was only the women who danced, in a circle."

"Ach, show me, Fritz!" said Frieda, getting up and making moves to dance with him.

"I will try. OK, Hubie?"

"Ja, Ja," he said. "Frieda loves to dance. I don't…" pouring himself another Opsaal and beginning to slur his words.

'Stoughton' asked the others to tap out the rhythm with their fingers on a table, which Toby and Donald tried to do, resulting in a confused clatter compounded by both dogs sitting up and howling. Frieda insisted that each of them danced with her in turn. Hubie had fallen asleep. Fritz broke away to pick out the melody while the other guest not dancing continued to clatter out the rhythm.

The end of the evening became blurred. Donald distinctly remembered coming across Fritz and Frieda, tightly embraced and kissing in the passage to their bedrooms. "So she's seducible," Donald thought, stumbling past.

The night engulfed him when he slumped onto the bed, and the nightmares were quick to return, full of Wellsian one-eyed squids overwhelming a ship he was on.

The dogs followed von Weldenburg everywhere, and the guests found them slumped beside him at early breakfast on the verandah, served by a surly and unshod Indian kitchen maid. The pleasant smell of thatch was all-pervasive. Frieda was not yet awake and Fritz had elected to sleep off his Opsaal, or so they were told.

"Zopf?" asked the host, offering them braided white bread and an array of butter, jam, honey and cheese, after they had polished off bowls of muesli, followed by fried eggs and bacon.

"I taught the baker in Empangeni how to make Zopf. Goet, Ja? All Swiss eat this."

At the end of the meal Hubie said: "Let us ride to the fields in Kelpie! OK? I've never been in one. But first we go to the shed and collect my binoculars. The shed's behind the house. Then we have to come back through the kitchen again. OK?"

Finding them he said, "I like the Dutch-Afrikaans word 'Verkykers' better. 'Far-lookers' says more than the English 'two-eyes'."

The corrugated iron shed bore all the marks of a meticulous Swiss. Tools were all marked and clipped to their places in racks and even the ox-drawn farm machinery was lined up like a squadron. It was then that Donald spotted something tell-tale – for on the bench, among other bits and pieces awaiting repair, was a disassembled radio-telegraph keypad. Most of the parts mounted on a small wooden base were of brass except for the return spring which had rusted and snapped. Repair had been interrupted at a point when sundry replacement springs lay on the bench beside a pair of snout pliers.

Expressing interest in an American plough, in for repair, he deliberately left the Kelpie's keys on the vast bench, a good distance away from his main interest.

On reaching the Kelpie again and making a show of fumbling in his pockets for the keys he exclaimed, "Oh, my

God. I put them down on the bench in the shed. I was so interested in your machinery. Won't be a moment."

He strode back through the kitchen, saw the kitchen maid and said, "Tell the wife of the man who ran away to wait for us at the gate to the farm. We will have some food for them. What's her name?"

"Deepika."

"We will leave in about one hour. Tell her to watch out for our car."

Reaching the shed, he quickly looked for any evidence of a radio telegraph transmitter, and located it under a piece of tarpaulin in a far corner behind agricultural machinery and masked by a rack of batteries. He discovered a box of Leyden Jars and a spark gap linked together by electrical wires and, separately, a headset. From these, a twisted pair of wires led out of the shed at the back towards very tall twin poles about 150 feet apart which he glimpsed in a small clearing among a cluster of gum trees. They were well out of sight from any road or path and were masquerading as the lightning conductors to which Frieda had referred. A wire was slung between them to which one of the wires from the shed seemed to be attached halfway between the two poles, although much of its length was concealed by weeds and thorny undergrowth. He assumed that the other would go to ground as the earthwire. This suggested that there was no necessity to utilise message couriers because long-wave radio telegraph contact could be maintained with an offshore base – perhaps with a sympathetic radio operator on a liner of the Holland East Africa Line which had taken over seventeen German war reparations ships. Cash and material would still have to find their way overland, of course, Donald realised, but as Dutch vessels were calling at South African ports again this would not be insurmountable.

He had just enough time to replace the cover and make a move of returning to the car, jangling the keys, when von Weldenburg appeared at the entrance saying "Ah! You find them?"

"Yes, careless of me! Too much Opsaal last night. Got to my noggin."

"Your 'noggin'?"

"My head. Still fuzzy."

"Oh. Ha-ha. Come, we ride in Lizzie!"

In the fields they visited, the soil had been harrowed and ploughed by ox-drawn machinery, and Indian women with their older children were dotted about the fields removing pebbles and stones thrown up by the harrow into small heaps. On one stretch, a driller was being coupled to a span of two oxen in preparation for seeding with a winter crop of beans. Legume growth accelerates and fixes nitrogen in the soil as the days become shorter.

"So we make money! Winter beans help sugar cane to grow when the days grow hotter, longer and wetter again."

"Late August, before we plant the new cane, we plough in kraal manure for fertiliser. In fields over there we just re-grow the cane after cutting it down to stubble, and take away the trash when winter is over. We can do that for three years, maybe a bit more; then we must replant. This is what we will do in this field."

"But the nagana sickness is becoming bad for our oxen and there is no known cure. Then there are the ticks. We have to dip our cattle every three days when it starts to rain again. I should have bought nguni oxen, but didn't. Mein Gott! Africa is so full of disease. I am thinking about buying a Fordson tractor from a dealer in Durban, a man called Chapard."

"Oh? Yes, I know him. We bought our Model Ts from him," said Donald, as they walked into the next field.

"Ja. Here, already, we cut cane stems into short pieces for storage over winter. We cover them so that light doesn't start – how you say – germination? Then we re-plant in some fields later. Let me show you," he said, leading them over to an Indian cutting cane into short lengths. There was a pile of cut stems at his feet.

"Nein, nein, nein!" he yelled. "You've cut them on the joints, you fool!" and kicked the makeshift stool away from him then punched him in the face, sending the worker sprawling.

"You have wasted the cane!" he shouted.

Toby immediately jumped between Hubie and the Indian and said "Stop, Hubie. Stop! Stop! This is not good." It took some time for Hubie to simmer down.

After taking their leave Donald stopped the Kelpie out of sight of the house, near the entrance, where an Indian woman in a ragged sari was waiting.

"Are you Deepika?" he asked. "Here. Bags of rice and sugar for your family. They should last for a month," whereupon Deepika sobbed with tears of relief.

"Can you write in English?" he asked.

"Little bit."

"What's your husband's name?"

"Vishnu."

"Write to me in a month to say if all is well. Here is my address in Ntambanana and here is money to buy stamps. Here is some paper, too, and a pencil."

"Bit over the top, don't you think?" said Toby, after they drove away. "Hidden motives?"

"Perhaps," Donald said.

Chapter Three

Dearest Emily,

I am writing this at night in a rather bleak bedroom under a worse-for-wear mosquito net at the Masonic, smelly with old tobacco and other odours of past tenants. Excuse my wiggly writing. It's difficult to get enough light to see as the oil-lamp is feeble. The generator gets switched off at ten unless there is a special function. But at least I am in Zululand again, although those heavenly days and nights in Cavendish Chambers will linger with me forever.

You are constantly in my thoughts, and thank you for your letter and telegramme. 'Fatknickers' (at the bank) had obviously read the 'gramme before she handed it to me, so I wonder what rumour that started! Please look after yourself now you're back in Cape Town. Bad newspaper reports about the Spanish continue to come out of that city even now. Study hard, stay away from fascinating young men with glittering teeth and everyone who sneezes.

Toby and I spent last night at the von Weldenburgs. Frieda is nice but I agree with everything you said about her husband. Although it is hardly good form to speak ill of a host, the brutality to his workers became pretty evident. Not like the average Swiss at all. His daft ideas about 'Ubermenschen' kept on surfacing again and he had a runaway coolie flogged while we were there.

Only ill will come of him, I am sure, and I was glad to leave the next day. Met a brandy salesman there, a Boer. He related some wild stories about Brazil. Interesting fellow.

We had visited the Broccardos shortly after our arrival in Empangeni and my heart goes out to them, but I think they get irritated by a regular stream of 'comforters'. Also called in to your mother and father and met your brothers Andrew and Nigel. Great lads.

Your family has been dragged into a huge community fund-raising effort next month in aid of children orphaned by the flu. We and your brothers have been roped in to raise money by playing rugby against a Boer side, and there's talk of large bets being placed on us. This means we will have to drive in to Empangeni from Tam if we are to keep our promise. I just hope my leg doesn't let me down. The coolies have been coerced into running in an egg-and-spoon race and suchlike, and I'll be placing my money on Masheila's father, not that I think he has a chance of winning. Loftheim's have put up three large prizes of rice and children's clothing vouchers.

Lucy and your mother are planning to bake cakes for sale if they manage to get round present flour shortages. The whole shebang will take place in the field opposite the church, and the stammering minister was at the farm when we visited, discussing details. There is wild talk of a ball at the Masonic with prizes of fertiliser and suchlike for the lucky couples. I think I may give that one a miss, although I would have liked to witness the demonstration of the Tickeydraai.

Tomorrow I start out for Yonder in the Kelpie, fairly well stocked up with much tinned food, string, paraffin and things. So it's back to the bush and tent life until I can build the beginnings of a house. I'll keep you informed about that! Toby has acquired a Model T truck and we plan to drive to Tam in convoy. I am really looking forward to seeing the Dlomodlomo Mountain again and am becoming accustomed to the idea that Tam is my home and hoping (dear God, how I hope!) it will be yours too.

No sign of any rain for at least the next three months or more, so all that luscious grass from the summer rains this year has turned yellow.

I yearn for you, body and soul. Are you still wearing the ring?

Donald

PS: Can you send me photographs?

Donald then wrote a somewhat reserved note to Prue conveying his observations about the von Weldenburgs and 'Stoughton':

Dear Dodo,

I am back in the bundu and making preparations for the farm. The bird life in these parts is abundant and fascinating and one of the very first things I plan to do is to set up a bird-feeder at Yonder and record what varieties visit it during a fixed period, just as an experiment. As we share a common interest in these

creatures I'll keep you posted on what I have observed, if you would like that?
I don't know much about local species yet but, thanks to that list of birds you gave me and that magnificent book, studying them will while away the time as the crops grow (hopefully). But lest you suspect idleness, rest assured that days – nay, years – will be filled with toil from dawn to dusk, and there will be moments when I will wonder what on earth I have got into.

One visitor I have already noticed is the laughing dove – yes, I can recognise that! – which pecked away at seeds on the von Weldenburg's verandah when I visited. You may remember that I planned to visit them when I reached Empangeni before going on to Tam? They had an interesting fellow staying there called Stoughton (can't remember his first name). He told us that he was going to catch the train north in the afternoon to Mtubatuba, to be fetched by friends from Hluhluwe. Well, more later. Please give my fond regards to your parents.
   Much love
           Donald

After reading through it several times he realised that the letter was hardly convincing to anyone intercepting it. It was far too 'stiff'. He was torn between his loyalty to Emily and the need to introduce a more intimate note, so he added, after 'later', "I treasure those moments with you in the mu-se-um." He hoped that the alert by mentioning the laughing dove would imply that more details would be sent soon in code.

Sleep came slowly under the mosquito-net. It was a still night and the late voices tumbling out of the bar kept him awake. His slumber was filled with distorted incidents of childhood; then a wind sprang up in the early hours and rattled a loose piece of corrugated iron which became the rapid chatter of a German machine-gun at Kondoa Irangi.

Going down to breakfast next day among the heads of dead herbivores staring down at starched table napkins and damp bread rolls, Donald saw that the wooden foot and false teeth in the lost property cabinet were still there, now joined by a pair of black cami-knickers, a safety razor, a small teddy bear, a couple of tobacco pipes, and a battered copy of *The Thirty-Nine Steps*.

It was the last item which sent a shiver down his spine, until he reflected that this was a singularly popular and topical book and its landing up as a piece of hotel flotsam was inevitable, sooner or later.

The dining room remained redolent of after-dinner cigars, curry and many bacon and fried egg mornings. Toby, who had joined him, said, "I can't help wondering why the owners of country hotel dining rooms such as this one seem hell-bent on making them so absolutely gloomy, dark, smelly and bloody morose at this time of the morning. Even the waiter looks miserable."

"I think the owners resent the intrusion of daylight. Our waiter is deeply concentrating on the art of not noticing us. Perhaps it's so dark in here that he hasn't seen us."

While settling up at Reception afterwards Donald asked to whom the copy of *The Thirty-Nine Steps* belonged, and after a fiddle of keys and consulting of the hotel register the Indian said: "It was forgotten few days ago in room of Mr. and Mrs. Stoughton in Number 12."

"Oh, really? Mrs. Stoughton was there too?"

"Yes, yes. That is what it says. I remember her. Very pretty lady. She give me nice tip."

Toby and Donald exchanged glances.

"Lady with dark hair? Thin? I think I know her."

"No. Not so dark hair. Not so thin. Not so tall. They speak together funny language. Like Dutch but not."

"May I see the book?"

When it was handed to him Donald saw that a bookmark protruded from it marked 'Hotel Wagendrift, Hoog Straat, Vryheid', marking page 78 which started 'A fisherman came up from the waterside…'

"Wily fox" muttered Donald. "Wonder who the popsie was. Well – shall we be off to Tam, then?"

"See you in Tam, dongas permitting," Toby said. "Perhaps we can take a breather about half-way along at that giant tree. I remember spotting it growing beside a rocky outcrop."

"Excellent idea."

And so they did. At Model T speed over hazardous terrain, the tree came into sight an hour later.

"Any snakes?" asked Toby, opening a packet of sandwiches they had cadged from the hotel.

"Can't see any. I'll rattle around with my stick for a bit. Not keen on puffadders. Then I'll brew up the tea."

There was a very small rivulet near the tree, almost overgrown by grass, from which came the sound of a small fall of water. A solitary acacia tree stood among aloes in the middle distance.

"Beautiful view."

The view from the knoll where the tree stood was one of a rolling vista of grass, parched thatch-colour in the dry season, stretching into the heat haze, relieved only by flat-topped acacia trees, a distant cluster of native cattle, and beehive huts protruding above an outer ring-fence of branches.

"Strange to realise that as we sit here we are being watched by so many eyes…those vultures circling up there, the bulbuls and weavers in this tree, and probably by the lizards. I'm sure that a native or two is also monitoring our movements."

"Smith's Law, if there was one, would state that if a white man settles down to eat a sandwich in the bundu he will be surrounded by young Zulu children within ten minutes," Toby muttered, "and sure enough, here they come! And they have eyes too. What do you think they really want?"

"First, they want food," he said as he handed out some 'bon-bons' he took from a packet of them he had in the Kelpie. "Secondly, to satisfy a burning curiosity…something to pass the time. There's a rumour going around that we are wizards and are really black, taking off our white skins overnight to hang them up before we go to sleep. Thirdly, they will want a ride in one of the wizards' machines."

Some of them had brought simple representations of cattle modelled in clay dug from the bank of the spruit and hardened in the embers of a kraal fire.

"Who can speak little bit English?" Toby asked them. When one of them came forward, he asked, "What is the name of this tree?" slapping the trunk.

"Indwandwazane."

"Hmmmm…In-dwan-dwa-ZA-neh?"

At which they giggled.

The English name of the tree was White Stinkwood, ubiquitous from the Cape to Ethiopia. It acquired its English name from the unpleasant smell exuded when the wood is cut. It remains ideal for planking and yokes.

Recalling listening to the word-patterns of a Japanese harbour pilot years ago Toby, as a naval man, sensed a shared rhythm between Japanese port names and those of Zulu, as in 'Yo-ko-hama, 'O-ki-ma-nu', 'O-fu-na-to' and the local 'N-tam-ba-na-na' and 'Em-pan-ge-ni'.

"I think we had better get going. Agreed?" asked Donald.

Upon rising, the umfaans scrambled onto the back of Toby's truck and tried to cram into the Kelpie.

"OK. I was right! The third reason was to get a ride on our new gadgets. After all, our Tin Lizzies must be even more novel than the steamela which some have seen chugging along. We'll let them ride for a mile then chuck them off."

"Ride slowly. Don't bump them off."

A mile further on, over yet another veld detour to avoid dongas, they stopped and Donald shouted loudly the only other Zulu words he had learnt: "Hamba ekhaya!" [Go home!] to which they responded reluctantly, scrambling noisily off the back of the truck and turning to stand and wave from the edge of a donga, like a row of meerkats. He was startled that the few Zulu words he had picked up had had such an effect.

In those days, Tam was more a state of mind than a place – unless the small wood-and-iron store belonging to Piet van Jaarsveld could be considered the centre of the settlement, with its meandering footpaths radiating from the cracked front stoep. The rest of the development, not counting the faraway Norwegian Mission, comprised scattered farms, mostly still at the start-up stage, and a small wood-and-iron Natal Mounted Police station.

Van Jaarsveld came from a long farming tradition. His father Kosie and his grandfather, Gerhardus Jacobus van Jaarsveld, had been farming successfully for many years in the Orange Free State, until two successive droughts had destroyed their crops. It was Piet, the son, who persuaded them to start again with sugar cane near Stanger. In due course, Piet came to realise that he would never share the same point of view with his father, so decided to branch out on his own.

He had met his wife at a quarterly Nagmaal gathering held on the De Jagersdrift farm some miles from Vryheid, where there was a modest church building. Nagmaal, the Dutch Reformed Church form of Communion, was celebrated at these gatherings as well as weddings, christenings and related goings-on. It was one of the few opportunities for mingling and meeting when a tent and wagon-town would spring up, drawing families together from remote farms. The Nagmaal wagons were smaller and designed to carry family and belongings a comparatively short distance. The spans were also smaller.

Emma Hannatjie Badenhorst was only eighteen and Piet twenty-three when they had first met. She recalled often to the children their being allowed to sit alone together holding hands and talking in a covered wagon while the rest of the Badenhorst family discreetly chattered with their van Jaarsveld wagon neighbours outside a large tent they had pitched beside their vehicle. Papa Badenhorst treated humorously his lighting of the opsitkers before he stepped down from the wagon, but shyness could not conceal Piet and Hannatjie's natural attraction, and it was there that Emma exchanged her first real kiss. The purpose of the opsitkers was to bring to an end such meetings when the candle burnt down and spluttered out.

Reports were filtering down that more areas in Zululand were about to be thrown open to white settlers, and he could see good opportunities for establishing a trading store specialising in agricultural and building supplies as well as general goods. He would be able to advise fledgling farmers and attract sound custom over the years, despite the fact that they were mainly English-speakers. Turnover could also cater for the domestic needs of the natives and Indians living in the area. Also foreseen was that petrol-driven cars and tractors were in the ascendency and, although they were few and far between in Zululand in 1919, he saw that the decimation of oxen by nagana would drive farmers to adopt mechanical alternatives more quickly than would otherwise have been the case. He reasoned that installing a Pegasus petrol pump (the only one between Ntambanana and Empangeni) beside the water-troughs and outspan fodder shed would add to turnover in the years to come. Thus, although he didn't yet own a car himself, he could hardly restrain his delight when Donald and Toby arrived with their Tin Lizzies, vindicating, once again, his vision, as other settlers were also acquiring vehicles.

"These are slim [clever] things," he said, coming out onto the stoep, attracted by the Kelpie backfiring when Donald turned off the ignition, and catching sight of the dust-coated vehicles which had drawn up in front of the store, scattering native customers. "Wragtig. A rooi Tin Lizzie!" he said. "Hanna!" he shouted to his wife in the store, "Kom kyk!" which she did. "Hemel! Hoeveel sulke toestellen kos?" [Heavens! How much do such contraptions cost?] a question lost on the men. Hanna possessed a built-in resistance to new-fangled things mechanical that inhibited Piet from taking the plunge and buying a car. The ox-wagon remained embedded in Hanna's soul even though she was prepared for her husband to sell petrol to the foolhardy.

After buying petrol and a few provisions, they drove off in convoy in a cloud of dust to the Schnurrs, where Marie greeted them warmly.

"We've been expecting you, and welcome!" she said. "Eric is away somewhere talking to remote farmers as usual, but two letters arrived for you, Donald, by ox-wagon express. I'll make some tea and we can sit under the flamboyant tree while you read them and I catch up on the world with Toby. Just shoo the hens away."

Both letters were postmarked 'Durban'. The first was a

short little note from Judy wishing him well but the second, from Prue, which had crossed his in the post, made him pause and reread it. He read:

Dear Donald

The Dodo has become somewhat mustier in your absence, although I revisited it the day after you left for wildest Zululand, perhaps to recapture that moment beside the extinct old fowl. Although, as a blushing maiden, I should not be writing thus, I must confess that I am already missing you. We shared a lot in the short time we had together.

Not much news from Durban while everyone's struggling to get back to normal after the flu, those of us who have survived, except that Ivan Filatov came into the library with his children to say goodbye – you remember him at the League of Nations presentation and how he spluttered garlic-fumes behind his flu mask? He said that he had wangled a way to get to Russia in time to help in preparations for the second Communist Party International in Petrograd and Moscow in mid-July next year; that is, if it ever takes place, there being such turmoil going on, what with the war against Poland and all. I believe that the German, French and Czechoslovakian 'democratic' parties have been invited to attend, but not the Ukrainians. Russia is blockaded so the only legal way will be for him to enter through Revel. Lenin is projecting himself as the new 'Father of the Nation'. The proletariat is expecting to be given a fish but I think this demagogue will trick them into accepting a poisonous serpent. His 'Bread & Peace' slogan is a hypnotic spell if you are starving, however – as most of them seem to be.

Filatov maintains that the Russians have far more 'soul'. He wrote it down for me in Cyrillic like this: Русская душа! Sounded like Ruskea-hyah dooSHAH. He says that Durbanites have little soul by comparison. He's brave but foolhardy and left the care of his children to a very disgruntled wife. He plans to go through Germany first, now the Allied blockade has been relaxed to allow through American food supplies. I think he is planning to work as a deck hand.

Another snippet – a local native Josiah Gumede has been stirring up more trouble among the Durban Zulus over the new Native Lands Act, which limits African access to 7% of the country. He founded the South African Native National Congress through which this dissatisfaction is being voiced. Mummy has been flailing about injustice as usual and corresponding with that rabble-rouser poet Roy Campbell at Oxford, much to Daddy's despair, especially after Campbell failed his Oxford entrance exam.

Do write soon and let me know how Yonder is progressing. Seen many birds? The mynahs here have taken to diving on the cat. They sit and wait for it up in that coconut tree close to the house.

With love,

Dodo

PS: Daddy and Mummy send their regards. They rather liked you.
Mummy says please be kind to the coolies."

Chapter Four

Donald first encountered Layani sitting on his haunches near the new borehole. He was barefoot and wore a ragged vest, a pair of old shorts and an ancient felt hat, battered shapeless. Although Donald had little knowledge of tribal differences at this stage, he suspected that he was not a Zulu but rather a Shangaan because of the pattern of cut-marks on his face. He had learnt that these tribal incisions were made at initiation, and evolved in the hope that Arab slavers would reject such youths in the old days as being 'unsaleable'. Layani had a quasi-Arab nose, intelligent eyes and a wide mouth harbouring the whitest of white teeth. He kept his eyes downcast according to tribal custom, indicating respect.

("Watch out for any native that looks you straight in the eye, unless he's a chief," Jim had advised.)

"I will work for you, Nkosi," he said, stated in such a way that he expected this to be a fait accompli. Donald had learnt by this time to be circuitous in such meetings and realised that it would be a long time before he would be able to establish with any certainty where he came from and why he wanted to work for him; so asked, "Lambele? [Are you hungry?]"

"Yes, Nkosi. Eu estou com fome," he replied, half in what sounded like Portuguese, so he offered him a large mugful of mieliemeal and some of the lychees he had been given by Marie.

"You can take amanzi from the pump." (The hand-pump was on loan until Donald elected to replace it with a wind or steam-pump.)

Donald told him in English, with suitable gestures, that he could use his old three-legged cooking pot made of cast-iron, and indicated that he should light his fire for cooking a substantial distance away from the tent ("Don't get too friendly. Stay aloof," Jim Bell had advised, "or you won't be respected.")

"Ufuna usawoti?" [want salt?] "Ushukela?" [sugar] asked Donald in the same stumbling Zulu he thought he remembered from the primer; words which, almost unaccountably, had stuck in his mind. He had been studying basic Zulu from a very second-hand grammar he had bought at Loftheim's, titled 'isiZulu'.

"Hau," Layani said, either in surprise that the white man was attempting to speak in Zulu, which he could understand, although his tongue was a variety of Tsonga; or in surprise that the white man was kind, unlike the one he had run away from who farmed on the ocean side of Empangeni. He held out cupped hands as he was taught at initiation, indicating that he accepted the salt and sugar with gratitude, a gesture lost on Donald.

Layani went in search of firewood without another word, taking the cooking pot (Donald had a newer spare), mieliemeal and condiments with him, the latter held in twists of 'Sausage Wrap'.

Out of immediate sight of Donald, Layani poured a pyramid of mieliemeal into the centre of the pot after splashing in several mugfuls of water, added some of Donald's salt, then put the lid on and half removed the pot from the fire, leaving the mielie-meal to absorb the water while simmering. He mashed the end of a stick by pounding it with a stone, then used the stick to prod and stir the mieliemeal when he judged it was time to do so, stirring in more water to be absorbed.

Before he started to eat, he dug a small hole with a stick and let fall a dollop of putu followed by a trickle of water, covered it with earth, then pushed a stone on top of it. It was his way of expressing gratitude to the field's subterranean spirits who dwelt there, and the hope that he had found a home, for, to Layani's way of thinking, this putu was the nearest food to paradise, even though there was no nyama (meat) to round it out. It was the first time his stomach promised to feel satisfied since he had run away from von Weldenburg's farm.

Donald had pitched his tent close to the new borehole. On this occasion he had spent the remains of the day preparing the usual defensive fire near the entrance and tackling the promised message to Prue, and had gestured to Layani that he could sleep beside the same fire. He considered suspending a paraffin lamp near the tent on this occasion so he could see clearly enough to write, until he recalled memories of the clouds of flying insects it would attract, so penned the note unaided in the fading light, sitting on a box near the entrance and using as a writing board the Woodward birdbook Prue had given him.

He reached for the battered Buchan novel and opened it at random, noting the page number and choosing the line 'the desolation of the waves of a tarn lapped on their greygranite'. Next was the labour of applying the twenty-six letters of the alphabet, starting four letters in from the start of the line. Thus A became E, B became S, C became O and so on. This was followed by his starting a letter to Prue which read, after pondering on whether or not he should include the phrase 'heartily reciprocate':

> *"Dear Dodo. I am writing this at the entrance to my tent at Yonder, as the daylight begins to fade. The crickets and frogs are due to start up in about an hour, followed by the nightjars when it becomes completely dark. Thank you for your note and the sentiments expressed which I heartily reciprocate. This is a quick note to catch the cleft stick early tomorrow. To explain…the enterprising storekeeper here has introduced an effective postal distribution service for us in the new settlement.*
>
> *"A barefoot messenger, letters in a cleft stick (actually a post bag), arrives fairly early in the day, now and then (the frequency is a bit haphazard) to collect and deliver post, and it works very well. My deliveries and letters for posting are left in a sideways-mounted Huntley & Palmers tin box facing away from the prevailing wind and secured to a post, out of reach of ants and other nunus. Verily a Post Box. Ahead, I buy stamps when I visit the store. Strange to think that a letter posted months ago – say, in a remote part of Scotland – should find its way by rail, steamer and ox-wagon to a tent in Africa, delivered on the last leg by a barefoot messenger, who may not be able to read very well.*
>
> *"I am still at the early stages of living in a tent again and am about to overcome the challenge of clearing fields of trees and stones – with the help, hopefully, of some Zulu stalwarts and my interpreter, Layani, who is Shangaan.*
>
> *"I have managed to set up a modest bird feeder table; but keeping it stocked is a challenge as the most*

populous birds – particularly varieties of pigeons and doves – descend ferociously and clean the platter of practically everything before the smaller birds can even get near. The tiddlers are developing a 'crumbs from the table' approach, however, and have figured out how to position themselves under the feeder and wait for seeds to fall from the 'dogfight' above. The larger fowl spray seed everywhere in their ferocity and spend half their time fighting off their own number and flapping about, so a lot of seed falls below.

"*I am only now beginning to work out what eats what, and it dawned on me slowly that, generally speaking, small birds with stubby beaks eat on flat surfaces whereas those with long beaks peck from hanging food. It also dawned on me slowly to consult that magnificent Woodward book you gave me – I only 'clicked' when I saw a 'toppie' pecking away at the remains of a plum I had left. So I am now learning what range of morsels should be on offer.*

"*Nevertheless, true to our arrangement to give your Durban ornithologist-friend some sort of an occasional sampling of the variety of birdlife in the Ntambanana area, I sat for several hours carefully noting bird visitors which I hope I have managed to identify correctly (no guarantees!). Please ask him to forgive any notation mistakes I might well have made. You will recall we share his identical lists of most populous Natal birds, marked A, B, C and so on, so we can communicate in 'shorthand'. Here goes, recorded between 6 am and 9am yesterday (I'll explain the numbers afterwards):*

"75/15/4. OELNVAAEAIOEEOLWEFA-FAAVARAELAASTOITEHAENIOAANAIO-

ALTOAAVOFFAVTIOAVAAITIFALAEEO-
AALOETOETRATONLF!"

What Donald hoped he had written in code was, without word-breaks, "RadioTelegraph MastsVonWeldenburgFarm-FakeLightning ConductorMastsStoughtonGuestDeparted-HluhluweFriends."

> *The numbers refer to the number of beetles and other things that also visited the feeder and were duly gobbled up. I won't go into any details, except to say that Zululand is teeming with insects, let alone wild animals.* [In reality, 75 was for Page 75, 15 was for 15 Lines Down and the 4 was for Four Letters in From The Left, all referring to the Buchan book.]
>
> *Establishing this farm from scratch is daunting. While the Schnurrs are immensely supportive (you may remember my mentioning them during our League of Nations afternoon, after we escaped from Ivanov and his garlic fumes) I can see that finding and pinning down labour will be a constant concern. We are all chasing after the same labour pool – more of a puddle, really, with the natives showing little wish to work for the white man. I have about thirty trees to remove and thousands of stones to extract and haul away even before ploughing can begin, and without labour I am banjaxed. That was a word I heard an Indian use at the store. He explained it was a corruption of an Urdu expression – something like 'Bahngehecked' – when a flimsy earthen pot collapses, and these often do, it appears. Good word that, Banjaxed.*
>
> *It's getting too dark to see properly so all for now.*

Will you ever come up this way? With love, Donald.
PS: Please give my best regards to your parents. I liked
them too.

This was the first time Donald had slept under canvas since the East African campaign and he found it immensely satisfying to be lulled to sleep on a stretcher beneath his mosquito net and be serenaded by the chorus of the African night.

A snuffling sound at the side of the tent in the wee hours woke him, on one occasion. He thought that, while it might be a kraal dog, it could as well be a stray hyena or jackal. Both beasts have bone-crushing jaws capable of tearing off an arm, given the chance. He kept his loaded rifle beside his stretcher so got up slowly and quietly, poked it skywards out of the tent, and let off a shot, making the hyena scamper away with a howling growl, its tail between its legs. Layani had been far more vulnerable and, although he had woken minutes earlier, jumped up startled by the racket.

After helping him haul several more heavy logs to the fire Donald spent the rest of that night drifting in and out of sleep.

His interrupted dreams were haunted by failure. In his dawn dream, he was standing on a mound of sand within the walls of a vast but derelict wood-and-iron house where he had sown unidentifiable seeds. These sprang up, turned black and withered before his eyes. Somewhere in the dream, Creighton appeared eating gingernuts with a roll of old newspaper cuttings under his arm. Cole and Fatknickers were also there from his Durban bank. The latter was much fatter in his dream and had nothing on except a mauve hat and gloves. Creighton said that "it was the birds that got them." Turning to Donald, he muttered, with the mad logic of dreams, "You should be more careful of birthmarks; this is really not good enough." Prue was standing behind him, but there was no sign of Emily.

Donald had planned to pace out the site of a modest dwelling and shed that day to be built near the borehole, allowing for yard space, and then to walk as much of the arable land as he could cover in the morning, before making himself some breakfast. This he set out to do after staking out the position of the house, yard and sheds with the help of Layani, when he was halted mid-field by the sight of Toby standing on a fallen branch in the far distance. He had stopped in the middle of a clearing and discharged a rifle in the air without any apparent intention of taking aim at anything. Staring around him and turning away without seeing Donald and Layani, he did the same thing again, pointing his rifle in the air and letting off another shot.

After the third shot, it dawned on Donald that Toby was lost, so, after chuckling his head off, he bellowed, "What are you doing?"

Toby, spying his distant figure, walked towards him shamefacedly and said, "I hate to tell you, but I was absolutely lost. I'm rather short-sighted and every tuft of grass looked like the next one. I had intended to walk over to see you and suggest that mutual porridge and fried eggs might be a good idea."

"Good thinking," Donald said. "We can mull over ways to find each other's farms without wasting ammo. I have a compass which might help, as would a glance at the way the trees are bent. You can see that most wind blows North-North East and so bends the trees in that direction (one can check that on the compass). On the other hand, most rain-storms come from the South-South-West. Once you know how the farms are positioned you can get a compass fix from the trees. Moss also tends to grow on the lee side of the prevailing wind too. It's a rough guide, but it works. I had to rely on that sometimes when I was in East Africa. How was your first night under canvas?"

"Got tangled up in my mosquito-net first, then I found the chorus of the night disturbing. Then I kept on waking up worrying about the fire in front of the opening going out, then struggling out to feed the big logs into the fire. Not quite like sleeping on a ship – but I dare say I'll get used to it, in about a year or so. Aboard a ship one comes to recognise every slap, creak and groan of the hull; but wildest Africa is different – despite the short stint in crop production I did at Cedara, I still get the night-time heebie-jeebies in the bundu. However, something pleasant happened at first light this morning. I heard a woman's voice outside the tent saying something like 'Ghoiyamoorah! which made me jerk awake…I assumed it was a native woman jabbering away but when I looked out there was little Mrs Potgieter and Susannah. Remember them from the Spanish Flu? She rescued Susannah when Mrs Myburgh was dying and the husband was going off his rocker. They had come over by horse, with Susannah riding pillion. After I emerged from the tent she gestured to Susannah who presented me with a small contraption of wire holding a dozen eggs, each wrapped in pieces of old newspaper, and said something which sounded like 'Vellcom bay tam. Sesis furyo frind' [Welcome to 'Tam'. Six are for your friend] so I spoke the only words I had learned to utter in the lingo which sound like 'buy a donkey', but which I gather means 'many thanks'. Mrs Potgieter's English seems to be as lacking as my knowledge of Dutch, I think, or possibly she just doesn't like the language."

"Susannah said something like 'yaymoet dit teroogheer' [you must give it back] with suitable gestures which I guess means something like 'return the wire basket'.

"By the way, I saw a list of new settlers at Eric's last time we were there, and do you know what? There's only one Dutch surname among the lot of them, all sixty-seven of us ex-servicemen. Someone called Wessels; there was an Irish-looking one – Ryan -and the rest are names like Hamilton, Smith and Blackbeard (that's a helluva surname): I remember those. Schnurr did tell me that an Irishman called O'Grady, married to an Afrikaans girl, had settled in the vicinity many years earlier and he was not pleased at the 'English inval', as he called it. Bit belligerent. But it does make the Dutch look like endangered species in these parts, though this can't be said of the Vryheid area.

"I think that we 'English' should nurture our friendly relations with the Dutch families near Tam, though – and near Empangeni, even with that belligerent Afrikaans-speaking Irishman. The few Boers that we have met are built like rhinos, and we'll be playing some of them at rugby very soon. Besides, we liked the ones we rode up with on the ox-wagon express."

The divide was marked between the predominantly English-speaking new farmers in places like Ntambanana, and the Natal interior centred on the town of Vryheid, less than fourteen and a half miles away as the crow flies, where Dutch-Afrikaans was the lingua franca. 'Vryheid' is the Dutch for 'Freedom'. There remained serious 'distancing' between the two camps exacerbated by the permanent presence of Natal German residents who spoke in a dialect called Natalerdeutsch.

The establishing of Vryheid as its capital took its rise from the Boer founding of the Nieuwe Republiek in 1884 in Northern Natal. It was absorbed into the Dutch republic of the Transvaal in 1888, becoming part of Natal only after the second Anglo-Boer War in 1902.

While place names in the rest of Natal sounded predominantly English or Zulu, the villages in the Vryheid region remain Dutch-Afrikaans. Those that do have Dutch names in other parts of Natal are often anglicised – for example, Winkelspruit (pronounced in Dutch-Afrikaans as 'Vunkelsprait') is 'Winkle-sproot' to Rooineks.

The little Nieuwe Republiek centred on Vryheid was recognised upon its foundation by Germany and Portugal, but not by the Transvaal Republic and Britain, and occupied land granted to the Boers by the Zulu Prince Dinizulu, after an extraordinary ceremony when the prince was crowned King of the Zulus. This took place at Nyati Hill on the 21st May 1884, upon the death of the defeated Zulu King Cetshwayo.

After his installation by Zulu rites, a Boer leader, Andreas Laas, anointed him with castor oil in the presence of the Boer Commando, several princes of the Zulu Royal Household and about 9000 tribesmen, after which representatives of the Commando, the Comité van Bestuur, swore to uphold his sovereignty.

The outcome was that, in the turmoil following the Anglo-Zulu wars and the dithering of the British, the Boers, joined by some German settlers from Luneburg near the Transvaal border, contrived to carve out a substantial slice of rich Zululand pasturelands, almost incorporating St Lucia Bay before the British hastily annexed it.

"What's that native doing over there?" asked Toby, while the eggs sizzled.

"That's my first employee. He's a Shangaan, or so I think," replied Donald. "He just showed up and announced that he was going to work here; though I'm pretty sure that Schnurr directed him to me. At least he's not a Zulu so won't have qualms about being a general factotum. I'm going to need him and some of his friends to dig foundations...mix concrete and so on. He speaks rudimentary English, although he tucks in a few Portuguese words when he can't think of an English one and a Zulu one when he can think of neither. Still haven't worked out how much to pay him and still don't know the details about Indian payment."

"Schnurr'll be able to give a guideline."

"We've all got mountains to climb during the next few years, haven't we? Houses, lines for the Indians, Shangaan labour – or Zulus, if we're lucky; cultivation, employment paperwork and everything that goes with it; and in the midst of all that we must both negotiate with the Protector of Indians' Office and the Department of Agriculture. Shall we pop over to the Schnurr's and pick Eric's brains again? I'll need to get a lot of building material and God knows what else on the way back – as I'm sure you will too. I need a harrow, plough, picks, cement, sand, shovels, corrugated iron, wood and so on. Every time I look at my list it grows another foot's worth, while my bank balance shrivels as I slumber. Perhaps we can work out some system of sharing the bigger items like the harrows and ploughs?"

"Yes, of course, anything to save money."

"Layani! Woza!" Donald shouted to him, beckoning him to ride in the back seat of the Kelpie. As Layani clambered in it was clear that he had never been in a motor car before. His eyes were full of excitement and nervousness as Donald drove bumpily and very slowly over the veld to Toby's farm to collect his truck.

At the end of the visit to van Jaarsveld's store the truck had accumulated mounds of building materials, substantial lengths of timber, a bag-full of roofing bolts and nails, and a layered pile of corrugated iron sheets.

The clearing of Tam's virgin land for cultivation was going to be labour-intensive and time-consuming, demanding the removal of seemingly endless rocks and stones and trees.

After the lopping of branches and felling, earth had to be dug away from the tree-stump roots before they could be chopped free and wrenched out – ideally by a span of oxen. However, as nagana was attacking all but the hardiest nguni cattle, Donald realised that the Kelpie might have to be inspanned instead. The only other alternative was manual labour.

Thus began the long-winded process of getting permission from the nearest induna to employ some Zulu men – if they would agree.

The induna, known as the isigodi, acted as the head of the district or settlement, under whose sway were the umnumzane, the household heads, to whom the umuzi (individual householders) were likewise answerable. The isigodi was responsible for regional law and order and ruled by a hereditary inkosi, directly responsible to the Zulu king.

The tradition of clearing tribal land for agriculture was 'men's work'. Women's work in the fields was restricted to cultivation and the gathering and removal of small stones and pebbles. Children were enlisted to assist.

The first step in negotiating for labour was a waiting game to speak to the induna, initiated by an adequate introductory inducement, which took into account the preservation of the headman's dignity. Donald knew that the most attractive present would be of meat, but without access to refrigeration or ice and no venison to hand, a large sack of mieliemeal would have to do in his first approach. He considered taking along army-sized tins of meat and openers as well, but rejected the idea because of the risk of introducing ptomaine poisoning. The meat would deteriorate rapidly if left in opened cans at the kraal, as it surely would have been.

The terrain was so rough that Donald wondered how foolhardy he had been to take the Kelpie so far off the beaten track, and after a further mile had decided to turn back just as he was spotted by a group of umfaans.

They ran over the veld towards him, shouting with the hope of scrambling onto the car. With Layani translating, Donald said that he had a sack of mieliemeal for the induna and expressed the wish to talk to him. As this was happening, he looked down and saw that his trouser legs and socks were smothered in blackjacks – the ferocious clusters of black barbed seeds of the ubiquitous khakibos which hook onto clothes and animals.

An age of waiting followed, which he utilised to remove the blackjacks one by one while endeavouring to find out more about Layani. He established that this first employee of his had made his way from João Belo in Mozambique on foot, seeking work further south across the Natal border, driven by rumours of an abundance of great employment opportunities, unlike his home area which was enduring a prolonged drought. It led him to a sugar farm on the coast side of Empangeni, where the farmer he worked for treated him very badly. "Muito desagradavel!" he said, so he had fled and followed the road inland, skirting Empangeni. He was close to starving by the time he had presented himself at the Schnurrs. Eric had suggested he should offer his services at Yonder.

Eventually, the umfaans did re-appear with a very thin donkey on which to load the mieliemeal sack, thereupon the odd little party walked the considerable distance to the kraal with Donald doing his best to avoid brushing against more blackjacks.

He was curious to see the inside of the settlement, and found that the layout conformed to description, the main feature being the big central cattle kraal made of interwoven tree branches supported by stakes.

He was shown where to sit (on a carved low wooden stool, Layani more at a distance) where one of the induna's young wives knelt beside an earthen pot of beer. After skimming off the froth with a wooden spoon, she poured some of it onto the ground close to a clay pot, the Ukhamba. This was an offering to the ancestors in the spirit world, who always drank first.

Layani indicated to Donald to take off his hat.

The woman then poured the beer into a hollowed-out gourd before drinking a measure in the presence of the headman. Other wives and their children peeped around the huts to witness the strange visit of a white man and his assistant. The induna tested the beer to ensure that it was of a quality to offer the guests, and only then was the gourd offered to Donald and Layani and three middle-aged men, each wearing snakeskin head-rings woven into their hair, indicating that they were married. Induna kaJama was clad with a leopard skin about his shoulders. Strips of furry animal hides hung from his waist to his knees, front and back. Hairy cows' tail tips were tethered below his knees.

After an exchange about the weather and the fineness of the induna's cattle, though plagued by the evil nagana, and the sad loss of his son from the Umkhuhlwane [Spanish Flu], the discussion turned to the virility of his grown sons. This led to the possibility of their displaying their strength by clearing the fields of trees and large boulders, ready for planting.

What the chief really said in his reply was, "Why are you bringing this white wizard to me? My son fought in the white man's war and then brought the Umkhuhlwane home to die. Before that, he told me of many bad things he saw. The land this invader wants to grow crops on was there for my cattle to graze. However, as my beasts are dying and I will have no use of the land until this curse passes, you can tell him we will allow some men to help build walls and pull out the trees. You need not tell him that there will be a time when I will come to reclaim this land, but in the meantime, he can grow his plants, on the condition that he sends three biggest sacks of mieliemeal every time the moon returns to shine again in the night sky, until all the men's work is finished. I will send some men to collect more sacks of mieliemeal. This is before work can commence."

Thus, Layani turned to Donald and said, "The induna he say yes. He will send men for dois sacos mielie before men take trees out and other work wanting great strength. You must send three sacos mielie, Nkosi, every time moon comes back in sky, sebenza esta terminado [until the work is finished]," winding up in a jumble of English, Zulu and Portuguese.

Donald said, "Tell the chief that I will do that and to thank him. Ask him now if he would like to ride in the car for a little distance. Say to him I cannot bring the car any closer for him. Ask if he wishes his first wife to come with him. He can bring four of his children but they can only ride after him and his First Wife."

"He say yes."

And so with great dignity the headman did, after summoning his First Wife to accompany him and bring their children. He shouted at the elders and his lesser wives not to follow him but only to stand far off to watch. Arriving at the Kelpie, Donald pulled the primer ring beside the radiator and turned the crank to raise the fuel; after which he switched on and rotated the crank with his left hand several times. Miraculously, the engine started at the first attempt, then repeatedly tooting the two-tone horn (which sounded like an out-of-breath buffalo) Donald drove the Kelpie forward in a wide bumpy circle many times until the chief signalled that he and his wife had had enough. Layani had been instructed to keep his eyes peeled for hidden rocks and other hazards.

After dismounting with care the headman turned to Layani, who was doing his best to give the impression that he rode in this kind of mechanical beast every day, and said, "This is a wonderful thing. Now I go," and walked away, beckoning to his wife and offspring to follow.

"Well? How did it go with the chief?" asked Toby, when they next met.

"Not bad. Arranged for some men to come and take the trees out and perhaps help with the building work. Chief's name is something like 'pyjamas'. Now it's your turn, and good luck. Let me know how it goes. Approach the purpose of your visit slowly and take an offering with you. The chief demanded three sacks of mieliemeal from me before work would begin, with more to follow every month. You'd better take Layani with you. Offer some of the wives and children a ride. Easy how you go; don't break an axle. Don't get lost or shoot anything and good luck. Remember; the rugby match looms!"

Chapter Five

A letter had arrived at the Schnurrs for Toby from Phoebe, his older sister in London. It was travel-worn by its lengthy journey around the Cape, by rail to Empangeni and then by ox-wagon-express to the store at Ntambanana, which also served as a postal agency. In addition to the usual stamps, the envelope was franked 'Bullard King & Company Natal Direct Line'. Eric was in the store when the post arrived, and used it as a reason for riding over to see how the new settlers were getting on. His horses' legs had accumulated a swarm of blackjacks by the time he swung out of the saddle. One of his ridgebacks had accompanied him and ticks had lodged in the dog's ears.

Several photographs dropped out when Toby opened the letter. They were of his sisters, Phoebe and Hannah, who had bobbed their hair although the picture of his mother must have been taken before the war. She was still in corseted Edwardian dress, posed against a fireplace, with one forearm across the mantelpiece, her left arm akimbo. The sight of them took him back to blissful summer days on the Irish farm playing with his sisters, the boreen, hedgerows heady with meadowsweet beside fields full of barley. The wolfhound that always tagged along was called 'Smoke'.

"Dear Sausage," Toby read (for this is what Phoebe

had called him from early childhood), *"I am really beginning to feel that I have lost my little brother for good. First the war, and now Africa. Please do write in lots more detail. Your postcard merely said that you were in Zululand and your farm is called Hadeda but you were thinking of changing the name to Yola. That's hardly the whole story!*

Mummy's not getting any younger, you know, and although she remains as bright as a button, there are signs of ailing. A tremor has developed in her hands and she is becoming harder of hearing. She makes a joke of 'getting to First Base' when she reaches a landing and gets out of breath.

You must understand that she is pining too, like your sisters, for more news of you, and it would be a good idea to start planning a visit once the pressure on passenger berths begins to ease, and before it's too late. The strain of letting the farm go and leaving Ireland in the middle of the war, the fear of being torpedoed, finding a home and living in wartime London, Daddy's death and not least the Zeppelin raids, have all taken their toll – plus the urgency of making those sphagnum moss wound dressings for the Front. Hannah, Mummy and I had all volunteered for making them at the Church hall. There were at least sixty of us, working away at long trestle tables under supervision, and we all began to smell like an Irish bog after a while.

But that was my spare-time work. Remember my taking Spanish lessons after school? Well, they bore useful fruit as my remaining hours were spent censoring letters to and from the Argentine. Boring family correspondence predominated, but there was much anxious commercial stuff about Argentinian beef upon which Britain came to rely to 'flesh out' (!) local production – especially after Germany started torpedoing Argentinian merchant ships. I didn't realise how strong the German voice was there until I came across a copy of the Argentinisches Tageblatt sent to someone called Hefner in Lancaster. (He never received it!)

Nanny – you remember Nanny? – has died. Mummy could not bear leaving her in Ireland, so she had brought her with us to London. She collapsed very quickly from pneumonia brought on by the flu in her little flat downstairs three weeks ago. Much distress. We all sobbed; she was so much a part of the family. Eventually, we gathered up her belongings, such as they were, including several rosaries and a strange picture of the 'sacred heart' (I was told that's what it's called by one of the maids.) and Mummy sent them with a kind letter to her family's address somewhere near a place called Taghmon in County Wexford, in the hope that the Flanagan family would treasure them. I saw Mummy putting fifty pounds into the envelope when she thought we weren't looking. She managed to make contact with the local Roman Catholic priest to arrange a little funeral; which we attended. Dismal. We weren't used to all those bells and smells in a cold dark church full of plaster icons, but a gratifying number of Irish cooks and housemaids came and we all wept. A personal era ended with stale grey bread sandwiches, beer and tea.

During the war, it was very difficult to get servants because most of the men were away fighting and the girls had taken over their jobs. Now it's over it's a different story as a lot of the girls are being kicked out in favour of the returning men. In the light of that, Mummy has employed a housemaid to help Cook and perform the usual cleaning duties. Her name is Jenny. She comes from a pre-war service tradition so we had to explain that we didn't expect her to 'give room' every time we encountered her on the stairs.

Rationing of meat, butter, margarine, lard and sugar was introduced last July and you can be fined if caught eating more than two lunchtime courses of awful food in a restaurant. Now there's the growing trouble of demobilised soldiers roaming the streets in numbers and we no longer feel safe to venture out, so we have taken to getting about in those new-fangled Beardmore taxis – when one can be found.

There are newspaper reports of rioting between white demobbed soldiers and South Asians because jobs are so hard to find. The idea being provoked by the unions is that these 'aliens' are stealing what little work there is because they accept lower wages. The Home for Asiatic seamen in West India Dock Road was surrounded by a violent crowd of demobs a few months ago, which tried to burn it down. Mary's husband, back from the Front, told us that there is a growing hatred of the leaders who dragged us into war, and now that it's over there could be a revolution if they're not careful. He said that the demobs feel they are not getting a fair deal, and there have been many unreported mutinies all over Britain, he claimed.

What the newspapers are full of is stories about nightclubs springing up in the West End like mushrooms. We're dying to go to one dressed as flappers just for the fun, but Mummy won't hear of it and is horrified at the thought. Mind you, most of them are just rackets to sell overpriced booze after midnight, they say. Three guineas for a bottle of champagne and one guinea for a supper!

A serious type of flu is going the rounds and some people are dying from it. It's a bit frightening. There are notices warning people to avoid 'thronging and spitting' anyway so perhaps we will have to put off our nightclub adventure until it dies down. Many pedestrians have taken to wearing muslin nose and mouth masks as a protection from the germs – including a lot of demobs whom, it is said, resort to wearing them to conceal facial disfigurements that can't be operated on. My heart goes out to them. There's a silly child's ditty going around:

*I had a little bird
His name was Enza
I opened the Window
And in-flew Enza.*

This type of flu is different and there doesn't seem to be any cure. You either survive it and build up immunity or you succumb.

Sorry about this tale of woe. We are so relieved you have survived and are starting afresh in a land of promise, but we do miss you so. Write soon, soon, soon and send photographs! And come home as soon as you can. We do rather need you.

Yours ever, Pheebs"

Hearing such news from a home so far away reminded

Donald of the last evening spent on the old Scottish farm with his father and sisters. He had travelled down from London with his brother Andrew to be with them over the Hogmanay and a few weeks into 1914. Andrew had been persuaded to 'first-foot' over the threshold at midnight, requiring him to leave the house and shiver in the cold before re-entering, a stroke after midnight, bearing a lump of coal and a bottle of whisky. He forgot that the coal had dirtied his hands in coal dust when he shook hands with the McAlpines and friends who had ridden over on horseback from neighbouring farms. One family brought a young German girl called Gisela, a 'working-guest' on their Fada Farm (it was a very long piece of land, hence the name). Donald wondered what had happened to her after the declaration of war on the 4th of August. She wore a red and black tartan skirt and laughed a lot.

The farm, Yonder, was becoming more of a hobby for his father and a relaxing bolthole from the cares of the City. Many weeks of the year were spent in his London sales office, yet the farm remained an important source of income, managed by the McAlpine family who lived in the yard house.

His father's interests lay in coal merchanting and a lace factory in Darvel, in which he held an important share.

It was cold and overcast on Donald's last day, with leaden clouds and the approach of early darkness bringing snow. Andrew had already left for London. Although the household had plenty of coal for the winter, his father preferred the homely smell of peat and wood logs for the living room fire, so Donald had spent much of the afternoon chopping up more logs with one of the McAlpine boys, a friend from early boyhood.

Part of the farm was under tillage, and he remembered that during harvest and the sowing seasons, hired hands used to sleep in the hayloft above the byre, the barn in which the animals slept, their warmth rising to heat the loft.

It was still early lambing time, as his father liked to be one of the first to market with spring lambs born in midwinter. This meant getting up at all hours of the night to check conditions and help with deliveries. Angus McAlpine, Andrew (while he was there), Donald's older sister, his father and he had taken turns to be present and assist.

Most days were spent creating quartering pens for individual ewes and their new offspring and seeing to providing adequate bedding straw, fodder and water. There were the inevitable stillborns and a few orphans, the latter being the responsibility of the girls to mix up milk substitute and give them bottles, although his father and McAlpine did lend a hand when they could.

"We might be snowed in by morning," said his father. They were in deep easy chairs about the fireplace, except for little Jean who sat on the rug close to Donald. "As you're leaving us to live among the savages, I thought I should go over a few things you ought to know. And it's good for your sisters to hear this too.

"The Kirkwood family are really MacGregors 'in disguise'. The clan had a running feud with the Campbells for generations and I'll tell you about that in a moment. Well before that, our ancestors can be traced to King Dalriada born in 835 and King Donald, a descendent born in 858. That's why your mother and I decided to call you Donald. The motto of our clan is 'Royal is our Race!'

"After the Wars of Independence, the MacGregor lands were given to the Chief of Clan Campbell by Robert the Bruce, despite the courage shown by the MacGregors at the Battle of Bannockburn. The Campbells hounded the McGregors heartlessly, to the point that they were forced to flee to the fastnesses of Glenstrae and became known as the Children of the Mist. Many of those who did not leave were murdered.

"Our families were obliged to change their names after the Campbells had persuaded King James the Sixth of Scotland to 'altogether abolish and destroy the name and peoples of MacGregor'. To avoid this persecution your ancestors adopted the name of Kirkwood. After the lifting of the Proscription in 1774, the Kirkwoods decided to keep the name as their own. Yet an ancestor of yours, Rob Roy Macgregor, fought on without changing his name and survived by guerrilla warfare and cattle-rustling, until he was pardoned late in life.

"I must ask you to remember us often, to write to your sisters and respect your Scottish roots. Treat Campbells forever with caution, even though Rob Roy's mother was a Campbell. If it's possible to grow such things in Natal, plant a few Scots Pine near your new home in Africa – the emblem of the MacGregors and thus the Kirkwoods. It will help you to remember us, who will forever hold you dear.

"And now for the keepsakes. Here is your mother's wedding ring. Only allow it to be worn by the girl you marry; and here's a small string of Scottish river pearls, most loved by your mother. They are valuable. Keep it safe."

Winnie, his older sister, piped up then and said, "Here's a book from me – see I've inscribed it on the flyleaf. It's *Rob Roy* by Sir Walter Scott." She had written 'With love to Donald Dubh from Wee Winnie'. Dubh is Gaelic for 'black'; all four Kirkwood children had dark, almost Spanish-black hair, and he was known teasingly as 'Black Donald'.

Then Jean, his younger sister, said, "And here's one from me. It's a copy of *Waverley* by Walter Scott too." All she had written on the flyleaf was 'With love from Jeanie'. When he looked at her and smiled, her eyes were wet with tears.

They sat for a long while in silence, kept company by the crackle and slide of the fire, a distant bleating of ewes and new-born lambs, cloaked by the falling snow and the sense of family that goes beyond words.

Donald departed the next day and was never to see his father again after the Caledonian Line train pulled out of the Lockerbie station. His father had looked forlorn. Although cars were still a rarity, his father had been able to afford a brand new Beardmore Country & Colonial, of which he was very proud. Donald had persuaded him to slither the car to a halt in the snowy road beside the long stone wall that bordered the farm, so that he might pry loose a small piece of the red, lichen-encrusted sandstone. He had dusted away most of the snow and put it on top of his cabin trunk.

On the train, he warmed it on the compartment heater where it left a miniature puddle of snowmelt.

Chapter Six

"Be careful of these crowbars," Piet van Jaarsveld had said at the store while heaving them over the counter along with an assortment of shovels and picks. "They break 'em," and although Donald realised that he was jesting, he did indeed witness, in the days to come, how the combination of great strength and an ignorance of the fragility of mechanical things often led to an implement's speedy destruction. What's more, the rural Zulu at that time had not embraced the idea that when Western things were broken they might be repairable. They were merely cast aside and left to rust away in the weeds of remote Ntambanana undergrowth.

Being so remote, a broken harrow or plough could be disastrous, so van Jaarsveld had encouraged his Indian assistant to start a primitive smithy in the yard behind the store.

Clement was a thin and sinewy Asian who radiated garlic, olive oil and sweat, and displayed a remarkable talent for metalwork and was able to repair broken equipment, often producing new metal devices to a customer's specifications. He could turn his hand to tin-smithery too, and had even repaired Mrs Potgieter's broken ear-trumpet, leading her to say loudly, "Ek hou nie van Indiërs, maar hierdie een is die uitsondering!" [I don't like Indians, but this one's the exception.]

Donald had encountered him while investigating the drifts of smoke and clanking sounds emanating from a soot-dark shed. The only light that came in was from the door and a smudged fanlight, which had made it difficult to see him in the gloom.

"Hello," said Donald. "I'm starting to farm near here."

"Yes, me see. Plenty crowbars!"

"I'm looking for Indian men, to help build housing lines and work in fields."

"You meaning 'indenture wukkers'?"

"No, that's all finished, but I'm looking for good Indians who don't want to go back to India; to live and work on the farm."

"How much you pay?"

"Whatever is reasonable. It includes food and lodging. I will ask Mr Schnurr's advice and let you know."

"What is lodging?"

"Rooms to live."

"Where farm?"

Donald described where.

"Yes. I know place. Near Schnurr."

"My friend needs Indian workers too, for long time."

"Married wukkers?"

"That's OK. But not all."

"How many? Ten?"

"No, no, no, five or six. Not so many. No drinkers. Better one family to begin. Build rooms. Then build next rooms, next family."

"OK."

"OK?"

"Be here one week. Then you can talk them. Take them your farm."

"No, no. I must talk boss-man for Indians first."

"OK. Talk me later, but I talk friends."

"Why do you work like this in almost dark?"
"We all work same way. Need dark to see hot red metal."
"I see."

Clearing the fields of trees on Yonder started well enough, and Donald was impressed with the way the Zulu men tackled the extraction of each tree as a team puzzle which had to be solved by debate. Once a course of action was decided upon, they would address the extraction with gusto.

First, each tree had to be cut down to the stump, and this was done with two-man saws and choppers. Once felled, the top parts were dragged away to the field's perimeter to be reduced for firewood and building by the older umfaans accompanying the men.

Then the digging out of these hardy old Zululand trunks would commence – first by delving down to the roots all around the trunk and chopping away bothersome extensions. When done, crowbars and choppers came into play to loosen and break the remaining roots, before chains were wound about the stump and attached to the Kelpie. The reverse gear was the best for this kind of work, and here Clement's ingenuity had been called upon to forge and fit a temporary tow bar to the front of the Kelpie's body (and also to the rear, in the same manner).

Thick branches were laid beneath the rear wheels to inhibit spinning. While the technique was sound, Donald realised that the strategy could cause a gear to be stripped, leaving him transport-less and miles from anywhere, so he resigned himself to the long-winded process of buying a six-span of Afrikander oxen and a second-hand open dray for haulage, with all the yokes, chain and tackle that went with it, as the government steam tractor was not available for this type of work.

Chapter Seven

A breeze fluttered the tent flaps and wafted ash from the spent fire into the early light which glittered through the foliage.

Donald's dream was a nightmare of barbed wire entanglement and stakes during bombardment by a German mountain battery, amid swarms of flies and mosquitoes and men dying. Captain Whittaker was helping to harness mules when he was blown to pieces with three men from the Kings African Rifles, whose body parts splattered Donald. As he woke, the buzzing of flies became those caught up in his mosquito net and the boom of the mountain battery became the sound of ground hornbills courting. It took him a while to accept that he was still alive while looking around for the remains of Whittaker and before realising it was a dream.

He found Layani standing at the remains of the fire when he poked his head through the tent entrance. "Hau, nKosi! You shouting, shouting. I think que foram chacais."

"Chacais?"

"Big dentes. Go Hahahaha," pointing at his teeth and then imitating the jackal's trot.

"Jackals?"

"Izimpungushe," said Layani in the hope this Zulu word might describe the animals better.

"No. I was dreaming," said Donald, putting his palms together beside his right cheek.

"Aaaahh, pesadelo. Muito mal."

"So here I am," thought Donald, "still living in a tent in the middle of nowhere, with a Man Friday who I can barely understand and no ploughing or planting started, and still throwing money into a bottomless pit. Emily is likely to have forgotten me down in Cape Town and, on top of that, the oxen I buy will probably die of nagana in time."

Layani started blowing on the embers to get the fire going again, after gathering some kindling and drawing water from the borehole. Some time back, Donald had indicated that it was more practical for him to cook at the same fire. For security against animal prowlers he could sleep beside the fire, wrapped in an old blanket Donald had given him. There was safety in numbers, after all.

The tree fellers made their own arrangements further off. He heard them chanting sometimes.

On inspecting progress in the main field (which came to be called the Thunder Field for reasons that will become clear), he was irritated to see that one of the trees had been left untouched, and took Layani along with him to interpret his ire to the workers.

As they approached, the men stopped working and rested on their picks and shovels to see what the Umlungu would do next. When Layani saw the offending tree he mangled English and Portuguese to say: "Nkosi, that is Arvore Trovão,…tree for relâmpago," gesturing at the sky and as if protecting himself from the heavens he said, "Boomf! Boomf! Zulu call tree 'umvithi'. Don't cut. Bring bad. If you cut make bad smell. Bad relâmpago."

The Zulus seemed satisfied that the ignorant white man now understood the significance of the tree and picked up their implements again.

"So I must just plough around it?"

"Yes, Nkosi."

"What's all this about an Umvithi tree?" Donald asked Eric when he went to consult him about Indian labour wages. "I was told not to remove it from the field nearest the borehole because it provided protection from lightning and thunder. It's umbrella-shaped with a single stem."

Eric said that Donald was wise to leave the tree standing. Special sticks were made from its branches by the Zulu 'weather doctors' who also used the bark for associated practices. It was said that they were used to kill the lightning bird, and the tree was left standing near Zulu kraals for this reason. "It's the *Boscia albitrunca*. We call it the Tugela Shepherd's Tree. Don't know how it got that name. Do you know that so strong was the European concern about the power of the Zulu 'weather doctors' in the nineteenth century that the Natal government tried to introduce a regulation preventing them from tinkering with the rain-pattern?"

The Umvithi tree has flexible branches rather like a willow and its blooms are odiferous. Long thorns ooze a blood-like sap.

"They also believe in a Lightning Bird called the *Inyoni yezulu*. It's said to appear as the lightning strikes and has a red bill and tail. We 'white wizards' have somehow spirited the power of this sky-devil to make electricity. If the wires are touched it bites like a snake."

"Now you're here, I would like to talk to you about the idea of forming a co-operative, and it's time you met the rest of the families settling here. There're a few rum ones, but in the main they're a good lot and they've all 'been through it', even an Irishman called Padraic O'Grady. He's an old-time settler but fought on the Boer side. He has strong views about Ireland, so forewarn Toby.

"The general thinking about a cooperative is that, as the farms around here develop, there will be an expanding need for agricultural supplies and equipment as well as the usual domestic things, and it will consolidate crop purchases.

"The idea is rather delicate because Piet's store is the sole provisioner for miles around and he'll feel challenged. Presently he can charge whatever he likes. If the cost of something seems unrealistic, the only alternative for us is to buy whatever it is in Empangeni and pay for its transport to Ntambanana, courtesy of his friend Jan Mocke's ox-wagon express; with the upshot that it could prove far more costly than buying from Piet.

"He's a good man and provides a good service as best he can, so I suggest that the farming community should consult with him first and devise a way of incorporating his store in a cooperative, while ensuring that he retains ownership of his original investment. It's all a matter of tact, paperwork and written agreements. He may not like this at first glance so we'll have to tread gently – especially with his wife.

"For farmers' cooperatives, Pretoria offers tax concessions, attractive credit and interest rates, and price supports. You know the drill, Donald; you've been a banker," Schnurr said. "It means that by taking small shares in the co-operative, farmers can receive regular payments ahead of harvest, benefit from bulk-buying and profit-share. It also gives negotiating muscle for dealing with the gin and mill managements."

When Donald mentioned that he was resigned to acquiring some oxen and a cart, Schnurr said, "So you've decided to de-mechanise! Yes, I heard about your efforts to extract tree stumps with your Tin Lizzie. Very risky. Something is sure to snap sooner rather than later and you can't rely on the government steam tractor to be around when you need it. It's wise to go back to animal-power until paraffin tractors become available – and I can't see that happening any time soon. It'll be a long time before someone designs anything reliable enough. War brought forth the tank, but it will take a long time for Peace to bring forth a reliable tractor! Nagana could stymie us though. You can't plough with dead oxen!

"You've got to be careful when you buy them. It needs someone with a lot of experience to go along with you," said Schnurr. "An ox has to be big and an ox must be healthy and it mustn't be too old – about four years is the best, provided it has been trained."

"How do you judge its age?"

"By its teeth – just take a look at the incisors. In between four and five years the incisors should be worn a little below the level of the grinders, but not too much. Don't judge its age by the horn rings. Unreliable. The first three rings disappear with age. The neck must be short and strong, but, even more important, the animals must breathe easily and not cough. Take a critical look at the hakke too. Got to be well formed."

"Sorry – but what are the hakke?"

"Oh, Dutch for hocks…the leg joints…and the animal must walk easily too. No limping or stumbling. Oxen are like people. Each one has its own personality and you will have to spot vicious or lazy animals as these are impossible to train properly."

This led to Donald's first encounter with O'Grady, the Boer-Irishman, red Viking hair and all, who was recommended by Eric Schnurr as someone who knew a lot about oxen. Eric had mentioned that a farmer near Mabhensa, about twelve miles south-west of Ntambanana, had decided to sell up his small Afrikander span, a decision precipitated by the death of his wife from Spanish Flu. Many of his workers had suffered the same fate. His span had survived nagana, probably because Mabhensa was out of the fly-belt and Afrikanders were more nagana-resistant.

Padraic O'Grady was busy supervising the dipping of cattle near a wind pump with some Shangaan helpers and a few umfaans when Donald found him, after picking his way in the Kelpie over the uneven ground, then walking the rest of the way, accompanied by Layani.

Cattle to be dipped were penned in a kraal left open at a narrow dipping channel built of concrete, wide enough to allow passage of only one beast at a time. The animals were persuaded by the high-pitched whistles of the natives and sundry prodding to plunge up to their noses into the dosed water at the deepest point. They escaped at the rising shallow end to drain in an extensive pen on the far side, after passing along a draining race. There was a rickety catwalk along the length of the plunge to provide access to beasts, particularly calves, which might get into difficulties.

"Hello."

"Ja?"

This did not seem to be a good beginning, but Donald persisted.

"I've come to ask your advice."

"Oh, yes. Can't you see I'm busy?"

"Yes. Can I help?"

"We have another twelve to dip, then the calves, so you and your 'Umslopogaas' can stand with sticks at that weak point over there, just to make sure they don't try to break out. Hold the sticks out straight so they can see them... Pasop ukuthi isilwane!" he shouted suddenly at one of his assistants in a mangled mixture of Dutch and Zulu, when an animal looked as if it was planning to crash through the fence of the enclosure. The calves were penned separately and were restless. Generous troughs of fodder lay enticingly on the far side of the dip.

"They don't like it. Instinctive. Never been dipped before. I told Shepstone that they didn't need dipping yet because they're Nguni cattle. Dipping interferes with their natural resistance to tick bite; but he's a mompara and wouldn't listen – so…why argue with a fool when there's money to be made, so it is? We'll talk after I'm finished."

O'Grady was built like an ancient Irish tree, with a beard and moustache reminiscent of a Kommando Boer. Schnurr had mentioned that he was married to Sarie Marais, a Dutch-Afrikaans girl, who was brought up on a dairy farm called Welverdiend beside the Mooi River in the Midlands of Natal. He used to charm her by calling her Mooinooi (pretty girl) and singing 'Sarie Marais', a Boer War song. Her ancient grandfather had been present, as a very young lad, in a battle between attacking Zulus and Boers shielded by their laagered ox-wagons at the cliff edge of a hippo pool on the Ncome River. The grand old man used to electrify Padraic and Sarie, Schnurr told Donald, with stories of the day when about twenty thousand Zulus attacked a group of 470 Boers. "Always keep a gun loaded with buckshot. You never know when you might have to defend yourself," he would say – a reference back to that battle when thousands of Zulus perished. Only three Boers were wounded.

O'Grady had been a demolition expert at a Randfontein gold mine and a member of the Celtic Literary Society before joining 'Foxy Jack' MacBride's Irish Transvaal Brigade, known as the Wreckers Corps, at the outbreak of the second Boer War. When the conflict ended, Padraic chose exile rather than signing an undertaking to abide by the peace terms, and found work as a transport rider over the border in Mozambique.

It was as well that he did as the British regarded Irishmen who had fought against them as traitors, Ireland still being part of the British Empire.

His Commander, John MacBride, vanished to Paris where, in 1903, he married Maud Gonne, the Irish patriot, much to the fury of the poet William Butler Yeats who regarded Maud as his personal muse. During the Boer War, Gonne had sent an Irish flag to the Irish Transvaal Brigade and it was passed on by MacBride to Padraic with the words "Mind the Flag," before he departed for Paris. It is said that those were the last words that MacBride uttered again before facing the Dublin firing squad in Kilmainham Gaol on the 5th of May, 1916, after the uprising was crushed. Schnurr told Donald that the flag was displayed proudly on a wall in O'Grady's sitting room, next to an indifferent painting of wild geese.

He trickled back to South Africa, years later after Union, to become the farm manager at Welverdiend, where he had married his Sarie before migrating to new pastures at Ntambanana to raise cattle. This was before the curse of nagana began to take hold and threaten his livelihood, though theft of his cattle by native rustlers was also an ever-present risk.

He was appalled when the vicinity of his splendidly isolated Zululand farm was 'swamped' by the allocation of new stretches of land to demobbed soldiers turned untutored farmers, and who neither shared his views on Irish independence nor the ambition to help terminate British dominion over South Africa – still strongly desired by the 'bittereinders' among Boer-Afrikaans society.

But Padraic was a practical man and couldn't resist the attraction of his guidance being sought – for a fee.

"Right. What is it you want to know?"

"Eric Schnurr said you were the best man he knew when it came to oxen. I have to buy a few oxen and Eric told me that I should ask your advice – and to come with me to buy them. I'm told that there is a span for sale at Mabhensa. Too many for me but I believe he will be prepared to split it up for a quick sale."

"Did he now? What breed are they?"

"Afrikanders."

"How old?"

"I don't know – I hope four years old."

"Afrikanders are almost as disease-resistant as Nguni, so they are. Well, that means travelling to and from Mabhensa, selecting the best, branding them on the day of purchase and arranging to herd them with a dray, if one is suitable, all the way back to Tam. For that my fee will be £25, half ahead and half when the job is finished. You'll also have to pay the herdsmen to drive the cattle (not very much) – and arrange for their food. It could be a two-day job. Have you built a kraal yet?"

"I'm about to."

"Build it strong and not too far from your camp and very close to a good water supply, yes indeed. You must build a rain-shelter for them too, and they must have access and be able to drink at will. Seeing it's winter, you'll have to arrange for fodder along the route and enough to see you through the rest of the cold season. That's quite a lot."

"I'll have to buy a dray from him, too, plus all the tackle."

"Then let's see what he has and is prepared to let go at a reasonable price – and perhaps you can buy fodder for the journey from him too. We'll go to Mabhensa when I've finished up here and done several other things. Say Friday?"

Donald nodded assent.

"Best to go on horseback. You can hire one of our horses.

Should take about three hours…let's say four. I take it you'll find out if the farmer will be available. What's his name?"

"Frikkie Mouton."

"Oh yes. I heard his wife died from the Spanish. Some of his kaffirs died too…mostly men. You can send your umslopogaas with a note to let me know if all has been arranged and we'll meet here at my house at daybreak. OK? Sarie'll have coffee and rusks ready. Bring your own padkos."

Donald left the guns and strongbox from the Kelpie with Eric Schnurr and the basics of the farm in the care of Layani, who seemed loyal enough.

The whine of the Kelpie and the barking of the dogs heralded his arrival at the O'Grady farm just before sunrise. Steam was rising off two horses, already saddled.

"Good morning, Englishman; did you bring your branding irons?" called O'Grady when he clattered out of the kitchen door. "Kom binne [come in]. Sarie's got our coffee ready."

Sarie came in with the coffee followed by another young woman who was introduced as Minnie Botha, a friend and visitor from Vryheid. Sarie was slight and practical, while Minnie was a beauty, and Donald struggled to conceal his attraction by making much of Sarie's rusks.

They sat in the kitchen, slurping from mugs.

"Sarie made these rusks this morning. Magtig! Hard enough to break your teeth, eh? You dip them in the coffee to soften them up."

"They're very, very good…but I'm not English."

"Well, what are you then?"

"I'm Scottish. We were forced to unite with England in 1707 because we lost most of our money in Panama. We were broke."

"It's too early for politics. We'll talk some more as we ride,

Scotsman; yes, indeed." O'Grady's accent was a strange blend of Afrikaans and Irish. Donald caught sight of the Irish flag in the sitkamer.

After locking away the dogs to prevent their following the horses, they were off, with a wave to the women in the still morning; past the cattle dip and along a rutted trail still cloaked in morning mist. They were joined by some picannins for a while, near naked as they were born except for a few beads and moochies.

Kraal dogs turned out to be a nuisance to the horses until Padraic cracked a short saddle whip at them. One of the dogs had barked, its breath made visible in a string of vapour puffs.

Conversation came slowly and when it did it was accompanied by wisps of vapour every time a word was mouthed. The horses were likewise breathing out little steam balloons. After the picannins tailed off into the mist they were followed by a whydah bird with long tail feathers, which swooped ahead then lingered to watch the horses go by.

"They've graded the path ahead where we join it, so the going will be easier," Padraic said.

Where the ways joined, a figure emerged out of the mist, cloaked in a blanket and walking quickly. "Sawubona," the figure said.

"Sikhona," both Donald and Padraic replied.

"Uyaphi?" asked Padraic.

"Ngithwala izinhlamvu," [I am carrying the letters] the blanketed Zulu postman replied, revealing a satchel and a water bottle. He was hatted but barefooted, and carried a knobkerrie.

"Hamba kahle," [Go well] Donald said, proud of his few words of Zulu.

"Hamba ngokucophelela," [Ride with care] called the man, disappearing into the mist.

Donald was quite happy to follow O'Grady, who clearly knew the lie of the land to the Mabhensa farm – connecting with native paths and game trails which led in the general direction from time to time – even a simple road towards the end of the ride which had been scraped smooth by a steam grader.

On approaching a thicket of castor oil trees they could hear the doo-doo-doo-doo of tambourine doves, and spotted a flock of them on the ground pecking away at fallen seeds, before the horses flushed them to fly away on chestnut wings, only a few feet above the path.

"Unusual to see more than one at a time. Look, look, there! See? Duiker," said Padraic quietly. "It always grazes alone on misty mornings. You could almost miss it, it's so small. Always by itself. It accepts the horses so it ignores us, sitting on them...unless we get too close. It's in good condition. Silky coat...What's the matter with you? You jolted. Looked as you've seen a spoek."

Inexplicably, Donald saw a German officer in everyday German East African uniform standing in the middle distance near a fever tree. The horse sensed his alarm and halted, trembling. Just as soon as the man was there, he was gone, when Donald looked again.

"During the Boer War did you ever see the ghosts of men you had killed?" asked Donald.

There was a long pause before Padraic answered: "Yes."

He said nothing more for quite a long time, then: "It will fade over time. It did for me. When I started out fighting in Jack's Brigade I hated your lot and everything the British stood for, but towards the end, I couldn't feel enmity for its soldiers. After one encounter at Hlangwane, near Colenso, we walked over to look at the bodies. You know what it's like. They were just young boys, eyes staring, many shot in the head defending one of their howitzers…dead and far from home. The dum-dum bullets from our Mausers did terrible damage to bodies. Rotting meat for the flies and vultures. I couldn't hate them anymore. Some I helped to bury. We took their guns and ammunition and put whatever was in their pockets in a satchel, but kept the food and the medicine and the money. We marked their graves as best we could. I don't know what MacBride did with their personal stuff. Letters to parents…the locks of hair of sweethearts. Some said he ordered that belongings were to be left where the Brits would find them…on a path to a rooinek field hospital…I don't know. I used to see their faces in the middle of the night. Sometimes during the day, in the beginning, I'd be supervising the milking when I would see a group of them, standing in the shed behind the milk cans."

"Do you hate the British?"

"It's not the people, it's the system. Lookit, how would you like living under occupation for seven hundred and fifty years – being treated as second-class citizens in the land that is rightfully yours just because you're Irish – almost like we're treating the kaffirs? First it was the Normans from Wales… all those castles, although they tended to intermarry so their presence became more benign…but then came Cromwell."

"I know very little about Ireland."

"Then here's a lot to learn – far too much for one man in his time. It goes back, far beyond the suppression of anything that was Catholic and the Penal Laws. But if you were Catholic in the Penal times you couldn't own a horse worth more than five pounds; you couldn't vote and you couldn't buy Protestant land. And that was just the start of it. They don't allow Gaelic to be spoken to this day – let alone taught, except in the 'ignorant far west', where they can't speak English at all. But there were many Anglicans who objected to British suppression too – especially in the hundred and fifty years or so, like Minnie's grandfather."

"Tell me more?"

"I prefer to leave it to her to tell you, if you ever meet again. A brother of his died for Irish independence, a man by the name of Emmet."

"So where do you stand now?"

"It's left a residue of hate of anything imposed by Britain, and the Catholic priests, especially, have capitalised on that. They've come to represent the Irish tribe, which is only half true. For myself I don't believe all their churchy mumbo-jumbo. But now…all Sarie and I want to do is farm, though I can see exactly what is happening in this new South Africa. Even in Zululand. The Government speakers mouth fine words about 'unity between the Dutch and the English', since the end of the Independence War (that's what we call your 'Boer' war), but it's not like that really. There's still a lot of poverty among the Dutch and there's much resentment. Try speaking Dutch-Afrikaans to some Englishman in authority and he'll look down his nose at you and ask you to speak in English. They don't even allow Afrikaans to be taught in schools…only High Dutch…and that, with reluctance. Afrikaans is seen as inferior, a kind of patois, a sort of kitchen-Dutch. It's sneered at."

"Don't you miss Ireland?"

"Well, it's a long way from Timoleague to here, but feck it, with Sarie and our children I'm content. We speak Afrikaans at home. Not like you newcomers, all speaking English. In the Boer mind you will be forever 'apart'. It would be interesting to peer into the future and see who eventually will come out on top. I'd put my money on the Boer."

The Mabhensa farm was sparse and Frikkie Mouton had the look of determined resignation. They had passed a plantation of cultivated avocado trees on the approach, sacking protecting the swelling fruit from birds. Further on there was a plantation of pineapples. His dwelling was a 'hartebees huisie' made of sticks and reeds which had been plastered with clay and cow-dung. The simple kitchen-cum-store-room was in a thatched rondavel attached to the main dwelling, the latter roofed in rusting corrugated iron. The ghost of a woman's touch was still there…withered flowers in a window vase…a crocheted doily trimmed with beads covering a milk jug…a sewing basket on a chair near the hearth. Farm implements lay scattered about the yard untidily, some broken and rusting among tall weeds. The oxen had been kept close in a circular stake-and-barbed-wire enclosure in anticipation of Donald and Padraic's visit. They settled on the stoep to talk, after seeing to the horses.

The Spanish Flu deaths had been sudden and devastating, taking a mere three days for his wife and the natives to die. Mouton's command of English was minimal so he and O'Grady conversed mainly in Dutch-Afrikaans, leaving Donald feeling marginalised until he received a translation from O'Grady. Mouton had gestured to a place marked by a small iron cross in the shade of some peach trees on the other side of the house as he said simply: "She lie there, daaronder."

There was no mention of what happened to the native labourers.

Padraic explained to Donald that Mouton had abandoned sugar cultivation and had decided to fall back on avocado pear and pineapple production, and was set to employ Indians who had completed their indenture contracts. He was one of the few in the area who possessed a truck and was convinced that that would be sufficient for his moderate transport needs.

Eight of the Afrikander oxen they looked at proved 'good

enough', according to Padraic, although he rejected the rest. The dray, while worse for wear, was satisfactory. The plan to hire an experienced wagon crew had to be abandoned as they had died in the pandemic. This left Donald, Padraic and one inexperienced Shangaan on loan from the farm to inspan the oxen and help trundle the dray the twelve miles back to Ntambanana over the same haphazard trails, their horses tethered on long leads to the back of the wagon. Donald spotted that the central yoke chain had been made in Scotland and the wagon bore the brass seal of the Durbanville Wagon Works, a long way away in the Western Cape.

Before leaving, they had manoeuvred each beast into the pinch pen to hold it still while it was branded 'DK'. Mouton had prepared a wood fire for the purpose, as "Jy kan nie 'n steenkoolbrand [coalfire] gebruik nie, because makes iron te warm," he said in mangled 'Afriklish'. He demonstrated how the branding iron ends should be an ash grey colour, not bright red. They applied Donald's initials in a rolling motion for about five seconds and with firm pressure on the haunches of each beast. It was clear that the branding was painful, judging from the wild head movements, bellowing and tail flicks. Donald decided to move out of view of each beast so that future associations and control would not be beset by memory of the pain.

Mouton had stood on the stoep to watch them go, satisfactorily enriched by the transaction, not least by the reasonable price Donald had paid for a cartload of fodder. The inexperienced Shangaan was ordered to be the 'voorloper', and Padraic assumed the task of the driver, turning out to be quite good at the job. He had taken the precaution of learning the names of the leading and rear oxen he was to walk beside and understood how to encourage them in Irish-tainted 'oxpraat' ('ox-speak'). He knew how to crack the long ox-whip above their heads without ever touching them, from his days as a fighter in the Brigade. Donald became the brakeman and sat on the wagon beside the wooden lever. The enormous horns of the Afrikander oxen made positioning the yokes and skeis (securing pegs) hazardous. A sudden swipe by an ox can do permanent damage – or worse.

Upon their arrival at O'Grady's house, it was left to Padraic to finish the journey to Yonder, with Donald leading the way in the Kelpie, grinding away in high gear. Their procession passing the van Jaarsveld's store brought out the family and the Indian smithy to watch the curious parade go by.

Chapter Eight

"I'm told that Armitage is giving advances of two or three months to whatever native workers he can find," Barnes muttered to Bennett. "That's thirty shillings a month, even before he can get any work out of them!"

The men were sitting amid an assemblage of chairs and packing cases on the stoep at Piet van Jaarsveld's little store, waiting for the first co-op meeting, while planters, with a few of their wives, continued to appear. Many of the settlers' horses had collapsed from East Coast Fever by this time so some farmers had to walk or share rides in mule carts, mules being marginally less susceptible to the fever.

"He bribes 'em, eh? So that's how it's done."

"Except the last lot he lent money to simply vamoosed and then came around to me. We're all doing the same thing. Most of us, anyway, and they're still just downing tools – those that do stay on, wandering off for a wedding or funeral every two or three days…or just wandering off forever. I know of one skellum who's managed to get advances from three different planters, without working for any of them. The police refuse to act as they said he was not a contract-breaker, not a deserter and not absent without leave. Here's Muller."

"Hey, Sergeant Muller! Why don't you arrest these skellums who don't pitch up for work after they get advances?"

"Man, if we did," replied Muller, "the gaols would be full

to overflowing. You're a fool to give 'em money in advance and if they vamoose, it's not our job to act as your tracing agents."

The stoep was filling up with much scraping of chairs, those that there were; the rest – men and women, but mostly men – having to stand, some leaning against the stoep posts, or sitting on the edge, their legs dangling. A few sat on the cases, elevating them from the rest. Out of the group of thirty-one, twenty-six wore hats of every description, setting Toby to thinking (he had counted the hats and the number of people so far) that van Jaarsveld had missed a trading opportunity by not stocking head-coverings, although girls' cloches were useless in the Zululand sun, he thought, looking at one woman's impractical headgear. "No brim at all. What's the use of that?" he thought.

A tableau of native onlookers sat crouched in the distance. This was an entertainment which would be talked about in the distant kraal for weeks afterwards. No one had bothered to explain to them what the gathering was about, so they were left to their own conjectures.

A few of the planters' wives, those that arrived in some form of transport, had dressed up a bit for the occasion. Their husbands had been argued and sulked into wearing cotton jackets and ties. Donald had tinkered with the idea of wearing his black and purple Old Alleynian tie, but had thought better of it.

The presentation on forming a farmers' cooperative was to be made by Morkel, one of the three men sitting on chairs atop an open wagon parked parallel to the stoep – Schnurr, Mocke and the Pretoria man, André Morkel, from the Tobacco and Cotton Division in the Union's new Department of Agriculture. Marie Schnurr was sitting at a little table to the side of the wagon, preparing to take notes and keeping her hand on a fluttering jotter, until a farmer handed her a small stone to weigh the papers down. She had brought along dip pens, blotting paper and a precious bottle of blue-black ink; precious because the nearest replacement for it was in Durban, more than two hundred miles away.

"Do you think she's expecting?" whispered one of the women to the plump friend sitting next to her.

"Perhaps. It's about time, isn't it?"

Morkel had negotiated with Piet van Jaarsveld for the Department's two steam tractors, with their enormous steel wheels, to be stationed permanently beside the store, and there they stood, near the water tower, a symbol of progress and robust engineering, ranged beside a small forest of hessian bags of Somkhele coal. Puffs of wistful smoke continued to waft upwards, joined by the vapour from a smouldering heap of fig tree leaves.

Mocke and Morkel were chatting in an English so heavily accented and punctuated by Afrikaans phrases that the few settlers within earshot couldn't follow what they were saying, if they had felt so inclined. After a while, Morkel switched entirely to the Taal, amidst hostile glances from most of those present.

"So this is the voice of the new South Africa, eh?" Rutherford muttered to Begbie. "I suppose we'll just have to get used to it, but I wish they spoke comprehensible English instead."

"That Irishman, O'Grady, could practice taming his accent as well. He's almost unfathomable most of the time," said Begbie. "The Indians pronounce his name as Oggriddy. You know he fought with the Boers, eh? Bloody Irish. His children struggle at the farm school because their home language is Afrikaans and he's always complaining that they should be taught separately, so my wife says. I bet he'll put a spoke in things in the months to come. They always cause trouble.

Keeps on talking about his parents' dairy farm in a place called Timoleague. He says he and his relations have been fighting the English in Ireland since 1798 and can't wait to get rid of 'em…knows a thing or two about dynamite though, I'm told. Used to help the Boers fire their Long Tom into Ladysmith…dynamiting could be useful if we have to build a dam. Schnurr says he still hates the British, but doesn't seem to mind the Americans or the French. One of these Dutchmen over there says it's funny to hear an Irishman speaking Dutch-Afrikaans. Terrible temper."

"And did you hear about Mowat? Miracle, eh? He was mad enough to drive his cattle right through a fly area in the Umfolozi game reserve and they survived! They should have got nagana, but he said that the wind was very strong so he chanced it. Man, that could have been an expensive gamble. He should at least have taken them through at night. He did drive them to O'Grady's for dipping the next day, though."

"Crazy idea anyway, creating a game reservoir in a tsetse-fly area just to placate the natives and a few sports licence holders."

Actually, the pressures to create the Umfolozi and Hluhluwe reserves were far more complex than that, and partly took their rise from a deer park tradition of the English gentry preserving 'game' for sport and trophy hunting. The custom was imported into Zululand by the Natal Government for those who aspired to the status of sport hunters. It also developed a set of Natal Game Laws in 1884 modelled on English custom to protect certain species, setting down what was 'game', to be nurtured as sporting and trophy stock. Open and closed hunting seasons for 'game' were likewise introduced. Francolins, guineafowl, small antelope and hares acquired special protection under these laws, whereas carnivores which threatened 'game', such as lions, leopards, hyenas, jackals, crocodiles and wild dogs, were regarded as vermin. Bush pigs and monkeys were similarly disposable. The ground hornbill and the secretary-bird were protected because they kept down the snake population. Rhinos and elephant did not appear on the list at all because they had been shot out by the turn of the century, not in Umfolozi but certainly to the north in what became Kruger National Park in 1926.

The game laws (and the Natal government's introduction of the hut tax which provoked the Bambatha Rebellion) were completely foreign to the Zulus and enraged them, especially when they were hauled before a magistrate and punished for killing 'game' or for failing to pay the hut tax. The game laws also enraged the Boers for the same reason. They killed game for meat, not sport.

The motive for introducing the reserves was to placate the Zulu chiefs by accepting (rightly or wrongly) that nagana was carried by wild animals and transferred to cattle when they grazed among them. Zulus were convinced that the infection was passed by wild animals through their saliva to domestic cattle grazing on the same grasses. Although nagana flourished in areas strongly infested by the tsetse fly, the scientific explanation of infection through protozoa transfer had not been established. Reinforcing the native view, one Zulu observed at the time, "where cattle once lived there is now the fly and no cattle" – the so-called fly belts.

It was the arrival of an enlightened new Resident Commissioner Sir James Clarke in 1893 that helped to placate the Zulus. He recognised that the natives were close to starvation due to stock losses resulting from the ravages of nagana, forcing them to abandon traditional grazing grounds. He took into account that the natives were convinced that wild herbivores should be separated from domestic cattle to reduce exposure to the disease. He also listened to reports by old-hand hunters and transport riders who expressed similar opinions. Consequently, he decided to relax the Game Laws and initiate the driving of wild animals into a reserve, away from native cattle. This earned the co-operation of the chiefs who helped mount wild animal drives away from their herds and into the areas of poor vegetation and fever trees. It was these moves which brought into existence the Umfolozi and Hluhluwe game reserves by the end of the nineteenth century, well ahead of modern-day altruism, wildlife photographers and game viewing.

"I think we can get started," said Eric loudly, looking at his pocket watch and tinkling on a glass of water with a pen. "But first of all, may we just stand for a minute and think of those who couldn't join us today, those of our little community who died from Spanish Flu."

He was about to include a reference to war casualties but thought better of it after noticing the number of Boer-Afrikaners present.

While they were standing in silence, Piet van Jaarsveld's chattering children rushed around the corner of the building and pulled up short at the sight of so many grownups standing silently. The Pretoria agricultural man was holding his right hand to his heart, thumb closed, as were many others. It was an odd sight in the African sun, with the silence broken only by birdcalls and scented by a pile of smouldering leaves. Forever afterwards, the pleasant reek would remind Toby of that day outside the small Ntambanana store.

After Schnurr broke the silence with a "Thank you," he introduced the man from Pretoria who embarked immediately on a prepared speech speaking in High-Dutch, which was interrupted almost immediately by shouts of protest.

"We can't understand you!" shouted Barnes, Bennett and several other farmers. "Speak in English!"

Morkel went on talking for a few more moments before shouts of protest drowned out his best efforts to follow the official line, then hurriedly glanced at Mocke, while saying in stumbling English to Schnurr, "I vill trrry my best in English, but Dutch must have a voice in official meetings, so minutes must be (wat is 'uitgereik' in Engels?" he asked Mocke, who said, "issued") "in both official languages." He was beginning to sweat as he fumbled the pages looking for the English version.

Schnurr replied quietly that this might be difficult but that he and Marie would get together with Jan Mocke after the meeting to see how this could be done. "I foresee that translating into both official languages will be a growth industry!" he said, then more loudly: "Meneer Morkel accepts that most of us here don't understand the Taal…yet, so has agreed to speak in English and asks you to forgive his mistakes. Mr Morkel…?"

With a heavy Dutch colouring to every word, sentences liberally sprinkled with 'inter alias' and interrupted only by substantial nose-blowing in a large handkerchief, Morkel began to grind his way through the advantages of creating a farmer's cooperative, expressed in stifling officialese. The sentences were so convoluted and so long that many had difficulty in following the winding threads.

"What the hell does he mean 'inter alia'?" muttered Barnes to Bennett.

"Dunno. Perhaps it's something religious like 'Hail Mary' which I heard O'Grady say once. Ask him."

"It's Latin. It means 'among other things'. Our new Pretoria speech-writers love using it…implying that they are educated and we are not," O'Grady said. "You should've asked that Anglo-Irishman over there," pointing at Toby. "He learnt Latin in one of those snooty Protestant schools that sort goes to in Ireland."

Morkel ground on with details about how such organisations operated and the role of his department in assisting them. Then, with visible relief, he said abruptly, "Veel dank" and sat down, handing over to Eric to explain how Piet van Jaarsveld's store would continue to play an important part. Being a large man, Morkel's thighs overlapped the bentwood kitchen chair that Hannah had provided. It squeaked and swayed whenever he stirred.

"I'd like to thank Piet and his good wife for the considerate way our provisional negotiations leading up to this meeting were conducted," Schnurr said, while trying to wrench his gaze away from a centipede that had been heading over the planks for Morkel's shoes.

At a point, he drew Morkel's attention to it by tapping his arm and pointing at it whereupon Morkel promptly crushed it into oblivion.

He said that a small portion of land immediately abutting the van Jaarsveld store would be purchased on leasehold by the cooperative and developed to accommodate stock to cope with the growing needs of the farming community in such essentials as fodder, seed, fertiliser and farm equipment at the best wholesale prices. The premises would interlead with the original store which would continue to stock household goods for the whole community. Trade with the natives would also remain in the hands of Mr and Mrs van Jaarsveld, as would the smithy and the petrol pump. The land on which the van Jaarsveld's house and outbuildings stood and the rest of the property would likewise remain in the hands of Piet and Hannah.

"The co-operative will buy your crops and pay you in

tranches during the season with an agterskot at the end of the season – which means you will enjoy regular income as long as you actively farm."

"What the hell's a tranche and an agterskot?" shouted Begbie. He had a reason for needing clarity since he had misread a long legal document of agreement some years ago.

"Tranches are portion-payments for the crops you are growing and agterskot is the final deferred payment, being the difference between payments made and the balance due for the season."

There was a general stirring of approval by the farmers, some of them already beginning to feel far-stretched.

"What happens if we're wiped out by locusts or floods?"

"Then you'll owe the cooperative for any moneys due, which will be assessed and offset against next year's season, subject to negotiation. Crop insurance will be on offer and, although not cheap, you should consider it as a safeguard against such occurrences."

"What happens if we have two years of crop failures?"

"Then you'll have a problem. The cooperative will be able to support within reason, but no further."

The farmers were invited to join for a modest fee and hold equal shares as members of the co-operative, on the understanding that the van Jaarsvelds would also hold an adequate number of permanent shares. In addition to profit from crops, income from item sales would be shared equally among the members at the end of each financial year, yet to be established. The co-operative would be administered by a board which would appoint one of its members as Chairman for the year.

"When are you going to fix the road?" shouted O'Grady. "How the hell do you expect us to operate anything while we still have to negotiate that string of dongas? Sugar cane must reach the Empangeni mill within twelve hours before losing sucrose content – and we have to rely on ox-wagon express which usually takes far longer." His outburst brought out other angry voices agreeing.

"My Department will talk to the Natal Roads Department about it," said Morkel.

"We've been talking to them for years! Talk is cheap! Natal's broke after the war," said Barnes. "That's the problem. It hasn't got any money for anything, so it's taxing everything. If it could tax the number of stones and snakes on our farms, it would."

"I promise to talk to Pretoria. I promise. Let me see what can be done."

Schnurr cut short the distraction with, "May we get on with the main purpose of our meeting? We can buttonhole Meneer Morkel about other issues later. He's come all the way from Pretoria to help, remember, and a farmer's co-op will be a great step forward. Can we have a show of hands in favour?"; and a majority of hands were raised.

Many more words were spoken while Sarah and an Indian servant girl began setting out platters of sandwiches, rows of clinking tea cups, glasses and mugs on a not-altogether-level trestle table under the huge fig tree, accompanied by bottles of Opsaal brandy, a large urn of hot water, several giant metal teapots, and beer bottles swimming with chunks of ice in a tin bath.

"Where did the 'Opsaal' come from?" asked Barnes.

"There was an Opsaal brandy salesman here recently and donated them…as a goodwill gesture to celebrate the future Co-op."

"Did he now?" thought Donald. "Is he still here?" he asked; "I think I've met him and would like to say hello again."

"No, I don't think so. Piet told me he'd got a lift here and had gone back the same way to get to Mtubatuba by train and then cadge a lift to Hluhluwe, lugging brandy samples all the way in a large suitcase."

"Seems we're going to have quite a party…some of them will be as tight as ticks by this afternoon. Watch out for George Macfarlane," muttered Barnes. "The rest of the world is out of step except George…chip on shoulder. Suspects everyone is doing him down. Flies into rages after booze and makes wild accusations. He talks grandiosely of pie-in-the-sky ideas that'll make his fortune…would have been flung out of the army if the war hadn't ended. They say he got serious malaria near the Usambara Railway in German East Africa and has never been the same since."

Mocke had earlier arranged for three-foot blocks of ice, cocooned in straw and wooden boxes, to be brought up from Empangeni Rail by wagon. It was chunks off this block that swam in the bath. The ice had been railed up from Durban.

"I have a list of twelve names of those willing to serve on the board, which we propose to keep to seven (including Piet van Jaarsveld and myself). That means we have places for five other board members. To keep the election secret, Marie and Hannah have prepared twelve boxes each with the name of a candidate and left them in the care of Mrs van Jaarsveld in the store. Please would you file in (gentlemen only) one by one, where you'll find a bowl of beans. Please put the five beans which Marie will hand you into the candidate boxes of your choice. We'll then count the totals and the top five will have been voted onto the board.

"But before we do that I'll read out the candidates' names one by one, and ask them to stand for a moment when their names are called, so we'll all know who they are. So here we go: Dent…Shepstone…Kirkwood…Jackson…Jackson? Where are you? Jackson?"

"Oh, gosh. Sorry," said Jackson, as he shot to his feet. He had been distracted by speaking in a low voice to his wife, the one wearing the cloche.

"He's a dreamer, that one," muttered Barnes. "Absent-minded."

"O'Grady."

"Here comes trouble," Barnes muttered. Donald was not sure if he was talking to him or just himself, in a reflective way.

"Oh, I don't know. He knows his oxen and has been farming in the area well before we got here."

"He'll be in league with van Jaarsveld and Mocke if he gets in, mark my words."

"Well, I'd be prepared to give him my vote," Donald said.

Barnes fixed him with a glassy stare and said nothing, but turned away…and all conversation between them ceased.

"Cadman…Mowat…James…Curry…Curry?"

"He's fallen asleep listening to that man from Pretoria. Hey, Curry. Stand up!"

"Pearse…and Norgaard. Thank you, gentlemen. The results of the selection will be pinned up at the store next Friday. The delay will be caused by our interviewing those elected before making the names public. That concludes our meeting; but, before we slake our thirsts, please take it in turns to vote inside the store. A special thanks must go to Mr and Mrs van Jaarsveld for their hospitality and to Meneer Morkel who has travelled such a long way to be with us."

After the applause, a general clattering and scraping of chairs and boxes ensued as the meeting broke up, before Schnurr shouted above the chatter: "And finally to Captain Stoughton for donating a generous supply of Opsaal Brandy."

The door behind the store counter was ajar and led immediately into the van Jaarsveld sitkamer. Hannah was house-proud, it was clear. As Toby prepared to vote he glimpsed through the door a framed daguerreotype of what might have been Piet or Hannah's parents. The woman was substantial and homely while the husband was gaunt and bald. They had fixed stares, caused by the concealed neck-braces holding their heads in place during the long exposure. The glassy stares reminded him of the antelope heads glaring down at diners in the Masonic Hotel.

The other brown-framed picture he saw was of three Boers, standing before a farmhouse wall, their chests crisscrossed with ammunition bandoliers. Two hatted and bearded men, one much older than the other, flanked a boy of about sixteen, likewise bandoliered and capped with a particularly wide-brimmed farmer's hat. All three were holding long-barrelled rifles. Facial features were similar – suggesting that this was the entire male side of the family prepared to defend their endangered way of life against perfidious Albion. There was no uniform; they were just dressed randomly in farming clothes.

"So you're standing for election?" Toby said to Donald. "That should be fun. What started that off?"

"My limited experience as a banker – and I wanted to ensure that we English speakers retain our voice…you saw how things could swing in favour of Boer control by the way that Morkel launched off into Dutch. Sorry I forgot to mention it when we last met. We'll see. I may not be elected. I'll keep you posted.

"How did you get on with O'Grady? I see he helped you with the oxen."

"He knows the territory well but has his demons – aftermath of the Boer War and his long-term dislike of the English Occupation of Ireland – as he calls it. A bit obsessed about it. Be careful how you treat him. His Irish friends are hell-bent on disinheriting English absentee landlords from their Ireland estates – and it's likely to turn even uglier than it is at the moment. Your family were not absentee landlords but they could have risked being tarred with the same brush and it was wise of them to transfer to London for the time being. Shouldn't affect you much, remote as we are, but he will traditionally regard you as related to the Occupiers. There's no trust there…calls them all sleeveens, whatever that means."

"A sleeveen is a sly and untrustworthy person."

"Good word, that. But he called that man de Valera a sleeveen too, which spoils my ability to understand Irish politics. Up until now, I thought that all Irish rebels were united. Now I know otherwise. I think…"

"If Ireland manages to evict the English, there'll be fighting over the spoils…rather like pigs fighting for territory in the truck on the way to the slaughter-house."

Come Friday, Donald found he was elected, along with van Jaarsveld, Schnurr, O'Grady, Wilson, Cadman and Curry, but further discussions about the Co-op were held over until the fund-raising weekend in Empangeni was out of the way.

Chapter Nine

It had all started quietly enough. A small Empangeni Region Spanish Flu Survivors Trust committee was formed to represent the regional interests of the Dutch-Afrikaners, the English-speaking settler-farmers (the majority), the Indians and the natives. Pastor Henrik Louw and Reverend Robert Short were co-opted and in the absence of her Pastor, Nurse Eriksen from the Norwegian Mission Station had agreed to represent the interests of the Zulus, while the District Magistrate, Colonel Tanner, volunteered to represent the Indians. It was agreed that the bank manager, Allan Bustros, should serve as Chairman. The presence of people of colour actually serving on the panel was not even thought of or discussed.

The apportionment of income raised was agreed upon in advance, a bank account in the name of the trust was opened and Paolo Broccardo was appointed as treasurer. The fundraising weekend date was set, and preparations began.

Eric and Marie Schnurr had arranged to ride to Empangeni with Donald and Toby in a convoy with twenty other Ntambanana settlers who could afford to tear themselves away from their fledgling farms at that time, including the ferocious–looking William Blackbeard (all beard and bellowing voice) who had been chosen as the Rednecks' rugby captain. Myburgh had settled down after the loss of his wife to the drie-dagsiekte, and nowadays nursed his grief privately and agreed to participate in the rugby tourney.

Mrs Potgieter had offered to stay back to look after the Myburgh children.

As many depended upon shared wagons and drays for those without motorcars, progress over the rutted road from Tam to Empangeni was agreeably slow. The convoy had set out soon after sunrise while Donald, Toby and the Schnurrs had left hours later, passing the ox-wagon column just ahead of reaching the Bell farm.

Durban Corporation only started radio broadcasting in 1924, five years after the start of this tale. Before that time, newspapers were the sole source of general news and eagerly read.

"Hey, Donald, seen these?" asked Toby. They were sitting on the Bell's front verandah waiting for Andrew and Nigel Bell to come in from the farm. Donald had spotted unsettling news stories in the Natal Advertiser, which had come up from Durban by rail the day before along with the Pietermaritzburg paper, The Natal Witness.

"Remembering that you were shunted around East Africa by Smuts chasing the Huns…" he said, as he handed him the paper.

SMUTS FAVOURS HUN FRIENDSHIP

Before the signing of the Treaty of Versailles which ended the state of war between Germany and the Allied Powers, Lieutenant General Jan Smuts, a member of the British peace delegation, has once again advocated appeasement and reconciliation with Germany, according to a telegraphed report. He went on to declare that: "British statesmen should apply the same medicine to Ireland that I applied to Bohemia – appeasement and reconciliation."

He urged the Allies to leave Russia alone, remove the blockade and adopt a policy of friendly neutrality, saying that a soviet system might well be better than barbarism."

Returning to the topic of Germany, Smuts said: "It's a brutal fact that Britain is a very small island on the face of a continent in which seventy million Germans represent a most important and formidable factor. You cannot have a stable Europe without a stable and settled Germany. You cannot have a stable and settled Britain while Germany is weltering in confusion. Therefore the appeasement of Germany becomes of first importance.

Smuts wound up by quoting from Jeremiah, saying, "We looked for peace, but no good came."

IRISH QUESTION PRESSING

Concerning the Empire and dominions, General Smuts said the most pressing of all is the Irish Question. 'It has become a chronic wound whose septic effects are spreading to our whole system. Through its influence on America it is beginning to poison our most vital foreign relations.'

"So what do you make of that?"

"He's saying it's a Carthaginian Peace...but I think that the powers-that-be will just ignore him until it dawns on them in years to come that he was right. They're so committed to supporting the Russian White Army against the Bolsheviks that it's a panjandrum that will be hard to stop – especially with that fellow Churchill standing in the way."

"Here's another...mmmm, seems the Krauts are truly reaping the whirlwind. Slipping Lenin into Russia has come back to bite them."

THE GERMAN CRISIS

A New Plot for Soviet Republic throughout the Country.

A plot has been discovered in Berlin to overthrow the government and proclaim a Soviet Republic throughout Germany, but the Red Regime seems to be confined to the Southern provinces.

Reports from Munich state that the Bavarian Soviet Republic has been proclaimed. The Workers' Councils declare that the entire labouring population in Bavaria is solidly united and is assuming all public power through the Soviet Council.

Advices from Wurzberg reveal that the Communist troops have seized telephones, telegraphs and newspaper offices and a general strike has begun, excepting food shops. Regensburg has declared for the Soviet Republic."

"And here's one for that Irishman, Padraic..."

Unveils Emmet Statue

San Francisco: "You have unveiled a monument to liberty here today as great as that famous monument in the harbour of New York," Eamon de Valera, president of the 'Irish Republic' said in addressing a crowd of more than 60,000 at the dedication of the statue of Emmet in Golden Gate Park. De Valera was received uproariously by the throng.

"See this one? This'll make our Shinner friend rather sad."
"Why?"
"Well, it turns out that Louis Botha has died."
"I don't see the connection."
"Neither did I until this moment. May I read it to you?"
"Go ahead."

The first Prime Minister of South Africa died in Pretoria today. Although limiting political rights of natives and Indians, Louis Botha advocated reconciliation between Boers and Britons.

He was born in the Orange Free State, the son of a pioneer Boer settler, and received his only formal education at a German mission school.

"Louis Botha was the founder of the New Republic in the Vryheid region of Zululand, purchasing a farm there and marrying Annie Emmet, granddaughter of Emmet, an Irish patriot.

"Did he, now. Couldn't have been Robert Emmet because he wasn't married by the time he was executed in Dublin."

"Well, let's face it. Botha was a patriot and a gentleman. He was the one who helped capture Winston Churchill when his troop held up that armoured train near Ladysmith…and he lived in Zululand for a time only seventeen miles away from Tam. General Smuts will be the next Prime Minister. There's a whole long obituary about Botha if you'd like to read it."

"Later. What else is there?"

"Well, you Irish are still in the news overseas. Parts of the population seem to be going about murdering policemen. See this –

THE IRISH QUESTION: POLICE MURDERS IN DUBLIN

The shooting of Detective-Sergeant Barton in Dublin was the fourteenth police murder this year. He was young and popular and recently transferred to the political section of the detective force.

It is believed that the murderer tracked him through the crowded streets and fired four shots in College Street, one shot penetrating Barton's back.

"Good lord! Here's one that will disturb your naval soul…"

"What?"

"Well, the Germans have managed to scuttle most of their navy at Scapa Flow except for the subs they surrendered at Harwich. It seems they just pulled the plugs when no one was looking. Even the Hindenburg was scuttled. They hoisted the Imperial German Ensign as they sank. See… there's the report."

"Now that *is* a disaster. What a miserable waste."

"Anything in the Witless?" 'The Witless' was the fond nickname for The Natal Witness, Natal's oldest paper, published in Pietermaritzburg.

"Yes, on the local front. There's this bit about a native girl, for example. There'll be Indian and native unrest again sooner or *later.*"

GIRL FLOGGED TO DEATH

Police reported that a native girl at Wessels Nek had been buried without the necessary report of her death being given.

The body was exhumed and a post-mortem held by the District Surgeon. He reported that, in his opinion, the deceased girl had been flogged so severely that she had died from injuries inflicted.

"And here's something about labour – or lack of it…"

ANTI-INDIAN LEAGUE STARTED

A League has been established in Johannesburg by Sir Abe Bailey for the expropriation of Indian land and building ownership. This is in response to Indians sidestepping the strictures on their owning property by registering premises and land in the names of companies.

Such ownership had been declared lawful in 1916 although there are plans to appeal against this ruling. An anti-Asiatic League congress met in Pretoria this week, attended by twenty-six local authorities, thirty chambers of commerce, nine agricultural societies, twelve religious congregations and forty trade unions. General Jan Smuts is said to regard the undesirable granting of rights to Indians as 'the thin edge of the wedge which would open the way to rights for the African majority'.

The South African Indian Congress has protested to the Union Government and the British Government, and has appealed to the aid of prominent Indians including Srinivasa Sastri, Tej Bahadur Sapru and Mrs Sarojini Naidu.

A scheme has been mooted to subsidise the repatriation of Indians.

"Well, we're not exactly overrun with Indians in Ntambanana, are we? Perhaps we should quietly encourage a few to repatriate themselves down our way…anything to alleviate the labour shortage. But look what's happening with workers in Cape Town! There's a huge strike going on down at the docks. The natives and Coloureds have formed a trade union and are blocking the export of food to Europe. It's said that a native called Clements Kadalie is behind it.

"And – it's being supported by the National Union of Railwaymen – and they're all White! Ah, here they are," he said, as Andrew and Nigel stepped onto the verandah.

"Ready to beat the Boers?"

"Do any of us remember all the rules?" asked Nigel, as he was pulling off his wellies. "My memory of play is stuck at school level – I can barely recall the names of some positions, although I do remember how my ears got mangled in the scrum when playing second row lock. What's the scoring again?"

Donald said: "It's three for a try and two for a converting kick between the poles. As for rules, I think the game's more fun if you can't remember them very well. Why on earth the ball has to be oval is beyond me. The most important rules are 'don't pass the ball forward, and don't tackle around the neck', and the principle is to keep the ball in play except when kicking to touch to gain ground. You're playing scrum-half so you'll have to dig the ball out of the scrum when it comes your way. The unofficial rules are run like hell and bash on regardless but pass the ball along the line when doomed.

"I grew away from the game because we had to memorise the names of every bloody team member at school and got chastised for memory lapses. What an absolutely pointless waste of time!

"Tiny van Rensburg is playing – remember that giant who drilled the waterholes for us, Toby? Well, Eric Schnurr told me that the rest of their team matches his size. All built by the makers of Stonehenge. We'll need a cunning plan to bring them down.

"I remember a neat trick we had at college because our rivals from Wellington always seemed to be bulkier than we were," he said. "One of us would charge in front of the monster with the ball, kneel down quickly on all fours while the other player pushed the fellow hard…with another tackling him. Worked a charm – and there was nothing obvious in the rules against it."

"We'll try it – anything to beat 'em – I'm told they're hell bent on making this afternoon a bloodbath…and the man who told me didn't seem to be joking. We'll just have to retaliate in kind."

"Let's choose an easy code-word for the Stonehenge manoeuvre."

"How about 'Shaka Zulu'?"

"Shaka Zulu it is. Good one that. Who's our Captain?"

"Blackbeard."

"We'd better tell him as soon as we see him. And the ref?"

"A Portuguese man by the name of Ferreira."

"Where on earth did he come from?"

"I believe he's quite a prominent trader. He travels about."

"One wonders what he can know about the rules of rugby."

"Says he played it in Lisbon in 1903. The club name was 'Cruz' something-or-other. Rumour has it that he fancies O'Grady's wife, Sarie."

"He'll come short if he tries anything there," Donald said.

When they chugged into Empangeni, they found the manager of the Masonic Hotel stringing up fluttering bunting from the balcony, aided by one of his Indian waiters. Donald recognised the Indian from his first stay. He was the one who served them with a bandaged thumb sticking into the soup.

"Good lord, whose car is that?" asked Toby, admiring the cream-coloured Ford parked outside the entrance to the hotel and recently washed so that the metalwork sparkled.

"It's the manager's – Tom Legge, up on the ladder over there. Don't know where his money's come from; a manager's not paid all that much. Paid cash. Some said he'd won quite a lot on Fahfee."

"Fahfee? What's that?"

"Never heard of it? It's a numbers racket usually run by a Chinaman. Native women are the usual customers but some Indians play it, as well as the odd White."

"How does it work?"

"I don't really know much about it, but I believe that it's based on thirty-six digits, and operates every day in most towns and even villages like 'Pangeni. The operator uses runners to collect bets and names, and announce the winners for each session. It's illegal, so standardised signals are used instead. Each number is communicated by a special gesture. Number nine is a moon and the runner indicates this winning number by taking off his hat…so keep your eyes peeled for a hat-doffing Zulu."

"Ah. Or it could be because he thinks better with his hat off."

"Number two's a monkey and the runner indicates this by scratching himself under the arm. A gesture as if cutting across the throat is 'chicken', number thirty – and so on.

The winning ratio is about twenty-eight to one...so it can become addictive. News of occasional windfalls keeps the punters coming back – although the House, in this case the Chinaman, is the ultimate winner as he will choose the number least popular on that day. Some get so caught up in the game that they place ever larger bets, even borrowing large sums to do that. Inevitably that leads to huge debts."

"Perhaps we can persuade the Chink to contribute to the orphans' fund."

"That'll be the day! You wouldn't be able to identify him anyway. His kind is usually tucked away in a little room somewhere."

Bunting flew from the low roof of the railway station, and Loftheim's shared a string of fluttering streamers with the bottle store, both being on the other side of the road.

The white population of Empangeni in 1919 was under three hundred (the majority holding no parliamentary right to vote). This was less than seven percent of the region's indigenous humanity, to which could be added the large number of indentured and 'free' Indians. More than half of the white settlers converged on the fair that day, while natives and Indians were excluded, except for their many servants. They were allowed to watch from afar.

Marshals were charging for admission to the village then directing the new arrivals to the fields behind the hotel, where the Bell party discovered a scattering of tents, ox-wagons – many of them belonging to the Afrikaners – and a modest sprinkling of cars. Children were darting in and out and jumping over the stays. One tripped and nearly brought a tent down – much to the fury of the beery owner. Most of the horses had been tethered and watered in a long row beside the entrance to the hotel, although a few were tethered to the rear of the wagons. There was the smell of steaks and boerewors grilling over many braaivleis fires, the smoke drifting into people's eyes.

In one part of the grounds was a khaki marquee loaned by the Natal Police, full of chattering women, with trestle tables still being erected by a few marginalised men, as the women set out stalls of jam preserves (jars labelled, dated and sealed with butcher paper, string and candlewax), Meccano sets, needlework, cast-off women's and children's clothes, a clutter of well-used primus stoves, shoes, non-matching cups and saucers, a miscellany of cutlery (the bone handles already yellowing with age), snakes made of bamboo segments, tired-looking teddy bears, pies and embroidery; jumble of all kinds.

Close to the marquee entrance and next to a man frying and selling sausages in buns sat a stone-deaf old farmer with a wide brimmed hat made of rhino-hide, offering lettuce seedlings and repaired bicycle tyres.

Eben Brink, the Vet, already togged out in rugby clothes, was supervising his son and golden-haired daughter setting up a tombola drum near the jumble marquee, while looking bemused at the number of people continuing to flow into the grounds.

The oxen and a few untethered ponies had been released to graze further back, on the remains of the winter grass through which tiny shoots were peeping. Closer, a flat piece of ground had been kept clear for the three-legged and mieliebag races, jukskei- tossing at a tickey a throw, and an impromptu rugby field, with rugby posts made from wattle trunks already erected and whitewashed at the base. The three-legged and mieliebag races were for the children and were in progress. A small drinks and snacks pavilion (courtesy Gyn & Belcher), the canvas sides rolled up for ventilation, was beginning to crowd with thirsty and noisy patrons.

The Bell party drifted into the jumble marquee and it was there, when Donald was drawn to the tables of second-hand books, that he came across Hubie von Weldenburg studying a copy of *Auch dem Wege Nach Atlantis* by Leo Frobenius.

"Helloo!" exclaimed von Weldenburg, warmly. "We meet yet again," shaking his hand. "This is a strange book to find in the usual heap. You know about him?"

"Can't say that I do, Hubie."

"He is an ethnographer who explored southern Africa and other places. In this book he records relics of cultural greatness among some tribes and suggests that this was because they were exposed to a vanished white civilisation, an Atlantis."

"He writes (OK I translate?) about the present black primitives, saying 'I am disheartened that this degenerate and feeble-minded posterity should be the legitimate guardians of so much elegance'."

"Perhaps," said Donald, "it might be that Africa went to his head. He's not the first – 'white man's grave' and all that…all these African diseases. Frankly it sounds like a lot of twaddle, or an excuse for colonial powers to dispossess the natives. We could be accused of that too."

"But he's a great scientist! He explored much more of Africa than we will ever do. I must buy this book. Ah, look! See inside; it used to belong to the previous owner of our farm, see 'Rudolph von Breitenberg, 1903! What a coincidence. That lady behind the counter doesn't realise that this is a collectors' item…Excuse me. How much for this?"

"A shilling – it's all for a good cause."

"A shilling?"

"You can give more if you like."

"I will do so. Please. Here is five shillings."

"That's very good of you."

"My pleasure." Turning to Donald, Hubie said: "You will remember that discussion we had at the Bell's farm about eugenics and Pygmalion?"

"Yes."

"Well, my view about the need for an Ubermenschen society has not changed – though Frieda can never agree…. So I see you play rugby this afternoon?" he remarked, gesturing at Donald's rugby togs and boots.

"Yes. You must bet at the tote over there. We expect you to place at least £50 that we will win!"

"What are the odds?"

"I don't know – they change all the time. You'll have to ask the bookies but expect to lose it all for charity anyway. There are all sorts of variants – for example the player who scores the most tries, what side scores the first try, what the first half score will be, the second half score and the final score. There's even one for the player for the knobbliest knees (as decided by the committee after the match)."

"That is interesting. I have never seen a game of rugby. I am more used to ice-hockey and football."

"Rugby's a bit like schoolboy cowboys-and-Indians with a few rules thrown in and a funny-shaped ball."

"Cowboys and Indians?"

"You probably played something like that in Switzerland when you were a child. You know the sort of thing – two sides line up on opposite sides of the school grounds then run shouting at each other. The goal is to reach the other side by struggling a way through. In rugby, if the opponent clutching the ball manages to break through the enemy side and touch the ball on the ground behind the line of the goalposts he is said to have scored a Try."

"I see. You have been practising this 'struggling'? I was told that the Dutch side has been drilling all week. They kept on running up and down and throwing that funny-looking ball to each other."

"No. We haven't been practising and most of us have half-forgotten the rules, if they were ever known," said Donald. "Well now, you must excuse me, I need to have a chat with Andrew over there. By the way – that brandy salesman… interesting fellow. That was quite a night we had at your farm! Have you seen him again?"

"Yes! He's back here again, over in the drinks tent."

"I'll go and say hello later. Is Frieda here?"

"She will come with a friend, later."

They were interrupted by an unearthly screeching coming from the top of the drinks tent and then an extremely loud voice, interrupted by more squeaks.

"Good heavens, what's that?"

"Loftheim's have railed up from Durban one of those new voice magnifiers just for the event."

"Life will never be the same again. What a racket!"

The source of the noise was Pastor Hendrik Louw and Reverend Robert Short sharing a teachers' platform borrowed from the school, with a strange circular device atop a pole from which wires trailed behind the drinks pavilion. Short's wife had attached a few ribbons to the microphone "just to dress it up a bit," she had said.

Between the feedback howls and squeals produced by the speaker system, Louw addressed members of his tribe in Dutch-Afrikaans first, then switched to stumbling English, as an acknowledgement that most of those present wouldn't understand what he was saying. Short followed and brought forth cheers from some of the boerewors-munchers with a few sentences in Afrikaans which he had been practising for days while taking his dogs for a walk in the veld every morning.

Those who attended his church services were accustomed to helping him over his stammers but were confounded by his stammering in Afrikaans over a word starting with a 'p', until one of the boerewors brigade came to the rescue by shouting 'plesier!' [pleasure]. With cheers from the crowd, and while a marshal began to line up twelve Indian men on the playing field, each wearing a numbered vest, Short wound up by declaring the Fundraising Fête open, while ever mindful of the loved ones lost in the war, on behalf of the 'many hundreds of families afflicted by this new flu tragedy'.

"First off, I hope you've all placed your generous bets for the egg-and-spoon race, ladies and gentlemen, in aid of the Indian families, especially the orphaned children. Competing for a month's supply of extra rice and spices donated by Loftheim's are…(here he fumbled with a page and began to struggle through unfamiliar–sounding names) One: Naigum, Two: Kaghery, Three: Esack, Four: Reddy, Five: Nagoodoo, Six: Rungapen, Seven: Chinapen, Eight: Veerasamy, Nine: Perumal, Ten: Poolathah, Eleven: Nunchee, and Twelve: Thondroyah." These men represent the hardship of many… Are they ready, marshal? All of them have eggs?" It was a barefoot race.

The marshal waved, then fired the starting pistol.

The Bell family cheered and shouted as their man, Reddy, raced in a stumbling helter-skelter style to break the finishing ribbon.

"And now we have another surprise for you before the first game of rugby to be played in Empangeni since before the war," Short said, and bellowed into the microphone: "Madoda! Woza udansa ngathi!"

A group of Zulu warriors in full war regalia had been

assembling out of sight at the far end of the rugby field, and suddenly ran on and started to drum and stamp a war dance.

"I'm glad they're performing with sticks, not spears," Meiring said to his wife. "My God! Imagine that lot getting out of control again," as the ground shuddered with stamping feet. The air was filled with the sound of whistles and voices and sticks being beaten in rhythm against cowhide shields.

"I saw Sergeant Muller and some of his men wandering around, so I expect he's keeping an eye on things."

Once the warriors got started it was difficult to persuade them to stop, until one of the marshals brought on a wheelbarrow loaded with portions of cooked meat on butcher paper and a large bowl of putu borne by his Indian assistant. The marshal went on wheeling it across the field to the other side until they disappeared from view, after beckoning the warriors to follow – which they did, rather like a flock of sheep following a bucket of feed pellets carried by a farmer.

His assistant detoured on his return to where Donald was standing and stood for a moment beside him before discreetly handing him a small folded piece of paper saying, "From Deepika," then walked away quickly. Puzzled, Donald opened it to discover a pencilled note in childish lettering, so popped it into his rugger shorts pocket, deciding to read it later.

Most of the crowd had gathered along the nearest touch line now, and the volume of shouted encouragements increased to a crescendo when the teams ran on to the field.

Loftheim's had sponsored the jerseys – blue and white stripes for the Boers, red and white for the Rednecks. Donald spotted players on the Boer side that he knew – including Padraic O'Grady and Karl Lindqvist, the Vet's assistant, and an image of Nietzsche's 'Blond Beast' sprang to mind. While Creighton's references to Nietzsche's metaphor had flown over his head at the time, the mention of the Blond Beast had stuck in his memory, and when he looked at Lindqvist, he recalled the occasion in that little Pickering Street office in Durban when Howard Creighton warned Donald about the growth of German 'Social Darwinism' influenced, undeservedly, by Nietzsche's utterances, even while the West was preoccupied with the threat of Bolshevism. Lindqvist was Nordic and gigantic, after all, and certainly a formidable opponent, in rugby terms.

Karl nodded to him, as did Padraic. True to the rumour, most of the opposition were giants, with Lindqvist leading the pack.

The natives had been marshalled to view the match on the far side of the field upon a little rise of ground, as had the Indians, who were limited to a separate, distant part.

The tote was lively, with punters demonstrating not only their support of the 'flu-orphans' cause but of their team of choice, and the temptation to show off a bit, oiled by liquor.

Referee Chico Ferreira was short, from Portuguese Mozambique, and spoke dense nasalised and laryngealised English, embroidered by Afrikaans adjectives. Before he tossed the coin, Blackbeard asked him to pause to allow the Rednecks to break into a war dance of their own, stamping their boots in unison, raising their right fists and shouting "Kuhlasela! Kuhlasela! Kuhlasela!" [Attack!] which took the Boers off-guard and set off the distant native watchers to giggling at the umlungu employing a Zulu word to strike awe into their opponents.

The Boers rallied quickly and shouted a defiant "Vrystaat!" in response, harking back to the ancient struggle. They won the toss, chose to defend the northern side, and started the match with a drop-kick from the halfway, followed up a by a formidable rush of the forwards. Andrew, being fleet of foot and an accurate booter who was playing full-back, was able to catch the ball far inside the reds' quarter, then made urgent efforts to dodge and dive his way up-field, desperately looking around for support, which was not forthcoming. He was soon felled and a ruck ensued, the whole multilegged muddle being pushed back towards the reds' goalposts by the force of the opposition before the ball was released and scooped into the large hands of Eben Brink, the vet, a giant known to have wrestled a bullock to the ground.

Around towards the Reds Brink waded, his rugger shorts dragged half off as three Rednecks hung on in a struggle to bring him down, as ineffectively as lion cubs might try to claw a rhino to the ground. A fourth man had to run to the rescue before he could be felled.

There were not many baths or showers in Zululand at that time and the combined smell of sweating bodies in close proximity during the scrums and rucks was pungent indeed.

And so the match went on to the roars of Empangeni spectators, with the Reds kicking to touch whenever they managed to snatch the ball, in desperate attempts to regain ground, although the resulting line-outs were invariably snatched by the towering Boers, until half-time saw a score of 13-nil to the Boers, made up of three Tries and two Conversions (a Try was worth three points in 1919 and a converting kick between the goalposts, two). The last attempt at a Conversion bounced off one of the uprights.

At half time, a tin bath of water clattering with mugs was rushed onto the field by the marshals, along with a basin full of quartered oranges.

"It's time to switch to 'Shaka Zulu'," Blackbeard muttered to his panting side, all huddled together, mostly stooped forward with hands resting on knees or squelching oranges. "Because they'll wise up after a couple of times I'll switch the password to 'Sugar!' later. The manoeuvre's identical, OK? And we've got to break through by better feinting – you know, pretending to pass the ball one way then passing to the other side to get them off-balance. And kick to touch as far down the field as possible whenever we get the chance." (Even a full-back was allowed to kick to touch in the good old days.)

Some players on the Boer side were stretched full out on their backs to take maximum advantage of the ten-minute break.

The second half was not quite the earlier disaster, until a mule, spying its master, cantered onto the field among the players, causing them to scatter, then trotted to and fro with the ebb and flow of the game. The Blond Beast and Eben Brink had been felled with the Shaka Zulu manoeuvre while this was going on, until Ferreira stopped the game and shouted to the vet to "get thet blerry enimal off the goddam field!" allowing the Rooineks to scrape together some of their honour when the game restarted by scoring two tries in rapid succession, with Andrew managing to convert once, though the first kick went wide of the mark.

The rest of the match was marred by injuries, with Dr Lombard and Nurse Jenkins fully occupied attending to a broken nose, several serious sprains and a major cramp, with some players, including Donald, having to limp off the field, as his troublesome knee had given in again.

At Ferreira's final whistle, no more tries had been scored, allowing the Boers to walk off the field triumphantly with a score of thirteen against the Rednecks' eight.

"We'll have to challenge them to a return match at some time," said Blackbeard, "but frankly, we were a bit of a shambles. What we need is a permanent rugby ground and a lot of practice before we do that." Some of the team, including Andrew and Nigel Bell as well as Toby and Donald, had escaped from the embers of the fair and were sitting in the Masonic's beer-garden staring morosely into their beers, when Blackbeard joined them.

"I believe there's a spot of land big enough for a permanent rugger field near the sugar mill. But what we need is an organiser to sort it out and lick a team into shape; and that's not me. No time and too far away at 'Tam."

"Well, when we were passing Kelly's farm on the 'Tam road, he was waiting on horseback at the entrance and wished us well – explaining bitterly that he couldn't leave the farm, much as he wanted to, because some of his cattle seemed to be going down with nagana. He's rugby mad and a good organiser. Why don't we rope him in? No objections?"

"Over to you, Blackbeard. Have a talk to him."

The fundraising day petered out officially not much beyond sunset, when the Natal Mounted Police came to retrieve their marquee and the drinks tent had run out of liquor. Tired children were being carried back to tents and wagons – and what cars there were – until all that was left were the rugby posts, standing out against the fading sky, and the usual debris of an abandoned fairground and families sitting beside small fires, chatting with friends. The Zulu workers had gone back to their quarters and the Indians had wandered off to their domestic duties.

The focus had shifted to the Masonic Hotel which was doing a booming and noisy trade in the beer garden. A small group of whiskered men had arrived and offloaded trumpets, trombones, an unwieldy drum set and a 'squashbox'. In the dining room a pianist was tuning the dark, care-worn Blüthner upright which had been wheeled squeakily from the back meeting room and parked under the glaring herbivore heads, in preparation for the dinner-dance that evening. The hotel management had managed to replace the chef who had succumbed to Spanish Flu with a man from Mauritius, Max Pitot.

Andrew and Nigel Bell had already arranged to attend the event with their current girlfriends Janet Chisholm and Jane Sissmore, both daughters of sugar cane farmers in the vicinity, and had prevailed upon Donald and Toby to sit with them. As they had been given a lift into Empangeni in one of the Bell cars they had to go along with arrangements, whether they liked it or not.

The dining room had been transformed. Coloured paper streamers flowed from the central light (powered by the generator which made the electric light throb) to points around the walls, including the herbivore antlers. The glow was softened by candles at each table. Loftheim's microphone, which worked off batteries, had been moved to the dining room, along with the schoolroom platform, where the band was now installed. The dancing area close to the band was surrounded by round dinner tables.

In the event, the young women brought along two more girls from the same social set and, for one, Donald groaned inwardly at the prospect of having to shuffle them politely around the dance floor in the hours ahead. His limp was more pronounced after the rugby, the room was already beginning to fill with cigarette smoke and chatter, and he wondered what Emily was doing way down in rainy Cape Town. He was paired with a Beatrix Miller, a bony girl in a shiny pink dress which reached to the floor, who talked incessantly about her horse; it liked apples offered in halves, he learnt, and these were presently hard to come by. From a pre-war experience he knew that sooner or later he would trip on the hem of her long dress when the time came to take to the floor.

As a means of drawing her away from her horse, he asked her, flippantly, "Do you agree with George Bernard Shaw's remark that dancing is a 'vertical expression of a horizontal desire'?" which shut her up for a while, so he could talk to the others. Turning to her again, he found her looking at him curiously.

When, before the war, he had been confronted with the requirement to dance, he was given hurried lessons ahead of the event by a friend's well-endowed sister, Joy Migliorini, on their back verandah. It had not gone well, but he enjoyed the pneumatic proximity of the sister, so endured attempts to respond to the beat blared out with Germanic efficiency by a large wind-up Parlofone and the tugging this way and that by a determined girl. He had refused to attempt the turkey-trot (it was so absurd, all that elbow-flapping) but had done better with the waltz, while Joy kept on repeating, "Don't look at your feet. Look at me! Hold me closer! One, two three, one, two three, look at me, one, two three." She was seventeen and had a small mole on one cheekbone, wideset brown eyes and a full mouth.

Hints of London's post-war abandonment had begun to appear in the mode of some girls' dresses and behaviour, even in remote post-war Zululand. One of the girls at the table wore a broad ribbon across her forehead, rather like a sweatband, to which was attached a small artificial flower. Another smoked cigarettes from a lengthy mother-of-pearl cigarette-holder, flicking the ash with insouciance into a sloganed ashtray. The girl with the slightest figure at their table wore a flapper-dress sent out to her by her London aunt, causing a middle-aged woman at the next table to glare at her with disapproval. "She's half-naked!" she said loudly while getting up from her chair to walk across the floor to other friends. Donald thought that the woman's gait was close to that of a pigeon when walking, because she bobbed her head forward with each step. His sister Winnie had a mare and foal that did the same thing, he remembered, nodding their heads as they approached the fence for a handful of oats.

Donald realised that he was not paying sufficient attention to his partner during dinner. He was tired from the match, his knee was playing up and he was even further distracted by the import of Deepika's note written in a large childish hand which he had reread: "Masta. You ask me rite. My husben die but tankyu for food. This Masta bad man. I want cook for you. Plees anser. Deepika." It was significant, in that if he could persuade Deepika to stay in place he would be able to help Prue monitor the goings-on at the von Weldenburgs. There remained the puzzle of how to make contact with Deepika, until he realised that the Indian waiter attending his table was the man who had brought him the message.

"Are you full-time here?" he asked.

"No, sir. At bottle store, sir. Daytimes. My name's 'Freddie' Reddy…cousin Reddy who work Bell farm."

This exchange was interpreted by his table companions merely as a pleasantry, although between Reddy and Donald it established an unspoken understanding that Donald could contact Deepika by this route. Donald nodded. Later that evening, he managed to ask the waiter to tell her that he, or a friend (he was thinking of Prue), would be in touch.

Little Miss Tatham, the voluntary librarian, now all perfumed and a-glitter, called at Donald's table with her portly husband in tow, and succeeded in selling the men raffle tickets. The prizes were around one of the potted palm trees, draped with tinsel saved from the hotel's Christmas tree.

There were bags of mieliemeal, very large tins of vegetables and meat, presentation boxes of ladies' toilet soap, gift bottles of cologne, a tea set, a big green cardboard box labelled

FERTILISER, a child's bicycle and a cast-iron meat-mincer, each tagged with the name of its donor.

The speech of welcome between the main course and the dessert was given by Lt. Colonel Tanner, D.S.O., who kept it short and pro-forma, addressing both camps – in Dutch and English – with equal courtesy, although the gathering was predominately English and most of the Afrikaners came from farms closer to Vryheid.

Tanner had been wounded during the Battle of Delville Wood where thousands of South African soldiers had lost their lives.

Part of the menu was in English and 'chef-French' (no Dutch) and comprised 'La soupe aux pois' (good old hotel pea soup dressed up in French).

OR

'Richard's Bay Oysters Mignonette, cradled in avocado' (served in crushed ice chipped from a large block railed up from Durban).

The first option for the main course where, for no obvious reason, the chef had switched to mangled 'franglaise', was:

'Umhlathuze Grunter poisson à la sauce mangue and pepper' (A group of Dr Lombard's friends had caught the fish in the Richard's Bay lagoon and had presented a large number to the hotel as a gesture to mark the occasion).

OR

Madras Mutton Curry and Rice ('one can't Frenchify that', the new chef had thought; 'too Raj by a long chalk').

AND

Légumes en saison (surely they would understand that, even in Empangeni?)

Dessert alternatives were:

Apple crumble with warm Crème Anglaise

OR

Crème Brulée
followed by
Fromages assortis (Pitot was dreaming of his Mauritian grandmother's fromagerie near Port Louis when he scribbled that on the menu cards.)

As the smoke-filled evening progressed, the dance floor began to crowd with couples bumping into each other, until a player stepped forward with a button concertina and launched into the sakkie-sakkie rhythm of boeremusiek, backed by the others on guitars and drums.

Almost immediately, couples rose at the Afrikaner table and began to dance the tikkiedraai, the English couples escaping to their seats to watch. Captain Stoughton, the brandy salesman, was one of the first to dance, with an attractive dark-haired girl. The only couple at the Afrikaans table who didn't move to the floor was the von Weldenburgs, who sat there smiling and tapping their feet. Nevertheless, Frieda succeeded in turning heads by wearing a black frock with a hint of flapper hemline, but not enough to shock her conservative Afrikaans companions. As Hubie was disinclined to dance at all, it was inevitable that Stoughton would sweep her onto the dance floor in due course, after escorting his partner to her place. Captain Claude Stoughton and Frieda were good dancers and introduced their own style into the step. Whereas other couples would link hands and spin around on the spot at a point in the dance, Stoughton whirled Frieda about while clasped together as if for the foxtrot.

Chico Ferreira, the referee, was a guest at the Afrikaans table. When he stood up and invited Padraic O'Grady's wife, Marie, to dance the tikkiedraai, Padraic stood up too, bristling with brandy-fuelled rage, and objected strongly. Chico had contrived to sit on the other side of Marie and as the evening wore on his overtures to her were becoming noticed by Padraic and the others. It was over quickly when Padraic pushed him to the floor, planted a foot on his chest and bellowed at him: "Fág Maria aonar nó beidh mé tú a mharú!" – reverting to childhood Irish in his rage. Ferreira got the drift, although he would not have understood the words.

Lt. Colonel Tanner waded through the dancers, quickly assessed the situation and said, "Gentlemen. This must stop! Chico. You must leave. Now! Padraic, sit down!" all delivered in the commanding voice that he had last used before the Battle of Delville Wood. He remained there until they obeyed, after helping the crestfallen Ferreira to his feet. He was last seen climbing into his car and driving off.

The dance stopped at midnight after the gathering stood and sang the first verse of 'God Save the King', except for the Dutch-Afrikaans table which remained stubbornly seated; although the von Weldenburgs did make to rise before being pulled down to their seats by frowning companions. (South Africa was a British Dominion in 1919 and George V was king and emperor of India from May 1910, the very year that the Union was established. It was sung until 1957 when it was displaced by the Afrikaans language, 'Die Stem', a straw in the wind for what was to come.)

Cash from the day's events had been brought up the winding backstairs to the hotel office and stored in the wall safe by the manager, Tom Legge, under the watchful eye of Lt. Colonel Tanner. He counted out twenty-seven Treasury one-pound gold certificates inscribed in copperplate Dutch and English script and placed them in one of the safe's pigeon-holes. There was one five-pound certificate among them, a large sum in those days. The huge pile of farthings, halfpennies, pennies, minute silver tickeys, sixpences, shillings, 'godless florins' and half-crowns was poured into coin bags and stored for counting later on, stacked well away from the hotel float which was in its own large tin cash box.

It had been agreed beforehand for some members of the committee to count the cash after the ball to provide a total to be announced on Sunday in the Anglican Church services. Pastor Louw of the Dutch Reformed Church was reluctant to do likewise as the total of the field day takings included those from liquor and games of chance, but was persuaded that the cause was a good one and so could be condoned as an exceptional circumstance.

Thus Allan Bustros, the bank manager, Paolo Broccardo, little Miss Tatham, William Tanner and Nurse Eriksen stayed behind for the count and sat impatiently waiting for Tom Legge to appear with the keys which he had mislaid, he said, 'downstairs somewhere'. The wait became so prolonged that Bustros went down to find him and was surprised to discover him sitting in the kitchen munching a sandwich.

"Why aren't you looking for the safe key?" asked Bustros in exasperation. "Have you found it? How on earth could you mislay it so easily?"

"I'm sitting here trying to remember where I put it. There was so much to-ing and fro-ing with the takings that I must have put it down somewhere. Why not leave it for tonight and I'll make a good search tomorrow?"

"That is impossible! You have half the committee waiting upstairs for you and we agreed to total the takings so that announcements can be made tomorrow! Here, let me help you find it. Think back. When did you last hold it in your hands?" he said as he opened and shut various drawers in the kitchen table and found a large heavy key under some paperwork. "What's this?"

"Oh, good heavens! That's it."

"Well, come on man, upstairs we go."

Legge was strangely slow in following Bustros up the stairs and halted half way, saying, "Hold on, I must let the rest of the staff go," and started to go down the stairs again when Bustros stopped him, grabbed the key and rushed up the stairs impatiently with Legge shouting, "You can't do that! Only I may open the safe. Here, give the key to me," but Bustros was obdurate, shook him off and left him standing on the stairs.

Bustros's suspicions were confirmed when he opened the safe in the presence of the others and Tanner exclaimed, "But all the notes have gone! I put them there in that cubbyhole myself just before the safe was locked in my presence. We had better get hold of Legge to find out what has happened – although we can guess."

Tanner and Bustros found Legge sitting alone in the kitchen with his head in his hands. There was only a single light left burning in the corner, the others having been switched off to save precious light bulbs after the kitchen staff had left. The figure at the table cast an enormous shadow on the wall where a sink tap, which had not been turned off properly, was still spluttering.

"Where's the charity money you took from the safe?" Tanner roared.

With his head still in his hands and avoiding Tanner's gaze, Legge mumbled, "I only borrowed it. I was going to put it back first thing on Monday morning…there'll be a big win coming my way; but I had to pay someone tonight for a betting debt I owed. They were threatening to cut my fingers off."

"My God, what a mess you've got into, and the committee," said Tanner. "After all our efforts you have gone and spoiled everything. Well, you've got twelve hours to return that cash. Failing which, we'll have to lay a charge of theft against you and as I'm the District Magistrate I don't have to emphasize what would happen to you. If proven, you could face a long prison sentence and all the disgrace that goes with it. And consider your wife and child. What would happen to them?"

The last image in Legge's mind's eye, before pieces of his cranium and brain splattered the wall of the hotel ironing room, were of his father. He was bending down to the small boy and smiling, as he helped him cast for trout just below the Old Bridge weir on the River Nith, Dumfries. They were standing in the shallows.

The upshot was that an estimate had to be made of the stolen money, with the acceptance that it would probably never be recovered from persons unknown. Legge's car was attached by the committee, after a legal rigmarole, and in due course used as surety to raise an overdraft in the name of the fund. Later, the car was auctioned off by Chapard's in Durban and the proceeds, less the amount to clear the overdraft, was paid to Legge's wife, who left the district. She was last heard of living with her child in Mtubatuba.

But this was not the end of it. Next day, the hotel housekeeper, Mrs Maytom, took one of the maids, Jabulisile (the name means 'Joy') with her to clean up the mess in the ironing room and swab off the blood stains with petrol. Later, Jabulisile was sent in again to tackle the mountain of ironing that had built up. Old coal-heated laundry irons were still in use and without a thought for the consequences, she lit the small fire in the grate to heat up the coals.

The explosion shook the hotel. Mrs Maytom and an Indian waiter rushed to the laundry room to find Jabulisile collapsed and unconscious on the shabby granolithic floor. The skin of her face, chest and arms had erupted in huge yellow and black blisters.

Neither of them knew what to do, but instinctively, the waiter ran to fetch a sheet and wetted blankets, then between them they rolled the still unconscious body in them.

Mrs Maytom tried to get hold of Dr Lombard by phone but there was no answer; then she remembered that there was an old and curling First Aid manual kept under the counter at Reception. From scrabbling through the pages with trembling fingers she learnt that it was important to replace fluids and to persuade the patient, if conscious, to keep sipping mild saline solution with added drops of lemon juice, so then she charged to the kitchen and back again to the ironing room with a full mug.

Jabulisile died later that evening.

When she had started to work in the hotel she had been given accommodation in a small back room in the servant quarters. On gathering up her effects Mrs Maytom went into her quarters and found that Jabulisile had slept on an iron bed that had been raised higher with bricks beneath each leg – as protection from the Tokoloshe. The native Africans believe this small hairy dwarf of the night becomes invisible by drinking water.

There was little else in the room, save a small and rickety bamboo table covered with an embroidered cloth, some beadwork, a mug and an illustrated Sunday-school pamphlet.

At least she received a traditional Zulu burial after her stony-faced father and brothers came to collect the body. Mrs Maytom was crying when she gave them a young goat and money. The family had not only lost a daughter, but the bride-price of ten head of cattle which went with it.

Legge was not so fortunate, as Reverend Short would neither permit a funeral for him nor allow him to be buried in a marked grave in the little churchyard. "I am tremendously saddened, but my hands are tied," he stammered, when questioned by a distressed Mrs Maytom. "The church cannot condone suicide." A friend of Legge, who had a farm on the Ntambanana road, offered to inter his body in a marked grave, near an old thorn tree on the farm. The family, Mrs Legge, and several other friends (for he was a popular man among the fishing fraternity) attended a little ceremony of their own, with a few readings from the bible. He was buried with his favourite fishing hat and his book of Robert Burns' poems which he had won at school.

Later, a gravestone marked the spot with his name, the dates that spanned his life, and the words of the Scottish Bard:

'In Heaven itself, I'll ask no more
Than just a Highland welcome.'

Chapter Ten

Donald awoke before dawn to a world of mist, spider webs and the liquid call of a robin-chat, which was almost immediately joined by another.

His stretcher was pitched among the incomplete flooring pillars of the house and his blanket covering was damp with dew. For a few moments he was waking as a child on his father's farm in Scotland, before the starlings in the coille melted into the call of the chats.

He thought of Emily. They had sat on a bench of decaying concrete at the end of the Mole, as the swell rose and withdrew over the barnacled rocks below with a glistening, bubbling sound. The sounds of the harbour were all about them.

He thought again of her in their bed, just before dawn. She was naked and curled up beside him. He had drawn the blanket over her and propped himself up on an elbow to watch fishermen far below, swathed in mist, launching their rowing boat from the yacht club slipway. That morning was so still that he had heard a big fish leap and plop, further out in Durban bay.

The embers of last night's fire still glowed, releasing wisps of drifting wood smoke. It was lit before sundown in a corner of the roofless room where it crackled, slipped and grumbled all night to discourage visits by snakes and other night creatures. He could hear Layani moving about outside gathering tinder and sticks to bring it back to life for hot water and breakfast. This had become an established routine.

Donald determined to write a short message to Prue, before work started for the day, so opened the Thirty-Nine Steps at random on page 59 and chose sixteen lines down and four letters in, which read 'I scrambled to the top of the ridge.' Then began the laborious process of encoding his message: *'Befriended maid Deepika. Maybe amenable monitor von Weld. Friend Reddy works 'Pangeni bottle store.'* After this he composed a short chatty letter around it and the birds he had observed. He kept the letter in its envelope until he could post it at the store.

Building a farmhouse in the middle of nowhere-in-particular hardly required supervision and signing off by a building inspector stage by stage. There were no rules. You just went ahead and built one with available materials, and this is how the dwelling at Yonder came into being. Common-sense and the experienced advice of others ruled the day. Cement was expensive to transport from source, so was reserved for essential uses, such as a component of concrete for pillars to support floors. Bricks were also too costly. They would have had to be railed up from the Umgeni Brick Works in Durban and transported the rest of the way to Tam by wagon. These were pioneering days and corrugated iron was the settlers' choice for roofing and cladding, if they could afford it, as it was readily available from van Jaarsveld's store. Many other settlers made do with wattle and daub construction as the first move up from a tent.

(Wattle is made by weaving young gum-tree branches between upright stakes, to form a wall. Reeds are used as well. Daub, made of a mixture of cattle dung, wet clay, straw, sand and soil is daubed on to the framework, while sticky, to make a rugged and long-lasting wall. These land up so thick they offer attractive deep window ledges and good heat insulation.)

Donald kept to the local wood-and-iron convention (such as it was) of a squarish room at each end, separated by a smaller room in between and fronted by a verandah. A kitchen extended out at the back. Roofing was a simple matter but he had persuaded Clement, the Indian metal worker at van Jaarsveld's, to put in some hours, when the time came, to help assemble the guttering and water tanks at both ends of the house.

Layani had built himself a hut afar off – a circular construction of stripped branches with a conical roof. He had started to collect grasses for the roof with components for daub being assembled beside them.

The number of mouths to feed was growing exponentially, not forgetting the cattle and the Zulu men, who had built a temporary beehive hut of wood and thatching at the edge of the Thunder Tree field. They were hard workers, once they got started, with tremendous appetites. Feeding the men was not mentioned in the negotiations but was just taken for granted. The regular supply of mieliemeal sacks bartered for their labour went to the chief. Other new mouths demanding nurture were presented by Layani one day when he appeared at the back entrance to the unfinished building with a young Shangaan woman, saying in a mixture of English, Dutch and Portuguese, "This minha vrou, o nome dela é 'Fanisa'. 'Kotani' is baby."

Donald assumed a matter-of-fact expression, but still found it difficult to be completely at ease talking to bare-breasted native women like Fanisa. who did not notice his discomfort. Barefoot, she wore a multi-layered grass skirt and a 'choker' of brightly coloured beads. Her infant was held in a bundle of rags against her left breast. Balanced on her head was a grass basket, within which was another small basket, and she kept her eyes cast down as a sign of respect.

"Now what do I do?" thought Donald. "Is this the start of an invasion of sorts? I'll have to stop it before it starts, but I'll let her stay and discuss the protocol with Eric Schnurr."

"Has Fanisa travelled far?" he asked.

"Ela andou muitos dias," Layani replied, emphasising the last two words from which Donald construed that 'muitos dies' meant many days. He was mystified as to how she had found her husband four hundred miles away and wondered at the dangers she must have encountered on the way from other tribes, wild animals, snakes and the hardship of food deprivation. Here was a woman of great courage, he thought.

"Your wife and umfaan can stay, but no more people. Do you understand? No more! Abantu awasekho!…and I will have to talk about this with the 'big boss' here." (There was no 'big boss' but he decided to imply that such decisions were not his to make, even though he was sure that some guttural meddler from Pretoria would come snooping around sooner or later.)

He put into her cupped hands paper twists of extra sugar, tea, mielie meal and some powered milk, and then indicated that Layani and he had work to do for the day. For the first time, Fanisa smiled, and it was a beautiful open smile in a face of wide-set eyes, a Tsonga nose and a generous mouth revealing a pianoful of bright white teeth. After some rummaging he found a careworn blanket for the child, for the mornings were still chilly.

Building barracks for the Indian families was another challenge, and Donald had no idea of what the Protector of Indian Immigrants might have specified in 1902 and how these applied in 1919; so he just used common-sense.

He had seen distressing examples of Indian families being accommodated in wood-and-iron rows where overcrowding in poorly ventilated rooms was commonplace, compounded by fumes from cooking fires burning within. Poultry and other small farmyard animals were often kept inside the lines – contributing to unhealthy and insanitary environments conducive to tuberculosis – and worse. Venereal disease was rife and women did not have their own ablutions. He knew from Prue's mother that, by 1888, Indians had to carry identity passes and could not live outside designated areas. In 1891, Act 25 withdrew the promise of land and citizenship. With the undertaking given to Prue's mother, Cordelia Jardine, ringing in his ears, Donald was determined to create conditions for his workers which were sufficient and sanitary.

Although the scheme of indenture was terminated by 1911, many workers had signed up for another five-year period and then stayed on afterwards out of choice on the same farms, instead of returning to India. Being an entrepreneurial people, some of those who did remain moved away to start small enterprises of their own. They became clerks in the postal service, court interpreters, market gardeners, general traders, carpenters and railway workers.

There were other Indian immigrants who were not indentured, known as 'passenger Indians'. Mainly Muslim, they travelled as British subjects and paid their own fares.

The motivation for Hindu coolies to leave their villages and sign up for indenture 'across the Dark Water' was complex, but primarily due to the devastating decline in self-supporting village economies in India.

For the most part, this was caused by Britain flooding India with cheap domestic finished goods while restricting similar Indian imports. For example, in 1835 duty on cotton cloth imported from Britain was only 2.5%, whereas a punitive 15% was levied on Indian cotton cloth exported to Britain. The accumulative ruin of millions of artisans and craftsmen was the result, as conditions in India (unlike those in Britain's industrial revolution) were not accompanied by alternative industrial growth. In fact, during the same period English imports of unworked raw materials from India were encouraged, and local industrialisation discouraged.

Another aspect for women was that, for certain castes, it was taboo for widows to remarry after a husband died. Such women saw a way out of this stricture by migrating 'Across the Kala Pani' to a land where the caste system was blurred and the mandated ratio of immigrant Indian men to women was 100 to 40, introducing very good opportunities to marry again.

The accompanying of indentured Indian men by women and children was regarded with resentment by many planters, who saw women merely as a means of reproducing labour over time. But as time passed, estate owners began to realise that they had a valuable labour asset, for which they could pay half of what the men earned. Another bonus was that they were not obliged to pay repatriation or settlement costs at the end of the indenture period.

Willing to work long hours, Indian women were seen as nimble weeders and pluckers on tea estates. By contrast, Zulu women and girls were far less willing to be employed on the estates, and were discouraged by the Zulu hierarchy.

Some planters allowed their coolies ground to cultivate vegetables and fruit on Sundays to supplement their mandatory rations. The word 'coolie' is nowadays regarded as a pejorative; but in 1919, less so. It is thought to stem from the Tamil word 'kuli', meaning 'labourer'.

Chapter Eleven

Dust on the Kelpie's windscreen made driving into the setting sun over the random tracks in the veld even more hazardous than it usually was, so progress to the Schnurrs was at a snail's pace. The dogs started barking well before the car came to a stop in front of the house, as they had recognised the familiar sound of the Kelpie car engine. The barking soon changed to a panting and tail-wagging reception as they climbed out of the car. Their arrival had set off the geese as well, which started a chorus of honking as the geese crowded to the fence in a phalanx, in the hope of being fed.

Earlier, Donald had instructed Layani to gather some fireball lilies. Their blossoming had been triggered by the rising temperatures and the extending sunlight hours of early spring, and they were now flowering in the veld. He had gathered clumsy armfuls of them which Donald had battled to contain in page-spreads of old 'Sausage Wrap' and string. These he now presented to Marie, who was beginning to waddle very slightly with her pregnancy, a little like a petite penguin. He had collected Toby on the way.

They had been told that the Rutherfords and the Morrisons would be joining them for Saturday sundowners outside, with supper to follow in the dining room. Eric and an Indian helper were busy splitting logs and throwing them onto a young fire near the huge 'doringboom' tree at the front, while sparks and early smoke flew up as it hissed and crackled. Toby handed him a bottle of Opsaal brandy.

"Welcome to 'Pamplemousse' yet again, and yeah, thanks for the hooch," said Eric, with a broad smile, dismissing his helper with a 'thanks' and a wave. "You've arrived just in time to lug out some camp chairs from the shed. Just follow the noise of the generator, and here's our torch. Switch it off when you don't need it. Batteries are in short supply."

"Hello," said Marie warmly. "You've brought so many lilies, Donald; I'll run out of vases. I'll have to use a tin bath for the rest. They'll be in the entrance to greet visitors; and thank you."

It always took visitors a few moments to adjust to Eric's mid-Atlantic drawl when he said, "The advantage of living in the bundu is that we can always hear visitors coming a mile off. The dogs heard you, then the geese did, so we figured you were on the way. Look, there are all the geese at the fence. I've had to roof their pen with extra-strong chicken wire to protect them from predators…had to shoot a caracal last week in the middle of the night, trying to get in. Amazing cats…they can leap up nine feet to catch birds."

"My good wife, who knows about these things, has instructed the cook to roast a goose, something about stubble geese being eaten to celebrate harvest. But that's a European custom…unfamiliar to me as an ignorant American. What gets me is that, despite the fact that our seasons are all inverted, we still cling to northern hemisphere habits. We're stick-in-the-muds. You watch. At Christmas, at the height of summer, we'll be decorating a wag-'n'-bietjie thorn bush with cotton wool blobs for snow and eating a boiling hot Christmas dinner in sweltering Zululand – not forgetting the tinned Christmas pudding blazing with Opsaal brandy.

That's on my insistence, but, being French, Marie has a tiny tin of foie gras she was given by a Frenchman in Durban who trades with Madagascar."

"Good heavens! That must be my friend I go sailing with. It's a small world."

"Yes, indeed, if you're right. She's been keeping the foie gras to serve with Richard's Bay oysters which she likes to eat raw…but perhaps she'll be more concentrating on the infant by that time – and I'll have to make do with a ham sandwich decorated with tinsel. How's the building going?"

"As well as can be expected; we're both muddling along, but for me (and I understand Toby as well) the roof wettings for both houses should be in a month or so – or as near as dammit. You and Marie will be the first to know. Perhaps we can arrange a travelling roof wetting between the two dwellings? But labour uncertainties are a bit tricky and Toby and I would like to pick your brains about Indian working conditions and so on."

"Sure, but hang on until I can get the fire sorted out and settle the guests. We'll find a moment to chat."

As the clatter and thumps of a vehicle negotiating its bumpy way towards the house over uneven ground grew louder, Schnurr said, "That'll be them, and there go the dogs and geese again! You must've met them briefly at the Co-op meeting? Bob and Kate Rutherford have said they'd be more comfortable bringing their two children with them rather than leaving them at the farm with their nanny. Conditions are still a bit primitive. I think the children's names are Philip and Alice. We'll have to tuck them into a bed somewhere later. Henry and Grizel Morrison haven't any children – yet. They're all coming in the same car. Bit of a squeeze, especially if the Rutherfords bring their Indian nanny along too, and I predict they will. Bob's got a glass eye – war injury – never know which eye to look at. The families are farm neighbours living about a mile west of you. Both men managed to survive Delville Wood. Over seven hundred died, I'm told."

"You're forgetting the eleven hundred black stretcher bearers and trench diggers who also came unstuck."

"Yes, yes, of course, you're right. Should remember them, I suppose. By the way, all that barking reminded me – have you got any dogs yet?"

"No, not yet."

"Well, one of ours has just had a litter and they're about to be weaned. Like a couple? Ours are short-haired but not purebreds…more disease-resistant that way. Long-haired dogs pick up more ticks, get distemper. They're Rhodesian ridgebacks and you get intelligence, loyalty and length of leg. Better be quick, although there's one runt in the pack I'll have to drown…putting it off. We've some day-old goslings too and some chickens. You might want to have a look at 'em as well. Access to drinking water for the geese is important and goose-heaven is a shallow pond as well, with easy access for goslings. You could keep them happy on a pond near your windpump, provided their shelter is caracal-proof. The same applies to chickens, but I'm sure you know all that."

The women had all met before but not the men, so after introductions and during the shaking of hands, Toby said, "HMS *Galloway*, Singapore Station."

Rutherford replied, "First South African Infantry Brigade, 9th (Scottish) Division, both of us; and you, Donald?"

"BSAP B Company, East Africa. Eric, we know you served in France even before America came into the war."

"Yup – First Field Hospital, 2nd Division, AEF mostly at Bezu de Geury."

A bond was established, and no more needed to be said.

Although Rutherford was only twenty-seven, he looked war-weary and disinclined to speak much. Kate, his wife, and their son Philip, aged seven, on the other hand made up for that, each in their own way. Both were chatterers, while the daughter Alice took after her father. She arrived clutching a rag doll that had seen better days and the first edition of Arthur Mee's Children's Encyclopaedia, and soon stole away to sit reading on a pouffe in a corner of the verandah. When Donald drifted over later to include her in the circle, he saw that she had turned to a chapter titled 'Other Races' by Dr Caleb Saleeby. It was illustrated with pictures of a Hindu porter, a seated Fijian mountain warrior (with much fuzzy hair and wearing a loincloth, glaring glassy-eyed at the camera) and sari-clad women, cane workers near Georgetown, British Guiana. The pictures were printed in sepia tones, fashionable at the time. Donald said, "They look very interesting. What does it say about them?"

"I can't read every big word yet, but I think it's saying something like the other races aren't as grown up as us yet, so we must look after them."

"Ah," said Donald, rather at a loss for words, but thinking, "It's the bloody British Empire at work again, weaseling into the minds even of our youngest children. We're still suffering from the belief that we know what's best for the natives. Perhaps we do – although Emily would say differently. If only she were here!"

Marie whisked the women away to view the future nursery, leaving the men around the fire to their brandy and pipes for a while. Philip, the Rutherford's son, was left to sit at his father's feet. Henry Morrison, the other husband, was the less reticent of the two and was the first to raise the subject of coolie pay, after the usual pleasantries.

"Eric, we need a spot of guidance about coolie regulations. I should know all that, but things have changed since the end of the indenture scheme. Bit of a free-for-all…on some estates they're encouraged to cultivate vegetables and even keep chickens."

"Hang on a minute and I'll go in and fetch my notes," Eric said, and returned with a small ring-binder of collected papers. Sitting down, he said, "Now I can speak with authority. These are from Natal Government Notice Number 34 of 1866."

"That's archaic. Haven't you anything more up to date?" asked Morrison.

Eric said that the Notice prevailed right up to 1911 and wages and rations specified remained unchanged even after then.

"Right! Wages. First thing to know is that from 1860 (when the scheme of indenture started) and 1911, when it ended, there was no official change in the scales of pay – and here they are; but hang on, let me give you the rations first for ten years and over. This could be handy as well. I'll write it out for you later. Two and a half pounds-weight of rice daily, then the rest is for monthly rations…two pounds of dhal (that's another word for split peas), two pounds of salted fish, one pound of ghee (that's a kind of fat made from boiled milk solids; cooking oil is an alternative) and a pound of salt. Females and children under ten get half ration."

"And that's all?"

"That's all. No, not quite. They get paid every second month and receive double rations on paydays on some estates. That's the theory anyway."

"Why do women get half rations?"

"Beats me. On most sugar estates they only got rations when they worked. On the tea estates it was different because the women were more prized. They were considered nimble tea pluckers."

"My God," said Donald, "that explains why most of them look as if they're half-starved. They are."

"That's what labourers live on in India – if they're lucky," Eric said.

"And what about wages?" asked Toby, who had remained silent until then.

"Well, there was (and is, because the same customs continue) a big difference between wages for the skilled and unskilled. The unskilled man was and is paid on average fifteen shillings a month on the estates, but a bit more at the mills. A skilled worker could get twenty to twenty-five – or even more, in some cases at the mills. The same applied to Natal Railways. The pay-packet was increased by a shilling per month per year over the five-year contract, and employment arrangements still remain just about the same."

"No wonder they die like flies," said Donald.

"That's so on some estates, not all, but mainly caused by their living conditions; too many crammed into rooms, too many children…breed like flies; lousy ventilation and hopelessly inadequate sanitation. You can add no protection against malaria mosquitoes and uncertain access to a doctor, though things have improved a lot, thanks to Polkinghorne."

"Who's he?"

"He was the protector of Indian Immigrants and made himself highly unpopular on the Reynolds Estates near Umzinto, down on the south coast. The Indians were exploited ruthlessly for years and years – long hours, seven days a week, irregular rations, floggings and so on – resulting in reports of assaults, deaths, suicides and desertions, flowing continually from that quarter. Polkinghorne eventually succeeded in getting the chairman of the Reynolds board removed and things improved; but Reynolds got his revenge by getting Polkinghorne removed from office later on and the whole scandal was covered up."

Donald started suddenly when a log exploded with a series of bangs, and crouched away from his chair as if he had seen ghosts – which in fact he had. He was back in East Africa, with the ghosts of his men dying from German machine-gun fire in a swamp. Slowly the image faded as he stammered that he thought an ant had bitten him. Rutherford and Morrison exchanged knowing glances. They understood and sympathised.

Before Eric could say, "Well, I wonder where the women are," Igawe, the Schnurr's accomplished cook, came out of the kitchen door and clanged a piece of metal hanging from an outside rafter with a tureen spoon.

"It's actually an old German howitzer shell we found lying around," Eric said, as they rose and made their way through the outer door which clattered closed every time someone let it go. Over the entrance the weak electric light had attracted a halo of moths and other night insects

The house was a cluster of interlinked rondavels and an oblong sitting room hung about with paintings of Mauritius scenes. One was of Marie's parental sugar estate dwelling before they moved to Zululand. It was at the end of an avenue of tall coconut palms.

There was another of giant Pamplemousse water lilies by Xavier Le Juge and another of a Sega dancer.

"I see you're looking for the engraving of 'Paul et Virgine', Toby. We moved it to pride of place over the sideboard. See," said Marie, pointing. "Over here. Toby, come and sit to my right. I want to hear all about your sisters in London. I believe they had a challenging time after they moved from Ireland. Did you ever manage to read the novel about Paul ct Virgine by de Saint-Pierre? Katherine, I'm sure you see quite enough of your husband all week so I refuse to allow you and Robert to sit together for dinner; so, Robert, come and sit on my other side. Katherine, do sit beside Donald, to prevent him getting on to the subject of banking. Ask him about Scotland and lace factories instead, and tell him about your parents' tea planting experiment near Kandla."

And thus the seating arrangements continued, with the children being given a separate little table. The electric light had been turned off to allow candles in their tin wall reflectors to contribute warmth to the candle glow on the centre of the table. Donald noticed that Marie had decorated the candlestick bases with a few of the fireball lilies he had brought.

As she tinkled the small brass table bell, Eric said, "Be advised. We're in for a French-style meal with a good old piece of British goose in the middle. Donald, you went to one of those fancy schools; would you like to say grace? (I was teasing you when I said 'fancy')." Whereupon Donald stood and said, after everyone had bowed their heads to stare at their table setting, "Benedictus benedicat," and sat down again.

"My word, that was quick! What does it mean?"

"Something like, 'May the Blessed One give a Blessing', but that is inadequate to thank our hosts for their continuing kindness."

"Hear, hear," the guests said, as the door from the kitchen creaked open to reveal Igawe bearing a tureen of French onion soup. He was accompanied by a young Indian girl in a sari carrying a shallow grass basket of warm bread rolls. The door was half closed again by an unseen hand in the kitchen.

"This is the nearest South African alternative we could find to claret, said to go well with the soup," said Eric. "It's an early red we got up from Durban…the 'Pangeni liquor store doesn't run to such things. Igawe has been trying to keep it as chilled as possible by running water over the bottles. You'll be sampling a cabernet with the goose later."

"You obviously know a lot about wines, Eric."

"I don't. Read it all up to impress guests. But cabernet does go with goose, the book says. It's from a wine co-operative founded in the Western Cape last year, I read on the label."

The children had finished their food by this time and had been led away by the nanny to curl up, blanketed, on a verandah sofa, far enough away from the grown-up chatter.

Donald turned to Rutherford and said, "I see your daughter was reading a chapter in the encyclopaedia entitled 'Races of the World' by a Dr Caleb Saleeby. Isn't he the fellow who founded the Eugenics Education Society before the war – something to do with sterilising 'backward' humans and developing a superior race through selective breeding?"

"Something like that. He's all for educating women, but only to improve the cultural environment for the offspring." (Marie smiled a private smile.) "Nevertheless, I read that he couldn't see any reason why women should be allowed to vote."

"That should appeal to that Swiss fellow, what's'is name… something like von Weldenburg. I bumped into him at the rugby match. After a drink or two he rambled on about Übermensch, the 'super-man', above conventional Christian morality. He showed me an old German book he had just bought…something about Atlantis, I think…couldn't really make out what he was going on about."

Donald said, "I met him playing tennis at the Bell's some time back, before all this Spanish Flu business, and then again at his farm. A good host, but, for a Swiss, he does seem to have some rather cracked German views about racial superiority. The author of the book he was clutching at the rugby weekend proposed that the present indigenous people must have been ruled by a race of vanished Aryans...a weird lot of twaddle."

"On that line of thought, didn't the sister of that philosopher fellow who went mad, Nietzsche, try to found a colony of Aryans in Paraguay?"

"The very one; someone quipped, unfairly, that Nietzsche just issued aphorisms of profound superficiality. His sister's husband hated Jews. I seem to recall that a Paraguayan military man, someone called Stroessner, I think, helped them to get it started. They called it Nueva Germania, but it fizzled out, thank God."

"But there's a Neu-Deutschland near Durban!"

"Ah, that's a horse of an entirely different colour," said Eric. "This settlement was started by a Bavarian Jew with peasants from Hanover. His idea was to farm cotton, applying solid German cultivation skills; but the enterprise on Martin West's farm fizzled too, so the settlers switched to growing vegetables and flowers. Isn't it called New Germany nowadays?"

Marie cut short the conversation by ringing the table bell for the soupbowls to be cleared and the roast to be borne in from the kitchen by Igawe, the girl following him with the vegetables. Igawe remained while the girl left to fetch the gravy bowl and a glass jug of dilute grenadine for between-course clearing of palates.

After the servants had left the room, Grizel Morrison said, "My word, Marie, where did you find your cook?"

"We nicked him from the Royal Hotel in Stanger," Eric said. "We were visiting sugar farm friends in the neighbourhood when we spotted him. Even then Igawe's food preparation was outstanding. We learnt later that he'd been trained as a chef at the Norwegian Mission Station near here. When he expressed a wish to re-settle nearby we 'charmed him with smiles and soap'. He brought his wife with him and his umfaan who helps in the kitchen occasionally, like tonight. With encouragement, they expanded our kitchen garden, some of which you are eating this evening. Now, we understand, there's another child on the way…Marie has womanly chats with her."

Marie said, "What on earth do you mean, Eric…'smiles and soap'!?"

"I was being whimsical, or at least trying to be, and quoting from 'the Hunting of the Snark'. It's about the only piece of poetry written by an Englishman I know, but we Americans are not very good at whimsy."

"Really, Eric. Really," Marie said, with mock severity. Turning to her guests, she said, "Igawe says you must remove the legs and wings of the goose and roast them separately because they cook at different speeds," by which time Eric had risen to carve and separate both generous breasts from the bird so that he could then slice them finely, before addressing the legs and wings.

"Well, let's seek satisfaction 'with forks and hope'," Eric said, smiling to himself, knowing that few would spot the reference. "Who's for breast?"

The young sari girl had reappeared, as if to a signal, to offer the diners bread sauce, roast half-potatoes, sprouts and red cabbage, while Marie saw to it that the gravy boat circulated.

After the kitchen door had closed behind the servants again, Katherine Rutherford asked Marie about the young Indian girl.

"Her name is Aahna and this is her permanent home for as long as she wishes. Her father and mother and aunt, her only other relative, died of the Driedagsiekte within days of each other. The two women worked in the fields and the father was our odd-job man. We found the girl distressed and near starving, so encouraged her to move here. She's made a home for herself in a small room we have out at the back, and attends the little schoolroom on the Siedle's farm. Ethel Siedle says she's doing well. Thank heavens Ethel was a teacher in Stanger before she married Siedle, otherwise we'd have to send our little treasures to boarding school miles and miles away – and where would that leave the Indian children?"

"Of course, Padraic O'Grady's wife complained about having Indian children and a couple of natives at the school, and that all lessons were in English, so she yanked the Boer children out and now teaches them in Dutch-Afrikaans at Mrs Potgieter's. Ethel just smiled and carries on. No doubt some mompara from Pretoria will interfere in the years to come, but in the meantime we're too remote for Pretoria to worry about us. The thin edge of the wedge was that man Morkel. Pretoria is excessively bureaucratic because it inherited all those Dutch clerks Kruger imported from Holland before the Boer War. Now they've got the bit between their teeth…swarming down from the old Transvaal Republic into pastures new."

A black cat squeaked the kitchen door open sufficiently to push through, and Katherine said, "And I see you have a cat too," as the animal rubbed its body around the legs of the diners. "That's Schrodinger," said Marie. "She's a brilliant mouse-catcher, even though she brings them into the house and then plays with them; though she's rather scared of cane-rats."

"Odd name, Schrodinger. Why?"

"Because she was only half alive when we found her – and full of fleas. Don't worry, no more fleas. You know the joke about Schrodinger's cat, of course? Well…the cat walks into the room – and doesn't. Second helpings, anyone? Henry? Toby? Well, then, I'll ask Igawe to bring in the cheeses," leaving Katherine mystified.

"This is when we revert to being French again," said Eric as he circulated the table, filling glasses (but not Marie's, who consistently put her finger on the rim of hers. There was a jug of water on the table and, after offering the jug to the others, she poured herself a glass.) "They eat their cheeses before dessert, so it gives us a good excuse to savour another glass of cabernet. Some of them came from Jean-Pierre Meyer's parents in Madagascar…well-travelled but still very good. The parents sent them wrapped in waxed paper with small holes here and there. I'm told it allows the cheese to breathe but not dry out."

Rutherford's parents were from Jedburgh in the Scottish Borders and he had inherited the Border abruptness from his father. Changing the subject impatiently from food, he said, "Last time we were in Durban we met someone staying at the Marine who had just got off a Lloyd Triestino boat from Mombasa…been in Nairobi talking to people about exporting coffee to South Africa. He said that Nairobi was buzzing with retired Guards officers and Indian Army Colonels. Most are involved in a Land Settlement Scheme which covers over two million acres of government land. It's being sold cheaply to non-locals of what the Colonial Office calls 'pure European extract'. To qualify, they must be British and have served in the war. There's only one exception to that, a Dane who was awarded a VC while serving in the Canadian Army. This contrasts to the Boers at Eldoret, way in extreme west Kenya, who settled after the Boer War in 1902. They trekked there by ox-wagon after landing in Mombasa. The Protectorate admin is ambivalent about them – classifying them as poor whites, but some of them are receiving grants to stop them grumbling…not like the new English settlers who only qualify for land on a 999-year lease if they are able to invest £1000 or more. That can't be more than three percent of the whole British population in all its possessions…mainly landed gentry and other toffs."

"Phew, that's setting the bar very high. Why, I wonder," said one of the men.

"I was told that the plan is to plant coffee on an industrial scale…build up the economy. Because the crop takes four years to grow, the admin needs investors with deep pockets who can afford to wait out the first growing period without going bust. There's big money to be made for those who do, though. They're restricting the influx to British citizens as part of the usual empire-building process…Cape to Cairo and all that. It's a way of keeping the natives under control after the war."

"Yes, I heard about the Kenya scheme. There's been talk of some rich Durbanites wanting to apply, but finding it impossible to convert their investments in time. How many people are there after a war who have a thousand pounds jangling in their pockets? Very few…war-profiteers, mostly. [The current equivalent of the £1,000 in 2020 is just over £50,000, or $65,000.] It doesn't bear thinking about, but the ancestors of some of the same gentry are likely to have made their millions from the slave trade."

"What part of East Africa?"

"The best part – the Highlands; that's about a quarter of all the good land there is. The Protectorate is clearing out the natives there, taking away most of the Masai grazing in the process and shoving the rest into reserves. Apparently the soil is rich and they've had to rule out cattle, in the main, because of nagana. Coffee's a good option although the altitude could be against them."

"That all sounds rather familiar, doesn't it? We squashed the Zulus into reserves, leaving us the rich bits. Perhaps they got the idea from us…it's a new twist to the Scottish Highland Clearances."

"The worst part about the Scottish clearances – highland and lowland – was that members of the clan were betrayed and evicted by their own chiefs," Donald said. "In Natal and Kenya, at least it's a case of the invaders kicking out the natives. Not the same thing at all. No better, but less inbred. The only good thing to say about us is that at least we didn't shunt the natives off to Flinters Island, as they did in Tasmania, and allow them to die off from introduced diseases."

While Eric circulated the grenadine Marie rang the table bell again and said, "I think we should change the subject. Let's see how Igawe copes with having to make do with cream out of a tin. His warnings have been dire…but we're doomed to live out of tins for the foreseeable future anyway, aren't we? We've just adapted and learned to cope. He was taught how to make crème brûlée in the Stanger kitchen – but that was from real raw cream almost straight from the cow, before nagana took hold – although little Mrs Potgieter still has a few milk-producing cows. Afrikanders."

"My word, Marie, we didn't expect such a feast in this last outpost," Toby said. "I'll remember it as a highlight of the early days."

"Well, merci beaucoup, Toby. Eric has a new-fangled gadget which fires a flash when he takes a night photograph. He's been trying to take pictures of bats and he would like to take a photograph of 'this highlight' with his Voigtländer – he bartered it from a German prisoner for cigarettes. Is that all right? After the brûlée then? The flash produces some smoke and we can't spoil the taste of the food."

"I read that dessert wine from Constantia in the Cape goes very well with our bowls of 'burnt custard', so here it is," said Eric.

Accompanied by the diners' drumming of caramelised sugar with their spoons and murmurings of satisfaction as they broke through and reached the custard beneath, Rutherford asked Eric when they could expect rain.

"That's a bit like asking whether the price of gold will go up or down, the answer being that there is a fifty percent chance either way. I don't know, but as spring's on the way, it should be within weeks. Donald, will you end the meal with grace? Short version again?"

Everyone stared at the remains of their crème brûlée as Donald stood to say, "Benedicto benedicatur," and after a pause, "Perhaps we should congratulate the chef?"

"Good idea, but first the photograph...perhaps we should include him in it. Eric?"

The meal ended with coffee being served in the circular sitting room. It was Donald's favourite room in the rambling Schnurr house, with thick rondavel window ledges clustered with Eric's collection of clay models of cattle made by picannins and Marie's silver snuff boxes. There were other wonders besides.

"We're travelling to Durban in three weeks' time and Marie'll be staying with her cousins in Morningside until the baby arrives," Eric said. "For that, she's booked in at the Berea Maternity Home. I'll be travelling up and down in between times, so it's going to be an interesting few months! I need to get Marie to Empangeni before the spring rains turn our road into a quagmire again.

"Talking of spring rains, how are your land clearances going? You have to be ready to plough. If only we had some way of forecasting a month ahead! I'm on good terms with a khehla and he seems to have an uncanny knack of forecasting…says I should watch the weaver birds. They've started to nest high up in the weeping willows by the river, so heavy rain could arrive within a fortnight…although he can't read and hasn't got a calendar so his idea of a fortnight and mine could differ greatly; but he indicated all fingers of both hands, then another hand of five and said, 'Leyo nombolo ilanga'…that many sunrises."

Marie said that hours before a thunderstorm, and well before the arrival of the gusts and rumble of distant thunder, Schrodinger would race around the house and garden, hair standing on end, a berserk look in her eyes. She knew what was coming well ahead of humans.

"This khehla told me to keep a look-out for the appearance of red ants and for rapidly rising anthills," Eric said. They're sure indicators of good rains approaching. The first appearance of sparrows – he called them 'ondlunkulu'- and the excessive sprouting of aloes on hillsides also pointed to full water tanks ahead. He said that he also knew when rain was a few days away by experiencing sharp sudden pains in his leg bones – saying, "Phurrzz! Phurrzz!" and making stabbing gestures at his lower limbs."

Grizel Morrison said brightly, "It's a bit frightening, really. We're beholden to the whims of the clouds. It can bring us bounty or punish us, and we don't really know what it's going to do. All we can do is assume anecdotal evidence is reasonably reliable. If only life was easier and we could farm by the calendar."

"Donald has a bird table so he'll be able to spot the arrival of sparrows. Seen any yet, Donald?"

"Not yet, but I do keep a record of bird visitors. I'll tip you off when the sparrows arrive."

"Good idea. We'll test their infallibility."

Donald thought with satisfaction how his expressed interest in bird monitoring would become common knowledge and mask the secret shared with Prue. At the same time, he thought back to that unexpected moment of pleasure in the Durban bank, when the small staff who had presented him with a barometer and wished him bountiful harvests.

"My barometer forecasts changes in the weather," Donald said. "Unfortunately, it only looks a few days ahead, so perhaps we should keep our best weather eye on nature. Now, if we could communicate daily by telegraph with everyone in the country who had one of these we could build up a very good countrywide pattern of what the season is planning to throw at us."

"A dream for the distant future, perhaps, bearing in mind that it took years for Umzinto to get a telegraph line down to them on the South Coast," Eric said. "I've one of those crystal sets and found I could increase the signal strength by clipping the aerial to our bedsprings. It has to be grounded as well, of course, so I attach the lead to a water pipe. Works wonders. When a storm brews I pick up crackles from distant lightning…I think the French call them parasites. One can't tell how far away the storm is, though. I learnt Morse Code in the ambulance corps and could swear I was receiving signals from ships, judging by the content; but there's one very powerful station which breaks through now and then and drowns out other signals. It's so strong I could almost swear it was quite close by. Can't make out the Morse. Just a string of numbers. Unusual."

Donald pricked up his ears and thought of von Weldenburg's transmitter.

"Perhaps we should form a society; you know, we could call it something like the Ntambanana Weather Forecasters, and issue predictions based on the appearance of red ants and so on," Kate Rutherford said brightly. "Come on, Bob, we must get the children to bed. Would you call the nanny? Marie and Eric, thank you. It was an utterly scrumptious evening. Donald and Toby – a pleasure to meet you both and we hope to see you again soon. Now all we have to do is find our bumpy way home. Morrisons! Come on."

After waving them goodbye, Eric turned to Donald and said, "Would you like to take those goslings and puppies right away? No time like the present!"

"Thank you, yes, I would."

As Toby was sharing transport in Donald's Kelpie, the three went off to a shed, with Eric lighting the way with an oil lamp.

"That's the runt I'll have to drown," Eric said.

Donald was stirred with pity and said, "No, don't do that. I'll take him, and one of his sisters."

"Are you sure now? He'll never come to anything."

"I'll take that chance. I'll come back for the goslings in a few days, when I have knocked up a goose run."

Toby also took away a pup, but declined, for the moment, the offer of goslings.

The Kelpie smelt of 'puppy' for days after...

Chapter Twelve

Clement, van Jaarsveld's metal-worker, had assembled the corrugated iron water tanks so that they now sat, roundly shining and elevated on stilts, on either side of the timber-framed skeleton of the half-clad cottage. There was no water in them yet, so they boomed satisfactorily when struck. Donald had attached the gutters all the way around the main roof of the house, allowing Clement to work away at soldering the metal drainpipes to them and the tanks.

"Big roof, plenty water. Is good but cook water for drink," said Clement. "Pasop mozzies in gutters, bird-shit and lizards on roof. Borehole better for drink." The pipes would supply rainwater to the tanks and, in turn, from the nearest tank, to the cold water tap and the boiler outside the future kitchen.

Pipes also protruded through the scullery wall, ready for brass taps. The tank on the other side of the house was to supply water to the vegetable garden.

In the distance stood girder-work for the tall windmill, and another accompanying water tank. Wind power was to take over the task of the original hand pump.

"Ja. Die windpomp is 'n wonderlike ding," Jan Mocke had said, as parts, metal sails and girder-work were being unloaded, with a prolonged clatter, from his 'ox-wagon express'."

(Halliday's Self-Governing Windmill was indeed a

wonderful thing. This simple nineteenth-century invention opened up parched lands to farming and steam locomotion in South Africa, Australia and the United States. The inventor developed a simple mechanism that would turn the windmill to face the wind automatically, regulate the revolution of its metal sails, and pump ground water to the surface, year after year, without a human in sight, except for routine greasing and maintenance. Strictly speaking, they are wind-propelled borehole water pumps, but no-one calls them that.)

The installing of the cottage boiler promised to satisfy Donald's longing for a hot bath, ever since enjoying them again at the Masonic Hotel. After the mud and insects of East Africa, a hot bath had become his idea of civilised heaven. He had grown accustomed to them again after the war, while staying at the Barbican, the genteel boarding house on Durban's Berea. It was customary for worthy Durban citizens to bathe away the perspiration of high humidity summers, every day.

Clement seemed to be at home with the complex art of plumbing, but clambered down to ask, "Where you put bath?" making Donald realise that his plan for ablutions, and the scullery, had been vague on detail, even though the foundations had been laid for them and the extended framework erected, if still unclad.

The Zulus had departed for their kraal, having completed the herculean task of removing all the tree stumps. Many sacks of mieliemeal went with them along with a bonsela of a Nguni first-calf heifer for the chief. Donald had acquired the animal for an indifferent price from a neighbouring farmer. He had to assume that he was not trampling on Zulu custom, but as the chief had lost so many cattle to nagana, he thought the gift would build good relations. It seemed so, as the men had clapped their hands and chorused, "Ngiyabonga,

Numzaan!" and went off chanting with voices as vibrant as any Welsh choir. He learnt only later that 'Numzaan' was a sign of respect, and this was despite the white man's stupidity about the Thunder Tree.

The equipment shed and barracks for the Indian labourers had been completed ahead of the house, and the Indian women and oldest children had been set to work in the fields, removing small stones and pebbles. These were loaded onto the ox-drawn dray for disposal at field edges. The biggest stones and boulders were set aside to half-fill the pits left after the tree stumps had been dragged away. Substantial layers of earth were to be shovelled in on top and pressed down by stamping feet. The boulder-work was for the men.

One day, Donald woke to the chirp of sparrows. They were all over and below the feeding tray. The fields still lay dry and hard when Schnurr rode over. "You're going to find it difficult to plough all these fields with your oxen in time to plant after the first rain," he said. "It's coming soon. Although one can't farm by the calendar, as Grizel observed, the fifteenth of October is usually the time to start seeding and that day has passed already."

"Yes, for the first time, I woke up to the sound of sparrows…wasn't that one of your khehla's rain-alerts?"

"It was indeed, and I came over to suggest that I ask Frikkie and his gang to bring over the government Geiser tractors in readiness. The one stationed at the store is the twin of one based seven miles away. It'll only take a couple of days – if that – to plough the lot after the first rains…and you'll understand, as the state entirely funds the first virgin-land plough, there'll be the rest of Ntambanana clamouring for the same service."

"Thank you very much for thinking of that – but why twin tractors?"

"Can you imagine turning one of those behemoths around at the end of each field length, as well as decoupling and recoupling the plough? It would chew up half the farm and compress the rest as good as any steam-roller. Your workers would be hard put to dig up the soil compressed by twenty tons of machinery.

"They work in parallel – one at each end of the furrow. Under the belly of each tractor there's a cable drum. To plough, a cable is stretched between them, with the plough hooked up to the nearest tractor. A whistle blows, and the tractor at the other side of the field winds the cable, so pulling the plough along with the cable unwinding on the nearside tractor. The action of the plough can be reversed – so, bingo, no uncoupling. Then the twin tractors advance to the next unploughed section…and so on."

"I see you've left one large field fallow. Wise man…crop rotation and all that. The geisers can turn over as much soil as six ox-drawn spans in the same time and to a uniform depth, as these machines have twelve bottoms. Nevertheless, your oxen will remain as useful as they have ever been, not least in providing manure for natural fertiliser…non-stop, the best. Shall we go ahead immediately after the first rain?"

"Yes, good thinking,"

"Well then, Frikkie and Hans (don't know their surnames) will pitch up with the tractor gang, plough, and all the clobber that goes with it…a pile of stuff, as soon as possible. After the first rains, Marie'll be in touch with them and make them sandwiches, for the first day– then it's over to you. They'll have to camp overnight in your shed…and they like their Opsaal, so be prepared. They consume much boerewors too. I'll ask van Jaarsveld's wife to provide some and you can pay me later. The Empangeni butcher keeps Sarah supplied and she has quite a little boerewors business going.

"As Toby's farm is next to yours I guess his'll be next in line for the geisers. You might like to arrange a shared braaivleis?"

Donald nodded.

"Well. After the rain, then. It could be a few merry days and evenings ahead!...Oh, I forgot: it's £5 a day all in. They'll bring coal as well, ahead of time, by ox-wagon. Just watch out where they dump it. They can draw boiler-water from your borehole. Here's a spare soil thermometer of mine. Perhaps share it with Toby? Don't plant after rain until the soil temperature is constantly above sixty-three degrees Fahrenheit, and the soil is moist over an inch deep. May I suggest that you keep your coolies weeding in the meantime until conditions are ripe? Get them to get rid of the morning glory creeper in particular– it's cotton's nemesis...spreads like the devil, as well as the Maria-Maria...and let's hope we don't get locusts swarming after the rain. They'll eat anything green."

"If that happens, what's the protection?"

"Nothing effective once they're on the wing; but they can be attacked while they're still ground-hoppers. I'm told that way back in 1906 the farmers near Amatikulu recruited native labourers from the reserves at sixpence a day to dig trenches ahead of the hopper swarms. Long screens were erected to funnel them into the trenches which were laced with poisoned treacle. After that, they smothered them with earth. That was reasonably effective; but once they're on the wing they just land and eat everything...closest thing I've ever seen to what I saw in France after a bombardment.

"Well, cheerio," he said, walking away towards his horse, and then, looking up at the structure, asked, "You are going to fix a lightning conductor to the roof, are you? All that iron could attract lighting strikes."

"It's next on the list – see, over there, that spike in the roof will be attached to a thick copper wire leading to a buried copper plate."

"Good man. Better do it soon. Wouldn't like to see you sizzled. Remember to attach one to your windpump too. I remember, last year, coming across the carcasses of twenty-four cattle up against a barbed wire fence in the hills near the native reserve. It was after a terrible storm the night before…not a pretty sight. I first thought that they'd been poisoned, but no – it was lightning. The chief was enraged with his herd boys for allowing the beasts to wander up the ridge when a storm was brewing. The boys were beaten severely. He eventually decided just to abandon the carcasses to the wild animals – and in fact, jackals had got to them overnight and were joined by vultures the next morning. It was a helluva loss for him in property, as well as prestige."

As Eric was talking, Donald's thoughts wandered to his constantly dwindling bank account, with no income yet to replenish it. His bonds were locked away for ten years, as they should be, and his working capital was substantial, but not there just for dribbling away on bits and pieces. He would have to spend lightly until the first harvest, and that would be a long time coming. Thank heavens, he reflected, for the co-operative's tranches, ahead-of-harvest payments. He wondered what his father would have thought. Pater, as he called him, a style of address he picked up at Dulwich, had been a warm-hearted frugalist; a characteristic Donald used to taunt him with, whenever the matter of pocket money arose while on holiday. His father would jokingly assume the vernacular and say "Ye can have all of it at the end of the dee, all five shillings, me lad, after yeu've finished mucking out the stables. That's yuer job." He remembered the tone of his voice when he said, "There's no free money here. Yeu must earn yuer keep."

It became a practice for Toby and Donald to meet up over a pleasant breakfast on Sundays – a time for Mrs Potgieter's eggs, fried up with tomatoes, brinjals, and bacon out of a tin. It was Toby's job to bring over the eggs. Donald supplied the tinned bacon and vegetables. The latter were cultivated by Layani's wife, encouraged by Donald. Bread had to come by ox-wagon from the bakery in Empangeni to the store, and was always stale by the time 'Tam farmers could get their teeth into it, until Hannah, the storekeeper's wife began to bake bread for the wider community. Soon, the pleasant morning smell of it would mingle with others, of leather, soap, Jeyes fluid, bicycle tyres and sweat.

Toby and Donald took turns in collecting the latest papers from van Jaarsveld's store on Saturdays. They were always a week old by the time they reached Ntambanana, but the contents of their pages were devoured eagerly. After breakfast the two friends would sit beside the windbreak and read, from cover to cover, front-page advertisements and all, the Zululand Times, the Natal Witness from Pietermaritzburg, and the Natal (Shipping) Advertiser from Durban.

Mrs Potgieter continued to arrive once a fortnight or so at Toby's farm, on horseback, with Susannah riding pillion and clutching eggs in the little wire cage. It was a steady business, supplying the neighbourhood with eggs, thought Toby, but he paid gladly, pleased to see that little Susannah had learned to cope with the death of her mother, thanks to Mrs. Potgieter, or rather 'Mevrouw' Potgieter, as she firmly corrected him. (He was yet to discover what her Christian names were and what happened to her husband.) She seemed to take amusement in forcing him to stumble along in the few mispronounced Dutch words he had learnt, expanded by what he could remember of his schoolboy German.

Routinely, Toby would leave the egg container at the store, to join the clutter of returned egg cages from other farmers, but on one recent occasion he forgot, so decided to find out where she lived and return the basket himself.

During his trudge across the field close to her wattle-and-daub house, he had had to skirt several Afrikander cows, with their beautiful curved horns. Afrikander, like their veld-cousins, the Nguni, were far more resistant to nagana than imported stock. Two of the cows were accompanied by young calves and all of the cows were in milk. Toby wondered who had the task of milking them twice a day. Surely she had assistance?

Hens scratched and pecked away in a poultry enclosure with its henhouse in the corner. One hen had a brood of chirruping chicks, which followed her closely. The mother would pause, scratch the ground and cluck-cluck to show her offspring how to find worms and seeds. There was no necessity for the hen to look down while scratching, as its wide-angle vision allowed it to see the ground and keep a weather-eye out for predators.

Surprisingly, there were no dogs to bark at his arrival, so he had startled her in her rambling kitchen – bright where light poured through a modest window and the door, gloomy where light struggled to reach. He found her furiously turning the big handle of a milk separator which sat atop a cast iron stand, making it almost as tall as herself. She was throwing all her small might into building up the speed of the fly wheel. After protesting, she allowed him to take over until the cream and buttermilk began to splutter out of the flat tin spouts. A small wooden step was to hand, in order for her to reach the top of the separator and her laden pantry shelves, of which there were many.

A round of butter, on a wooden board and squeezed free of buttermilk, sat on the broad yellowwood table beside jars of curing salt and sugar. The butterball would be turned into an oblong with butter pats, then stored in a pan of very salty water, and weighed down with a small stone. At the door, pails of milk stood in a tin bath filled to the brim, with a large cloth half in and half out of the water. Evaporation would draw up fresh water, so keeping the milk cool.

Unlike his sisters, who were always pestering the cook when they were children, Toby had seldom lingered in a domestic kitchen, let alone a remote Boer kitchen, and he was fascinated by Mevrouw Potgieter's organised clutter. There were mincers, jars of vinegar, paraffin lamps, a biltong box, spices, mixing bowls, tins of sugar, shelves of preserves, mottled blue soap, flypaper hanging from the rafters, a tin bath on a peg, scrubbing boards, and much else besides in the darker reaches of the room among the brooms and scuttles. Her cast-iron gnome of a three-plate stove squatted beside its basket of logs and the preparation table.

Two small pictures watched over her – one, a framed portrait of Queen Wilhelmina of the Netherlands, cut from a Dutch newspaper; the other, a poster of Paul Kruger. His face loomed out of an oval, framed by many flags. Beneath was the legend, 'Eendragt Maakt Magt' (Dutch: Unity Makes Strength); atop the oval frame was a winged eagle, as if sitting on top of his head.

(Kruger was President of the Transvaal Republic, which was annexed by the British at the end of the second Anglo-Boer war in 1902, along with the Orange Free State. During 1900, while the tide of war was turning against the Boers,

Kruger had moved to Waterval Onder, a hamlet close to the border of neutral Portuguese East Africa, and near the foot of a seventy-five-foot waterfall – hence its name – and it was from there that he entrained for Mozambican territory. Kruger's intention was to tour the Continent to raise support for the Boer cause, but he was detained under house arrest for a month at the behest of the British Consul in Mozambique. It was Queen Wilhelmina of the Netherlands who brought this impasse to an end by interceding on his behalf with the British government, and arranging for Kruger to depart for neutral France aboard the Dutch warship, HNLMS *Gelderland*.

Kruger went on to receive an exuberant reception in Paris and again in Cologne, although Kaiser Wilhelm II refused to meet him in Berlin, much to Kruger's chagrin and sensing betrayal, bearing in mind that Kruger's ancestors were Germans from Berlin. He went on to receive another rapturous welcome in neutral Holland where the Kruger party was given permanent sanctuary in Hilversulm by Queen Wilhelmina. He died of pneumonia in Clarens, Switzerland, at the age of seventy-eight. His body was first interred at the Hague, but later returned to Pretoria for a state funeral.)

Mevrouw Potgieter's smile was merely a transitory glimmer across a wrinkled face and she communicated only in Dutch, very loudly because she was deaf, with Toby stumbling over his replies, which he had to shout. Nevertheless, there was a mutual respect which arose from those moments when he and Donald assisted Nurse Schwitter, from the Norwegian Mission. As a desperate last resort, she had struggled to keep Susannah and her mother alive with makeshift blood transfusions from them. The men had recovered from Spanish Flu, contracted in different theatres of war. There was of course no flu vaccine at the time, and the medical profession was unable to stem the rising tide of casualties. There was anecdotal evidence, however, that blood transfused from a recovered patient could transfer resistance to a Spanish Flu sufferer. Research in blood types had only just begun, so there were many fatal reactions as a result. Nevertheless, Susannah and her mother had not reacted catastrophically, though the mother, Herina, was too far gone to survive.

Three hundred thousand South Africans died of Spanish Flu over six weeks. This was about 6 percent of the population – more than 127,000 blacks and 11,000 whites – and it created an unprecedented number of widows, widowers and orphans almost overnight. Although the first and third waves of the pandemic were comparatively mild, the second wave was vicious and became known as the three-day sickness – from infection to death.

"Funny to think that Susannah probably has a pint of my blood coursing through her veins," Donald would muse – casting his mind back to childhood and the occasion when he and young Angus McAlpine, son of the farm manager in Scotland, became blood brothers by pressing small cut veins on their palms together and swearing a blood-curdling oath of fealty, 'like the Red Indians'.

Donald had agreed to employ Chinnamama, one of the young Indian women, as junior housekeeper and cook, and it was she who was frying the breakfast. He and Layani had built an elevated open grill from a few bricks brought from the store. It was positioned so that the smoke drifted away in the general direction of the prevailing wind.

After Chinnamama withdrew, Toby said, "One of the troubles of farming in the bundu is that there're no available women. It takes the gilt off the gingerbread, somewhat. They're either married, or far too old or far too young, and

I confess that, if it wasn't so taboo, even your Chinnamama is beginning to look enticing. Bachelorhood in London or even Durban, by comparison, is gilded gingerbread with extra butter and jam."

"I couldn't have expressed it better myself," said Donald, thinking of Emily...

"Oh, here we go," he said, rattling his newspaper and thinking back to when Prue introduced him to the spluttering Ivan Filatov at a Durban League of Nations presentation. Filatov had pushed a copy into his hands of The Socialist Spark in which was declared: 'The black people of South Africa are the true proletariat of the working class', under the general heading of 'Equal Rights for All!'

He read out:

> ***"Africans to join International Socialist League. A Communist Party mooted…*** *Cape Town. 12th October, 1919*
>
> *"At an open meeting of members in Cape Town last night, the founder of the International Socialist League of South Africa (ISL), William H Andrews, declared that members of the South African Native National Congress were welcome to join the League. He said that the invitation automatically extended to prominent Coloureds and Indians.*
>
> *"First to join would be Reuben Alfred Cetiwa, Hamilton Kraai, Ble Digamoney and Thomas William Thibedi. Prominent white members of the ISL include Julius First and Matilda Leveton. The Secretary is David Ivon Jones.*
>
> *"Andrews told the paper that his league had helped in the formation of the first black trade union, the Industrial Workers of Africa, but remained sympathetic*

to the plight of the white miners, where semi-skilled jobs are being given to lower-paid black workers, for the first time, as a result of gold production costs soaring while the ounce price of the metal continues to plummet.

"Since the Russian revolution in 1917, the league has supported the interests of the Bolsheviks. Andrews said that efforts were being made to merge several socialist organisations to form a Communist Party of South Africa in the near future. It reflected "the dawn of a world-wide commonwealth of labour."

"I suppose they ended the meeting by singing 'The Red Flag', like those Lahitzsky meetings in Johannesburg. Remember our discussing him – he with the pet monkey we laughed about in the Durban Club?"

"Yes, I very well remember. There's going to be more labour trouble ahead…as if we didn't have enough to worry about. This communism junket is worldwide now. Here's a piece in the Witness in that vein:

"China refuses to sign at Versailles. *Fury over Japanese continued presence in Shandong. Tiananmen Square mobs spark Chinese Communist Party formation…Paris. 15th October, 1919.*

"Chinese delegates to the Paris Peace Conference in Versailles have refused to sign the accord. China has reacted strongly to the favouring of Japan's post-war continuing occupancy of Germany's considerable possessions in Shandong, including railways, mines and Tsingtao port. The Chinese were outraged by the Allies favouring Japan's interests over China's at Versailles.

"The Chinese Ambassador to France, Wellington

Koo, said that his country could no more relinquish Shandong than Christians would give up Jerusalem, pointing out that the area was the birthplace of Confucius, the nation's greatest philosopher.

"When asked for comment, the de facto leader of the Japanese delegation of the Peace Conference, Baron Makino Nabuaki, declined to discuss Chinese demands.

"The favouring of Japanese interests over the Chinese has led to huge anti-West demonstrations in Tiananmen Square, Peking. A worker at the demonstrations said foreign nations were 'selfish, militaristic, and great liars'. This has led to reactionary Chinese nationalists forming the Chinese Communist Party.

"China supported the Allies during the war on condition that the Kiautschou Bay in the Shandong peninsula should be returned to it after the war. The bay area was part of the pre-war German Empire, but the region was occupied by Japan on the outbreak of hostilities.

"Although China remained neutral until 1917, when it declared war against Germany, Chinese workers had been recruited during 1916 to dig trenches in France and Belgium during the conflict. They also unloaded ships and trains, laid tracks and built roads.

"Many lives were lost during their transport from the Chinese interior via Shanghai, by ship across the Pacific, by rail across Canada and then on to Liverpool, before departing from Folkstone for France and Belgium. It is thought that 20,000 died in Europe."

"Well, off mind-numbing politics for a moment, here's something cheerful…according to the Natal Witness, the

UK Daily Mail has offered a prize of £10,000 for the first non-stop flight across the Atlantic."

"But that's been done already. It was in the papers quite recently! Those airship wallahs...they flew from England to Long Island in the 'States, but didn't know how to moor it to the mast, so one of them parachuted down to capture the glory of being the first to fly east to west between the two continents."

"No, I think the prize is for winged aircraft. Now they're all offering prizes. The Australian Prime Minister has matched that £10,000 for the first flight to Australia and – as if we had the money to fling around – our government is offering the equivalent for the first flight from Croydon to Cape Town."

"That would have pleased Rhodes. I bet that Pierre van Ryneveld could do it – y'know, that air-ace. I read he suggested that the Vickers Vimy bomber could stay the distance...just imagine...being able to be in London within days instead of a fortnight by mail boat! That explains the report I read about preparing landing ports and strips all the way down the east coast., places like Nimule, Abercorn and Broken Hill."

"Where's Nimule?

"I think that's in the Sudan."

"And Abercorn?"

"Near Lake Tanganyika. That's where von Lettow-Vorbeck surrendered last year...marched his men all the way from the Chambeshi River, a tributary of the Congo. They have small earthquakes in Abercorn, every now and then...so they keep the buildings to single-storey."

Donald and Layani were occupied with riveting the remaining roofing sheets to the rafters when they heard a far-off steam engine chord, heralding the arrival of two huge metal-wheeled tractor-beasts of a furnace, boiler and flywheel, huffing and puffing their way onto the farm and crushing all vegetation before them.

After the monsters had come to a halt near the windpump, where Donald had guided them, Frikkie and the other men clambered from their machines and uncoupled trailers loaded with Somkhele coal and came across to them, while the engines continued to steam.

Frikkie said, "Allo!" casting a critical eye towards the Thunder Tree field. "Man! Why've you left that bloody big tree in the field over there?" asked Frikkie, who was in charge. "We'll have to plough around it somehow. Can't you pull it out?"

"No. It's the Thunder Tree," said Donald, with assumed insouciance, as if expecting Frikkie to accept the fact with no further discussion.

"Wragtig! Every time you come to plough you'll have the same problem."

"Yes, but I'll be using oxen next time, if they're still alive. Much easier to move them around. Look, when you come to plough, you'll be able to sleep in the shed, over there. It'll stay nice and dry. After work, each evening, we'll have a braai. I've arranged for the boerewors. If it rains we can move to the shed."

Beef, the main component of boerewors, was in short supply caused by the current nagana pandemic, so it had become a tempting luxury. 'Farmer's sausage' was developed with a high proportion of fat and was preserved with salt and vinegar, and heavily spiced. it is still eaten in large quantities at the traditional braai.

> *"Darling Emily."* Donald wrote, that evening: *"I have managed to rig up a mosquito-proof 'roomlet',*

made of a wooden frame and mosquito netting, which means I can sit inside it at an empty packing case with my knees inside the box. The page I am writing on is illuminated by an oil lamp, which is attracting moths and other night insects trying to get in. There is no moon, so 'The Box' must make a strange sight in the Zululand night. It's a temporary measure until the dwelling is complete, which is far too modest to be called a bungalow... more of a 'bugnallow'!

"I haven't had a letter from you for quite a while, but I suppose I can blame your silence on your Lobola dissertation. Is it finished at last? I would love to read it. May I see a copy? Or is that not possible while it is still being reviewed? Did you have space in your studies to investigate the additional impact of Spanish Flu? Schnurr mentioned there were many cases of newly-wed husbands claiming a return of the bride price they had struggled to gather, where the bride had died of the flu before producing offspring.

"Those wonderful few days we shared in Jean-Pierre's flat overlooking Durban Bay seem so very far away. Do you remember the misty morning when we heard the sound of that big fish plopping far out, when the water was as calm as a millpond? And the sounds coming to us from the harbour, way over the water – our leitmotif, as you called them... Would that they might lead us together, forever!"

Unable, he felt, to express his yearnings for her adequately, he resorted to writing about the farm.

"We're all waiting for the first rains, which are late; we can't start ploughing and planting before they

arrive. Do you remember the storm and lightning on the night we first met at your parent's farm? Well, I have been warned to prepare for something like that, to start spring with a bang, sooner or later. When it arrives I'll be thinking of you. The signs of coming rains are everywhere...aloes in early bloom and fruit-trees blossoming. One of the first things we did, as soon as the roof was up, was to fix a lightning conductor at the top. I say 'we' meaning Man Friday 'Layani' and I. He only speaks a muddle of Portuguese and Shangaan, so it's surprising that we can communicate, but we do, by muttered words and acting out the intended action. I often wonder what the reaction of a visitor might be while witnessing our acting out construction decisions and Layani's gesticulations offering alternative ways of doing something, all in deaf-and-dumb show. We have managed to establish a group of set gestures including touching a forefinger to the forehead, meaning 'I think'; a charade for a handful of nails, by holding the left hand cupped and the right making a hammering motion, meaning 'fetch more nails' and so on. Occasionally, when I get completely stuck, I call on our local artificer of metals, Clement, who has been soldering the drains and suchlike, to clamber down and interpret. Clement can speak what sounds like fluent Zulu. Layani is a Shangaan but also understands Zulu...so between the three of us we get the work done.

But this is not the only charade we enjoy out in the bundu! It's great fun, for example, witnessing neighbour Toby communicating with little Mevrouw Potgieter, who cannot, or refuses to, speak English... and is very deaf. My neighbour, Toby, tells me that he has to shout very loudly with bits of Dutch he has managed to pick up (and mis-pronounce hideously) muddled up with words of German and all pushed along with much gesticulation...yet, believe it or not, they seem to understand each other, assisted sometimes by the presence of young Susannah, who is quick-witted and has learnt some English.

"All that is needed now is for me to absorb basic Tamil, so as to interact more effectively with my Indians. Fortunately, there are a lot of English words mixed up in the so-called 'Madras language', so I'm finding we can communicate for the moment in limited form in pidgin English. They've been settled into their new barracks, ablution block and all – not too many families...just three, plus three bachelors and a couple of single women – and that will be the limit...don't want to be overwhelmed by them, but they are already proving an asset. They work hard and for modest payment (I am inhibited from paying them much more than the going rate by local pressure), but I will try to ensure their life on the farm will be a ++++ = good one. They seem to have an outstanding knack for growing things, so I've allotted them reasonably-sized plots for cultivating their own vegetables on Sundays. Already, the faint whiff of Madras vegetable curry wafts this way when the wind is in the right quarter. They seem to eat nothing else but curried everything. I had to draw the line, though, when it came to keeping poultry and a goat in one family's quarters. That had to be stopped.

"However...and this is a big 'however'...I realise that my farm management skills will be tested to the limit in the days – and years – ahead. An intelligent woman's touch is very much needed to turn the house

into a home and do all the sensible things at which any man is a bit of an idiot, including social contact. You, of course, would do all this beautifully. I have already proposed to you and you have my mother's wedding ring to prove it, but I have no intention of disturbing your final studies for an answer. I love you, Emily.

Donald."

Chapter Thirteen

A report as loud as a dynamite blast, followed swiftly by a series of tumbling crackles and bangs, announced the end of the dry season, and jerked Donald awake. There was a smell of ozone in the air. His first thought was that he was under fire, and he threw himself to the floor, dragging the blanket with him. When he realised where he was, he thought of his oxen and the safety of his workers. The next flash struck the earth beside the far-off Thunder Tree, which was lit up for a moment, as if it were a stage flat. The tree remained unscathed – a good omen which would not be lost on Layani and the distant Zulus. He had moved his camp bed into the now-roofed dwelling some days previously, and was relieved that all the lightning conductors on the farm buildings and the windmill had been connected up in time

On the night of the puppies' arrival, Donald had made a temporary home for them with a frayed blanket in a wicker basket, close to his bed. He had given them an old veldskoen to chew on. At the first crack of thunder the two puppies shot under his stretcher and into the basket, where they huddled against the old shoe until the storm had abated. In adult life, the dogs would never grow accustomed to thunder storms, and behaved in the same manner, even before the first rumble was audible to human ears…. He had decided to call the runt Jesse and the bitch, Bess – after the border collies of his Scottish childhood. They were easy names to call.

Swirls of wind came next, making the foliage of the trees perform a sudden swaying and agitated jig, as a heap of leaves rose up in a berserk pirouette. The landscape flickered with each flash. Everywhere was movement…not least of a leftover sheet of corrugated iron which clattered and scraped along to crash and rattle against one of the tractors, before dislodging and flying off into the night. Then came the rain, first as a gentle fluttering on the iron roof accompanied by the petrichor of dampened soil, and then swelling to a permanent roar, overflowing the gutters and gushing into the water-tanks. It created an instant pond around the letterbox and started rivulets wherever the land slanted away; rivulets which pushed ahead of them little collections of old winter leaves and twigs, as they fingered through little dips and valleys of the soil.

Donald lay under the blankets, listening to the roar of the storm and inhaling that unique smell of earth, after a long, parched season is broken by the first rains. He reached down to pat the dogs and felt two canine tongues lick his hand.

The hail started during a pause in the downpour, first with the bang of a few pebbles hitting the iron roof, increasing in frequency until the roar of hail wiped out all other noises, except the boom of thunder. It was during another lightning flash that he saw the distant figures of Layani, his wife and child running towards the sheds. He learnt later that they had been flooded out of their hut.

"That's just as well," thought Donald. "At least they won't be electrocuted." He made up his mind to install a lightning mast beside their hut, if they preferred to continue living under grass.

The clouds had drifted away before sunrise, and Donald

awoke to a dawn chorus of frogs and bird-calls, supplemented by the distant crunch of coal being shovelled. When he splashed out to investigate he found Frikkie standing at the tractors, watching an Indian assistant shovelling coal onto burning kindling and logs in one of the fireboxes. Grey-brown smoke was beginning to drift out of the chimney as sparkles flew up.

As he approached, Frikkie was lifting down a three-legged cooking pot and said, "Môre!" [Morning!] and pointing to the pot said, "Potjie kos." In a jumble of Afrikaans and English he explained that the lidded pot of stew would be left to cook very slowly, overnight, in the dying embers of the firebox, after the day's work was done. Embers would be left on the upended lid as a supplementary source of heat.

(The custom of slow-cooking venison stew in a small cast iron pot, with a tight-fitting lid, was imported to the Cape from the Netherlands over four centuries earlier. It was adopted by the Boers as compact kitchen equipment to accompany their very long treks by ox-wagon. Wild game was shot for the pot, along the way, and cooked with spices. Vegetables were added, whenever they were available.)

"You're early!" Donald said.

"Ons moet [We must]…drie uurfull steam…neem water from borehole. Lekker rain, eh?"

The tractors were stationed, parallel, on either side of the Thunder Tree field, with a cable strung between them and connected to motorised drums between each machine. The combined harrow and plough was connected up and dragged from one side to the other, guided by his assistant, manning a steering wheel on the contraption. He was soon covered in dust, which stuck to his sweating face and arms. Two other men had to sit on the cultivator, to add weight and control the harrow levers. It was a dramatic sight to watch how quickly the character of the unremarkable veld was converted into dark and fertile farmland.

The tractors were repositioned later, to cope with the intrusion of the Thunder Tree and, in later years, this part of the field would always prove more fertile, the soil having been reworked so thoroughly.

Labourers spread out over the ploughed and furrowed sections armed with measuring sticks and hemp satchels of cotton seed. They were soon planting a theoretical three seeds per hole, one inch deep and four inches apart; but in practice, it was far more haphazard. Planting seeds by hand was time consuming and wearisome, and required the labourers to crawl on their knees along the furrows, dragging their small bags of seed. After a day of supervising the work, Donald realised that, sooner or later, he would have to appoint someone to supervise so that he could be released for other farm duties.

While they were working that field, a custom soon developed for the labourers to gather under the Thunder Tree for their lunch break. It was on such occasion he would occasionally wander over and talk to them. He soon noticed that one of the Indians spoke up as their representative. It was always he who put forward ideas and requests voiced in Tamil to him by the other workers. A more effective allocation of the workers' time was one of them. His English was more advanced than the others, so he acquired the mantle of spokesman on their behalf. The Indian's long name was Malika Ramaswamy, but he was satisfied to be called Ramsammy…and, even later, Sammy.

Donald decided to let this informal arrangement develop, without giving voice to it, with the intention of appointing him as some minor form of supervisor at some time in the future, if his behaviour justified it.

On the final day of ploughing, Eric Schnurr arrived on horseback halfway through the morning, and was joined by Toby to watch the last field to be cultivated. Frikkie and his men had made short work of ploughing and Donald could already see how the day would end – with much braaivleis, boerewors and brandy being consumed around a camp fire. The liquor would loosen their tongues and he would listen with fascination to the old Boer stories…about the uncle who said that he would not get his hair cut until the fighting was over. When the man managed to slip home to see his wife, he found that the farmhouse had been burnt to the ground by the British troops and his family taken to the Louwsburg concentration camp where his wife and younger son later died (he learnt this after the fighting stopped). He was never the same man again, and spent the rest of his days in a Pietermaritzburg lunatic asylum. He resisted all attempts to cut his hair and eventually died, still unshorn.

Other stories tumbled out, but the ones that sent his own mind racing resembled most closely his East African experiences – like the one in which Frikkie's older cousin was involved in fighting the Australians. He had come across a clearing littered with the corpses of rotting horses and mules and freshly dug graves.

Eric said, "I see you've left the Thunder Tree standing… wise man. I'm afraid I'm the bearer of bad news…you know the Bell's, well…they've received some awful news by telegram; Marie was telephoned just before I left to see you. Their daughter, Emily, died from Spanish Flu yesterday; so James and Edna are catching the first train they can down to Cape Town, via Durban. It's going to be a miserable trip for them. Of course, we're all very upset. Such a lovely girl… such a waste of a young life. They've already decided to bring her body home and bury her on the farm. Their sons are perfectly capable of managing the farm while they're away, but I said I'd look in on my way back from Durban. As luck would have it, Marie and I couldn't leave 'Tam before the rains broke, so it's going to be a difficult ride to Empangeni. Poor Marie, not the easiest ride in her condition…she'll be staying with her cousins in Morningside until it's time to admit her to the maternity home.

"While we're away I'd appreciate it if you or Toby could drift over to our house from time to time? I'm pretty sure Igawe will have everything in hand, but it's always wise to establish a presence….mice will play and all that."

"The Bells' will be staying at the Mount Nelson while in the Cape, so you might wish to write to them there."

Donald went numb while listening. He had become inured to the sudden deaths of war. There was nothing noble in the sight of disfigured body parts, smashed faces and spewed guts, only stench and horror. He had learned to accept the slow deaths of close friends from dysentery and sleeping sickness, or the quicker deaths from snake bite; so, outwardly, his reaction to the news of Emily would seem to be one of sympathetic indifference. In his heart, though, love wrenched into grief.

Emily had been a balm that soothed the weals of war, and now she was gone.

"I'm very sorry to hear that," he heard himself saying, realising that Emily and he had managed to keep the secret of their relationship to themselves. No doubt this would change when Jim and Edna went through Emily's belongings and correspondence.

A week passed before Donald spotted a stone on top of his post tin. There were several letters – one from Scotland in Winnie's handwriting. She had covered the top of the envelope with low denomination stamps to add excitement; her handwriting a graceful feminine copperplate with large loops...Another was from Prue, and the third, a registered letter, more a soft packet than a letter, postmarked Cape Town, he opened first. It enclosed a much smaller envelope padded with cotton wool and containing his mother's wedding ring. He read:

> Hope Mill Women's Residence,
> University of Cape Town
> Government Avenue, Cape Town
>
> *Dear Mr Kirkwood,*
>
> *By now you will have received the dreadful news about poor Emily. She and I were close friends and shared accommodation at Res. When she took ill and suspected that she was not going to recover from this awful three-day Spanish Flu, she made me promise, before being transferred to an isolation ward at the San, that I would return the ring you gave her with a simple message; it was "Yes." She was already experiencing difficulty breathing but managed to say, in little more than a whisper, that you would understand. She also told me that there was a red scarf in a cupboard shelf, in which was wrapped some patterned Zulu beadwork. She had written on a slip of paper 'Ibheque' and 'Longing'. The beads are in a pattern of black, white, yellow and blue. I have boxed up the scarf and things and have sent them by parcel post, but I thought that the ring, being of highest sentimental value, should be sent to you separately.*

Donald thought back to his last sight of her. She was

standing at the upper deck rail as the liner slid out of Durban harbour. She waved when she had caught sight of him, standing beside the Kelpie on the north pier. The red scarf was about her neck and streaming in the breeze and she had pointed at her left hand, as if to imply that she was wearing the ring he had given her.

> *Emily was a good friend and I miss her dreadfully. Although a private person, she did discuss knowing you and her hopes for the future. She was hard-working and I have no doubt that she will have passed with a first-class degree, when we get the results, despite her faint dislike of the essential but irksome statistical element required for anthropological studies…*
>
> *She spoke with warmth of her parents and the farm, and that sense of pioneering which pervaded Empangeni settlers. With that said, she also spoke frequently about the Zulus, and the savage destruction of their traditions and way of tribal life by the intrusion of the whites and, as she saw it, them grabbing their land.*
>
> *I come from Johannesburg and, by contrast, was brought up in a far more conventional environment. My parents' house is high up on Pallinghurst Road in Westcliff, which overlooks the panorama of the new northern suburbs. My closest encounters with natives are of mistress-servant, black nannies and black kitchen and garden boys. We never mixed and hardly spoke, so listening to Emily speak what seemed to me to be fluent Zulu, and hearing her stories of Zululand, was exciting and refreshing.*
>
> *I particularly remember being with her when we went for tea one day in the Mount Nelson Hotel.*

We were walking through the gardens afterwards when, I can't recall how it came about, she somehow recognised that one of the gardeners was a Zulu. They spoke at length in Zulu and I could see that his eyes were glistening – for here was someone from 'home' and who understood him. She told me later that Zulu tribesmen in Cape Town were few and far between. She undertook to relay a message to his family near, what sounded like, 'Felixtown'. Is there such a place? They parted the best of friends – and that was what your Emily was like. She was kind and could mix with anyone. She was also strong-willed and could be quite forceful, particularly when it came to defending students' rights, as a member of the SRC. Some students were demanding for certain subjects and lectures to be provided in Afrikaans, and she supported their cause (wrongly, I think!).

Emily was torn between continuing further studies at UCT and returning to Zululand to farm as well as ameliorate, in some way, the natives' plight. She also spoke of the distress of indentured Indians and their treatment on some farms (not theirs, but some others); but the strongest tug back to Zululand was the hope of marrying you.

*Yours in sadness,
Janet Anderson.*

Donald sat for a long while in the gloaming before moving to his makeshift writing desk in its square cocoon of lathes and mosquito-netting. He lit the paraffin lamp and settled down to read again, though with a heavy heart. The puppies had tumbled after him and he allowed them to settle at his feet, and opened the large padded envelope from Winnie. It was marked OVERSEAS MAIL, PLEASE DO NOT BEND!!!, below rows of green, orange and beige stamps bearing the bearded profile of King George V. A professional photograph on stiff card of the two girls dropped out, shot in front of a painted background, along with several Box Brownie snapshots of the girls with their frail-looking old father. On one, they were grouped beside his much-loved Beardmore motor car. His father never recovered fully from the shock of his son Andrew's death in France. A small brown packet also fell out. It was marked 'Scots Pine seeds'.

He saw that the London house address had changed, and was now 21, Richmond Hill Road, Richmond, TW10, blind-embossed on the letterhead.

Dearest faraway Donald Dubh,

Here are a few seeds from the Scottish farm, in the hope that they will grow beside your mud hut at Yonder. We are all so pleased that you chose the same name as the farm in Scotland. McAlpine told me how to prepare them. He picked an unopened cone off the ground and posted it to me in London. I was instructed to leave it in a lidless shoebox in the kitchen to open. When it did, the seeds could be shaken loose. Then I wrapped the seeds in greaseproof paper and popped them in the icebox. McAlpine said they have to be kept very cold for a few weeks to start the germination process. Seeing that the envelope has been aboard ship for a fortnight and then travelled to you in Zululand, I suggest you plant them right away!

We have changed homes and are now settled in a new-old house on Richmond Hill (there it is in the picture), shared with Auntie Evelyn. Do you remember her? Of course you do. Rather tweedy with wisps of hair on her upper lip, but we always viewed her as our substitute mother ever since Mummy died. Her husband was lost in France, you will remember.

Near the end of his life Daddy sold his interests in the lace factory to his partners, and his coal-merchandising business in London, and gave up the old home in Kew. He kept the farm in Scotland for us and saw an opportunity to buy this house for a song in our name a few weeks before he died. The McAlpines were given a minor share and still manage Yonder farm very well.

I won't go into describing the sadness and turmoil of those days, while you were out of reach in East Africa. So here we are. Daddy's old driver, Tommy, is still with us and he and his wife, Mrs Hopkins (our housekeeper) live in the carriage house.

Daddy consolidated his capital into a trust for us in Canadian government bonds and something to do with hydro-electric power, which now yield comfortable and secure dividends and a steady income for us. Moodie, the solicitor, handles the details monitored like a hawk by our Auntie Evelyn. (She has been provided for separately.)

All this must seem misleadingly prosperous, during very troubled times, and we are exceptionally fortunate that Daddy secured our future before he died; but there are hard years ahead for the average person. There is still coupon rationing of butter, meat, sugar and other things; and petrol for the motor car is very expensive indeed.

"Far, far worse than all that is the plight of

the wounded, the mutinying of the Canadian Expeditionary Force soldiers in Wales, demanding to be repatriated, the rioting in some midland towns – and the list goes on and on.

I do voluntary untrained nursing work every day, except Sundays, at Syon House, across the river from Kew. It continues to serve as an auxiliary military hospital and convalescent home. I get Hopkins to drop and collect me out of sight of the main building entrance, to avoid comments about our rather grand car. Auntie comes along too when she can break away from other work. So we're not idle…

Jean has been packed away to Queen Margaret's, a boarding school at Esrick Park, near York, on the insistence of Auntie Evelyn, as our little sister was getting out of hand. The school was evacuated to Pitlochry for the duration and only recently has it returned to its York 'home', so things haven't quite yet settled back into pre-war routine. Miss Fowler, the headmistress, startled the girls by announcing that very few of them stood any chance of marrying…there were just too few men left alive. Awful; she warned them that they must carve out their own careers, should study hard and aim for university…this was in the face of strong but weakening opposition, and she drew their attention, for example, to the Sex Disqualification (Removal) Act, passed last year, which has pushed the door ajar. [It became illegal to exclude women from jobs because of their gender.] *But returning soldiers are demanding their old jobs and a lot of unhappy girls have been dislodged back into domestic service; so there is now a confrontation between returning soldiers' rights and women's rights and there have been some ugly scenes.*

Donald Duhb, do please write!...and spare a letter for Jean; she does miss you so. Her school address is Duncan House, St Margaret's School, Esrick Park, near York, England.

Well, little brother, it's almost time for me to leave for Syon House. I have been writing this in the early morning in my bedroom overlooking a beautiful view of the Thames Valley. In fact, it's so beautiful that it's protected by an Act of Parliament.

With enduring love,
Wee Winnie

PS: Send photographs!
PPS: A sur-namesake of ours, David Kirkwood, has been causing quite a stir...blamed for a 40-hour strike at the Mile-End Shell Factory and was arrested in George Square, Glasgow. They call him Red Donald!

A fiery-necked nightjar startled him when it whooped and chirruped among the invisible bamboos. The lemon-peel moon had flitted behind the clouds and outside his cocoon it had grown very dark, even while the tumult of night sounds grew. Donald felt isolated and alone, mildly alleviated by a whiff of curry carried on the evening air. It reminded him that Chinnamama was preparing supper for him. Mutton (unless tinned) was in short supply and beef was shunned by her, resulting in a relentless daily diet of vegetable curry, supplemented occasionally with hard-boiled eggs. Donald allowed her to take part of the meal back to her room which she shared with her young son in the Indian lines. Coming from Madras, she had a working knowledge of English, but was not forthcoming about how she came to sign on as an indentured labourer; yet he gathered, from others during Thunder Tree conversations, that her Brahmin father had formed a relationship with her lower caste mother, and both parents had died. Chinnamama had given birth during the crossing to her premature son and had managed to survive on a distant sugar estate before she came to work for him. Donald would never know if she was a runaway, a widow, or merely a restless adventurer. (It was not considered irregular for a Madras woman to travel alone.) He made a point of maintaining a friendly, but aloof, master-servant relationship. By working in the house, her role was coveted, however, and she became socially isolated from the women field workers. Layani tolerated her, but they bickered, every now and then.

Flooring of the small bungalow had been started and Donald took great pleasure in sitting at a table to eat supper in the part of the dining room which had been planked. The barometer presented to him by the Durban bank was already hung on an upright beam. It fascinated Layani, as Donald had got into the habit of tapping the glass, to see if the needle would move to 'Rain', 'Fair' or 'Change'. Layani misinterpreted Donald's explanation of the device and told Zulu tribesmen that Donald had the power to control the weather by tapping the glass. The myth was reinforced by his tapping the barometer to demonstrate its purpose. The needle had jumped to Rain, and Donald had said, in stumbling Zulu, "Lentambama, iyovula." [It will rain this afternoon.] When it did, his reputation, unbeknownst to Donald, spread among the natives as a person who could make it rain.

Years later, during an extended drought, the local chief sent a senior delegation to him, requesting him to make it rain. He protested that this was not within his powers, and demonstrated that nothing would happen if he tapped the barometer glass. He had brought the device out onto the verandah where the elders had waited. When he tapped the glass the needle swung to the Rain side of Change and he had said, after consulting his Zulu primer, "Imvulaingase ifike maduzane." [Rain may come soon.]

His reputation was enhanced when, several days later, it rained so heavily that the White and Black Umfolozi rivers came down in flood. Thus Layani continued to bask in the glory of working for so powerful an employer.

Donald slit open the envelope from Prue with a dinner knife and yet more snapshots dropped out (Durban had not been left behind in the Box Brownie craze). Unusually for those times, some of Prue's group pictures, taken by another hand in front of the treble-storeyed Nimmo Road house, included 'Jeeves' and the garden-boy, standing discreetly to the side of Prue and her parents, the Jardines. The 'Beware of Coconuts' notice was still there, in the flowerbed. He remembered that the mother's name was Cordelia, and noted her remark that the Indian servant's nickname was 'Jeeves'; but for the life of him, he couldn't recall the nautically-bearded husband's Christian name. (He learned later that it was Keswick.)

Prue was at her prettiest in the pictures. Donald had almost forgotten her slight stammer (her letters were so fluent) and the small birthmark on the left of her neck, not visible at all in the photographs. Her arms were bare up to her shoulders and her slight figure-hugging dress became semi-transparent from mid-thigh to where it ended just below her knees. Her parents looked as if they had just come off a liner in hot and humid Singapore.

The garden boy was barefooted and clothed in standard issue – flax shirt and bermuda-style shorts, trimmed with dark tape. He was holding an upended garden rake, as if posing for an American Gothic painting. Only Jeeves had dressed for the occasion, sweating away in a dark waistcoated suit.

He read,

Dear Donald,

Sparrows (I think they're sparrows) have taken to nesting in the gutter outside my upstairs bedroom window and there is regular flitting to and fro. Each time a parent arrives there is a chorus of chirpings.

How are your bird-monitoring observations going, or are you too busy farming to spare the time? (My observations are set out below, as per our arrangement). Our garden is now full of early summer visitors. The barn swallows have arrived from Europe and some of them have detoured here, before going on to the wetland reed beds near Umhloti. I suppose they like our garden because there are so many flying insects to feed on at this time of the year. Daddy and I went to watch the sunset spectacle last week of millions of swallows swirling around to form extraordinary patterns in the sky before descending into the reeds, all of a sudden. What, one wonders, is in control, and how do the birds co-ordinate their movements? 'There are more things in heaven and earth, Horatio, than are dreamt of, in your philosophy' etc., although one wonders whose philosophy Horatio was studying in Wittenberg. Seneca, possibly?" [This observation went straight over Donald's head, leaving him baffled, and wondering whether it was some coded reference for him to puzzle out.]

The 'road' to get there was awful, and we nearly collided with a cane train, which suddenly steamed out of the sugar cane and cut across in front of us without any warning.

I'm writing this early in the morning," [another one choosing dawn for correspondence, thought Donald] *"before leaving for the children's library. I've a spot of leave coming up, so have to go in early this week to tidy up odds and ends before I vanish.*

My leave coincides with Daddy's planned visit to Zululand on business and I thought I might tag along some of the way.

May we visit? Mummy wants to see how the coolies are being treated on the sugar estates (you know how hell-bent reformist she is). The intention is to rail the car as far as Empangeni and base ourselves at the Masonic Hotel. From there the plan is a bit fluid although Papa will wander off to the bay for a while.

I had better explain that, as Daddy's the Durban harbour master, he's been asked to investigate the possibility of developing Richards Bay, initially, as a coaling port for steamers plying the East Coast and the Indian Ocean islands and Madagascar. Bunkering is expected to get even more cluttered in Durban harbour, now the war's over, and Richards Bay is seen as a relief valve. Heaven alone knows where the government intends to get the money. I understand there's an inactive coal mine at Somkhele. There's talk of reactivating the mine and building a rail spur from Empangeni to the bay. (As you know, there's already a spur to Somkhele from the Mtubatuba railhead but it only serves the new sugar and cotton initiatives near Hluhluwe, at the moment.)

Apparently, the Zululand bay is one of the deepest coastal waters in Africa, and has huge potential. By contrast, the sea approach to Durban tends to silt up and create a sand bar to the harbour, unless it's dredged constantly. Wasn't Richards Bay the place where your acquaintance was tragically taken by a shark? Awful.

The news from Durban is we are all doing our best to recover from the impact of the Spanish Flu – but of course, you know all about the orphanages that had to be expanded and trusts developed to assist stricken families – or what's left of them. I remember you had to set one up for bank employee dependents. Mother is flailing about, as usual, demanding that more be done for the natives and Indians, who were hardest hit. (She's right, of course.)

I know you get angry when there is talk of squandering money, in your view, on war memorials, instead of using it to assist the survivors, and you are not alone. Enclosed is a clipping from Ilanga Lase Natal, the Zulu paper, expressing the fury of demobbed African soldiers that the entire focus is on commemorating the whites who lost their lives at Delville Wood with no recognition of the blacks who lost their lives at the Front and East Africa.

The whole idea of constructing such a monument in South Africa is enraging Afrikaans right-wingers too, who were dead set against entering the war against the Germans in the first place.

The rumour has it that Smuts will erect the monument at Delville Wood itself and the other rumour is that it will be unveiled by Louis Botha's wife Annie. It won't go unnoticed by the Afrikaans that she stems from the Robert Emmett family tree and that Robert is considered as an Irish patriot, sentenced to death by the 'hated' British in 1803. But this doesn't address the growing crossness of the Africans and Indians who served and returned to an ungrateful nation. Trouble ahead.

Here are the latest birdfeeder results from 5am to 7am Monday to Saturday last week inclusive, I might have missed a few but the early hours are best for me.

10.39.13
WETTUSEKBULLDDHENWHSEELSKASENRT
I look forward to hearing from you and, hopefully, seeing you in the near future!

Much love, Dodo

After Chinnamama had washed up and repaired to her quarters, Donald reached for Buchan's novel and turned to page 10, counted thirty-nine lines down and thirteen letters in, to find the part-sentence which read 'would rake in the shekels and mak' and then, painstakingly, decoded Prue's message which turned out to read, 'Will contact Deepika monitor von Well'

He thought how devilishly effective the code was, for even if a single communiqué could be (conceivably) broken down by alphabetical letter frequency, and assuming the language in which it was written was known, the grid for each report was unique, so a decoder would have to start all over again with each new message. He realised that such reports could be made even more secure by enciphering the coded letters, and was relieved that such a tiresome challenge would not be required of him.

Brandy brought solace. In the night, the wind got up.

Emily was to be buried on the farm, near an outcrop of green Archaean granite and a small stream which welled up nearby. Weaver-birds had colonised a weeping willow that had taken root in its banks. Here, the water ran cool and clear, never running dry, even during the worst of droughts. Tiny crabs, no bigger than a thumb, had made a watery home there too,

"As a child, she loved to come and watch the weavers; it was her favourite spot on the farm," Jim Bell said to Donald, while standing a distance from the open grave. They were waiting for late-comers to arrive. Jim's hair had turned grey and he looked care-worn. His wife, Edna, was smoking one of her Turkish cigarettes and wondering, while talking to the Broccardos and Janet Anderson, whether she had catered for enough guests. Janet had accompanied the Bells on the long return rail journey from Cape Town. She was holding a guitar from which black ribbons fluttered. The Bell sons, Andrew and Nigel, were beside Emily's coffin, where seats had been arranged. Sonya had come up from Pietermaritzburg and stood beside Toby.

"She used to watch the weavers for hours with a pair of little binoculars we found for her," Jim Bell said. "After finishing each nest the male goes into a fluttering dance to attract a mate. If there are no takers he shreds the nest and starts again. He likes many wives, like the Zulus. She used to watch the little crabs in the stream as well. Emily will be content here." A desperate look came into his face and he turned away.

Toby suddenly remembered the time when, as a young boy, he and his father had set out to find the source of the Liffey River in the Irish Wicklow Hills. They found a small stream bubbling out of the bogs beneath Kippure Mountain, just under two thousand feet above sea level. His father, who liked the writings of James Joyce, mystified Toby by pointing at the stream and exclaiming, "There she is, the stream of consciousness."

Well-wishers continued to arrive, carrying chairs over the bumpy ground from where they had left their cars. For those who had come on horseback Jim had provided fodder and a temporary hitching rail, formed from gumtree branches.

The chairs were soon taken by farmers and their wives... little Miss Tatham, the librarian, Eric Schnurr, (his pregnant wife was stuck in Durban), the Lebanese banker, the vet, even Jan Mocke, the ox-wagon builder, with his wife. The house servants, Gorkil, Joseph and Jemima with Masheila Reddy and her father, were encouraged by the Bells to sit just behind them and in the same row as Toby, Donald, Janet and the Broccardos.

"You see?" Meiring muttered to his wife. "The natives and the churrahs'll be taking over the whole blarry countryside next. It's not right, it's not right. Hulle sal alles oorneem." [They'll take over everything.] A woman on a chair in front of them turned around and said, "Shush!"

"I think we had better begin," said Reverend Short loudly, who had been talking with Mary, his wife. "The Bell family thank you for coming out to the farm to share Emily's final homecoming...a young daughter so full of promise, struck down by this dreadful Spanish Flu. She loved this farm and everyone who worked so diligently on it. She used to visit this spot, from early childhood, to watch the weavers – see, there they are – and even study the little crabs in the stream...

"Emily's mother Edna told me that Emily disliked formality and convention. She said that it got in the way of analysis and facts. This principle inspired her to be one of the first students to enter the study of social anthropology in this country – at the University of Cape Town. Underscoring this pioneering insight, I'm told that the London School of Economics has just introduced a Department of Social Anthropology this year, led by another famous pioneer, Bronislaw Malinowski. Apparently, Emily was excited at the prospect of studying under him. The family wonders if she would have gone on to study there as she has received a first-class degree in her field, to be awarded posthumously. The subject of her dissertation was the practice of lobola (bride price paid only in cattle) during the intolerable climate of nagana we are experiencing, where most of the cattle are dying of it, with no cure in sight."

Then followed the Lord's Prayer and readings by Andrew Bell and her great friends Sonya Broccardo and Janet Anderson, interspersed by two hymns led by Mary Short, accompanied on the guitar by Janet. It was up to Edna and her other son, Nigel, to reminisce on Emily's growing up, and Jim to recall an occasion when the farm first got electric light from the new generator. Emily, as a child, had been fascinated by the way the outside light attracted the flying ants and had put out a basin to collect them as they fell to the ground. The chicks and ducks had been let out and made a bee-line for the basin to gobble up this cornucopia, joined by a hopping of frogs on the same mission.

During the burial itself, a small dust-devil had whirled across the field and shaken the foliage, before moving away and expiring. Donald caught Janet's eye as he cast Emily's beadwork onto the coffin, while earth began to cover it.

Boulders were to be rolled over the spot to deter wild animals.

"Going through her possessions, I came across your letters. Did you love her?"

"Yes, very much."

"I know she loved you. We were very proud of her and I'm comforted that she, at least, had the experience of falling in love. Would you have married her if she had agreed, instead of her going off to study in London?"

"Yes."

"We would have been very pleased, and you will always be especially welcome here...for her sake and ours. How's the farm going?"

"As you can expect, it's a challenge; we've (by 'we' I mean the workers and I) planted our first cotton and have almost finished building a small wood and iron cottage."

"You're progressing well. I must come and see it one day. When we first settled we lived in a rondavel Jim built. Nowadays it's Jim's office, where he keeps his butterfly collection and some chemicals. Whenever I walk in there that smell of thatch and daub takes me back instantly to the first day we moved in. We lived for months in a tent before that – right through the rainy season...we felt very cut-off and remote...in the beginning. You'd better find another girl tough enough to cope. Otherwise, it'll get very lonely."

Donald was startled by her matter-of-fact directness, so soon after Emily's burial. Probably it was her way of coping, he thought, along with the smoking of those Turkish cigarettes that smelt of cow-dung. It was only when he looked directly into her eyes that he saw the misery.

A few steps later on they were joined by Paula Broccardo, the mother of Zeno, who had died in the shark attack at Richards Bay. Paula took her arm and they walked on together.

"It gets easier, in time," she said.

In later months and years Jim and Edna would sit at the grave in the late afternoon, before the time when malaria mosquitoes became most active. A brass plaque had been set in one of the giant boulders, which read, 'Emily Adair Miranda Bell. 7th March 1900 – 27th October 1919 Phumani kahle, bathandekayo.' [Rest well, beloved.]

The stream at the willow tree was slow-moving, and dragonflies found it suitable for laying clumps of eggs where the reeds grew in one of its placid pools. In the season, they could be seen hovering and darting near the grave, along with dark, white-spotted butterflies. Jim, being a butterfly collector, had identified them as *Kedestes Mohozuza.*

During the dry season, natives reported seeing a leopard drinking at the stream. This was unusual, as they hunt by night and are rarely seen during the day.

Zulus respect the leopard for its cunning and agility. Its skin is worn only by a chief, when in traditional garb, although married men are permitted to wear a little, in the form of a head ring, the 'sicoco'. Only the king may wear as much leopard skin as he likes.

Chapter Fourteen

"We've been invited to visit the sugar estate owned by a charming Swiss owner and his wife, this afternoon, after bumping into them at the reception desk," Cordelia Jardine said. "We were told by others that they run their farm with commendable Swiss efficiency, so we're sorely tempted to go. Of course, my true intention is to see how the coolies and natives are being treated." Prue's expression remained inscrutable. She looked as nubile and attractive as ever, though somewhat bothered by the heat and humidity of Empangeni. It was difficult, after all, to remain looking nubile while the sweat trickled down one's neck.

The Jardines and Donald were sitting on the terrace of the Masonic Hotel, soon after their morning arrival on the train from Durban. They had railed up their car on the same train, and after the palaver of getting it off the truck and registering at the hotel, they had settled down to chat to Donald, who had driven up to meet them at the station. Cordelia was cooling herself, as best she could, with a rattan fan, and Prue was watching the ebb and flow of people, saying little. Keswick Jardine reminded Donald of a photograph he once saw of Lionel Greenstreet, First Officer of the 'Endurance' on Shackleton's expedition to the South Pole. A group picture of them was on display at his old school. Jardine was of the intrepid sort, thought Donald, the kind that would have taken on his share and more of the rowing in that race to Elephant Island.

Cordelia was perspiring under a straw sun hat matching her light cotton clothing.

"Prue and I are going back on Tuesday, but Keswick is trundling off to Richards Bay next week with a couple of harbour people."

"This time it's just to get the lie of the land," said Jardine. "It's a case of planning for the future."

"I think I'd better warn you, Mr Jardine, that the gravel road to the von Weldenburg farm peters out after that into a very rudimentary track, for the rest of the way to Richard's Bay. All you'll find when you get there is very basic accommodation and some fishing shacks. If the party line works it might be worth calling Mr Grantham. He runs the rudimentary accommodation there, with his wife, and knows the area like the back of his hand. You might bump into Dr Lombard, the Empangeni doctor, who likes to go surf-fishing over the weekend, to escape from his patients. The coolie fishermen are also very knowledgeable…know a lot about the ways of the tides, because they depend on them…superb anglers. They are usually there before sunrise. Apparently it's the best time."

"Good thinking. New bathymetrics will come later if the government decides to proceed, although heaven knows where it hopes to find the money. I predict nothing will happen for the next thirty years. What I do know is that the bay stretches over eleven and a half square miles, with huge potential as a deep-water port; I believe it measures ten fathoms deep in most parts. Compare that to our Durban harbour, which is steadily silting up. You can see the sandbanks everywhere at low tide; and the sand bar at the entrance has to be excavated all the time.

Prue observed how well the two men got on – and she liked that.

"The lagoon fed by the Mhlatuzi River is jumping with crocodiles and sharks, which get in over the sandbar at high tide. The sharks are quite at home in a mixture of sea and fresh water. I've been put off the place ever since Zeno Broccardo lost his life there in a shark attack, which I witnessed."

"Well, now you've put the wind up me, I'll be particularly careful." Keswick said as he lit his pipe. The pungent smoke drifted across the table and Cordelia said, "Darling, please sit downwind; can't stand the smell."

"It's important to take quinine, while you're here, as this area remains malarial – especially near the coast."

Tea and biscuits were brought by the same waiter who had slipped Donald the note from Deepika during the rugby match. There was a clean sticking plaster around his thumb.

"Please tell Deepika that I have a cook already so there's no job for her, but my friends may visit the von Weldenburg farm this afternoon and perhaps the young lady may talk to her," Donald said, looking queryingly at Prue as he spoke.

"Who's Deepika?" asked Cordelia.

"An Indian worker on the von Weldenburg estate; her husband died. When Toby (a fellow farmer) and I visited we discovered her in a near destitute state, because her main, very small, income had died with the husband. We helped her a bit without bothering to burden von Weldenburg with the news. The upshot was that she wrote to me through that waiter, who turns out to be a relative, asking to come and work for me. I had to refuse because the small complement of workers on such a fledgling farm is enough."

"What do-do you think of their es-es-estate?" asked Prue, keeping up the pretence of knowing nothing about von Weldenburg. She was suddenly highly conscious of her stammer which was unusually pronounced at that moment.

"Excellent, run by a cultured martinet with an obsession about eugenics; but you must judge for yourselves. His wife taught Braille at a sanatorium in neutral Switzerland for German, and a few grave cases of English, soldiers blinded by gas. I think she intends to teach Braille here, but has doubts that the version she knows can be taught to the natives – something about a lack of diacritics…whatever that means. Her husband is appalled at the idea of teaching braille to blind natives on his farm, anyway. It doesn't conform to his ramblings about 'Untermenschen'. She has a beautiful voice and sang Schumann lieder to us, accompanied by her husband, when Toby and I visited."

"I didn't realise that Braille had such marked variations… hadn't thought about it, really."

"Yes, she even struggled to master English Braille while working in Switzerland. Mind you, even frogs have different accents, region to region, I am told, and that's true of all animals."

"That suggests that an Ethiopian cheetah wouldn't understand a Natal one."

"With difficulty, I should think. It would be almost similar to the language barrier that exists between my Shangaan factotum and me, who communicates with me in a muddle of Portuguese, Zulu and the occasional English word plus simple signs thrown in between. In our case, however, we've managed to develop a lingua franca, unique to us, and seem to understand each other quite well – even though thousands would find it very funny, which I s'pose it is."

Prue broke into a delightful silvery giggle as Donald gave an imitation of how it sounded, with appropriate gestures.

"Can't you come along with us?" asked Cordelia.

"Alas, I'm committed to visiting the Bells for lunch. They lost their daughter to Spanish Flu earlier this year and were very kind to Toby and me when we first arrived. (The Bell's farm is in the opposite direction to the von Weldenburgs.) I also have some basic shopping to do; but as I'm booked to stay here tonight, at the Masonic, I was wondering if we could have dinner together?" – to which the Jardines readily agreed. "The food passes muster even though the new chef likes to confound us natives by writing the menu in 'brasserie French'. The next step will be bigger plates, smaller helpings and higher prices."

"What happened to the old chef?"

"Spanish Flu…a happier death than the previous manager, who flew too close to the sun…If we're lucky, Mr and Mrs Hammar will be dining here tonight. Are you in contact with August Hammar?" (This was directed at Keswick.)

"Do you mean the surveyor? No. I've heard of him, of course, and know of his important work in this region, but I thought he was dead."

"Not at all! He and his wife have retired here and have a manageable pineapple holding on the Ntambanana Road, just outside Empangeni. He's a mine of information about the coast, including the hydrographic survey done by HMS *Mutine* before the war. I'll ask the town's switchboard girls for their phone number, in case the Hammars don't appear for dinner; that is, if you'd like to make contact?

"Yes, of course, and thank you. I'd like to meet up and I'm sure Delia will have plenty to discuss with Mrs Hammar. She was a school teacher in Stanger."

"Then in that case I can ask her about schooling for the natives," Cordelia said. Prue caught Donald's eye and raised hers very slightly heavenward, as if to say 'here we go again,

Mother will be on the underdog rights rampage again, given a chance'.

★★★

Despite the heat and humidity, it was de rigueur to dress for dinner at Empangeni's only hotel, and Donald felt obliged to struggle into his striped blue-navy-and-black Old Alleynian blazer and tie for an evening more memorable than Chinnamama's solitary vegetable curries consumed in Yonder's faint lamplight.

While dressing for dinner, Cordelia said, "The conditions and state of those Indian lines at the von Weldenburg's were appalling."

"Agreed, but I'm glad you kept your mouth shut. The owners were charm itself, in a Teutonic way. The German Swiss seem to be more German than the Germans themselves, though I sympathise with Frieda's efforts to extricate her sister and son from all that Bolshevistic rioting and bloodletting going on in Germany. What were their names again?"

"She's Anna Werz and her son is called Luitpold. He's nine."

"How on earth do you winkle out these gems of intelligence?"

"Anna is obviously troubled by what she's seen, and the son likewise...couldn't understand what she was saying, most of the time. It'll take them months to adapt...Dodo got on quite well with Frieda, don't you think? All that talk about braille...apparently she had put Frieda in touch with a friend of hers through Donald. We've met her once...Afrikaans girl called Danielle. You remember her – bright and fluffy? Now we've met up again, what do you think of Donald?"

"Reserved, but straightforward. Seen things; do you know

that, of every man killed in East Africa, thirty died from snake bites, wild animal attacks and tropical diseases, even starvation? He's been through it. I like him."

"Have you noticed that Dodo is barely opening her mouth, in his presence?"

"Can't say that I have, but yes, now you come to mention it."

"I think she's got a crush on him."

"Well, it's about time she did develop a solid crush on someone worthwhile. I didn't take to the few she did bring home…still wet behind the ears or borderline Bolsheviks."

"There seems to be something else between them…I know they correspond, but…I can't put my finger on it…some sort of understanding."

"Are you secretly planning to marry her off? I know she jumped at the chance of coming away with us, and of course they got to know each other quite well on those tram rides and attending that League of Nations meeting…I'd miss her."

"No, I'm not plotting, but I'd like to see her happy, rather than just burying herself in books at the children's library… you can see how she loves children, and a good man is hard to find since the war…not enough to go around. Nowadays it's rather like musical chairs, with very few chairs. I believe it's worse in Britain."

"I wouldn't mind seeing some grandchildren hopping about, I must say…carrying on the line and so forth…but a farmer's wife in Zululand? Could Prue cope? And what was she doing talking to that coolie woman?"

"Didn't you hear Donald talking to the waiter? Just a message to her from Donald."

"Hmmm."

"Perhaps we should engineer some space for them tomorrow, allow them to drift off for a bit. Donald obviously likes her…bit old for her, but there you are. I notice he has a slight limp."

"He's lucky to have escaped with just that. It's the 'psychological limps' we should be more concerned about. I bet you that he and other such men will have war nightmares for years to come…but, whatever you say, you old schemer. We'll encourage them to drift off for a while and see what transpires."

"We'd better go down if we want to get in a drink before they sound the dinner gong. I heard the dressing gong at least half an hour ago. I'll tell Dodo."

Prue was wearing the same dress and looking even more desirable in the flesh. August and Elizabeth Hammar did indeed arrive, and welcomed the idea of dining together, during which August kept them agog with his experiences during the Anglo-Zulu war. He was a Swede, who immigrated to Natal in 1878 and got caught up in the conflict in which he served as a trooper. Soon after witnessing Lord Chelmsford's final crushing of the Zulu army at Ulundi, he was asked to visit and paint a watercolour of the scene where Napoléon, the Prince Imperial, met his death during a Zulu skirmish. The work was sent to his grief-stricken mother, the Empress Eugénie.

Before Hammar joined up, he had purchased a farm near Rorke's Drift, so named after an Irishman who owned a trading store there, on the banks of the Buffalo River. Rorke's widow had sold the buildings to a Norwegian mission after his death, where another Swede, the Reverend Otto Witt, became the incumbent. It was used as a hospital during the Zulu/ British conflict in 1879; Hammar was away in the hills when he spied the attack on the British troops defensively stationed there to defend the patients. Zulu impis returning from the slaughter of Lord Chelmsford's men on the slopes of Isandhlwana were attempting to polish off the rest of the enemy, despite King Cetshwayo's admonition not to attack entrenched British troops. Hammar made his escape by trudging the 170 miles to Durban.

In 1881, Hammar was admitted to practice as a land surveyor, after working at a practice in Verulam, near Durban, and this led to his sharing his time between surveying and farming at Rorke's Drift.

He joined a Dr Aurel Schultz to survey country as far as the Victoria Falls and west to the Okavango River and the Kalahari. Later, he prepared topographical maps of parts of Natal, after several smaller surveying expeditions, all the while illustrating his surveying work with water-colour landscapes. Four of these now hang in the Tatham Gallery in Pietermaritzburg.

The floorboards of the little Empangeni wood-and-iron church were fastened over wooden beams which were, in turn, supported on brick stilts. The disadvantage of this type of flooring was that footfalls were noisy and the floorboards creaked against each other, where the nails holding them down had worked loose. As the church began to fill, heads were turned every time newcomers walked to their pews. Donald sat with the Jardines and the Hammars in the row behind the Bell family. He could have sworn that Edna Bell winked at him when she turned and spotted Prue. Everyone knew each other, so the presence of the Jardines was a matter of discreet curiosity. He groaned inwardly at the number of hymns on the board, and made up his mind not to sing at all, as the same ageing harmonium player slurred away at barely-recognisable Bach.

He thought back to the first service he had attended there with the Bell family, when golden-haired Emily was alive. She remained alive in his mind's eye. An out-of-control child had worked her way through the backrest and stared at him, hanging upside down. He was mindful that the minister and Prue both stammered, although the former's was far more pronounced.

After the service had wound its way through psalms, mumbled hymns (some just mouthing the words) and bible readings, accompanied by the flurry of pages being turned backwards and forwards as members of the congregation struggled to find their places, the Reverend Short creaked and clumped his way to the pulpit. His sermon set off from the Bible account in 'Kings', of Hezekiah's illness, the addition of fifteen years to his life if he behaved himself, figs and a shadow that went back ten steps. He drew his perspiring congregation further and further into befuddlement, compounded by his finding the barrier of pronouncing anything starting with a 'p' as insurmountable, and upon encountering 'poultice' having to resort, in final desperation, to substituting it with 'mice', despite his flock's offering possible words that started with a 'p' (like 'pigs', 'prayer' and 'palms'). It turned his sermon into a game of deduction, rather like a particularly difficult crossword or a game of charades, and concluded suddenly when Short exhorted his startled congregation, still worrying about the shadow going back ten steps, to "put your houses in order!" As if to add divine emphasis, a troop of vervet monkeys chose that moment to thunder across the roof and swing into the huge flamboyant tree beside the building. Donald assumed it was the same troop that had woken him, rushing to and fro over the hotel roof, so many months ago.

When Donald peeked at Prue, he saw that she had bent over her prayer book, her body trembling with suppressed giggles.

It was as hot and humid as it could only be in a late

October Zululand; and the congregation almost burst out of the hot little church at the end of the service, seeking relief beneath the flamboyant from the heat. The monkeys had vanished. A few out-of-season Christmas beetles were already practising for their deafening December crescendo, a chorus so loud it destroys all conversation within twenty feet. They suddenly fell silent when a blue-headed agama lizard raced up the trunk towards them, head bobbing up and down whenever it paused.

General introductions had been made and Sonya Broccardo came over to Donald to ask after Toby, partially as an excuse to eye Prue at first hand, but particularly through her interest in Donald's farming neighbour. Some young children, released from the tiny Sunday school, were racing in and out of the adults until one of the small boys fell over and started to cry. Prue was the first to go to the young child's assistance and comfort him.

The Jardine parents had accepted the Hammars' invitation to lunch at their house and Prue had announced that she would accompany Donald back to Ntambanana for the afternoon to see his farm. He had arranged for the hotel to pack a picnic lunch.

"Keep your eye on the weather," Jim Bell advised. "If it storms – and it's sultry enough today – you might find it difficult to get back. The road turns into a quagmire after rain, as you know." This was said within earshot of the Jardines.

Prue had changed at the hotel into what she envisaged as 'farm-girl' clothes, before they had set out, and Donald felt a terrible yearning for her as she sat beside him in the Kelpie. Although not expressed, both were remembering those moments when they first embraced and kissed beside the Dodo in the museum,

They stopped on the way beneath a shade tree and Donald

said, "It's a relief to speak openly again. I find all this coded mumbo jumbo a strain."

This was hardly a romantic opening to discussion over a packed lunch in the middle of the African bundu, and reflected Donald's reticence. Nevertheless, Prue played along and said, "The m-messages you sent have been invaluable. Von Weldenburg is obviously a right w-wing German in Swiss clothing. Lots of them have emigrated to the Argentine and other places since the war, posing as Swiss and Swedes. My 'masters' w-won't do anything – just keep him under observation. As Creighton might have said to you (he used to repeat the quote from M-m-macbeth' often), 'we've scotched the snake, not killed it'. As for our Captain Stoughton – n-now there's a snake-in-the-grass if ever there was. He's m-managed to shed the skin of his actual identity (Duquesne), and cloak himself as a bilingual English brandy salesman, but he remains bitterly anti-English. I don't blame him after what Kitchener did to his parents' farm and family. He m-makes ideal recruitment m-material for another Boer uprising, like the one just before the war in 1914, supported again by guns and m-m-money from Germany. Von Weldenburg is ideally placed to act as broker…and yes, a 'responsible source' advised me that they're m-m-onitoring his transm-m-issions – thanks to you."

"Don't you think that Germany's a burnt-out case for a long, long time to come? Surely they're more consumed by hunger and survival, with the Bolsheviks swinging through parts of the country. Perhaps von Weldenburg's just a crank, living in the past, dabbling in eugenics philosophies, sending fanciful wireless messages to the old guard, smothered in golden Militär-Verdienstkreuzes, who don't accept the Weimar Republic, deluding themselves that they retain power behind the scenes?"

"Come on, Donald, with all your experience you know that's not true. It's the little-noticed, but lengthening tentacles of German national-socialism extending to this country that our m-masters are w-worrying about. Did you know that m-members of the National Socialist German W-workers' Party have been secretly circulated a 25-point plan that will be announced at the Hofbräuhaus in Munich next year? The first three points are: unification of all Germans, the abrogation of the peace treaties of Versailles and St. Germain, and a demand for land and colonies for German surplus population. Lebensraum, in other words grabbing neighbouring countries again. The same old story. The fourth addresses all those of pure German blood only, and excludes the Jews.

"The rest of the programme is along the same lines, including the demand that all writers and employees of newspapers published in German must be of pure German blood."

"Well, I can see where all that's heading, but I've developed a great deal of respect for the Afrikaners in our area and those I fought with, and I cannot believe that such concepts will rub off on them."

"Oh, but they have already. The formation of the Broederbond is a good example, which excludes all m-men not of 'pure' Boer stock'. It's based on m-many of the same principles imported from Germany, and will operate in secret. The aim is to gain control by stealth, and drive all the English and Jews into the sea."

"What about the Indians?"

"They'll try to make life so uncomfortable that most of them will return to India."

"And our black brethren?"

"The Broederbonders regard them as 'hewers of wood and drawers of water'; and that'll be their permanent lot."

"I think that's enough of politics for a month or more... I've chosen a cut-off life of fighting weeds and locusts instead of Germans...I've supped enough of horrors, ghastly times I want to forget...and being cut off helps, even though the nightmares return." (He didn't mention his flashbacks, of encountering men he had killed.)

"We get our newspapers seven days late and I embrace the idea that our only topical contact with the outside world is the party-line telephone, when it works. Even a telegram will take several days to reach me by proverbial cleft-stick messenger; so it saddens me that all this political nonsense is rumbling away behind the scenes, even here...Come, Prue...let's get on."

"Oh, don't call m-me Prue," she said, wrinkling her little retroussé nose. "Please call me Dodo."

"I thought that was reserved for your parents..."

"It's restricted to my nearest and dearest," she said, turning and looking directly into his eyes and colouring slightly.

There was a pause, and then he put his arm about her waist and drew her to him. Their kisses were warm and lingering. It brought to the surface all those emotions, in both of them, of wanting to love and be loved in return, so completely dashed in Donald's case by Emily's death. After a little while, she pushed him away and said gently, "That could be for later. I want to see Yonder."

As they rose and brushed themselves off, Donald saw, in the distance, vultures descending on a dead animal.

"Hold on," he said, "I think I'd better go and take a look."

What he discovered made him sick to the stomach. After shooing away the vultures as best he could, he found the carcass of a young giraffe. It had been mutilated while still alive; its genitals had been cut away and back leg tendons hacked to prevent it kicking out against its tormentors. The young animal had been in such agony that dark stains of tears had streamed from its eye sockets.

Prue had walked over to join him and they clung together, appalled at such cruelty.

"This is ghastly. I must report it at 'Tam," Donald said. "There's nothing we can do here, so now it's over to the vultures and jackals. We'd better move on."

★★★

As he brought the Kelpie to a halt at the store, Donald was suddenly conscious that his property, when they did get to it, might seem very 'small beer' in Prue's eyes, after Durban… just a modest tin cottage and outbuildings, at the end of a rough earthen track, a cluster of oxen staring at them, ploughed fields barely showing any growth, some labourers, a windmill and a pronounced smell of curry. She would not see the grinding labour that had brought it into being, or understand the relationship he had built with people like Layani and Chinnamama.

Serendipitously, Corporal Reynolds of the Natal Mounted Police was at the store when they arrived, to whom Donald reported coming across the dead mutilated giraffe.

"That's a muti killing," he said. "The animal must have strayed out of the reserve and the killers saw their chance."

"What's muti?" asked Prue.

"It's uMuthi, a Zulu word meaning tree. The inyanga [herbalist] usually prescribes medicine made from parts of a tree or other plants. But sometimes he may prescribe parts of animals – and that can include vulture brains – when a prophesy has to be made."

"But these parts were cut from a live giraffe!"

"The belief is that the muti is more powerful if cut from a live animal…or person."

"Or person!?"

"Ja, it's true! Particularly albinos. They just disappear and it's put about that they have magical powers and can vanish. We try very hard to catch and punish muti-killers, when we can find them, but they're clever…and these killings can happen anywhere – even in Durban."

Prue shuddered. Donald had been startled to hear Prue talking to the storekeeper, Piet van Jaarsveld, in Afrikaans, while he was briefing Reynolds.

"I could've tried to speak in High Dutch," she had said jokingly, when they got back into the car, "but only officials do that…The man at the shop said there's a big storm coming – did you hear that?"

Donald was becoming bewitched by Prue's slender young body as she climbed in and out of the Kelpie, her intelligence and her sense of fun.

"No, I didn't. You were chattering away in Afrikaans, remember. Where did you learn the lingo?"

"Hardly chattering…more like m-m-muttering, but the other lingo was part of my librarianship studies. Since Union, it's been m-mandatory to be able to serve library visitors in English and Dutch – even though, it being Durban after all, I'm seldom called on to break into the Taal. On the rare occasions I have had to, we have always conversed in Afrikaans. Do you know it's still regarded as a patoi and therefore banned in schools; yet written Afrikaans has been in existence since 1876? I used to drill myself by reading library file copies of the first Afrikaans newspaper, 'Die Patriot' published in Paarl at about that time. It lost readers and had to close down w-when the editor m- m-made the m-mistake of backing Cecil John Rhodes.

"I could ramble on about patois…"

"Go on."

"Well, to the French, patois is a kind of sneering word, referring to the dialects of the lower classes in various regions; but I don't think Afrikaans fits into that category, as it has ceased to be regional. It's spoken by most Boers – even in Pretoria by those pretentious government officials when their master is out of earshot. Stupidly, High Dutch remains in force for all official documents. And, on another tack… may I brag?"

"If you're capable of it."

"I love languages so I've taught m-myself a little bit of Zulu out of a 'Teach Yourself Zulu' book, and practise it on our garden boy and the library cleaners; m-my pronunciation is 'cleaner-standard' and m-m-y vocabulary is very limited indeed; but it's a beginning. It's a beautiful-sounding language, even at 'cleaner' level…and the natives are so instinctively musical too, perhaps that influences the m-m-elodic flow of the language…a bit like the Italians and opera. I used to enjoy listening to the native workmen digging up the road outside the Durban Town Hall. The leader would chant a phrase to the rest of the team standing in a row, with picks raised above their heads. At a point in the song they would join in, and then bring down their picks simultaneously, with an almighty thud. It sounded like a chanting steam-engine."

It was a long time before Donald started the car; they just sat talking, making Donald realise how much he had missed her easy company. By the time they got to Yonder, the sky had darkened with rumbling storm clouds and the vanes of the wind pump were turning rapidly.

"I should've thought of this before. Sorry, but we must go back to the store to phone your parents. It looks as if this storm will be a big one and flood the road most of the way to Empangeni, making it well-nigh impossible to get you back safely tonight," he said, while turning the Kelpie about and driving it as fast as it would allow him to go over the uneven ground. Prue was able to say little as they bumped along, except to blurt conventional concern between bumps. She was far more worried that she had no other clothes, if she did indeed need to linger overnight. Besides, this was exciting, so she gave herself up to the moment.

Donald noticed how warmly the van Jaarsvelds greeted them at the store, on the second time, where they were quickly ushered through to the dwelling area and into their daguerreotyped parlour. The phone was in the hall, and as Prue made the call to her father she found herself staring at another old framed family photograph taken in front of a wattle-and-daub farmhouse. The older of the two men was hatted and boasted a beard down to his chest. Seated were seven children and the mother, her hair, like those of the ouma and daughters, centre-parted. Prue had spoken to the van Jaarsvelds in Afrikaans again – and without a stammer – before switching to colonial English on the crackling party-line, to explain very loudly to her father, with some exaggeration, that the unexpected enormous, absolutely humungous storm would probably cut off 'Tam for at least the next twelve hours, but that she was safe and sound.

"Well, what do you make of that?" Piet said to Hannah, after they had left.

"I like her, even though she's Engelsprekende [English-speaking]. She bought some clothes from the shop for tomorrow, so you can tell that she didn't plan to stay overnight. But I could see…she's in love with him and I don't think it's dawned on Meneer Donald yet. She's pretty, but I think she could be tough enough to be a farmer's wife. We'll see. At least it could be someone we could talk to, among all these rooineks. The 'absolutely humungous' storm (imitating Prue's English voice) is coming, so are the children back inside? You'd better call them in quickly, before the lightning starts."

The storm clouds were so dense by the time they arrived back at Yonder, it had grown as dark as if an eclipse had masked the sun. The wind had dropped, but the rumbles of thunder were more pronounced. As they stepped onto the verandah, there was an almighty flash followed almost immediately by the crash of thunder, suggesting that the lightning was almost overhead. Chinnamama was in the kitchen preparing the inevitable curry and she greeted Prue warmly, as did Layani and his young son.

After the usual greetings and introductions, Donald said, "Chinnamama and Layani, better hamba kia before tempestade." Prue giggled, but he was rather proud of that word 'tempestade', which he had learned from Layani. "Better take your food now, Chinnamama. Missy Prue will take over." No doubt, thought Donald, Prue's visit would be the subject of much chatter and speculation.

"My God!" said Prue, after they had left. "You haven't any books!"

"Well, I do have that beautiful bird book you gave me, and *South* by Shackleton; then there's *The Thirty-Nine Steps* by that Buchan fellow and a whole lot of farming manuals, plus a few copies of *The Alleynian*."

"What on earth's that?"

"My Old Boys' school magazine."

"I'm shocked, as a librarian who lives among books every day, to find a home where there isn't even a bookshelf."

"Steady on; I've just put a roof on. I spend my days out in the fields and am so tired at the end of the day that there's pretty little time to read, after eating something and staggering off to bed. And try reading a book by candlelight while the world's moths are fluttering into the flame, into your face and all over the pages. Toby does bring the papers over on Sundays, and that's the only daylight time I have to read anything."

As if to add emphasis to his words, there was a crackle and crash as lightning struck the cattle shed. (Thank heavens for lightning conductors, Donald thought.)

"Of course, I'm sorry," Prue said, after recovering from the shock. "I was only mocking; but I'm committing m-myself to improving your access to good books – so m-much so, that soon your neighbours will stagger back to discover that not only has Yonder got a book shelf, but that it has become a centre of culture and learning in the bundu." She said all this, smiling broadly, but wincing every time the lightning crashed. Soon, sheets of rain began to roar on the corrugated iron roof, to the accompaniment of Wagnerian lightning flashes.

"If you can see it through the rain, there's the post box where your letters arrive at, and there's the bird feeder," he said. They had drifted to a window, arms about each other, to watch the curtain of rain. Prue shivered suddenly and asked for one of his jerseys. The puppies had long ago taken shelter under the bed.

Donald had opened one of the wines he had bought while the Jardines were away at the von Weldenburgs, and Prue tipped her glass to his and said, "To us."

"To us," he replied, as the roar of the rain increased and turned to deafening hail. Donald reflected with relief that the cotton was barely peeping above ground, so would be protected, for the most part, from damage.

"We'd better eat your cook's curry, before it burns," said Prue, starting to lay out the food, as Donald watched. "Does Chinnamm-m-a-m-a come back to wash up?"

"No, in the morning."

"You'd better lock the kitchen door…I assume the doors can lock?…ah, m-m-ango chutney. Any bananas? Where's the coconut? She made papadums but didn't make the sambals before you sent her home."

Donald poured her more wine as he watched.

"I'm not used to having someone, other than the maid, doing all this."

"It's called m-m-arried life…"

Their love-making was a natural progression. "He seduced her with m-m-angoes and chutney," she had murmured, as they lay entwined, before struggling out of their clothes. Donald was stirred by the smallness of her waist, the softness of her mouth and the small of her back, while they gave themselves up to the silent language of love, when the mind is withdrawn, until she cried out with joy.

"Could you bear to be a farmer's wife?"

"Rhetorical or actual?"

"This is an actual, heartfelt proposal."

"You had better get down on one knee beside the bed and ask me properly."

Donald rolled off the bed, knelt and said, "Dodo, I am head over heels in love with you. Please will you marry me? I love you for your beauty, your brains, and your chutzpah."

"Chutzpah? Sounds as if you're clearing your throat to spit."

"It's a good word a French friend in Durban introduced me to. He picked up the word from Jewish acquaintances."

"What does it mean?"

"Guts…boldness…determination."

"I've never been proposed to by a naked man, kneeling beside my bed, uttering spitting noises. I'll have to think about it. I think I could contribute to us and the farm…start a dynasty (we might have done that already)…teach children…

run a little library…write a book…guide a plough…control the domestic staff…help with bookkeeping and…continue my other duties…I've been in love with you for quite a while. I think about you every time I catch a tram to the library. Even in the library you're close. I often wander upstairs to the m-m-useum and gaze at the Dodo and think of our first kiss. Give me some time. I'll let you know from Durban. Why me?"

"Because of your chutzpah."

Later, lying entwined on the bed together, he told her about his sisters and the farm in Scotland, as the puppies were being allowed to snuggle onto the bed; of the last sight of his father on the platform as the train pulled out, and of his brother who died in France. He said little about Emily or the war, leaving that to another time. Prue talked about growing up in Singapore and how her life was saved by a naval officer, who swept her away from an advancing fatwa mob…they talked about the future…and her love of books, and reading Chekov's *Cherry Orchard* for the very first time.

"One day," she said, with prescience, "when the barbarians come, they'll chop down our orchards; our statues will fall, and they'll do their laundry in our fountains. I don't think my mother would like that. She's a sort of Fabian, not a revolutionary…only on the fringes of being a true socialist. She's a kind of capitalist – socialist, if there is such a thing. No dogs barking…just tortoises."

"You've lost me. Dogs? Tortoises?"

"I was being silly. D H Lawrence wrote a poem about the socialists coming to town and all the dogs barking. The tortoise was a reference to the Fabian icon symbolising gradual change towards equality. They abandoned their first symbol as undesirably sinister, of a wolf in sheep's clothing.

Mother is not sinister, she's just a gradualist, yet she's very uneasy with the Fabians' tinkering with eugenics. So am I. That way lies totalitarianism."

"And your father? He and I seem to get on rather well. How does he cope with all this political hand-wringing?"

"Yes, he approves of you. He just lets the whole socialist thing wash over him…water off a duck's back, although he sympathises with Mother's views. They respect each other, and that's a Good Thing. Daddy's a rugged man, with enormous vision…and a tremendous sense of humour. He loves his Durban harbour and I love him. I like rugged people who can laugh at themselves, and you're one of them."

When passion was spent, they had lain a long time, sharing their pasts and future together. Prue talked about her home, high up in Durban's Berea, her discovery as a young child that not everyone stammered and her near-fatal curiosity on seeing her cat, all hairs bushed as if by static electricity, hissing at a puffadder beside the bilbergias. She had called the garden boy to come and look, leading to her mother rushing down the front steps, pulling her away, then blowing the snake's head off with her husband's twelve-bore (her father had been down at the harbour at the time). It was only the second time that Donald had talked about the war in East Africa, and about his concerns for the farm, not least the threat of nagana. He even talked about Emily.

Chapter Fifteen

By mid-November the Scots pine seedlings had begun to prod through the soil, and the first squares of the cotton plants had developed. Thinning and weeding remained a full-time occupation for his Indian workers, who had to battle constantly with the encroachments of morning glory, maria-maria, and a host of other intruders. The women, aided by some of the older children, had to crawl along, between the cotton skip-rows, filling hessian bags dragged behind them.

Donald had devised a bonus system for filled bags that worked well. The communal piles of weeds were burnt when they reached hip-height.

It was one of those sparkling young mornings when the dew is caught in spider webs that the barefoot postman found Donald eating breakfast on the verandah. The man stood at the foot of the steps until Donald said, "Sawubona," [I see you] to which he replied, "Ngilapha ukubonwa." [I am here to be seen.]

Prue's letter had come up with the last train before the rail strike, a strike which was to paralyse rail services for many weeks. It was a sympathy action by the 5,000 native and coloured railway workers, expressing solidarity with the Cape Town dockers who were demanding eight shillings and sixpence a day. Native municipal workers followed suit throughout the country, for the same reason. She wrote:

Donald [there was no 'dearest', 'darling' or 'diddledums' about Prue], *I hope this letter reaches you before the railway strike takes hold. Everyone we know has gone into siege mode, expecting major supply disruption, and they are all stocking up. Between coping with chaos down at the harbour, Daddy has sent in a favourable report on Richards Bay, prepared with his colleagues, but said to us privately that the state is so broke after the war that he couldn't see anything happening for the next fifty years! So your doctor who likes to go fishing there can rest easy.*

I think of you constantly – especially when I wake up and just before I drop off to sleep…when I take the tram to the library every day; but I feel your presence most of all when I wander upstairs to the Dodo at lunchtime. I remember our first kiss there and then that crazy naked proposal at the farm. The answer is yes, yes, yes. I can think of nothing more fulfilling than to share a future with you. I realise that the post will have ground to a halt by the time you receive this letter, but oh, please try to phone me from the store; although I realise that you'll be inhibited in what you say, knowing that the whole of Zululand will be listening in on the party line.

I've not mentioned the subject to the parents yet, but I suspect that they will have guessed. I don't have to tell you, dear one, that all this will be a massive upheaval for me and them, as we are so close as a small family, but I look forward to it so very much.

Avian news…we've begun to see white woolly-necked storks in our garden. They no longer appear to be migrating and we've spotted a breeding pair which is quite settled. Perhaps it's a good omen? Here follows a report of other bird visitors over the last week, Sunday sunset to Saturday sunset. Where do you keep these schedules after making the comparison – in your bird book? 70.19.7. HEEI HSTC TPTH OOFT HCGT CCTP PHUC OOGP HTT

As usual, it'll be interesting to see how the pattern of their visits compares with their Zululand cousins. I pass on the info, regularly, to the ornithologist based at the museum, who gets quite excited about this type of anecdotal study. Have you seen any woolly-necked storks?

Call me soon, Mad Love, Dodo.

He tucked the letter into the bird book Prue had given him, with the intention of deciphering the coded part at the end of the day.

At suppertime, he was startled by the content of the message he decoded between forkfuls of curry and rice, which read, 'I'm expecting a baby – tell me now if you want to call it off,' which set his mind racing. It was too late in the day to set off to the store, but he jotted down the words; he would telephone a telegram through to the Empangeni post office to reach her at the library, so spent the rest of the evening deciding on various options and settled on: DELIGHTED NEWS PLAN VISIT TO ASK FATHER PERMISSION – SET DATE NUPTIALS OXEN SHOWING SIGNS NAGANA   DONALD.

★★★

"I'm glad to see you managed to get through!" Jardine said, after the mud-splattered Kelpie had been reversed, tyre chains clanking, up the steep drive to the house and abandoned beside the Jardine Nash.

"Well done. We were expecting you, but weren't sure when you would arrive," boomed Jardine, as he emerged from the French Windows. "You've appeared just in time for sundowners."

Donald introduced a weary Eric as he clambered out of the car and mentioned that a friend from Ntambanana, Toby Strafford, had managed to book them into the Durban Club, as his guests.

Eric Schnurr and Donald had agreed to share the slithery and bone-shaking drive all the way to Durban from Ntambanana – permitting Eric to be at Marie's side until the birth of her child, despite the obstacle thrown up by the railway strike.

"Our daughter's not home yet…it's the strike…the trams aren't running to time. It's awkward when the plebeians take to the hills. We're experiencing our very own 'secessio plebis' and 'mons sacer'. We patricians better tread carefully. Are your coolies striking?" asked Cordelia.

"Not that we're aware of, no Roman mobs, although a few of them are so idle that it might be the case that we haven't noticed yet; there's always the odd skellum, but most of them pull their weight."

"You must stay to dinner," Cordelia said, and was about to bustle away to alert Jeeves and to muster kitchen reinforcements, when Donald said, "Might we take up that dinner invitation for tomorrow? We're both pretty bushed and I think Eric is rather keen to see his wife at the maternity home early this evening. Of course, I'd like to wait for Prue to get home and the thought of a sundowner is pretty irresistible to both of us."

"Well, at least you must have some sandwiches while you wait. Our kitchen-slaves had prepared some anyway, as we didn't know what time you would make it."

Jeeves was quick to respond to Cordelia's bell-push summons, and appeared wheeling the drinks trolley onto the front verandah. She said to Eric, "This is Jeeves, our majordomo, without whom the Jardine household would fall apart. Jeeves, this is Master Schnurr, and of course you remember Master Kirkwood. They've just arrived from Zululand. Jeeves likes reading P G Wodehouse books ever since Prue brought home *Something New* from the library. I think you're looking 'gruntled' this evening, aren't you, Jeeves?" whereupon Jeeves giggled, then bowed to them before disappearing back down the hall.

"Wodehouse's playing around with words like 'disgruntled' and 'gruntled' is a great source of permanent merriment between us," Cordelia said. "And we're all gruntled this evening because you two have arrived, safe and sound. Eric, what is an American doing in the depths of wildest Zululand?"

"Eric and his wife Marie are the mainstays of our little community," Donald said, and mentioned Eric's role as ex-servicemen's representative, farmer, and cotton expert, and extolled on the splendour of Marie's catering.

"Yes, but that doesn't explain why he's American."

"I'm married to a South African girl of colonial French extraction whose parents farm sugar in Natal. I served in a voluntary ambulance corps in France while President Wilson was dithering; so that's how I wound up representing ex-servicemen's interests, by default, in Ntambanana."

"That explains it, then."

"Marie and I met in London."

"Ah, here's Dodo," said Keswick, brightening, as Prue walked up the steps to the verandah, clutching a gramophone record and a book. She kissed her father and mother – then Donald, who introduced her to Eric. Although houses high on the Berea escape the worst of the summer heat, Durban's November humidity is seldom kind to a girl's hair, and unless clothes are kept flimsy, heat and perspiration soon take their toll; yet Prue survived such challenges and appeared crisp and cool, despite having to walk from the tram stop and up the Jardine drive. The birthmark on her neck gave her away to her mother's perceptive eye, however, because she blushed when she kissed Donald, making the strawberry mark more pronounced.

"Hello," she said to all of them. "Gosh, it's sweltering in town," and then, turning to the two men, said, "I'm so pleased that you m-m-anaged to break away from your farms for a few days. You must be bushed after that drive. Damned strike, it's disrupted everything."

Donald explained that they were just staying for welcome drinks, then driving to Eric's wife's maternity home and that they were booked in at the club for an early night.

"Maternity home? Oh yes, of course…no facilities in Zululand for the usual home births. Dodo, they're coming to dinner tomorrow night," Cordelia said, as she studied the interplay between Prue and Donald.

"Mr Jardine, is there any opportunity we might meet up in town tomorrow?" asked Donald. "For lunch, perhaps? I'd like to ask your technical advice about something rather complicated…somewhere near your office at the docks? Eric will be away seeing his wife, so it'll be just me."

"Why, yes, I'd be pleased to, although I might not be the right man; but I'm sure I could put you in touch with someone. Light lunch at the Royal perhaps…in the palm court? It's not terribly far from my office…twelve-thirty then, although I won't be able to stay long. It's just across the road from the library, so is Dodo going to join us?" to which Prue quickly responded with, "I can't tomorrow, Daddy, I'll be in an endless, dreary m-m-meeting with booksellers which I can't get out of. It was arranged a long time ago, finger-lunch and all." Prue knew full well what Donald was up to and plotted to stay well clear.

"What's that record you were clutching, Prue, when you came in?" asked Keswick, as he poured another whisky for Cordelia and sandwiches were circulated.

"It's dynamite in the wrong hands. Filatov's wife – you remember Filatov, Donald – brought it into the library when she was changing the children's books and said I must listen to it, perhaps in the hope of turning me into a raving Bolshevik revolutionary. Her husband made it to Moscow and somehow got the record back to her. It's a speech by Lenin, read in English by a party faithful and titled: *How The Working People Can Be Saved From The Oppression Of The Landowners And Capitalists For Ever* by V. I. Lenin."

"Well, perhaps we can play a little bit of it before dinner tomorrow night. It could be an interesting topic of debate; your mother will love it," Jardine said, with eyes a-twinkling.

"It's very worn, having been listened to m-many times before it reached Mrs Filatov in Durban, and there is a crack in the record which makes the needle jump, she told me. It's a curiosity, but it's unsettling."

"But if Eric is to see his wife this evening, you two should be leaving almost immediately."

The palm court was quite full and the turbaned waiters were kept busy. The beautiful Indian girl with the betelnut-stained teeth was still there, behind the counter, and Jardine was late. Donald was mesmerised by the waiters having to push palm fronds aside every time they had to access the kitchen.

"Ah, Donald," he said, as he sat down. Jardine was a large man, and the bentwood chair squeaked in complaint.

"I was delayed by the shambles down at the docks. We've had to back up ships outside the harbour...beginning to look like wartime again. Even though the crane-drivers are working the manual labour isn't, so the army's helping out; but there's a certain skill to unloading, and the army lads are a bit green. Shall we order? What's the technical problem you want advice on?"

"I'm afraid I've got you here under false pretences. I really want to ask you if I may marry Prue."

"My dear fellow, what delightful news! Does Delia know? Obviously you've talked the whole thing over with Prue. Has she agreed? Prue's over twenty-one, so she can do as she pleases, so I appreciate your old-world courtesy in asking my permission."

"No, I haven't talked to Mrs Jardine about our intentions yet, and to answer your second question, yes, Prue has accepted, subject to your approval."

"Dodo is no hothouse flower, but do you think she'll cope as a farmer's wife? She does have a responsible job and loves books and her work. Do you not think that she might miss all that?"

"We've discussed that at length, and she said that it would indeed be a wrench, but an exciting challenge, which includes various opportunities, such as part-time teaching in the little school with Mrs Siedle, starting an extension library, farm responsibilities, and the routine of running a household. There is another important consideration – and I must emphasize that Prue accepted well before the next development...she's expecting our child."

"Ah. That puts another colour to it. Good heavens, two surprises over a lunch when I thought I was here to discuss farm machinery...of course Delia will be delighted, and so will I, as soon as it's all sunk in. I'll have to ask you, what security would you provide for Prue?"

"Well, first of all to co-sign an ante-nuptial contract, designed to protect her interests and whatever she brings into the marriage. I inherited a considerable sum when my father died. He went to great lengths to see that my two sisters were left comfortably off as well; so when I was working at the Durban bank, after I was discharged from the BSAP when von Lettow-Vorbeck surrendered, I bought a property here with a small portion of the capital, on the north side of the Umgeni River. The rest of the nest egg I put into gilts, except for funds reasonably reserved for the farm. The hilltop house is a bit remote for the while, but the town will expand northwards and inland in the years to come, so I think it was a secure investment. Farming is a hazardous business, and all sorts of things can go wrong – droughts, crop failures, locusts – and so I'll protect her from financial insecurity. The farm will remain in my name but I will put ownership of the Durban property into Prue's. It's an old colonial house in a five-acre garden overlooking the sea. It's securely rented out and brings in a small but steady income. I'll make her the beneficiary of that, pay a monthly housekeeping and personal allowance into her bank or post office savings account as well, and, obviously, make her the sole beneficiary of my life insurance policies and investments. When children come along, we can always review all that, in keeping with the usual demands of education and inheritance."

"I can hear the mind of a banker at work there! I can't say how pleased I am – I'll telephone through the news to Delia when I get back to the docks, although I suspect she will have guessed – y'know, female intuition – which reminds me, I must dash! We'll miss Dodo…tight-knit little family and all that. Do your best to keep close to us after marriage. We'll see you tonight."

"I predict that you'll be seeing a lot of us in the years

ahead...at the farm and down here – railways permitting!" Donald said, as they rose and shook hands warmly.

"The enemies of the people, the landowners and capitalists, say that the workers and peasants cannot live without them. 'If it were not for us,' they say, 'there would be nobody to maintain order, to give work, and to compel people to work. If it were not for us, everything would collapse, and the state would fall to pieces. We have been driven away, but chaos will bring us back again.' But this sort of talk by the landowners and capitalists will not confuse, intimidate, or deceive the workers and peasants," By this time, the needle had reached the damaged grooves and the voice repeatedly jumped to other parts of the recording, until it settled onto the word 'collapse' which it repeated and repeated, over and over again, until Keswick put it out of its misery by lifting the spindle and clicking the turntable to a halt, then closing the lid. It was a recent acquisition and still a novelty.

"Only in a Durban household like ours would a daughter start the evening by playing us the voice of a Russian forecasting a catastrophic and perhaps dystopian future for us!" Jardine said. "At least we were saved from listening to a full three minutes-worth."

"It sent shivers down my spine. Just imagine...all those Indians and Zulus rising up and executing us, like the Bolsheviks are doing in Russia!" said Cordelia.

Donald had collected Prue by car from the library earlier on, and the family was sitting on the Jardine front verandah enjoying sundowners, except for Prue, who stuck to tonic water. Eric had bowed out of the invitation to join them for dinner, pleading the need to be at his wife's side, so the gathering was limited to Donald and the family.

"Donald and Prue, I cannot say how delighted I am at the news. We can debate Lenin's diatribe against capitalism over dinner, but what we need to talk about is your plans. Oh, this is exciting!" Cordelia said. "Jeeves, we have some important news, Dodo and Mr Kirkwood are planning to get married!"

"Goodness gracious! That's jolly, jolly good, missy Dodo. Where are you going to live?"

"On Master Kirkwood's farm in Zululand."

"That's velly long way away. Will you come to see us sometime?"

"Of course, Jeeves. Remember I'm still working at the library for m-m-onths and you and your wife m-must come to the wedding. Not a big, big wedding, just with our special friends."

"Well, well, well," he said, and went away chuckling to the kitchen to tell his wife, Anaisha, the resident cook.

To Donald's relief, and despite the Jardine's high social ranking, it was agreed that it would be a relatively quiet wedding a fortnight into the New Year, on a Saturday ("Mother, January's the sweatiest time of the year!"). The ceremony would be in St Thomas Old Church on the Berea, with Prue warning Cordelia not to get carried away on an ever-expanding invitation list, ("Mother, the chapel can only seat thirty!")

"Where are you planning to take your bride for a honeymoon, Donald?" asked Cordelia. Donald was taken aback at the rapid development of these life-changing events, and replied, on the spur of the moment, that perhaps the Victoria Falls Hotel would be worth considering. "I believe that Union Castle Line has reintroduced the 'Round Africa' trip, with a breakaway included to the Vic Falls Hotel, by train from Cape Town or Beira through Bulawayo. We could return by train to Beira then back by liner to Durban. Just an immediate idea, but I need to know what Prue has in mind. We'll have to be back on the farm by mid-February.

I'm told that viewing the moonlight rainbow at the Falls is spell-binding."

"Ooh, that sounds lovely!" said Prue.

"I believe that Union Castle has introduced two new ships –the Arundel and the Windsor Castles. It could be a good trip...in calm weather!" Keswick said.

Keswick and Donald sat sipping their whiskies, saying little, as the particulars of wedding, guests, bridesmaid, banns, clothes, catering, flowers, banquet, speeches and honeymoon were addressed with brio by mother and daughter, particularly by Cordelia, who said that, while it would be an Anglican wedding, it would be appropriate to invite their friend, a Presbyterian minister, to participate, it being the blending of two Scottish clans, the Jardines and the McGregors. And thus elements of a Scottish wedding should be kept foremost.

"Who'll be your best man, Donald?"

"I hadn't thought about it yet...probably Toby Strafford or Jean-Pierre Meyer, although Toby might be stuck on his farm – he's managing my farm as well, while I'm away. Jean-Pierre Meyer and I go sailing on Durban Bay, when I'm down."

"I'm glad they've chosen the old chapel – that is, if they can get a booking," said Keswick. "No doubt, Delia'll be on the phone to Reverend Potter as soon as day breaks tomorrow. (We call him 'Juniper' because his initials are JNP). Although it's small, it's redolent with history, as many of Durban's founding families are buried there, including the Gardiners. The story is told that the congregation was once trapped inside the original structure because a lioness had chosen to sun herself outside the only entrance. The little side lane is named after Gardiner's daughter, Julia, who died at eleven and is buried there."

With the men marginalised, Keswick's attention wandered

and he asked Donald about the condition of his cattle, as Prue had mentioned the trouble with nagana.

"It's not good news. My small span has died, despite the efforts of the vet to save them. There's just no cure. Anaemia…gets into the heart, brain and skeletal muscle. It's the same news for my neighbours, and it's killing off their sheep and goats, as well. Toby and I are sharing his Model T truck for the moment as the ox-wagon can't be used. For ploughing next year, it looks as if I'll have to hire the state steam tractors, and that's going to be costly, this time. The best option would be to find a tractor of my own, but they're few and far between. I took advantage of my Durban visit to go and see Chapard, the Ford dealer, but there's not much hope of getting a Fordson tractor – they were all shipped to the UK for their war effort. I've heard of an invention by Ferguson, an Irishman. It's a plough that can be hitched to a Model T. It's a good idea and could be a stop-gap – that is, if I can locate one."

"I can't promise anything, but I'll make some enquiries among the shippers," Jardine said. "Who knows? Now the war's over, there might be surplus Fordson tractor stock knocking around in the UK. I'll see what I can find out about the Ferguson plough as well."

"Thank you. We could hire it out when not in use on our farm, as there are a lot of neighbouring farmers in the same predicament."

"That's the banker talking again! Ladies! There's the dinner gong and it's time to get behind the mosquito netting."

It was a practice, in the Jardine household, to introduce a challenging topic during dinner, be there guests present or not. It originated during Prue's early childhood in Singapore, to stimulate her cultural development and make family meal-times forever novel and attractive. The tradition of debate was continued when the Jardines settled in Durban. Guests were often taken off-guard, as was Donald, who was unaccustomed to be challenged for his opinions between mouthfuls.

"Meat's in short supply because of the strike so, after the soup, we're making do with roast chicken and the entire trimmings this evening, Donald; Anaishe's speciality, although Jeeves is the past master of the roast potatoes. No one's allowed near the kitchen area during preparation. Anaishe refuses to provide details of her secret ingredients, but Jeeves has hinted that they include avocado oil, rosemary, thyme and lemons…and, of course, garlic, deprived of which the entire Indian population here would expire. What do you think of Lenin's ideas, Donald?"

"First, a toast!" interrupted Jardine, after ensuring that glasses were filled, then, rising from his chair: "Donald and Dodo, may your marriage be the happiest in Zululand, blessed with many children and much prosperity! We will welcome you as our new-found son."

Cordelia remained seated but joined him in the toast, saying that he should join them for Christmas, before Donald rose in turn to reply, with "To my wonderful Prue, and her wonderful parents!" and then sat again. He was neither accustomed to making speeches, even at a family dinner table, nor able to embroider on matters of the heart.

"So what do you think of all this Lenin stuff, Donald? If our local proletariat rose up, butchered us and took over, would they be able to run the country?"

Donald was about to say, "No," when Prue interrupted and said, "There's another element, closer to home. The book I brought with me was an archive of Gandhi's correspondence with our administrators, and several speeches he m-m-ade.

I know it's not polite to read at the dinner table, but I'd like to, when the roast has been cleared away…so, may I?"

In due course, Prue fetched the archive to the table and handed it to Keswick, pointing to a passage for him to read.

> *The Indians and the English spring from a common Indo-Aryan stock, but a prevailing belief in the Colony is that the Indians are little better than the natives of Africa, with the result that the Indian is being dragged down to the position of a raw Kaffir* [I'm paraphrasing here]. *He describes the latter as being content to acquire enough cattle to buy a wife, and then pass life in indolence and nakedness. Elsewhere he demands that natives should not be allowed to live alongside Indians in a location, and that they should be withdrawn.*

Prue said that, in response to the White League's agitation against Indian immigration, he wrote elsewhere that the whites in South Africa should remain the dominant race.

"There's another entry which alludes to the separate entrances for whites and natives existing at the Durban Post Office. He objected to being classed as a native and demanded that there should be another separate entrance for Indians."

"Well, Donald, what do you think about all that?" asked Cordelia.

"They're caught in a sandwich, neither fish nor fowl, to mix metaphors," he replied. "Perhaps the Indian Congress should adopt the mushroom as its emblem, being neither animal nor vegetable."

"Ah, but Indians are of flesh!" Cordelia reflected.

"Then I'm flummoxed! I'm unaccustomed to enter such family debates over meals, though I find it very refreshing, so I'll do my best to offer a reasoned reply.... Not long after I arrived in Africa I realised that different race attitudes existed and this was underscored during the conflict in East Africa, where the native porters were regarded, on both sides, as expendable...there were plenty more where they came from...an attitude which I found very distasteful, as was our living off the land with impunity. But I think that lumping Indians with natives is a political mistake – even though granting them enhanced privileges will be resented by the Zulus, who regard them as intruders, as they do the whites. The Indians are going to remain in this country – most of them, whether the powers-that-be like it or not.

"Glancing at Lenin's Russia: while the 'plebeian' takeover is a frightening development, some form of restructuring was long overdue; yet it has led to chaos, genocide, destruction of the bourgeoisie and long-term misrule. The implication for us whites is pretty clear, that the long-term suppression of the labouring classes could result in our overthrow."

"I'm going to corroborate that view with an observation of my own," said Keswick. "And as it's now fashionable, in the Jardine household, to read out things while dining," (here he winked at Prue), "I'm going to read out something from this morning's *Advertiser*. I cut it out and here it is," he said, putting on his spectacles: "It's a report of what that economist said at the Paris Peace Conference. His name is John Maynard Keynes and he walked out of the gathering when his protestations were swept aside, during negotiations concerning the imposition of punitive sanctions against the Germans. I'll just read the juicy bits (excuse my interrupting you, Donald). *The policy of reducing Germany to servitude for a generation, of degrading the lives of millions of human beings...should be abhorrent and detestable, even if it enriched ourselves, even if it did not show the decay of the whole civilised life of Europe. If we aim, deliberately, at the impoverishment of Central Europe, vengeance, I dare predict, will not limp far behind. Nothing can then delay for very long that final war between the forces of Reaction and the despairing convulsions of Revolution, before which the horrors of the late German war will fade into nothing.*' It rambles on, but you get the picture. Sorry, Donald; please go on."

"In all cases, including the Irish 1916 revolt against British Rule, it's reaction to deprivation, suppression or marginalisation. Prue and I heard General Smuts saying much the same thing about the German predicament at the League of Nations briefing we attended here at the Arthur Smith Hall."

"I believe that the development of some form of qualified franchise in South Africa – a safety valve – should be the objective...qualification to vote, measured by reasonable economic and educational standards, applied to the entire population, Indian, native, Cape coloured and white – even if it would result in the exclusion of some whites (there could be a sunset clause to get around that). Aspiration to qualify should be stimulated by a uniform standard of education (while taking into account cultural variations) and the gradual levelling of living standards. That's the golden ideal, but, in the present circumstances, with such uneven literacy levels, built-in prejudices, primitive beliefs and horrific ignorance, it's highly unlikely ever to come about. In fact, I'm led to believe that powerful elements are at work," (here he glanced at Prue) "to reverse whatever benevolent reforms are being considered."

"You're right. I believe that the Durban Town Council is preparing a Land Alienation Ordinance which will exclude Indians from ownership or occupation of property in designated white areas," Prue said.

"Nevertheless, qualified franchise could be something worth working towards," Donald concluded.

There was a silence, broken by Prue who playfully nudged him gently in the ribs and said, "You see, Dear Parents, that's why I chose this farmer."

Jeeves and Anaishe had entered with the dessert and the cheeses while Donald was talking, and remained near the doorway until Donald had finished speaking. Keswick turned to the two and said, "What do you think about all that, Jeeves?"

"We would like to stay sandwiches – not mushrooms," Jovan said, and they both giggled.

Chapter Sixteen

The port of Durban divides the 'north coast' of Natal from the 'south coast'. Queen's Bridge over the Umgeni River marked the point where the very long Umgeni Road out of town became the North Coast Road on the far side of the bridge. The tram line from the Durban Post Office terminated before an ignominious mound of weed-covered ground just before the bridge and the level crossing. Trains heading for Zululand would pull out of Umgeni Station and hold up such traffic as there was at the winking red lights level crossing, before chuffing and chugging on, to clatter and whistle over the river on another girder bridge, a quarter of a mile upstream.

It was over Queen's Bridge that Donald drove Prue. They wheeled to the right along Riverside Road for a while, and then turned up steep Buttery Road to reach the cooler air of Umgeni Heights. Antelope and some smaller wildlife still clung on in clusters of remaining coastal forest, coping with urban advance, and the Kelpie startled a dappled bushbuck ewe and her lamb, which melted into the trees as they approached.

At the crest, and around another bend of the road, Prue saw an old colonial house nestled beside huge old fig trees at the end of a long laterite drive.

"This is Chelmsford," Donald said, as the car squeaked to a halt before the house. "I alerted the Buckles yesterday to our visit and to allay any fears they might have about security of tenure, I explained that we were engaged, in case she didn't notice your ring!"

Tea was served on the front verandah, with its panorama of the river estuary below and the Indian Ocean beyond. After tea, Verna Buckle said, "Let me show you the summer house," and led them down a path lined with forest mahogany trees to an open structure on the edge of the cliff, with a thatched roof.

It so happened that the Zululand train, far below, was crossing the Umgeni rail bridge, belching smoke from its chimney and steam from its nostrils, and whistling a rich Garratt chord while the carriage wheels set up a regular 'teDUM, teDUM…/ teDUM, teDUM…'

"That's the train to your new home," Donald said, turning to Prue.

"Some pedestrians like to take a short cut home on the railway bridge so the driver's giving everyone a warning. I watch our children crossing the nearer Queen's Bridge on their way to catch the tram, every school day morning. We always make a point of waving to each other…I do, holding a big white handkerchief…Can you see 'lovers' leap'? That's what we call the big flat boulder jutting out there, just below the edge…it'll dislodge one day, if they keep on quarrying," Verna continued.

"I love Chelmsford…especially when the valley fills with mist and we seem to be floating above the clouds… Bushbuck steal into the lower garden, when the mist drifts in, and they stand there like ghosts. I don't mind their eating some of my shrub leaves occasionally, but it annoys me when they take a liking to my flowers. They eat the bark of some trees too."

Prue was holding Donald's hand and she squeezed it.

When he glanced down at her he saw that her eyes were filled with tears.

"Of course, it's not all paradise. My husband had to shoot a boomslang he saw in one of our mango trees last weekend. I hope it hasn't got a mate – and then there's the blasting at the quarry down below…at noon every weekday. We get the occasional chip of bluestone landing in the garden, and you can't eat the guavas here because they're wormy, though the fruit bats like them. The children can hear the cry of bats, d'you know; they say they give high-pitched hoots, like very tiny steam-engines. But, with that said, the bush is alive with birds. Our bedroom faces the ocean and the dawn chorus wakes us. We can hear the chatter of thousands of birds wafting up from the valley, before the Indian mynahs wake up and drown out the other birds. Look! There's a paradise fly-catcher with long tail feathers fluttering along. How do they manage to fly like that during the mating season, one wonders? My husband can identify most of the birds, but I'm afraid I'm still far behind. Even the children know more than I do. Oh! Now I know where I've seen you! Aren't you the girl in the Children's Library?"

"Yes, that's me!"

"You're always so helpful to the children. Last time I was in with them, I couldn't help thinking 'now there's a fine catch for a young man!' – Donald, you're to be congratulated for your discernment!"

Driving home, Prue said, with eyes shining, "What a wonderful house – and I liked Verna too. How did you come across it?"

"I saw the house advertised while idling through the paper, during a lunch break. It was a deceased estate, standing empty and in a sorry state, when I visited, but I thought it would make a good investment if I renovated it…so I did.

The Buckles are excellent tenants...impeccable about the rent. Buckle served in East Africa, but, like most people after the war, didn't have the capital to buy. He holds down a good job at the sugar refinery, so circumstances might change in the long run. If they make an offer to buy it'll be over to you, after we're married, to decide what to do with it."

"I've fallen in love with the place and I know you have too, so I don't think I'd ever part with it."

It was an early December Sunday morning at Yonder and the wall-thermometer already stood at 70 degrees Fahrenheit. The workers had the day off to tend to their distant vegetable gardens. In the fields, the cotton had reached the height of an average potato plant, so Donald could expect them to double in size and flower at about Christmas time, if conditions remained favourable. This meant that the bolls would burst open in June, ripe for harvesting.

"It's going to be a scorcher," Toby said, tapping the thermometer. "It'll be 90 by this afternoon, if we don't get the usual thunderstorm." As had become the custom, he had motored over for one of Chinnamama's breakfast offerings, bringing Mrs Potgieter's eggs with him and the week's batch of papers from the store. Conversation on the front verandah, as they waited for breakfast, was desultory, punctuated by the occasional crackle and rustle of pages being turned and slapped flat for reading.

"I see Carter and Carnarvon are back in Thebes again, trying to find old Tutankhamun. They've been at it for years, digging up Egypt, despite 'belli intermititur'…"

"That's not exactly riveting. Anything else worth reporting?"

"Well, back in India, our little friend Gandhi has been protesting against the Black Act…meaning any perceived troublemaker or revolutionary can be locked up without trial and judicial review for two years. In protest he and his mates went and bathed in the sea at Bombay, as part of the non-cooperation movement. I can't quite see the significance of that. I think the Act is simply an extension of wartime measures, because the powers fear an uprising. With all those starving millions revolting, it could be the end of Britain in India."

"Well, suppression and exploitation never succeed in the long run."

"Suppression and exploitation…is that what you think?"

"Yes. Look at Russia. When are you expecting the Broccardos?"

"At about ten. They'd have had to set off from 'Pangeni at about eight, so I suggested that we should meet up here and then all go over to the Schnurrs together for the service and christening, if that's okay. Sonya's coming."

"I'd be very surprised if she wasn't," Donald said.

"Her mother has been invited to be godmother. Young Joy is coming too. I wouldn't be surprised if the Shorts will have decided to travel in convoy with them and the Bells, to cope with any breakdowns."

"Who's the godfather?"

"Jim Bell."

"She was born with a silver spoon in her mouth all right!"

Every third Sunday, Reverend Short and his wife, Mary, would travel to the Ntambanana settlement to conduct a service under the Schnurr's huge flamboyant tree. They never looked forward to these journeys, because negotiating the road challenged their endurance.

"Schnurr told me that Marie's parents are already there, but Eric's father is too old to travel from the States."

"How are your labour-management skills developing?" asked Donald, between page turnings. "I've identified supervisor-material in the Indian labour group, called Malika Ramsammy (he prefers to be called 'Sammy'). He's turned out to be the spokesman for the field labourers, and seems to be trusted by them, so I have appointed him as supervisor. This has meant a better wage and improved living conditions, subject to his performing well. I wrote out a contract (with penalty clauses), which he and I have signed, in front of our storekeeper and his blacksmith. I'm just about to attach that to his door…" (Here, Donald broke off and brought over a slat of wood marked 'कृषिपर्यवेक्षक'). "He'll have no jurisdiction over domestic staff – that's Layani's sphere. Only Layani and Chinnamama rule the roost here."

"Good heavens! What on earth do those squiggles mean?"

"I hope it means 'agricultural supervisor' in Hindi. Sammy read it out to me as something like 'krshi paryavekshak'. I got the Indian blacksmith to paint it on for me. It could be the words for an ancient Indian curse, for all I know; but it seemed to please him mightily. He visibly swelled with pride. Now I'll have to teach him how to be one."

"Sounds pretty shipshape; you'll be putting up a Hindi 'chief cook' in Chinnamama's kitchen next! But seriously though, let me know how it goes. So far, my arrangements are un-naval and pretty casual. I caught one in the kitchen the other day, stealing sugar and cutlery."

"So what did you do? Flog him?" It was said with irony, as on some estates this remained a form of punishment, which both Donald and Toby disavowed.

"I got Sergeant Muller to come over and give him a verbal blasting in public and a warning shot across the bows, but didn't lay a charge…got the cutlery back, not the sugar. Cut a week's worth of wages and left it at that. The thing is they don't care if they're put in jail. The thinking is that they don't have to work so hard, and the food, they say, is better; but he's been a model of good behaviour ever since."

"Leopards don't change their spots very often."

"Well, let's see."

Many of the petty crimes, and, far less frequent, major ones, committed by indentured Indians working on estates could be attributed to the expression of frustration, and evidenced in the excessive use of dagga (cannabis), alcoholism and petty theft. They could be seen as the physical production of despair, deprivation and escapism. From the early days of indentured labour, certain 'crimes' could be ascribed to the rigid conditions of employment – for example, before the scheme of indentured labour was abandoned in 1911, an indentured labourer was not permitted to travel outside the estate unless rare written permission was given by the estate manager. From that date, and until after the First World War, such conditions began to wither away, but it took a long time before old practices disappeared. Disdain by whites and a great deal of suspicion remained.

"I see your cotton is thriving, like mine," Donald said as Chinnamama's breakfast arrived with a motherly clatter and a "You must eat now. Food hot. Quick-quick."

"I sometimes think that she regards us as children, but there's nothing better than her fried bread and eggs with brinjals and tomatoes to start Sunday, even though there's no bacon. Schnurr forecasts that my cotton will flower by Christmas…that's about the standard seventy days; but I'll have to wait for another three months before the bolls burst open, and then there's another long wait. I won't be harvesting cotton before late June."

"Same here; but the Rutherfords are reporting poor early development."

"Well, Bob only planted in the middle of November, that's why. How's your banana grove coming on? You remember I put up trellises for the grenadilla vines? Not a good idea, as the Indians kept on telling me. They seem to be natural market gardeners...really have the knack. I suppose it's survival-knowledge, growing up in remote little villages in India...My vines were struggling from too little ground water over winter; but the pawpaw trees are thriving. I got wise and planted them in generous holes with a mixture of compost, ox-manure and soil. They'll be producing in a year – that's if the monkeys and birds don't eat the fruit first...so there's much to keep my few Indians gainfully employed in the interim, except one couple, who must go. They're always last with everything...erratic, I think they both drink cane spirit and smoke dagga. Bloodshot eyes...either aggressive or half asleep. She always looks dirty and untidy. Fortunately, they don't have any children. They could cause trouble when I dismiss them, but Sammy, my tame supervisor, agrees with me. His bonus is diminished by their erratic behaviour.... . What did you get for the Schnurr infant? I was at a bit of a loss, so ordered a pusher-and-spoon set from a jeweller I met in Durban, called Leo Ferrer. Aren't pushers what infants usually get? I hope the Schnurrs won't be awash with them!"

"Oh, hell, that's quite grand. I'm just giving a fiver in an envelope."

"Well, the pusher cost about the same – it was the registered postage which was the killer. Look, you and I have been through a lot together, so it's appropriate that you should be the first to know...in Zululand. I'm engaged to be married."

"Oh, Good Lord, another good man bites the dust! Who's the girl? She must be pretty exceptional after Emily."

"Yes, she is. Her name's Prue Jardine, and I've known her

almost as long as Emily. It's probable that Emily and I would have married, but the Spanish finished all that. I'll tell you more in due course, but would you consider being my Best Man? You're a good sort and, being a naval man, you're a good organiser. Prue's father is Durban's Harbour Master, so you'd have lots to talk about."

"Of course, I'd be honoured. When and where?"

"Durban, on the last Saturday in January."

"It'll be hot and steamy in Durban, in more ways than one, at that time of the year! Well, well, well! At least everything will be at a standstill on our farms, for the same reason."

The font was a fluted porcelain basin borrowed from Marie's kitchen, half-filled with rainwater, which Short had blessed on the spot, and set on a draped coffee table. The christening followed the 'bring your own folding chairs' Sunday service conducted under the spreading flamboyant tree in the Schnurr garden. The tree was now in full vermilion flower and shot through by mauve-blooming bougainvillea, which had grown its thorny vines about the tree trunk and lower branches. Mary Short had handed out a mimeographed Order of Service to the friends gathered there.

Coddled in generations-old christening robes, brought by Marie's mother, the infant squirmed and wrinkled her small face as the Reverend Short trickled water three times over her head and said, "Françoise Élisabeth Marguerite Schnurr, I baptise thee in the name of the Father, and of the Son, and of the Holy Ghost," and then made the sign of the cross on her forehead. Élisabeth was a family name in the Schnurr family, while the other two were in honour of Marie's parents, from whose shared ancestors the given names Françoise and Marguerite sprang. The godparents standing beside the font were given lit candles to hold as Short explained, "By baptism into Christ you pass from darkness to light." The impact of the symbolism was lessened by the ceremony taking place in broad daylight, rendering the candle flames invisible. Nevertheless, the godparents, reading from the order paper, dutifully responded with, "Shine as a light in the world, to the glory of God the Father." The ceremony ended with a short passage about welcoming the child into the family of the church.

Storekeepers Piet and Hannah van Jaarsveld and Padraig and Marie O'Grady had been invited to the reception after the christening, as had little Mrs Potgieter, and while they stood together for a while, it was clear that they felt out of place when the volume of English voices grew louder after drinks were circulated. They started to slip away discreetly, when Eric Schnurr caught up with them and thanked them effusively for their baptismal gifts and for their attendance.

Out of earshot, Hannah said to Mrs Potgieter, "Oof! Die geraas! Ons gaan oorval word deur al hierdie rooineks – nou is daar nog een." [The noise! We're going to be swamped by rooineks – and now there's another one of them.] They were members of the Nederduitsch Hervormde Kerk, the NHK, so could not countenance attending an Anglican service, but were not restricted from sharing in a social celebration.

(The NHK was a breakaway church from the NGK [Nederduitse Gereformeerde Kerk – Dutch Reformed Church] which had been brought to the Cape by the Dutch East India Company in 1652. When England annexed the Cape Colony in 1806, colony funds continued to provide support for the Dutch church. Ultimately, however, Dutch clerics refused to serve in a British-controlled colony, so were replaced by Dutch-speaking Scottish Presbyterians, sympathetic to English interests. Upon the great exoduses of 1830 and 1840 by Dutch farmers rejecting British rule,

NGK ministers declined to accompany them; thus the NHK came into being as an autonomous body when the trekkers ultimately established republics in the Orange Free State and the Transvaal, where it became recognised as the state religion. The original spelling of 'Nederduitsch Hervormde' was retained. Some Dutch ministers had been persuaded to join the treks and were instrumental in founding the new church movement.)

Liquor had begun to loosen tongues when Meiring joined the Bell and Broccardo party, after tripping over a tuft of grass and slopping his drink, and said, "Did you hear about that panga ashack?"

He had broken the top plate of his dentures and had had to leave it at home, so his pronunciation was affected; nevertheless he ploughed on.

Sonya had a desire to giggle, but then the import of what he was saying brought her up short.

"No, tell us," Toby said.

"Blarry kayers bwoke into the Hendershon's farmhoush while he wash away and attacked Julie Hendershon when she went to inwestigate. They were as high as kites on booze and dagga, slashed her wight arm and the fingersh of her left hand before she managed to shoot one of them dead. They wanted money, booze and guns, but ran away into the bushes, leaving the dead one in the kischen. Strange that the kitchen staff didn't hear anything. Julie said she shrieked her head off when they attacked. The maid discovered the body early the nexl morning…blood everywhere…he had socks over his hands to avoid leaving fingerprintsh, I shpose. Julie was so shtunned that she couldn't move for the rest of the night. They found her just sitting on the floor and shivering from shock, still holding the shotgun."

A shudder went through the group as many thought how remote and vulnerable their own farms were.

"My God! Lucky she had the gun ready. Did they catch them?"

"Not sho far. Dr Lombard got there quickly with a poleeshman, when Julia's kitchen boy managed to work out how to yewsh the party-line phone and told the wishboard operator who parshed on the meshage. Lombard patched her up. Dick Hendershon is shattered that he was away when it happened."

"Did they leave anything else?"

"The panga – apparently it belongs to one of the Hendershon's farmworkers."

"Well, with the body of one of them too, that's more than a head start – they must have left behind a lot of other evidence as well."

"I forgot you were a combat policeman in East Africa, Donald. I could hear that in your response," Bell said.

"Not that I care to remember it," Donald replied.

"There's fear in 'Pangeni that they might try again and the Zululand Timesh is already headlining them as Panga-men."

Few farms in the 'Tam region had a party-line telephone, and it was difficult for owners to leave their farms unattended for very long, other than to visit Piet van Jaarsveld's co-op store, so these brief gatherings always provided a welcome opportunity for the quick exchange of news, major, minor and mere tittle-tattle. Donald once again noticed Sonya's beautiful, luminous eyes as she turned to Toby, and he observed their growing attraction.

Layani let the dogs out when Donald managed to steal away, back to Yonder, and they bounded towards him, with squeals and barks of happiness. Commenting on their behaviour,

Layani said in the usual jumble of languages and gestures, "Izinja muito felizes ukukubona!" [The dogs are happy to see you!] With more gestures, and imitating the sound of the motor, he indicated that they had become restless when they picked up the faint sound of the Kelpie approaching, well before he, Layani, had sensed it.

Donald was glad to escape the chatter at the Schnurrs and sat in his writing box, brandy at hand, to revel in solitude and commence writing to his sisters.

Dearest Winnie and Jeanie,

I'm sitting in a kind of light-box, a wooden frame tacked with muslin and fine-mesh mosquito-netting, big enough to house my rickety writing desk and a folding camp-chair, which Bess and Jesse, the 'ex-puppies', are now struggling to find enough room to curl under. The paraffin lamp on the desk is attracting all sorts of night insects which are flying onto the netting, trying to get in, including particularly noisy insects, which look like large pinkish moths but buzz like a beetle. Beyond lie the cotton fields and the African bush. All sorts of frogs, the occasional nightjar, and insects are serenading me and I can hear an assortment of wild animal noises as well, mostly far off. Viewed from a distance, it must seem strange… this glowing box beside an unlit house. I could write inside, now that it's roofed and floored, but I have grown accustomed to my cocoon, so just go on using it. I like being close to the night sounds.

Thank you, wee-Winnie, for your letter received months ago, enclosing the Scots Pine seeds and photographs. I am ashamed that I haven't replied for so long, my only excuse being that the farm and some other things have gnawed away at my time. But I have much good news (and some bad) – firstly, that several of the Scots Pine seeds you posted me have actually begun to sprout! This means that they will be acclimatised by the time they are saplings. I planted them reasonably close to the house and I'll make sure they're protected from trampling.

Secondly, although it has been a huge effort – clearing land, preparing the soil, weeding and planting, the cotton plants have begun to grow! I'm told I can expect blossom by Christmas-time, although the cotton will only burst many months later.

Thirdly – and this is life-changing, I'm engaged to be married early in the new year to a wonderful, beautiful and intelligent girl called Prue Jardine. Prue lives with her parents in Durban. She heads up the children's municipal library there and her father is Durban's Harbour Master (ancestors from Aberdeen). More details in my next letter, with photographs.

Now... would you and Jeanie like to attend the wedding? It will be in Durban. Prue and I will then disappear on honeymoon, possibly to Lourenço Marques, then by train to Bulawayo (to visit the Matopos, about 45 miles away) and ultimately Victoria Falls Hotel in Rhodesia. If Prue goes along with this (mark you, much depends on her say-so), you might consider joining us there (after a wee pause). Our party could then return home by train to Beira, from where we'd sail by Union Castle liner down to Durban again, with your staying on board, homeward bound, in due course, to London (via Southampton).

My thought is that it would be a good opportunity for the families to get to know each other.

Don't make any moves until I've discussed the whole thing with Prue. Until then, it remains just a secret idea. Who knows? Prue might prefer, rather, to show me Singapore, where she grew up. After I've talked to her, I'll let you know by cable. If it's yes, we can start planning.

Now, the bad news (for me): all my oxen have sickened and died from nagana, an incurable disease spread by the tsetse fly. It was miserable watching them fading away.. Neighbouring farmers have had similar experiences with their cattle. I'll have to get a tractor to replace them very soon, and these are hard to come by.

But a good little piece of news is that Jesse and Bess (need I remind you, named after Father's dogs in Scotland) are doing well. Jesse was the runt of the pack and I saved him as a newborn pup from being drowned by the owner. Although he was smaller than usual to start with, his legs have begun to grow in proportion with the rest of him, and even at this early stage, he has begun to develop into a particularly intelligent animal, an excellent (still yappy) watch-dog, and potentially a loyal hunter. Bess, the bitch, is also developing in the same way. Her party trick is to present me with leaves in her mouth. The natives call Rhodesian ridgebacks 'Izinja zeNgonyama', meaning 'lion dogs' because it's said that two of such animals can keep a lion at bay. Although we don't have any lion left in this part of the country (all shot out), there are plenty of other dangers and threats, not least big venomous snakes, hyenas, wildcats, leopards, cheetahs, buffalo and even honey badgers. The latter are ferocious predators of poultry, when they're not busy raiding wild bee hives – so I'm glad of the dogs' companionship and protection.

Say hello to Tommy and Mrs Hopkins. Write again soon with an answer and send more pictures!

Much love,
Donald

Chapter Seventeen

"Of course, we do realise that Jeeves was a valet, not a butler, although Bertie Wooster claimed, in the Wodehouse books, that he could 'buttle' very well indeed when called upon to do so; a valet being a sort of officer's batman, isn't he, rather than a household manager," observed Keswick Jardine. "We just ignore all that, as does Jeevan. He has thought of himself as a butler ever since he started reading those Wodehouse novels, although he may have misinterpreted Jeeves' function somewhat. Now he's enlisted a small army of his Indian relatives to serve as temporary waiters at the reception. I gather they all work at the Marine and the Royal as part-time waiters...they wear turbans and sashes as part of their workaday kit, so our guests might get the sense that they're participating in some sort of post-imperial marriage durbar. Oh, well, it'll all add atmosphere. That hammering and shouting you hear is Jeeves and his helpers erecting the marquee on the back lawn." Prue caught Donald's eye, as if to imply, wouldn't be nice to escape all the fuss.

The group was enjoying sundowners on the Jardine front verandah. Winnie and Jean had arrived in Durban aboard the Edinburgh Castle on the previous Thursday, full of their adventures; not least, a ducking during the Crossing the Line ceremony. There was much talk of their enjoying afternoon tea at Reid's Palace Hotel, when the liner called at

Funchal – Winnie saying that she had sat in the very chair occupied by Lloyd George when he had visited the island; Jean remaining agog at how very dark youngsters had dived for coins flung by passengers, during a stop at Lobito Bay. Prue had already taken them under her wing and a lasting friendship was developing. Toby and Donald had come down, first in the Kelpie, then by rail, from Empangeni, along with Bianca Broccardo, who had been persuaded out of her despondent state to chaperone Sonya and young Joy during their stay at the Marine, where Toby and Donald were also quartering along with the Kirkwood sisters. The reunion at the docks with Donald's sisters, Toby's and Sonya's growing mutual attraction, and young Joy's excitement at visiting the 'big city', all led to a sense of pleasant anticipation of the days to come. Despite her short exposure to shipboard life, Jean, as a previously cloistered schoolgirl, was far less worldly-wise than Joy and began to look to her for friendly leadership. Being of a practical mind, and reminded of her upbringing on a Scottish farm, Winnie was fascinated by the functioning of the unloading cranes, strange stilted creatures, and had stood staring up at them for a while. They seemed to her reminiscent of the creatures described by Wells in his *War of the Worlds*, which she had read on board ship.

"Between fluttering around the minister concerning the calling of the banns and arguing about who was to do the flowers, Delia's managed to winkle out some musicians from the Symphony Orchestra to serenade us at the reception," Keswick said, "and, I gather, hot it up for a spot of ceilidh dancing later. Prue has found a sitar player to provide a bit of unexpected Singapore sizzle, between the courses and the speeches. Although it's an Indian instrument, it was popular in Sing. while Prue was growing up. That'll startle our stuffy anti-Indian Durbanites somewhat, after they've been blasted with a spot of bagpipes leading the party into the wedding feast...the sitar player is yet another relative of Jeeves. I'm told that the lady pianist for the orchestral group is one of Cohen's part-time tinklers. She plays at the Electric Theatre. Wouldn't it be marvellous if the actors could talk instead?"

"Well, it may well come to pass!" Donald said. "I believe there was a demonstration of talking films at the Paris Exposition some years ago. It's all a matter of difficult synchronisation, they say. Meanwhile, a theatre manager might consider concealing actors and actresses behind a screen, to speak the words...it would be fun if they ever got all muddled up, or dropped their scripts!"

"It'll be a long time before pictures and sound can be married – if ever!"

"Winnie and Jean, were you in London during Lowell Thomas's show at the Drury Lane?"

"We were, and attended his series of lectures followed by short 'movies' of veiled women, Arab men with what looked like dishcloths on their heads, and camels. Thomas even had exotic dancers, performing in front of projected images of the pyramids, accompanied by the band of the Welsh Guards. The whole theatre reeked of incense from burners in the foyer. Lawrence of Arabia attended that performance and commented on some of the picture slides, before the film. He was dressed in Arab clothes."

"With all that exposure I suppose visiting Egypt and Middle Eastern countries will become romantically popular again, among those who can afford it."

"Lawrence spoke much of a place called 'Wadi Rum' in Jordan where he was based much of the time while on many operations, and showed a picture of a rock formation at the entrance to the camp called 'The Seven Pillars'," Winnie said. "What came through was that he was ashamed that

Britain had let the Arabs down at the League of Nations, after promising them the establishment of an independent Palestine, as a reward for their uprising against the Ottoman Empire during the war."

"Of course, the Germans were equally duplicitous during the war," said Keswick. "They even spread the myth that the Kaiser had secretly converted to Islam. He was hell-bent on completing the Berlin to Baghdad railway which included a bridge across the Bosphorus, to transport ordnance as well as gain access to oil sources. He didn't succeed, as there was a gap of about 600 miles when war was declared."

"Keswick's a walking encyclopaedia, Donald, like Prue, among all her books. You must know that," Cordelia said.

"I look forward to that. The war interrupted my pursuit of knowledge in favour of learning parts of guns and things. I think I could assemble a rifle in my sleep."

As Prue was an only child, Donald had welcomed the idea of preserving the name of Jardine by her linking both surnames, Kirkwood-Jardine, after their marriage ('Jardine-Kirkwood' sounded clumsy, by comparison). Winnie had brought out a thin strip of clan tartan, neatly stitched, for the tying of the knot ceremony, along with their father's Clan Gregor kilt, sporran, dirk, sgian dubh, and jacket, all faintly smelling of tobacco and mothballs, for Donald to have altered and wear for the wedding; and it was agreed that Jardine would wear his full Clan attire too ("if I can still fit into it!"). Prue had been brought the second and longer string of Scottish river pearls that had belonged to Mrs Kirkwood, a silver sixpence for her shoe, and a sprig of heather to conceal in her bouquet. Added to that was a very small metal horseshoe, especially forged by McAlpine, the Scottish farm manager, for Prue to tuck into her sleeve.

It was a given that Donald would follow the Scottish

custom of paying for Prue's wedding dress and of the bridesmaids, the piper with a dram of whisky, and the engraved Quaich itself. While Keswick would be expected to foot the bill for the feast and all the drink, Donald and he had reached a compromise behind the scenes, when they had agreed to share aspects of the burden.

"I read in the paper this morning that Olive Schreiner has died of a severe asthma attack," said Cordelia, feeling temporarily marginalised and changing the subject away from the stream of wedding discussions for the moment. "Sad that she had to write under the pseudonym of a man's name, 'Ralph Iron', to get published; I suppose London's too far away for you girls to have come across *The Story of an African Farm?* She was a great friend of Emily Hobhouse and Elizabeth Molteno, both concerned with civil and women's rights. She turned against Cecil Rhodes, for example, when he supported the Strop Bill – permitting the flogging of black and coloured servants for relatively minor offences. Emily Hobhouse and the Molteno woman were equally active in attacking the British treatment of the Boers."

"Toby and Donald, do you flog your labourers and servants?"

"Oh, God," said Keswick, "here we go again. May I refresh anyone's glass?"

"We are sorely tempted to, sometimes, Mrs Jardine, but so far have managed to restrain ourselves," said Donald smiling and catching Prue's eye. In fact, he had difficulty in keeping his eyes off her. She was wearing a sleeveless V-necked frock of light cotton, to cope with the heat and humidity of Durban evenings in January. A matching headband set it off to make her the prettiest thing in the room.

"However, there are those who do – and worse, and their farms and estates are unhappy places to visit. The owner of the Swiss farm you visited does, by the way."

"I thought as much. You had better call me Delia, Donald. You're either too old or I'm too young to be called Mother or – worse still – Mater!" – at which point Jeevan sounded the dinner gong. As they walked towards the dining room, Delia said to Winnie, within earshot of Prue, "Olive Schreiner was a great champion of rights for the oppressed, the marginalised and the threatened, despite being faced with ridicule. When black women were excluded from joining the new Women's Enfranchisement League here, for example, she resigned. I have a copy of that book, if you would like to read it?"

"Indeed I would, and thank you. I did hear much talk about it while living in Scotland, but my mind was turned to other matters at the time," replied Winnie.

At the table, Prue said, "Schreiner had some pretty firm views about love." Smilingly, she turned to Donald sitting beside her, and said, mockingly, "Her view was that m-m-an's love was like a fire of olive wood which flared up and threatened to engulf a woman's 'icicle coolth' (at least, that's what she called it). The next day, when a woman goes to warm her hands a little, she is likely to find mere ashes. By comparison, she said that a woman's love was a long, cool love, while a m-m-an's was short and hot. What say you, Donald?"

"I'd say that she was speaking from personal disillusionment, rather than epitomising all such relationships, for if it were so, where would we be? Certainly it will have no place on *our* farm!"

"Well said, Donald!" said Keswick. "Winnie, I understand that you did a considerable amount of voluntary work, like Toby's sisters, during the war, and even now, so you can give us a first-hand account of current conditions…?"

"Well, thanks to the suffragette movement, women over thirty got the vote in 1918," Winnie said, smiling at Cordelia, recognising her reformist zeal. "There are even calls to lower the age-limit for women to twenty-one, but I can't see that happening. I needn't tell you about the post-war suffering brought down on us by the Germans, but one cannot escape evidence everywhere in London, of returned soldiers with terrible wounds. Certain foods like meat, sugar and margarine are still scarce, even though rationing has been lifted, yet butter is still rationed; so you can imagine what it's like staying at the Marine! Breakfast for Jean and me is sheer heaven, what with bacon, eggs, fruit and jam and butter…we're in the same paradise as was our experience in Madeira…as we are this evening; what a wonderful meal!

"Many manufacturers made fortunes from wartime production and now their adult children, those who were too young to fight, are flinging money about and living it up… London is full of new night clubs, and the same set is flashing Cosmos sports cars at 200 guineas a pop; but that applies only to certain wealthy middle- and upper-class families… the rest of the country's still suffering from post-war shock, poverty, poor housing and ill health. Frankly, you don't know how lucky you all are."

"I don't think you will find the coolies and natives agreeing with you!" Cordelia said quickly.

"Yes, of course, silly to say that."

"But I did read somewhere that Lloyd George's coalition government has developed a grand plan to rebuild the national life on a sounder footing," said Keswick. "That seems rather heartening. A founding factor is adult education for all, orientated (and I quote) to building a democratic and tolerant society."

"All well and good, but voters' rights and education don't put food on the plates of poor families tonight."

"Yes. It's a sorry world indeed in Europe at the moment."

The flow of conversation was interrupted by a very loud

cricket which had found its way into a dining room skirting board and suddenly started singing lustily. Although the sound was ear-splitting, they all laughed and Cordelia said, "Now, that's a sound of good luck, if ever there was! Do you remember Lucky Rajev and his pet crickets, Dodo?"

"Of course I do, He used to make them sing for me," Prue said.

"Rajev was one of our garden boys in Singapore," Cordelia explained. "He had an absolute gift for growing specially shaped gourds for cricket houses – the shape enhanced the sound; his gift extended to persuading them to sing. Apparently the cricket cult was started during the Chinese Qing dynasty."

"It's surprising the cricket idea has never caught on among Zulu children; they're inventive enough. Perhaps the natural sound of Christmas-beetles is enough…they're deafening here during the day at the moment. They cluster and dribble in the big flamboyant tree at the back. Perhaps we can ask the bagpiper to give them a blast to shut them up for the wedding day!"

"Before we repair for coffee, there's a little Jardine tradition we would like to share with you, Jean, Winnie and Donald – seeing we will shortly become one family. We started it when Prue was very young, to teach her how to pronounce the 'WH' words," Cordelia said. "She learnt how to blow out the dinner candles by pronouncing with us Who, What, When, Where, Why and How. 'How' was the most difficult, and it was left to Keswick to handle that one."

"Kipling would be pleased," Toby said, chuckling. "They are, after all, the armamentarium of any good journalist."

And thus this custom was perpetuated; so if you by any chance ever find yourself dining with descendants of the Kirkwoods, and the younger guests are invited to take part in the same little ceremony, it might be considered ill-bred to decline.

It rained on the night before the wedding, cleaning the air for a sparkling morning, but by the afternoon Durban had returned to its usual summer mugginess. When Donald put on his kilt, assisted by Toby, he felt as if he was dressing for a fancy dress party – which, after all, a wedding is a good excuse to be. The tailor, who had made the adjustments, was far more knowledgeable about the correct position of the dirk and other accoutrements than Donald himself. In the back of his mind was the constant thought that the girl he was about to marry bore his infant within her being.

He was unaware of the squabble that had broken out up in the Berea about who was in charge of the bridal bouquets and church flowers, as two friends of Cordelia's had both sworn that each had been assigned the duty by her some weeks earlier. Keswick had to step in and settle the matter, before leaving to the harbour on an important mission of his own,

Prue and Donald had agreed to make a point of inviting leading members of the Ntambanana community to the wedding, including, most importantly, the Schnurrs and their immediate 'rooinek' circle, but not neglecting such perimeter folk as Padraig and Marie O'Grady, the Mockes, and the storekeeper, fully aware that most of them would not care or be able to attend; but the upshot was that wedding gifts continued to arrive from upcountry, even on the day of the wedding, including a potjiekos pot, and an inevitable willow-pattern dinner service, so that a spare room in the Jardine house had to be set aside to accommodate them. But there was one gift for which there could be no room – a brightly painted Ferguson 'Eros' plough, which had to be parked at the entrance to the marquee, and prettied up by Cordelia with a garland of bougainvillea. The Eros was conceived by an Irish engineer and was designed to be attached to a Model T Ford car or truck by a unique three-point hitch. Ferguson was well ahead of his time; but animal-drawn farm machinery remained commonplace, and steam power was generally too cumbersome to replace animals. It took many years before petroleum-driven tractors came into common use, and diesel-fuelled tractors only came into their own well after the Second World War.

Unlike her usually composed self, Prue was tearfully fretting about her dress, the looming success of the ceremony…that she might be homesick…that she might be unable to cope with being a farmer's wife or of caring for an infant in a remote settler environment. She had begun to experience nausea on waking up, but this she kept to herself and her mother and neither of the maids was aware of her pregnancy. Grizel, one of her two bridesmaids, poured her a hearty slug of sherry, which Prue went through the motions of sipping before managing to empty it down the lavatory without arousing suspicion. Winnie gently patted some makeup over her birthmark, which had begun to flare – Donald's older sister had been invited to be the other bridesmaid. All in all, Prue's early-stage pregnancy had brought out her beauty and there was little need for any other makeup. She was indeed radiant.

The wedding ceremony flowed on as smoothly as any well-planned wedding should, until it came to the tying of the clan knots after the exchange of rings. Toby, being a naval man, had drilled the couple on the tying of the double fisherman's knot, but, in the event, they got into such a muddle that the concelebrating Presbyterian minister had to come to the rescue. There was a laugh and applause when the couple pulled the tartan cloths and the knots tightened. Winnie, as the groom's sister, had the privilege of tying a loose final knot signifying the commitment between the two families.

Their emergence from the church was the signal for every ship in the harbour (and a few waiting in the roadstead as well), to blow their fog horns for three minutes. Being harbour master, Jardine had found this reasonably easy to arrange and it was the responsibility of Kirkwood's sailing friend, Jean-Pierre, to slip out of the church and call the harbour office to give the signal. The extraordinary sound wafted up the Berea, making the Indian mynahs chatter excitedly, and Nellie the Mitchell Park elephant rock from side to side and wave her trunk about for a long time afterwards (or so her keeper reported later), as the bridal couple drove off to the Jardine house. It was the first time the chorus of horns had sounded since eleven o'clock on the 11th November, 1918.

It was Sonya who caught Prue's blue garter, although Winnie had wished so very much that it might have been her; but at least, she thought, it was not caught by far-too-young Jean or Joy. Before stepping into the car which would transport them back to the reception, Donald remembered to cast a handful of silver coins which were scrambled for by wedding guest children.

"Mother, I'm going to need you so much, in the months ahead," Prue said quietly in her mother's ear as they the couple slipped away from the reception at last.

"Well, that's over," said Donald as he threw the Kelpie into gear and the car began to whine away down Nimmo Road.

"It's only just begun," Prue said as she flung her arms about him, planted a warm soft kiss and nestled up against a shoulder, making the car wobble all over the road. "Let's go oyster-catching!"

Chapter Eighteen

The remote Oyster Lodge, as it was known then, sat at a point of the coast called Umhlanga Rocks about twelve miles north of Durban. It was an isolated structure of Burmese teak and corrugated iron built in 1853, primarily as a navigational aid. The lodge was rented by Mr and Mrs Edgerton, who had been given permission to set aside modest guest quarters for paying visitors, attracted to the isolation and by being awakened to the thump and roar of Indian Ocean breakers. Some of the occasional guests were weekend anglers who would clatter off with their rods and tackle, well before sunrise, to fish for shad from the shore, a saunter away from the rocky outcrops that protruded into the sea below the lodge. Half-submerged, even at low tide, the old rocks offered a perfect habitat for oysters, which had proliferated; in turn, providing shelter from predators, and other small creatures like anemones, barnacles and mussels; and the nooks between the shells gave shelter to even smaller creatures. At high tide, and well before the tide reversed, the rocks cradled a protected seawater pool. Low tide left a host of small rock pools, alive with tiny crabs and other miniature life.

They spied the lodge at the end of a sandy road, a little less than an Irish boreen, and spied it by a small pulsing light over the entrance, twinkling at a distance through the bougainvillea which smothered the entrance.

"So shines a good deed in a naughty world," sighed Prue, who was nearing exhaustion, in relief. "Our naughtiness might have to wait upon the early morrow, dear one."

Brian Edgerton came out as soon as he heard the tyres crunching in the driveway. He was tall, in shorts, with hair bedraggled by humidity and seawater. One tooth was capped in gold.

"Hello!" he said, while insisting on carrying the weekend suitcase into the house. "You both must be hungry and tired, after all that excitement, so you'll find tea and a plate of sandwiches under cover in your room. We'll talk tomorrow. When would you like breakfast? Just let us know when you'll be arising…aaah, your keys. We usually switch off the generator at nine, but let me know if you'd like the lights to stay on a bit longer."

"No, no!" said Prue. "W-w-e'll be as-s-leep in ten minutes. It really has been a tiring day, as you can imagine."

Donald noticed that Edgerton was eyeing her admiringly, while saying, "There are candles and matches beside the bed. Don't set fire to the mosquito nets, and there's a mozzi-spray on the dresser. Well…sleep well, and see you tomorrow, unless I've gone fishing. Eve will take care of you."

And thus began days of heaven, as they began to explore with greater curiosity each other's minds and erstwhile private memories. With bodies entwined, the memory of Emily began to slide into a gentle memory…as did Prue's memories of Singapore, old boyfriends, her childhood doll's house, *Anne of Green Gables*, and other young girl romances and trinkets in the Jardine bedroom, now replaced by the immediacy of crops, crocodiles and crockery, and an infant nursery in remote Zululand. New memories would spring up, some sparked by the pebbles and shells Prue collected, which would find their way to a Yonder window ledge, some time later.

Donald started awake in the early hours, one night, with a bright torchlight shining into his face through the mosquito netting, and was about to spring out of bed. All the fears of a midnight surprise attack welled up again and took some time to subside, before he realised it was the large moon hanging low over a slumbering sea, which rose and fell with Prue's quiet breathing.

It was then he realised that he had fallen in love more deeply than ever before, and a feeling welled up of wanting to protect this gentle 'other', with her occasional stammer and graceful body. It was too humid to remain clinging together after making love. Wherever their bodies touched, beads of perspiration wept between them.

"Be gentle tonight," Prue had said. "We have to consider Henry."

"Henry?"

"Well, we'll have to decide on names sooner or later."

"How do we know it's not a Sarah?"

"Women know these things. If it were a girl I'd suffer far more morning nausea. Something about lower hormone levels for a boy."

"Well, well, well! I wish my father was alive! He'd be such a proud and indulgent grandfather, though not as proud I will be…but can't we think of something less dull than Henry?"

"I just thought of it because it's a traditional Jardine name."

"By all means let's include one…why not Keswick again, somewhere?"

"Daddy would be very pleased…it'd be the son he never had. I sometimes think I must have been a disappointment, even though we're pretty close."

When he turned to look at her, he realised she had fallen asleep, with her silver-bangled arm tucked around the pillow.

He thought back to that first kiss beside the dodo in the Durban museum, and pondered their future; he thought of his father and the Scottish farm, and the last glimpse of his father standing on the railway platform all alone, as flakes of snow began to settle. He had set into the farmhouse step the small stone had removed from the drystone wall that day. It would be a rugged upbringing for a young boy, he thought, and equally challenging for Prue.

On their last day, a cyclone that swirled over Mauritius and the Mozambique Channel had torn at the ocean to create 'white-horses' which reached far out to sea, so that when the waves hit the shallower continental shelf, huge waves were formed to thud and crash mightily onto the Umhlanga rocks, sending water, spume and spray high up the beach to strew a broken rowing boat, jellyfish, an oar, and stinging bluebottles all over the beach. The wind accompanying the breaking waves swept sand onto bare ankles, rendering the beach an unwholesome place to be; so this, being the last day before they returned to Durban to catch the Beira boat, they decided to strike inland to watch the sunset murmurings of a million barn swallows settling in the reed beds at Victoria Lake (the region north of the Umgeni River was known as Victoria County – given over to rich green sugar cane farms.) They watched the bird-clouds forming mysterious patterns, before suddenly plunging into the reeds.

"And so, mon ami, we start all over again," Jean-Pierre said, while out of earshot of Prue. They were sitting in his office flat in Cavendish Chambers overlooking Durban Harbour. "It does not seem so very long ago, drinking wine like this, before seeing off Emily on the boat. Sweet sorrow mixed with happiness, eh? May it be Bon Chance indeed this time; and here we are again to catch a boat!"

"Yes, indeed," Donald said, as the women reappeared. Jean-Pierre and his wife Caroline had taken Donald's sisters under their wing while they were away, and little Jean was chattering excitedly about the Zulu huts they had seen in the strangely wrinkled Valley of a Thousand Hills, inland from Durban. It is an extraordinary area of steep sandstone hills and valleys eroded over millions of years by tributaries of the Inanda and Umgeni rivers.

And then started the excited tossing of cabin trunks and valises into the Meyer's car, driven by Caroline, followed by Jean-Pierre driving the rest of the party and luggage in the Kelpie. Once again there was the helter-skelter drive to the docks and over the railway lines to 'D' Shed and the customs desk.

When they reached the foot of the gangplank, uniformed Missions to Seamen supporters were selling streamers for passengers to fling to those left standing on the dock. The party – Winnie, little Jean, Donald and Prue – were booked in twin cabins, First Class, with an interleading verandah, on the port side of the vessel; so they were able to fling streamers and wave at the Jardines, who had arrived separately, and the Meyers.

The thundering foghorn which sounded as the ship was tugged away from the quay, steadily breaking the last-touch streamers, jolted Donald back to the last hugging kiss he had had with Emily as they had stood away from the crowds, on the bay side of the deck. "Those harbour sounds will always be our leitmotif," she had said. He was brought back with a jolt when Dodo (he had grown used to calling her that) linked her arm around him, with Jean caught up on her other side. Winnie waved desultorily, her thoughts sad and lonely when she glanced at her brother with his young bride. She looked along the deck of waving passengers and wondered what stories there would be to tell if she could have been a thought-reader. A hatted man in a light brown tropical suit stood without waving, and suddenly caught her eye before she quickly looked away; the *Blue Peter* was being pulled down and the ship began to heave a little, as it slipped past the Bluff and began to meet the swell at the harbour mouth.

The ship skipped past Lourenço Marques to dock at Beira the following day, where the disembarkation of passengers was more haphazard because the harbour tugs were late in putting in an appearance, so the ship had to ride in the roadstead for an hour.

Beira was even hotter and sweatier than Durban, and the jumble of local languages was unlike the Zulu cadences to which the travellers had grown accustomed. Rickshaws took them to the Grande Hotel which stood on a promontory, a modest version of the luxurious hotel which would replace it seven years later. Mozambique was still suffering from the economic ravages of the war, which contributed a 'make-do' air to Beira's seedy charm, to which electric trams contributed, clang-clanging their wobbly way past houses slumbered over by venerable trees. The Grande Hotel stood on a promontory, although not quite so grandly as the name implied. The rickshaw men had to ply a circuitous route to arrive at its arched entrance.

The man in the brown suit, whom Winnie had spied on the liner, had disembarked too and was booked in at the same hotel, where they encountered him again sitting alone in a corner near a slowly rotating ceiling fan in the hotel dining room. "Heavens," thought Winnie, "does he travel with a whole suitcase of similar wear?"

He had a clear Knightsbridge voice so they could hear him ordering wine, after glancing at the list, yet slipping into Portuguese to order "Segundo, chowder de lagosta peri-peri."

Donald had nodded to him as they entered, with the familiarity of fellow travellers in a foreign land. The stranger had raised his hand as a gesture of recognition, and then looked away to reach for a bread roll. Portuguese colonists dined late in Africa, but British colonials tended to dine punctually at seven, so the dining room was fairly empty, with fezzed waiters standing near the service swing doors waiting for more diners to arrive. He ignored Donald's party for the rest of the dinner, but looked intently at every new diner that entered – almost as if he expected someone in particular.

"That's a detective," thought Donald, knowing the signs, having served in Rhodes's British South Africa Police for four years (even though it was away in East Africa), "if ever there was one," before concentrating on what Prue and the other girls wished to order. He was old-fashioned enough to take their instructions and then place the entire order with the head waiter. Beira Bay was famous for its rich seafood bounty, so inevitably that was what everyone requested, partially because there was very little meat on the menu and it was far too hot for a three-course blowout, except perhaps for ices and coffee later.

Like the town itself, there was also an air of 'make-do' about the hotel, despite its efforts to appear grandiose. Winnie noticed that the tear in the tablecloth had been neatly stitched and starched, rather than it having been discarded; this could have been explained by Mozambique's depressed economy, which had been fractured by Spanish Flu following the wartime fighting and sacrifices, made even worse by the inefficiencies of the Portuguese military machine. Donald's encounters with them during the East African Campaign did not make for happy memories, notwithstanding the rugged bravery of the men.

Paradoxically, Portugal did not enter the European

fighting in 1914 and remained in a state of armed neutrality in Europe until 1916, when Germany declared war on Portugal after the latter seized all German ships in Portuguese ports, in response to a British request; yet matters in 1914 took a different turn in Africa, after German troops under Von Lettow-Vorbeck infringed Mozambican territory, leading to Portuguese colonies in Africa promptly declaring war.

There had been some sort of muddle at the marshalling yard, so that there was no train to be seen when the travellers arrived punctually at the station. Experienced porters parked their trolleys at the approximate positions they expected the First and Second Class carriages to stop, after guiding their charges through the grubby jumble of hoi polloi.

"I imagine you will have got used to the idea that clocks are erratic in Africa the closer you get to the Equator, and even more so when dealing with the indigenous. There is a saying in these parts that a white man must look at his watch to see if he is hungry," Donald said to his sisters. It was hot, even at that time of the morning, and Prue was trying to disguise as best she could that she was feeling faint. Winnie saw this and tucked her elbow into hers and, giving her an understanding look, drew her down to a bench, where they sat, saying little but enjoying a growing friendship. Young Jean had wandered down to the tobacconist and had returned in triumph with an English language newspaper, the Bulawayo Herald, among 'all the foreign stuff'. She was an inveterate reader and had the friendly reputation of finding something to read wherever they went. In a stage-whisper, she said, "There's that stranger again. Phew! Is it always as hot as this?" as beads of perspiration popped out on her forehead. As if in answer to her appeal, a sudden dustdevil whirled along the platform and snatched a page from the paper she had carelessly folded, to come to a sudden halt against the leg of the stranger.

He smiled and came down the platform to the group and, handing it back to her with a little bow, said, "Good morning. We seem to be doomed to run into each other continuously – first on the boat, then at the Grande, and now as fellow-travellers on the train!"

He introduced himself as 'Kim' Russell when he and Donald fell into easy conversation. It transpired that the stranger was a mining engineer headed for the Northern Rhodesia copper-fields. Although the yields were currently disappointing, there were hints that a rich seam of the metal might lie deeper down. Russell said he was to be assigned to investigate this possibility by making extensive core samples and testing. "I'm told that legumes struggle to grow in the region and that indicates copper toxicity. I plan to fly over those parts to see if there are vegetation patterns emerging."

The territory had only come into being in 1911, as an amalgamation of two protectorates, Barotziland and North-Eastern Rhodesia, in an effort to simplify administration by the British South Africa Company brought into being by Cecil Rhodes, and to consolidate meagre revenues.

The conversation was interrupted by the arrival of the train, the bustling of the porters awakened from their torpor, and the search for surnames on cards clipped to First and Second Class compartments. Rhodesian Railways offered four classes of travel, though compartment bookings were only taken for the top two classes. The fourth offered only wooden benches, though the third class did offer a modicum of comfort. The dining saloon, with steam already rising from the galley, was a carriage on its own, and reserved for First and Second Class passengers. The rest were left to fend for themselves, as evidenced by teeming wayside vendors encountered at every daylight stop on the way to Salisbury. Abundant fruit, chapatis and made-on-the-spot samosas were exchanged between grubby-fingered hands plucking crumpled notes and coins from between generous black breasts.

The train chugged across the flatlands, untidily covered in swathes by a local variety of sugarcane, until the sweltering heat reduced as it wound its way up across the Manicaland escarpment to Umtali, haunted by the distant Chimanimani Mountains, and then onwards, ever rising, to Fort Salisbury, founded just thirty years earlier.

The party had two adjacent coupés and there was much visiting between them. From time to time they would gather on the little balconies which joined each carriage. At other times, conversation would cease contentedly while Little Jean's newspaper was shared out, or Donald returned to his *Farmer's Weekly* to read about the latest farm machinery or smile at the paragraphs devoted to lonely farmers seeking brides. Prue had determined on *The Glass Bead Game* by Herman Hesse to read, but her mind kept returning to a book on maternity written by a missionary in West Africa. Little Jean had set aside the paper to take up *Anne of Green Gables* again, so Donald picked up the paper and read, with little interest, that an important conference was being held in the capital on Tropical and Subtropical Diseases, with a subsidiary workshop conference on Poisons and their Antidotes. The gathering was being convened by the Pharmaceutical Society of the Rhodesian Federation.

> *The conference has attracted several scientists from the Continent and the United Kingdom, in the light of the appalling casualties suffered in East Africa during the war,"* he read. "Untold numbers of lives were

shattered, not by bullets but by malaria, dysentery, and dengue fever, as well as snake and insect bites. The conference was seen as a way of reviewing the lessons learned and the treatments found to be most effective. Antidotes for poisonous plants eaten by starving combatants had their place in this three-day meeting of scientific minds.

"Why does Donald call you 'Dodo'?" asked little Jean of Prue. She had been bursting to ask that question ever since she heard the name used, but had been too shy to ask.

"Well," said Prue, glancing at Donald, "partially, it's because of my s-s-stammer and partially because of the stuffed Dodo in the Durban Museum, just a-a-above the libraries where I worked."

"Golly, all those books! I think I'd like to be a librarian too! But you're still answering me in riddles."

"Not really. You see m-m-my parents called me Dodo after Lewis Carroll, who wrote the 'Alice' books, and whose real surname was Dodgson. He had a stammer too, and would s-s-stammer when he introduced himself as Do-do-dodgson; so his friends started calling him Dodo. He-he even wrote about it somewhere, suggesting, humorously, that s-s-stammerers should insert dashes in words of the letters they wrote!"

"That doesn't explain the other part – about the stuffed Dodo."

Looking gently at Donald, who was out of hearing, she said softly, "That's where we first kissed…upstairs, beside the Dodo, before he left for Zululand and I thought I might never see him again."

Little Jean said nothing more, but turned to the windows to watch the telegraph lines swooping from pole to pole, a cyclist standing beside his bicycle watching the train go by, and white tickbirds riding on a small herd of African cattle.

Prue allowed her book to rest in her lap as she looked out of the window with her thoughts, and in her mind's eye images drifted away to a sleepy rhythm, as the sun slowly changed position in the sky.

Chapter Nineteen

"My God! My Remington! Archie, I left it on the platform beside the girl and the blanket!! We've left it on the platform near that man's blanket! Quick…run like the wind before it disappears!"

The party had changed trains for Bulawayo at Salisbury. During the muddle of gathering possessions and finding a porter, Winnie was the first to spot that all was not well with a girl who had just alighted. Her eyes were rolling skywards and her mouth hung open as she collapsed onto the platform. Her knees drew up and she began to shake uncontrollably. Another young couple with a little girl also came to the rescue and helped to turn the trembling body on her side while she was making rapid intakes of breath.

"Quick, lend me your little blanket, Rosie," the mother said to her daughter, and Winnie had helped to ensure that the sufferer's tongue would not curl back and obstruct her breathing. At that point the father arrived after searching for a porter, and they left after her father assured them that he was familiar with treating her condition, proof of which was evidenced when he pulled a spatula from his breast pocket and held it on her tongue, while she lay gasping and shuddering, her knees drawn up.

The group had left the coupé with the girl, who though exhausted was now slowly recovering, sitting on the porter's trolley, and the father helping the porter load a surprising number of suitcases beside her. Their last sight of the couple was of her sitting on the trolley as if on a sofa and her father's comforting arm about her.

The overnight journey to Bulawayo was pleasant, the dinner superior (although the vichyssoise did tend to slop to and fro with the rhythm of the train), with the Kirkwood party now on waving and nodding terms with the brown-suited Kim Russell and the couple who had almost lost their precious portable typewriter. Before drifting back to their respective compartments along the rocking corridors, they agreed to meet up for sundowners with the discovery that they were all bound for the Victoria Falls Hotel. The typewriter-couple had introduced themselves as Archie and Agatha Christie, with their little daughter Rosalind, momentarily tongue-tied, clutching to her mother's skirt.

In 1920, the hotel near the Falls was as much a state of mind as an hotel of repute. It started out as a hostelry for engineers supervising the laying of rail lines in the virgin bush and the construction of the spectacular bridge arching across the Zambezi River gorge, so linking Southern and Northern Rhodesia. The railway was part of the realisation of Cecil John Rhodes's Cape-to-Cairo dream, never fully to be realised in his lifetime. It stretches between Cape Town and Port Said in Egypt, some 6,800 miles away. Later, the hotel was converted into a resort, its jungle remoteness attracting wealthy visitors from abroad, becoming the jewel in the crown of the Union Castle's new Round Africa service. It took another twenty-seven years before British Overseas Airways Corporation opened up quicker access to the hotel, with its flying boats landing on the Zambezi, permitting passengers to overnight at the hotel, dine on legendary fare, and slumber luxuriously in mosquito-netted four posters before continuing up or down Africa the next morning. It was then that the hotel was dubbed Jungle Junction, a fond nickname that has stuck to this day, even though the flying boat service was discontinued some years later.

"Where's your charming wife?" asked Winnie. After passing a large portrait of King George V the Kirkwood party and their new-found friends had gathered on the hotel terrace to enjoy sundowners. They were within sight of the Victoria Falls Bridge and the 'clouds of spray' that floated up from the gorge.

"Here she comes now," said Archie as he rose to welcome her, "She's been hacking away at that infernal machine of hers. You may have been turned into an IDB detective, a damsel in distress, or a wicked poisoner by this time"

"What nonsense you do talk, Archie! Doesn't he, Rosie? Your father frightens our friends away with such talk, for fear of being captured in my next book"

"Ooh, are you really a writer? What kind of books?" little Jean asked excitedly.

"Jean's a real bookworm; she always has her head stuck in a book," said Winnie, fondly.

"Then Jean and I will get on famously. But Archie's the famous one. He was in the Royal Flying Corps during the war and was decorated. Now he's going to help assemble a British Empire Exhibition – travelling all over the place. I'm just a pharmacy assistant – that's where we met in a military hospital during the war. I found all those smells and mixtures in the hospital pharmacy endlessly fascinating, so much so that most of my murder victims are poisoned. But Archie was even more fascinating and that's how little Rosalind came to be. But when we planned this visit, I couldn't resist including a breakaway to attend the Tropical Medicines conference in Salisbury. I've come away bristling with ideas."

"That qualifies me to play a lot of golf. It keeps me out of mischief and out of her hair while she plots another murder."

"I'm not little any more," said Rosalind; "I'm nearly six."

"Prue's a librarian," Winnie said.

"That's enviable and you will know far more about writers and writing than I do. Who are your favourites?"

"The usual that one tends to be drawn to in one's third year, after sweating through Beowulf, Chaucer and Marlowe – the pre-revolution Russians, Turgenev, Tolstoy, Gogol, even Dostoevsky, although he suffers so badly in translation. I'm attracted to that feeling of restlessness among the Russian gentry – hinting and suspecting that something awful but undefined was about to happen. My dissertation focused on that."

"I'm awed. I never went to school – just had governesses and, later, tutors for my sister Madge and me. But I was captured by books in my father's library and just read anything that took my fancy, including bits out of *Paradise Lost* with those gruesome woodcuts by Gustav Doré. Won't you miss being surrounded by books on a Zululand farm?"

"I don't think so. There'll be plenty of fresh experiences to keep me busy," she said, smiling at Donald, "and I have made arrangements to start an exchange library based at the new co-op, as an extension of one in Empangeni, linked to the Durban Municipal libraries. The rail service for book exchanges is efficient, save for the usual interruptions of storms and floods, and even the remainder of the way to Ntambanana can be relied upon, though somewhat plodding."

"May I donate a few books?"

"That's very kind of you; thank you. I intend to include some basic English texts, in the hope of starting literacy classes for farm workers."

"You're likely to hit opposition to that idea," said Archie.

"We'll give it a good try and to hell with their prejudices," said Donald in defence of his new wife, though foreseeing troublesome resistance ahead.

"Teach the natives to read and that way lies revolution."

Before Donald or Prue could retort, Agatha headed off the subject by prodding Archie in the ribs, saying, "He foresees the end of Empire, if we do," and reverted to the subject of writing, saying, "The only reason I started writing, by the way, was my sister Madge. She challenged me to write a detective novel; so I did, then went through the usual humiliation of being rejected by six successive publishers till I found one mad enough to accept me…must have been a quiet day at the office. I just kept on writing compulsively after that, when my publisher discovered that people liked somewhat elegant murder mysteries.

"As for writers I admire, I'm afraid that I have not read many of your Russians, but I've come across Scott Fitzgerald who also has his moments. I like the atmosphere of restlessness he captures. Have you read his *This Side of Paradise*?"

"Not yet, but he's on my list."

"And you, Donald?"

"I'm afraid I'm still stuck with Percy Fitzgerald and Ryder Haggard – but I look forward to Prue expanding my horizons beyond those and the *Farmers Weekly*."

"How do you write a novel?" asked Winnie.

"Well, all English novels have a Beginning, a Muddle and an End. A detective novel – my kind – focuses on creating an almighty muddle with suspects and red herrings galloping off in all directions, to mix metaphors magnificently. Sometimes, in the writing, I'm as muddled as my readers. It helps, though, to make a few central characters, including the detective, unassailable; but to leave the rest of the characters in doubt, until the last minute…the dénouement."

Kim Russell, who had remained silent until then, said, "Where do all your settings and characters come from?"

" 'Circum-spi-ce': in other words, 'look about you'. I realised early on that the novel needed a central figure that would be able to survive from novel to novel. In my case, I was fortunate to come across a strange little Belgian man in the military hospital, with quirks and idiosyncrasies that I had no trouble in recording. But, additionally, here we are in the beating heart of Africa, riddled with stories of lost cities, of gold, diamonds and skulduggery that most of my readers will never be able to reach or experience, surrounded by wild elephant herds, within the sound of a mighty waterfall – a setting for a novel that almost writes itself, aided by chance happenings which trigger trains of thought...you, Kim,.if you don't mind my turning you into a mysterious man in the brown tropical suit, and you, Jean, I might turn into a pretty young dancer from Paris. That incident on the Salisbury railway station could be turned into a person collapsing on a railway platform – perhaps in Cairo – and you, Donald, fiddling with that roll of film for your Voigtlander, I might turn into a diamond smuggler hiding gems in the film canister. I notice how you knock your pipe on the heel of your shoe, and this could be made into something sinister. You also consulted a gold half-hunter during that incident on the railway platform in Salisbury. That could suggest your social standing; and so on. Of course, I speak in fun, but you will see how little gestures can be transformed by the stroke of a few taps on a typewriter keyboard."

The rest of the conversation was drowned out by an African xylophone band striking up with a tune reminiscent of 'After You've Gone', followed by others of that genre, somewhat similar.

"Do you feel the beat of Africa, Winnie?" shouted Donald.

She smiled and nodded in enjoyment. Donald wondered if the musicians knew the words. They had prescience for colonial rulers. He thought back to a moment at an officers' nightclub in Mombasa towards the war's end: one of the men had smuggled into the club a giant crab he had caught. Its release started a minor stampede. When he asked the Swahili band what they were singing after the crab had been despatched, a singer replied, "We singing 'Go Home'!"

They rode the servant-pushed hotel trolley next day, past trees broken by a herd of elephants which had mown through in the early morning. As they approached the protective rails to gaze at the Falls, they scattered a group of warthogs, which, together with a family of bushbuck with their distinctive spots, moved away indifferently to resume grazing further off, before they were all thoroughly drenched in the gorge-edge forest where a mist-cloud rose from the thundering water.

"It's like a daemonic Monkey's Wedding!" shouted Prue, above the noise, as the sun shone through the spray.

Then, tiring of the dripping rain-forest, they took the path along the edge of the gorge where two permanent rainbows hung in the sunlit mist. Rosalind asked her father, "Daddy, is this Fairyland?"

Prue heard her with joy and thought of her infant-to-be.

Chapter Twenty

Albert Zunkel, a descendant of German missionaries, stood on the tiny Estcourt railway platform with a uniformed Indian retainer and an African labourer, and Zunkel raised his enormous farmer's hat as a pre-arranged recognition signal for the Broccardo party.

"Hello, hello! It's quite a long way from Empangeni; I hope you enjoyed the trip," he greeted them, while Toby and Paolo attended to handing luggage out of carriage windows. "Our little shuttle bus is over there. I am afraid the road to the hotel is a bit corrugated and dusty, so be prepared to keep the windows only slightly open to keep out the worst of the dust. Jimmy, here," winking at the Indian, "understands the mysterious workings of the internal combustion engine, so he's a useful man to have on hand, if this new-fangled Renault engine plays up; and Punyaan is our 'Man Friday', and even Saturday and Sunday. His family live somewhere up in the hills where we are going. He just pitched up while we were building the hotel one day, and has been with us ever since…. Has the strength of Hercules and the temperament of a lamb."

The Broccardo family were keen walkers, and the Drakensberg range made a perfect setting for a short holiday. The Broccardo parents had grown fond of Toby, and, monitoring how his courtship of Sonya was going, invited him along, knowing he was also a keen walker.

The invitation to accompany them had thrown Toby into a quandary, as he was committed to supervising the Yonder farm while Donald and Prue were away on their honeymoon in Rhodesia. The dilemma was solved by asking the two Bell sons to supervise both his and Donald's farms while they were away. Andrew and Nigel leapt at the chance, as both of them were becoming restless under their father's traditional farm-management.

Toby sent a short telegram which had greeted the Kirkwoods on their arrival at the Victoria Falls Hotel; Donald understood perfectly and sent a telegram back, 'GO AHEAD LOCK UP BOOZE GUNS CASH BULK FOODS."

On the way to Estcourt, Toby and Paolo had shared a compartment, the women another, so it had been an ideal moment for Toby to ask Paolo's permission for his daughter's hand, to which he had agreed with pleasure.

On the road to the hotel, the vehicle splashed through a drift of shallow water, with Zunkel shouting, "Good fishing here for rainbow and yellowtail! But tricky after a thunderstorm in the mountains when the drift turns into a six-foot deep raging torrent. Cuts us off. Lots of people drowned, over the years. The other side of the drift you can see the peak – just under 10,000 feet."

The journey was paused for a Thermos-mug of tea and Baker's Biscuits; then on to the hotel itself, cradled in its ring of peaks.

After settling in, the younger members of the party, Toby, Sonya and Joy, announced they would go exploring, and this led them to a small chapel in the grounds with an enormous window behind the altar, where they found a single figure sitting in one of the pews. He turned out to be French, elderly and with only a modest command of English, who said, gesturing towards the altar window, "From here, to the mountains, to God."

Joy now wandered off on an exploration of her own, so Toby chose that moment to propose that they should get married – and perhaps even in this little chapel. The Frenchman, overhearing Donald's proposal and Sonya's simple, "Yes, my darling, I will," stood up, applauding, as Joy appeared at the chapel entrance while Toby and Sonya were embracing.

The wedding was organised for six weeks ahead; the wedding party travelled up by train to the Berg again, as this was the most convenient way to get to the hotel: disembarking at the Estcourt station, met again by Zunkel, and thus by hotel bus to their destination.

Their marriage took place with – inevitably – Donald being the best man, Prue maid-of-honour, and Joy one of the bridesmaids. Their honeymoon journey was traced with postcards along the way. From Estcourt they boarded the train to Bloemfontein, where they turned south, and with a generous contribution by Paolo, Toby decided to abandon parsimony.

The postcards read: "Passing through the original Gondwanaland. Staggering night sky, full of stars"; "Hired a car at Paarl. Bought a beautiful chair at Tulbagh, sending it, dismantled, for collection at Empangeni station"; "Discovering Franschhoek. Now we understand why most South African rugby players have French names...descendants of the Huguenots!"; "We got a bit tiddly here. Beautiful Dutch names for the wines – Rivier Sonderend...Alles Verloren...Twee Jonggazellen (River without end...All is lost...Two young gazelles). The wine farms here are quaintly named...for example, 'Rickety Bridge'."

The next batch came from Cape Town, with cards reading, "Staying here. Very grand," with a picture of the Mount Nelson Hotel on the reverse. Another read, "Climbed the Nursery Gorge to top of Table Mountain, descended on this cableway! Catching the *Union Castle* back to Durban on Wednesday."

Upon their return home, the original custom of Donald and Toby sharing breakfast on Sundays now expanded to include their wives. The content of the latest delivery of papers and magazines was discussed, as they sat about after their food.

"Good Lord, did you see this!" said Toby, after the plates were cleared away, "It seems as if we're sitting in the middle of a civil war without knowing about it! This is what it says in the *Advertiser*." He went on to read:

> *White miners have gone on strike in Brakpan and Fordsburg and there have been serious clashes with the police. The strikers have erected banners, proclaiming, 'Workers of the World Unite! Support the White Miners!*
>
> *The leader of the strikers, Jimmy Green, said that the mines were attempting to introduce cheap black labour for semi-skilled jobs presently being done by the white miners...at substantially lower wages.* (So you were right, Donald, in your prediction.)
>
> *Explaining the move to black labour in semi-skilled jobs, Manager John Plewman of Robinson Deep Gold Mine said that the gold price had plummeted from £6 19s in 1919 to a damaging £4 15s per troy ounce in December, 1921, rendering most goldmines unprofitable, to the point that several mines will be forced to close down unless production costs could*

> be reduced drastically. This explains why mines are introducing native Labour for semi-skilled work, at low wages.
>
> Until recently, the South African Communist Party supported the mine workers, but it has now reversed its position upon an instruction by the Com-intern. Now, they support the introduction of black labour and equality of pay.
>
> At last count, 135 miners have lost the lives. Prime Minister Jan Smuts has called in 20,000 troops to suppress the revolt and reinforced them by aerial bombardment and the employment of armoured cars. During the bombardment the church was destroyed by aerial bombing.

The seasons had rolled by and, despite such disturbances, the Ntambanana farming community remained relatively insulated by the boom in cotton production. Embroidered by family events, such as the birth of their children, the rhythm of farming took possession of their lives.

On 6th December, 1921, customers in the Ntambanana store were startled by an elated Padraig O'Grady riding up to the petrol pump clutching an orange, white, and green flag, tethering his horse, then shooting skywards both rounds of his double-barrelled shotgun. Opsaal brandy fuelled his wild excitement: that was evident when he rushed into the store and shook hands with everyone, excitedly, including a rather startled Toby who, before that moment, had been regarded with suspicion by Padraig, as an enemy to the cause of Irish freedom after 700 years of British oppression.

An express-rate telegram had arrived early that morning and had been sent to the O'Grady household with the words, "UK AGREES IRISH FREE STATER SAME STATUS

AS CANADIAN. CIARAN." (Ciaran O'Grady was his younger brother, still living in Limerick.)

"Look it! Today a new Ireland is born! Yes, indeed!"

6th December had another significance in the Yonder farmstead, and was the culmination of much preparation and apprehension. Against all exhortations by Cordelia to the contrary, Prue was resolute that she would give birth to her firstborn on the farm. "If their women can do it, so can I," she had said to her mother.

As a result, Keswick and Cordelia travelled to the farm, after trucking the Nash by rail to Empangeni, then tackling the donga-ridden road to Ntambanana. Cordelia, deploying her great powers of persuasion, had exhorted Dr Lombard to travel the same route, boarding at the van Schalkwyks, to be on standby if there were any extreme emergency. The district nurse had also been persuaded to stay in the vicinity for the same reason. The Jardines were accommodated at Yonder farm.

Donald and Keswick had been shunted away from the bedroom and resolutely barred access by Chinnamama, who had gained status as the supervisor of boiling of water and the supplier of towels, as she fussed about ensuring there was plenty of both.

The two men resorted to whisky and water brought to them by Chinnamama, with the strict instructions to stay where they were until the baby was delivered. In an attempt to keep their minds off the burning subject of childbirth, Keswick asked Donald his opinion about the aftermath of the war which was being demanded by the Allies and prevaricated against by Germany.

"Unlike you, I have never fought the Germans, so my perspective may not be as sound as yours, but the reparations mean that Germany will not be out of their debt before

1963, and the destruction of their naval vessels still under construction seemed an awful waste! Surely, the Allies should just take them over as part of reparations?"

Emilia Lucy Hannah Kirkwood-Jardine (whom Dr Lombard was to describe as 'onsekleinbloemertjie' van die plaas, our 'little farm flower'), a mouthful which would only be found on future legal documents concerning the family, would grow up, go to school and pursue life as Emilia Kirkwood.

She was joined by Ewan Keswick Kirkwood on 6th January, 1923.

In the early days of their childhood, when she was not preoccupied by them, Prue's focus was on the development of the little library, sharing teacher responsibilities with Ethel Siedle, and general supervision of the Yonder household. After the birth of Emilia her stammer almost disappeared, reduced to a mild hesitation on encountering certain words. Her birthmark remained, and her slender figure became more motherly.

She and Donald would emulate the shared Kirkwood and Jardine respect for reading to the children every bedtime… tales of Brer Fox, *The Jungle Book*, *Alice in Wonderland* and all the rest, unconscious of the fact that they were breeding in eurocentricity which would set the course for future political and cultural lives But they also learnt things to which few city children were ever exposed – the habits of insects and other invertebrates of all kinds; snakes and antelopes and everything else that moved on the surface of Zululand earth; and were taught to be curious and to wonder – at weavers stripping willow leaves to build nests, at dew caught on early morning cobwebs, and the industrious micro-mountains built by underground dwelling ants. They were taught to respect the culture of the Indians on the farm, and formed firm childhood friends. Children absorb new languages 'through the skin'; and they were soon able to converse in Zulu and simple Hindi with the warmth of pronunciation that never comes from books.

Donald was continually absorbed by the business of farming, of locating kraal manure from the Free State where cattle remained nagana-free (it had to be trucked in by rail) – and the hundred thousand other matters which preoccupy farmers. In between he made wooden cots, a double-storey dolls' house which swung open on sturdy hinges, a wooden push cart, and much else besides…and life was good.

Jan Mocke's ox-wagon shuttle gave way to a three-a-week bus service after the road between Empangeni and Ntambanana was at last repaired – or rather reconstructed, as the original had deteriorated so badly that it could no longer pass muster as a road. Cars became more frequent, although a seventeen-mile, bone-shaking ride on a corrugated road behind the clouds of dust thrown up by a coach reduced such attractions. The first glimmerings of Toby's vision of a countrywide network of petrol stations were beginning to appear, demand being evident by rising sales at Piet van Jaarsveld's petrol pump at the co-op store.

Much to the delight of the Broccardos, Sonya switched her studies in Pietermaritzburg from Law to Accountancy, so following in her father's footsteps; and, after marrying Toby, set up a small extension of Paulo Broccardo's practice to serve the book-keeping and accounting needs of the 'Tam farmers. She had persuaded Masheila Reddy, the young Indian girl from the Bell estate whom they had helped to educate, to assist in running the small practice, after learning that she had applied for a job at her father's Empangeni firm. She was as beautiful as ever, though she was obliged to seem remote to any white bachelor. She radiated a 'nihil me tangere' manner that made her even more attractive. She was aloof, too, to the rough Indian farm labourers. Privately, she yearned to escape the restrictions of race.

Mrs Potgieter was growing older and more absent-minded, but her adopted daughters loved and teased her when she was forgetful – like the time when she arrived at the store without the eggs that she had set out to deliver.

Greenacres, the department store the far side of Durban, and Henwoods (with convenient entrances in both West and Pine Streets), the hardware store, had combined to produce seasonal mail order catalogues for patronage by up-country account holders. Orders received by letter or telegram would be dispatched by train within a day, and extended to reach even Ntambanana within three days. Paper dress patterns, material bolts of cloth, clothes, artificial pearls and hats of every description, bottles of Eau de Cologne, cast-iron foot scrapers in the shape of scotty dogs, discreetly packaged 'Unmentionables', agricultural seed drilling machinery, Swedish crystal sets complete with headphones and tuning guide, Madison and Brunswick recordings of Enrico Caruso singing 'Una Furtiva Lagrima', batteries, corsets, the very latest in enormous anthracite stoves that would dominate kitchens ('Installation guaranteed by our skilled engineers at no extra cost, and fuel supplies assured'), corrugated iron cutters, and much else besides – so much that the owner of Loftheim's in Empangeni and the Ntambanana Co-op were worried that their sales would fall – and entered agency agreements warrantying 'deliveries from the station to your door'.

Booming cotton production with sales to a market deprived of American cotton was leaving its mark on the little community, as a creeping 'keeping up with the Jones' entered the hearts of many farmers' wives, while husbands envied neighbours' grander Model A cars.

Estate owners of sugarcane plantations were also

prospering and, for white farmers and tradesmen, Zululand was booming, almost insulated from the gathering economic and political storms beginning to swirl in the rest of the world. News that Stalin had expelled Trotsky from the Party, to await his brutal assassination in Mexico, and the worst-ever earthquake in China, killing thousands, occupied the minds far less than news of the first single-handed flight across the Atlantic from New York to Paris and the launch of 'The Jazz Singer', the first motion picture with synchronised sound. Closer to home, the Kirkwood's party line phone had grown familiar, with the ring…ring, ring,ring…ring,ring, meaning the call was for one of them. Chinnamama and Layani had been taught to recognise and answer a call meant for Yonder, although Layani's jumbled Portuguese, Shangaan and English – after his over-enthusiastic "Hello! Hello!" – left many callers puzzled and hanging on hoping that Prue or one of the children would take over.

The Natal Provisional Administration remained in a parlous financial position struggling to make ends meet. As a result the roads, such as they were, remained in a sorry state, however much prosperity in Zululand was filling private coffers.

For the natives, though, there was little improvement, with cattle still dying from nagana, and many falling foul to Indian money lenders; and many others drawn into joining the African National Congress.

It being no longer possible to use oxen as draft animals, tractors with huge and heavy metal wheels became quite common.

Donald's limp became more pronounced over the years, especially before a thunder storm; but his wartime flashbacks dwindled, although his dreams were troubled sometimes by unidentified wartime threats.

Prue had cajoled him into acquiring a piano. She had been brought up to play and had convinced Donald of the value of teaching the children, so at great cost, not least the delivery thereof, a Carl Ecke upright was dismantled and railed from Ivan Cohen's music shop, to be unloaded at Empangeni then strapped to Toby's Model T truck and finally to be manoeuvred into the sitting room. It was accompanied by Cohen's near-deaf piano tuner, Mr Goldblatt, who immediately set about reassembling the instrument. The house was filled next day with sounds of piano-tuning, as the tuner clapped his ear trumpet to the wooden casing and listened intently. It was the only piano in Ntambanana, leaving Layani and Chinnamama to burst with pride that their master's house had such a unique piece.

The American craze for fancy-dress parties, fuelled by alcohol, had even trickled into the Zululand hinterland, sparked by the Siedles who suggested that the ideal venue was Yonder, what with a piano and a parlophone and all, and it being Ethel Siedle's birthday.

For a week leading up to the day, the women of the village were in a frenzy of patterns, ostrich feathers and Singer sewmanship creativity, while keeping the secrets of their costumes hidden from each other. The children became drawn into this whirlpool of endeavour, so that by the day before the gathering, the sole topic of whispered conversation was the exotic party. There was less enthusiasm among the menfolk, but even they were prevailed upon to enter into the fun. Rudolph Valentino was the popular disguise, followed, inevitably, by pirate variations. Tramps were the third choice (á la Charlie Chaplin) trailed by variations on the theme of cowboys, Indians and squaws.

Donald used his limp to excuse himself from dancing and undertook to man the Parlophone.

On the actual night, it soon became evident that excessive hooch challenges monogamy, and towards the end of the evening, the sanctity of many a marriage was in doubt. The night was brought to an abrupt end by Morrison falling out of the big tree, after accepting a drunken challenge to climb the highest. He escaped major injury, but succeeded in breaking his left humerus, causing Grizel Morrison, not absolutely sober herself, to drive her husband to Dr Lombard at Empangeni, who was none too pleased to be woken up so early on a Sunday morning.

Donald used the accident to bring the increasingly wild birthday party to an end. Prue had dressed as a flapper – an attractive garb that suited her slender figure well. She also danced like a fairy, laughingly fending off the ardour of several married men.

The old Huntley & Palmer's letterbox still stood on its post, and one day he spotted a letter from Winnie plastered with stamps and containing surprising news. With the letter came several photographs, one of grown-up 'Little Jean', hugging the head of her new mare, its mane beautifully plaited. Others showed Winnie with a man whose face was vaguely familiar, standing before the Richmond Hill house.

> *Dear Donald and Prue,* he read. Her writing style was Scottish and restrained. *I am engaged to be married to the 'man in the brown suit'! You will remember Kim Russell whom we met on holiday in Rhodesia. We have been in communication ever since, leading to his coming over twice to visit. He has no siblings but I have got to know his very ancient parents very well, and charming they are too. Although Kim is not Scottish, the Russells (their complete surname*

is Russell-Charlewood, but seldom used in full) come from a good Anglo-Norman stock bordering Malahide, near Dublin. I have taken the ferry across several times. Their draughty old manor is on many acres overlooking the sea. The family is in good standing, even in these troubled Irish times, though Kim fears for the future. They are Roman Catholic but not particularly devout, and stagger along to Mass, more out of duty than overwhelming faith. While I am impressed by warmth of the congregation and how closely similar are Catholic and Anglican celebrations, I think all the iconoclasm of statues and symbols is out of step with modern-day enlightenment...too much mumbo-jumbo too, with which all those Virgin Mary, etc., statues are associated. Fear not! There is no conversion in this soul and our marriage will be in a wee Presbyterian chapel in Richmond and concelebrated with an Anglican minister with whom we have become friendly. Kim is well off, and you must know that our properties and investments remain firmly under my control.

Dates and honeymoon remain to be decided but I suspect that Africa beckons Kim.

Kim has undertaken to pay for various things, including the stabling of Little Jean's horse (or horses!), the cars and so on.

Donald Dubh, I am fortunate to have found a compatible man, as men are in very short supply nowadays.

Little Jean has set her sights on completing her studies (Archæology) at Peterhouse in Cambridge. She is pretty but not giddy and is set to do well, but stabling her horse just for the holidays is a bit silly, so I have taken up the habit of early morning rides again. Kim is a good rider too, so there is added pleasure when he is present. His Scotland Yard duties call him away regularly, and I don't cross-examine him too closely on his work. But I do know that he has close working contact with De Beers Diamonds. Something to do with illicit diamond buying. It was this work he was engaged in when we met him on the Beira railway station! (His geologist qualifications are real, however, as is his interest in locating the elusive copper seam in Northern Rhodesia. A complicated and attractive man.)

So there you are! My voluntary nursing work at SYON HOUSE continues. Our chauffeur and his wife are getting steadily older...and I suspect her housekeeping duties are becoming onerous. Retirement looms, sooner or later. We'll cross that bridge when we reach it.

My special love to Emilia and Ewan, Winnie.

PS: The film Metropolis *by Fritz Lang is causing quite a stir here. Some quarters dislike it simply because it's German, H.G. Wells regards it as silly and too simplistic, the tug between Good Maria and the Evil Frieda robot made in Maria's image, and The Heart uniting the overlords with the toiling masses. I went to see it with Kim and found it challenging, but found all that music from the pits extremely jangling. The 'anything goes' Weimar Republic is certainly a source of creativity out of the turmoil, which may be jackbooted out of existence by those Brownshirts, Kim predicts. He has expressed alarm about the rise of organised right wing thuggery.*

The cotton crop was particularly bountiful that year, and on the Sunday morning of 27th March, 1927, Donald awoke remembering it was Sunday and that he had promised to build the children a tree house ("Not too high off the ground," pleaded Prue.) A mild south-westerly wind was blowing; it had rained the night before (with that comforting soft roar on the corrugated iron roofs) leaving the next day sparkling but sultry, with accumulating clouds, when the phone rang and Layani answered it; then knocked on the bedroom door to summon Donald to speak. It was Fourie from the Andover Estates on the Swaziland border, far north, with whom Donald had remained friendly.

"Donald, Andover is smothered in hoppers, almost ready to take off and fly south," he heard over the crackling phone. "Our entire crop has gone and they're about to fly southwards. Heavy wind here and rain threatening. You'd better alert the neighbours and 'Pangeni – it could take a day or so, but by that time they will have joined other swarms."

"Thanks for the alert. What's the best way to stop them?"

"Damned if I know. The birds are having a field day. Try lighting fires…better keep everything closed and keep the pets inside.

"The airforce did send across a small plane hurriedly fitted with insecticide sprays…a bit Heath Robinson…the pilot tried spraying the swarms with paraffin and then igniting it with a flare from a Very pistol, causing a big explosion which almost blew his wings off. Then when he landed in a field to refuel, he pranged the undercart. So that's him out of the picture."

Soon the phones were jangling all over the district.

It was Layani who spotted the swarm that now filled half the sky, causing him to rush into the house, close the doors and windows and sound the dinner gong. Sammy, and his

Indian field workers, Layani, Prue, and Donald, followed by Emilia and Ewan, rushed to light oil-dowsed wood piles.

There was nothing more that could be done as the huge swarm settled on the fresh crop and munched their way across the fields, covered in a juicy green crop, though Prue rushed out again in a vain attempt to beat the locusts off her precious roses. Giving up and rushing back, clawing locusts out of her hair, she spied two little Indians crying with terror, and swept them up to carry them into the house with her.

For the rest of the afternoon, all the children had their noses to the windows, marvelling at the multicoloured patterns of these Egyptian beasties.

"The co-operative can carry you for this year, but the premium for next year will rocket and if you have another disaster like this, the co-op won't be able to pay again, and it could be 'tickets'," van Jaarsveld told the gathering.

"What about the Department of Agriculture?" asked Barnes. "It's their duty to support us."

"Morkel has advised me that its policy is that farming is a business risk and, while they have underwritten our insurance company to cover last year's locust damage, it regards this year's disaster as unsupportable, as the land has been rendered unfertile for the next five years. I suggest that even if you have access to private means, it would be throwing good money after bad. The insurance company will pay for destruction of structures and equipment damage, but nothing more."

"Bloody Pretoria!" said O'Grady angrily.

But there was another disaster the following year, not locusts, but water. January to midway through April are usually hot and blessed with bountiful rain. That year rain was infrequent and light although the days were hotter than usual. This led to a poor cotton crop. The Indian field workers continued to earn their keep for the next four months, fighting the maria-maria weed, then ploughing in the winter crop to enrich the soil for the next seed planting just before the first spring rains.

The rains arrived on time, heralded by strong winds, then a series of three-day thunderous downpours, often accompanied by golf ball-sized hail which roared and crashed on the corrugated iron roofs. It poured with rain throughout Zululand, leading to ferocious floods, sweeping away the topsoil and seeds, snakes, and many a dwelling, to join the river after which Ntambanana was named which flowed to join the Black and White Umfolozi rivers, so greatly swollen that valleys were filled with churning brown water, drowning people and animals and collapsing submerging buildings.

"The co-op's insurance company is not strong enough and cannot support Ntambanana farmers for another year. The land will be useless for another five years, so the farms will have no value. We have all suffered overwhelming devastation. If you have no private means to support another year, the company suggests you all find other employment…and that applies to your field workers as well."

When he got the Kelpie back to Yonder over a road that had turned into a donga, Donald's face told Prue all, before he could open his mouth.

"Well, at least we have Chelmsford."

"We have this homestead too."

"But not much use, if the reason we are here has gone. And the children are growing a bit gauche and wild…they'd have access to good schools."

"And your parents are dilly about them.. But if we did decide to walk away from all this, we'd have to let the house-servants go…. to starve, most likely."

"No, we'll bring them with us. Chelmsford has an array

of empty stables that can be converted.. with the oldest and unusable only fit enough to house a donkey. Why was it called Chelmsford?"

"At some time in the Anglo-Zulu war it was regarded as strategically north and grand enough for Chelmsford to commandeer. When he left, and his men took all the horses... they never came back; but the owners were paid a handsome compensation."

"It's a thought, on the condition I can – no, both of us – can lecture them effectively on family planning...Stopes and all that."

"Parallel to that you could run literacy classes for the adults, and basic training for the children of the hilltop neighbours' children."

Unknown to Prue, Donald had opened post office bank accounts into which he paid three months' wages (the store, by this time, had opened a little post office agency, with Marie van Jaarsveld the postmistress).

He had considered opening overdrafts on his substantial investments with which to battle on farming, but angry world economic storm clouds were gathering, so he thought better of it.

On stationery, blind-embossed 'Yonder, Ntamabanana, Zululand', Prue typed, *"'To whom it may concern: (name of worker) has been in our employ for (number) of years and he/she is a peaceful and productive worker. Our farm has had to close down, so he/she seeks employment, having acquired excellent technical skills over the years.*

For any further details write to me c/o Natal Bank, Durban Donald Ernest Paterson."

He signed the letters with a flourish (not his usual signature, reducing the risk of forgery), and stamped the letters under his signature.

The next step was to assemble the field workers beneath the Thunder Tree, after employing Layani and Chinnamama to assemble three months' rations. With Ramsamy as interpreter, he explained the closure, and that their best interests had been considered. How to use a savings bank was explained and the Postmistress would be very helpful. He said that his heart was heavy, and that they would receive the letter and the Savings Bank book a few days before the Kirkwoods' departure. Prue had taken along the Voigtlander to the Thunder Tree assembly and snapped away, with Donald and Sammie standing in the centre, Ewan and Emilia in amongst them.

Before the meeting broke up, they were told that they were welcome to the hill-rice, which miraculously survived.

The blacksmith was at hand to disassemble the wind pump, which Donald would reassemble at Chelmsford. Next was the corrugated iron of Yonder itself, half of which he gave to the blacksmith in payment, the other half would accompany them to Durban, to refurbish the stables.

The family moved to the Schnurrs while this was being done and the packing completed, in timber crates and swathes of *Zululand Times* overrun newsprint.

One day a huge Loftheim's truck and trailer arrived…and then they were gone. All that was left was the timber frame of Yonder, becoming steadily more rickety as pieces of wood were sawn off and carted away.

A wind struck one night and blew the frame akilter…and the next storm polished it off. Soon blackjacks and maria-maria overcame the land, though the Thunder tree stood proud and firm.

The End

Epilogue

Toby and Sonya (not expectant) migrated to Durban where they set up home on the Berea in Rosetta road. They continued their good friendship with Donald and Prue, and were also frequent visitors at the Jardines.

Eric and Mari Schnurr migrated to Pietermaritzburg and settled in Wembley in a beautiful house cantilevered over a stream at the foot of the property. They had three children, and Eric continued his work caring for the interests of ex-servicemen farmers by taking up a senior position with the Natal Agricultural Society.

Pádraig and Sarie O'Grady returned to take over Sarie's father's farm near Mooi River, in the Midlands of Natal. Pádraig soon earned an excellent reputation for animal husbandry.

The Ntambanana co-operative had to close and the establishment returned to be a native trading store.

Mrs Potgieter remained self-sufficient, and continued to deliver eggs in wire baskets and continued to insist on not reading the English *Zululand Times*, in which the eggs were wrapped. The three girls of her Herina (who had died of the Spanish Flu) grew up as wild as meerkats, until she managed to board them at a little Dutch school in Vryheid which, when the school inspector was not there, taught the girls in Afrikaans.

Hubie and Frieda carried on with the sugar farm, although, unbeknownst to them, their links with Germany continued to be monitored by Prue's "Pickering Street Irregulars".

Captain Stoughton moved to Bloemfontein and began to assemble the Nazi-sponsored Ossewa Brandwag clandestine network, closely monitored by a "neutral" Swiss optometrist with a successful optical practice in Pritchard Street. Information on the OB was trickled back to the "Pickering Street Irregulars".

Many of these characters reappear, from time to time, in the third book of the Kirkwood trilogy, titled *The Girl in the Summerhouse.*

Glossary

Compiled by Anna Baggallay
who also edited the manuscript.

AFRIKAANS – Two meanings:

Nationality: Descendants of early Dutch, German and Flemish settlers, whose language and customs blended into a new culture, plus French (after 1688 when Huguenot refugees from France arrived to settle); now less than 10% of the South African population.
Language: It evolved from many influences, as above, plus words from the San – the indigenous bushmen – and Khoi, the Hottentot farmers who had brought agriculture and livestock herding from central Africa; also Malay slaves brought from Batavia (Indonesia) to the Cape by the Dutch East India Company. The first Afrikaans grammar book appeared in 1876, and a bilingual dictionary in 1902. It was officially recognised as a new language by the South African Government in 1925; and is spoken as a first language by at least 14% of the population, including many coloured (mixed-race) people.

AFRIKANDER Cattle breed evolved to suit southern African conditions, of the Sanga type (humped), with lateral horns which sweep upwards.

ALLEYNIAN Eng. An Old Boy (former pupil) of Dulwich College, a private (known as 'public' in Britain) secondary school in South London – founded in 1619 by Edward Alleyn, an Elizabethan actor.

AMANZI Zulu. Water.

BILHARZIA Afr. Medically called Schistomiasis: debilitating disease carried by a small host snail in certain rivers and streams in southern Africa, the organism enters the bloodstream, causing physical and mental weaknesses in many African children. It can be treated if diagnosed. The name derives from T. Bilharz, the German physician who discovered the parasite and by whom the genus schistosoma was named in the nineteenth century.

BLACKJACKS The hooked seeds of 'Bidens pilosa', an alien from South America, now a widespread strong-smelling weed, known as khakibos. Seeds about 70 – 80mm. long, cling to clothing and animal pelts, and are thus distributed.

BOER Dutch. Farmer; later used as a term for those of Dutch/German ancestry who defied the British attempts to take over the country and trekked (q.v.) north.

BOEREWORS Afr. Farmers' sausage. Mixed meats and spices, usually cooked at a braaivleis (q.v.)

BONSELA Afr. Tip, small gift, bonus

BOOMSLANG Afr. Tree snake, very venomous.

BOREEN Irish. Lane, path – diminutive of road (bóthar, a road).

BOSBERAAD Afr. Bush Meetings – usually held in secret, e.g. by the Broederbond.
BRAAIVLEIS Afr. Barbecue. Literally, 'braised (braai) flesh (vleis)'.
BRINJAL Afr. The vegetable known as aubergine in Europe and eggplant in the USA and Australia, botanically the berry of 'Solanum melongena', a member of the nightshade family; thus related to the tomato and potato.
BROEDERBOND Afr. 'Brotherhood' – powerful secret society, founded in May, 1918, (as 'Jong Zuid Afrika' – changed its name in 1920) of male Calvinist Afrikaners dedicated to the advancement of Afrikaner interests and the erosion of British dominating interests. By 1948, all the members of government and apartheid supporters were members.
BRÖTCHEN Soup, broth.
BUCHU Zulu. Medicinal plant, 'Agathosma betulina', native to western South Africa; known by Africans for centuries, used for urinary tract infections, inflammation and intestinal ailments.

CEILIDH Gaelic. Social event with Scottish or Irish music, singing and dancing.
COILLE Gaelic. Wood, woodland; dense trees and undergrowth.
COLOURED People of mixed racial ancestry, specifically white and black, white and other races imported as labour. NOT used for indigenous black people of pure tribal ancestry. Mostly Afrikaans speaking, and mostly found in the Cape Province.
CONDY'S CRYSTALS Potassium permanganate – "the

most useful survival chemical"; purifies water for drinking, and is a healing agent for skin lesions, rashes, bites, etc.

DAARONDER Afr. Under there.
"DIESE DEINE GEBEN" "these thy gifts".
DONGA Zulu. Dry water course, eroded ditch.
DRAY   Flat wagon, usually narrow sides which can be let down for loading.
DRIEDAGSIEKLE Afr. Three-day sickness; i.e. the second wave of the Spanish Flu, a mutation of the original.
DRIFT   Eng. Crossing place of a river; ford.
DUBH   Gaelic. Black.
DUIKER Afr. Literally, a 'diver': a small, shy, mainly nocturnal antelope that dives into cover if it is disturbed.

ERHEBUNG A survey.
ERSATZ   Grmn. A substitute, replacement, usually inferior, for something else. From German Ersatzen = to replace.

FADA   Scottish. Possibly borrowed from the Irish, "long"; but has many meanings in Gaelic. "Fada Farm"- a long, extensive but narrow piece of land.
FAHFEE Chinese. Gambling game/ numbers racket, played illegally by Chinese indentured immigrants, but also by Africans and even some Europeans who are sucked into it hoping to 'get rich quick'.
FECK   Irish. Originally, to steal or to throw; now used as a mild swear word, to avoid the similar English word which is far stronger.
FECKLESS Irresponsible, useless.

FLUCH UND BELASTUNG Curse and burden.

GEBRUIK Afr. Used, made use of
GRAND MAL Fr. "Great sickness" – used to describe the worst type of epileptic fit, when the patient becomes unconscious, often with violent muscle contractions, and can injure him/herself in the process, which lasts several minutes and is due to an electrical disturbance in the brain.
GRÜSSE Grmn. Greetings, regards.

HAKKE Afr. Hocks (of an animal).
HAMBA Zulu Go; go away (imperative).
   – ekhaya Go home.
HAMBA KAHLE Go well – widely used by all Nguni (q.v.) speakers.
HAMBA NGO KUCOPHELELA Farewell, ride with care
HARTEBEEST Afr. Large antelope species; can run fast.
HERRSCHAFT und KNECHTSCHAFT "Lordship and bondage", Master and slave, as labelled by Hegel, a German philosopher.

I.D.B. (Acronym) Illicit Diamond Buyer.
IMPI   Zulu. A regiment in the Zulu army.
INDUNA Zulu Official functionary of king or chief; the Head Man of a district; "great advisor". Now somewhat derogatory.
INSPAN Afr. To harness, or yoke up beasts (oxen) to a wagon.
INVAL   Afr. Invasion.
INYANGA Afr. Herbalist, tribal doctor.
ISILWANE Zulu. Animal.
ISIGODI Zulu. Valley; district.

IZIMPUNGUSHLI Jackals.
IZINGANE Zulu. Young children.

JUKSKEI Dutch. Old (at least 270 years) Dutch boeresport; trying to knock a peg out of the ground by throwing other pegs, akin to tossing the horseshoe.

KAFFIR Arabic. Originally an infidel, unbeliever, not a follower of Allah; thus in South Africa came to be applied to black people. Now a word of great racial and political sensitivity, a slur, the use thereof punishable by law.
KHAKIBOS Afr. Bos = Bush. See BLACKJACKS.
KHAYA Zulu. Home, dwelling.
KHEHLA Zulu. Old man (term of respect).
KLEINE HÜGEL Hillocks.
KNOBKERRIE Swahili Club with a knob at the end; fighting stick.

LATERITE Eng. Rock / Soil, clay-like, usually red colour, full of iron compounds. Used for road and path-making.
LYSOL Eng. Powerful disinfectant used on the streets during the Spanish Flu epidemic.

MADODA Zulu. Boys or men (collectively).
MIELIE Maize, sweet corn; white or yellow.
MOGE ER IN FRIDEN RUHEN May he rest in peace.
MOMPARA Dutch. Fool, idiot – disparaging term, but not unkind. Originally an unsophisticated country bumpkin.
"MONKEY'S WEDDING" Phenomenon when the sun shines through rain, refracting it and producing

a rainbow. Strangely enough, many languages and nations have similar expressions for this oft-seen rainbow – in Afrikaans, a Jackal's wedding; in Zulu, Monkeys, as in English! Seen also at waterfalls when the sun shines through spray.

MOOCHIES Zulu. Loin cloths; beaded or animal skins.

MYNAH Asian bird, of the starling family, which can be taught to talk and thus was often caged as a pet. Imported to South Africa via trading ships calling into the Cape of Good Hope, and gradually spread northwards during the twentieth century; now almost a pest in much of S. Africa, outbreeding native birds.

NAGANA Disease, usually fatal, of cattle; a parasitic virus, which spreads quickly, carried by tsetse fly.

NAGMAAL Afr. Communion service in the Dutch Reformed Church in South Africa.

NATIVE Term used for an indigenous black African person, as opposed to an Indian or a Coloured person (one of mixed race).

NGOSI Zulu. Hereditary Chief.

NGUNI Zulu. A breed of native African cattle, remarkable for their varied coat patterns, by which they are individually known.
Also a group of similar African languages, including Zulu, Xhosa, Shangaan, Ndebele, Swazi, mutually comprehensible.

NUNU Afr. Bug, insect.

OPSAAL Afr. Saddle up; used as a Boer rallying cry to Boer forces in times of conflict.

OPSITKERS Afr. "Courting Candle", lit where a young couple are permitted to sit together but know they must part when the candle burns out.
OUMA   Afr. Grandmother.
OUTSPAN Afr. Unharness – oxen from wagon; a rest, camping spot, a pause in a journey.

PADKOS Afr. Literally "road food" – picnic food for a journey.
PANGA Zulu. Long-handled spear/ assegai.
PANJANDRUM Powerful person; important, influential, often pretentious, official. Invented name for a character in a work by Samuel Foote, playwright, in 1755.
PASOP   Afr. Beware, mind out, take care…
PICCANIN Young Zulu child
PUTU   Zulu/Xhosa. Pap; a stiff porridge made by cooking maize meal with water to the consistency of mashed potatoes.

QUAICH Scot. Shallow two-handled cup, often of wood, used in Scotland.

RIDGEBACK Br. Breed of large dog evolved in Rhodesia, originally for hunting lions. Bull mastiff type, bred with older hunting breeds, with distinctive ridge of hair along top of spine.
RONDAVEL Afr. Round hut of wattle-and-daub, widely used in southern Africa, conical with thatched grass roof.
ROOI   Afr. Red
ROOINEKS Afr. Rednecks; slang term for British, who tended to get sunburnt on their necks.

RUCK   Br. Used in rugby when the ball is on the ground and players of both teams are contesting it, using only their feet, and when it gets pushed to the back, the nearest player can grab it by hand and run with it.

RUSKS   Br. Hard-baked dry biscuits from a sweet bread mixture, taken on treks or journeys; often dunked in coffee and eaten first thing – traditional on safari.

SAWUBONA Zulu. "I see you" – greeting.

SEBENZA Zulu. Work (noun)

SGIAN DUBH Small single-edged knife worn as part of traditional Scottish dress, usually kept the sock.

SIKHONA Zulu. "I am here to be seen" – response to greeting.

SITKAMER Afr. Sitting room

SKELLUM Originally Scottish, of Danish origin – a ne'er-do-well; a rogue, rascal, scoundrel; now only commonly used in South Africa.

SLEEVEEN Irish Sly, untrustworthy person

SLIM   Afr. Clever

SPAN   Afr. Team of oxen; the yoke which couples them in harness.

SPRUIT Afr. Stream, brook; tributary to a river. Cf. English word 'Sprout', an offshoot. Used in many place names, indicating the importance of water as the trekkers went north and founded settlements.

STEAMELA Zulu Train, drawn by a steam engine

STERRETJIE Afr. "Little Star". " –tjie" is a diminutive ending in Afrikaans.

STOEP   Afr. Verandah, porch

SWAHILI Language used mainly in Kenya, Tanzania,

eastern DRC and Uganda – a mixture of African and Arabic influences, which had many different dialects; eventually standardised in 1928 from that spoken in Zanzibar, used by most races, including colonials of European origin.

TAAL Dutch, Afr. Language; a synecdoche for the evolving language of Afrikaans.
TARN Scot. A small lake, usually at high altitude
TICKEY Afr. Old name for a very small silver 3d. coin.
TICKEYDRAAI Afr. Boer dance, where couples "turn on a tickey", i.e. make tight turns. Favoured by car salesman to describe a car's wheel lock.
TOFF Br. Slang used derogatorily for an arrogant person assuming a superior air.
TOPPIE Afr. Nickname for a commonly-found bird, correctly a black-eyed bulbul.
TREK Afr. Verb: To pull. Noun: an arduous journey, often on foot, but associated with oxen pulling wagons; as in the Great Trek, the movement of Afrikaners (q.v.), northwards away from British-controlled territory near the Cape from 1834 onwards. (Cf. 'Star Trek', a modern usage from the 1960s; and also adopted by operators of walking trips in the foothills of the Himalayas).
TSONGA Bantu tribe found in South Africa, on the borders of Zululand and Mozambique.

UDANSA Zulu Danced.
UFUNA USAWATI Do you want some salt?
UKHAMBA Zulu. Clay pot, kept to offer drink to the spirits, or to test drink is not poisoned before giving to a chief or visitor.

UKUTHI Zulu. That.
UMFAAN Zulu. Young boys.
UMKHUHLWANE Zulu. Fever – used for Spanish Flu in 1919.
UMLUNGU Zulu. White man (originally the white foam that collects on the beach).
UMNUMZANE Zulu. Head of a household; lesser chief; respectful term for old man.
UMUZI Zulu. Individual householders, in a cluster or extended family kraal.
UMVITHI Zulu. Tree of the bushveld, Boscia Oleaides or B. Albitrunca; Shepherd's Tree in English. Zulus say it prevents lightning, so protect it. It has the deepest roots of any known root system.
USHUKELA Zulu. Sugar.
UYAPHI Zulu. Where are you going?

VELD Afr. Open countryside. (Cf. English, "Field")
VELDSKOEN Afr. Literally "field shoes" – usually short suede boots.
VÖLKISCHER BEOBACHTER The official paper of the NAZI party, from December, 1920.
VOORLOPER Afr. Forerunner, precursor, person leading the way; particularly used of the man leading a team of oxen.
VRYHEID Afr. 'Freedom'; capital of the Nieuwe Republiek in northern Natal, established 1884, after King Dinizulu gave the land in exchange for a promise of protection; but absorbed by the Transvaal Republic, the ZAR, in 1888. Now a town in KZN on the way to Durban from Johannesburg.
VRYSTAAT Afr. Free State (usually ref. to the Orange Free State; could be applied to southern Ireland. The Irish and Boers were close allies, both anti-

British!)
W. WELLIES Br. Short for wellington boots – named after Arthur Wellesley, first Duke of Wellington, who popularised a boot of leather, adapted from hessian, which then became rubber and waterproof; and is widely worn by gardeners, farm workers, etc.
WELVERDIEND Well done.
WOZA Zulu. Come!
WRAGTIG Afr. From Dutch "Waaraglig" – Really? Truly? Surely…Expresses surprise, emphasis, used as a mild expletive.

ZOPT Swiss. Traditional plaited loaf of bread; a plait.
ZULU Zulu. Heaven

Bibliography

Singh Anand & Balgobind Singh, Shanta. (2006). *The History of Crime Among People of Indian Origin in South Africa*. Anthropologist. 8. 147-156. 10.1080/09720073.2006.11890951.

Brooks, Shirley J. *Changing Nature: A Critical Historical Geography of the Umfolozi and Hluhluwe Game Reserves, Zululand, 1887 – 1947*. Ontario: Queen's University, 2001

Desai, Ashwan & Vahed, Goolam. *The South African Gandhi, stretcher-bearer of Empire*. Stanford: Stanford University Press, 2019.

Motse, Mmatshilo. *The Best Kept Secret: Violence against domestic workers*. Paper presented at the Centre for the Study of Violence and Reconciliation, No. 5, 25 July, 1990. University of the Witwatersrand, Johannesburg.

Du Bois, Duncan. *Collusion and conspiracy in colonial Natal: A case study of Reynolds Bros and indentured abuses 1884-1908*. Historia vol.60 n.1, Durban May. 2015

Minaar, Anthony deVilliers. *uShukela!* Pretoria: HSRC Publishers, 1992

Phillips, Howard. *Epidemics*. Athens: Ohio, 2012.

Schnurr, Mathew. *The Boom and Bust of Zululand Cotton 1910-1933*. Halifax: Journal of Southern African Studies. 37:01, 119-134: Dalhousie University: 201

Twenty-six birds of Natal

These are the names of the twenty-six common birds of Natal that served as a blind to mask secret communications between Prue and Donald. The list is meagre, as Kwa Zulu-Natal is home to about 470 bird species, to which can be added another two hundred visitors.

- A Red-eyed Turtle Dove
- B Cape Thrush
- C Diederick's Cuckoo
- D Laughing Dove
- E Spotted-backed Weaver
- F Crowned Hornbill
- G Tambourine Dove
- H Emerald-spotted Dove
- I Black-collared Barbet
- J Red-browned Tinker Barbet
- K Olive Sunbird
- L Bush Shrike
- M Knysna Lourie
- N Emerald Cuckoo
- O Bou-bou Shrike
- P Bleating Bush Warbler
- Q Bar-throated Warbler

R   Red-winged Shrike
S   Black-headed Warbler
T   Layard's Bulbul
U   Noisy Robin
V   Natal Robin
W   Glossy Ibis
X   Forest Weaver
Y   Fork-tailed Drongo
Z   Narina Trogon

Lightning Source UK Ltd.
Milton Keynes UK
UKHW011058020622
403826UK00005B/94